THE NEW WATCH

Also by Sergei Lukyanenko

The Night Watch
The Day Watch
The Twilight Watch
The Last Watch

THE NEW WATCH

SERGEI LUKYANENKO

Translated from the Russian by Andrew Bromfield

WILLIAM HEINEMANN: LONDON

Published by William Heinemann, 2013

2 4 6 8 10 9 7 5 3 1

First published in Great Britain in 2013 by
William Heinemann
Random House, 20 Vauxhall Bridge Road,
London SW1V 2SA

www.randomhouse.co.uk

Addresses for companies within The Random House Group Limited can be found at: www.randomhouse.co.uk/offices.htm

The Random House Group Limited Reg. No. 954009

A CIP catalogue record for this book
is available from the British Library

ISBN HB: 9780434022311
ISBN TPB: 9780434022243

The Random House Group Limited supports the Forest Stewardship Council® (FSC®), the leading international forest-certification organisation. Our books carrying the FSC label are printed on FSC®-certified paper. FSC is the only forest-certification scheme supported by the leading environmental organisations, including Greenpeace.
Our paper procurement policy can be found at
www.randomhouse.co.uk/environment

Typeset in Bembo by Palimpsest Book Production Limited,
Falkirk, Stirlingshire

Printed and bound in Great Britain by
Clays Ltd, St Ives plc

For my parents

This is a dubious text for the Cause of Light.
The Night Watch

This is a dubious text for the Cause of Darkness.
The Day Watch

Part One

DUBIOUS INTENT

PROLOGUE

SENIOR SERGEANT DMITRY Pastukhov was a good *polizei*.

Of course, for the purpose of enlightening drunks who got a bit above themselves he sometimes employed measures not actually prescribed by the regulations – a few good smacks in the teeth or well-aimed kicks, for instance. But only in cases where the dipso concerned was getting a bit too pushy about his rights, or refusing to proceed to the drunk tank. And Dima wouldn't actually spurn a five-hundred note shaken out of some lunk from the Ukraine or Central Asia who didn't have a residence permit – after all, what with police pay being so low, the offenders might just as well pay him their fines directly. Nor did he raise any objections when he was poured a shot of cognac instead of a glass of water in eating joints on the territory under his purview.

After all, it was a demanding job. It was dangerous and difficult. And at first glance people hardly even seemed to notice it. There had to be some material incentives.

But, on the other hand, Dima had never beaten money out of prostitutes and pimps. On principle. Something in the way he'd been raised wouldn't let him do it. Dima didn't waste time dragging slightly tipsy citizens off to the sobering-up station while they still retained a glimmer of reason. And when he uncovered a real crime he launched himself into pursuit of the perpetrators like a shot. He always searched conscientiously for clues and submitted reports on instances of petty theft (that was if the victims insisted on it, of course) and he made an effort to remember the faces of persons on the 'wanted' list. He had several significant arrests under his belt, including a genuine murderer – a man who had first stabbed his wife's lover (which was forgivable) and then his wife (which was understandable) and then, still brandishing the knife, had gone after the neighbour who had informed him about his wife's infidelity. Outraged at such black ingratitude, the neighbour had locked himself in his apartment and called the police on 02. Arriving in response to the summons, Dima Pastukhov had first detained the murderer, who was pounding impotently on the iron door with his blood-smeared, puny little intellectual's fists, and then struggled for a long time with his own desire to drag the whistle-blowing neighbour out onto the stairs and rearrange his face.

So Dima regarded himself as a good policeman – which wasn't really all that far from the truth. Compared with the example set by some of his colleagues, he stood out, seeming every bit as diligent as the militiaman Svistulkin in that old Soviet children's favourite *Dunno in Sunshine City*.

The only blot on Dima's service record dated back to January 1998: still young and green then, he had been on patrol in the Exhibition of Economic Achievements district with Sergeant Kaminsky, who was by way of being the young militiaman's mentor. (They were still called 'militiamen', or simply 'cops', back then: the fashionable word 'policeman' and the slightly offensive term '*polizei*' hadn't come into use yet.) Kaminsky was very proud to be playing this role, but his admonitions and advice all basically came down to where and how you could pick up a bit of easy money. On that particular evening, when Kaminsky spotted this half-cut young guy (he even had an open quarter-litre of vodka in his hand) dashing out of the metro station towards the pedestrian underpass, he whistled in delight and the two partners moved in to intercept their prey. All the indications were that this drunk was about to part with a fifty note, or maybe even a hundred.

And then everything went pear-shaped. It was some kind of black-magic voodoo. The tipsy suspect fixed the two partners with a surprisingly sober stare (that stare was sober all right, but there was something savage and chilling about it, like the look in the eyes of a stray dog that had lost all faith in people a very long time ago) and advised the militiamen to get drunk themselves.

And they did as he said. They walked over to the trading kiosks (Yeltsin's chaotic reign was already in its final years, but vodka was still sold openly in the street) and, giggling like lunatics, they each bought a bottle exactly like the one carried by the drunk who had given them such sound advice. Then they bought another two. And another two.

Three hours later Pastukhov and Kaminsky, feeling very witty and merry at this stage, were picked up by one of their own patrols – and that was what saved them. They caught it in the neck, all right, but they weren't flung out of the militia. After that Kaminsky gave up drinking altogether and swore blind that the drunk they'd met must have been a hypnotist or even some kind of psychic. Pastukhov himself didn't slander the man pointlessly or indulge in idle speculation. But he clung on very tightly to the memory of him . . . with the sole intention of making sure he never crossed his path again.

Perhaps it was the powerful memory of that shameful binge, or perhaps Pastukhov had simply developed some unusual abilities, but after a while he started noticing other people with strange eyes. To himself Pastukhov called these people 'wolves' and 'dogs'.

The first group had the calm indifference of the predator in their gaze: not malicious, no, the wolf harries the sheep without malice – more likely, in fact, with love. Pastukhov simply steered clear of their kind, trying hard not to attract any attention in the process.

The second group, who were more like that first young drunk, had a dog-like look in their eyes. Sometimes guilty, sometimes patient and concerned, sometimes sad. There was just one thing that bothered Pastukhov: that wasn't the way dogs looked at their masters, at best it was the way they looked at their master's whelp. And so Pastukhov tried to steer clear of them too.

And for quite a long time he managed it.

If children are life's flowers, then this child was a blooming cactus.

He started yelling the moment the doors of the Sheremetyevo-D terminal slid open and he came in. His mother, red-faced with anger and shame (the shouting was obviously a repeat performance), was dragging him along by the hand, but the boy was leaning backwards, bracing himself with both feet, and howling: 'I won't! I won't! I won't fly! Mummy, don't! The plane's going to crash!'

His mother let go of his hand and the boy slumped to the floor and stayed sitting there: a fat, hysterical, tear-stained, unattractive child, dressed a little bit too lightly for the Moscow weather in June – there was obviously a flight to warmer climes in prospect.

A man sitting at a cafe table about twenty metres away from them got up, almost knocking over his unfinished mug of beer. He looked for a few moments at the boy and the mother who was trying to din something into her son's head. Then he sat down and said in a quiet voice: 'That's appalling. What a nightmare!'

'I think so, too,' agreed the young woman sitting opposite him.

She put down her cup of coffee and gave the boy a hostile look. 'I'd call it sordid.'

'Well, I don't see anything sordid about it,' the man said gently. 'But it's certainly appalling . . . no doubt about that . . .'

'I personally—' the young woman began, but stopped when she saw the man wasn't listening.

He took out a phone. Dialled a number. Spoke in a quiet voice: 'I need a level-one clearance. One or two. No, I'm not joking. Try to find one . . .'

He broke off the call, looked at the young woman and nodded. 'I'm sorry, an urgent call . . . What were you saying?'

'I personally am child-free,' the young woman declared defiantly.

'Free of children? Are you infertile, then?'

The young woman shook her head. 'A common misapprehension. We child-free women are opposed to children because they enslave us. We have to choose – between being a proud, free individual or a social appendage to the population's reproductive mechanism!'

'Ah,' the man said, with a nod. 'And I thought . . . you had health problems. I was going to recommend a good doctor . . . But you do accept sex, though?'

The young woman smiled. 'Naturally! We're not asexual, are we? Sex and marriage – that's all very good and normal. It's just . . . tying yourself to those creatures that are always yelling and running around and—'

'And pooping,' the man suggested. 'They're always pooping as well, aren't they? And they can't even wipe their own backsides at first.'

'Pooping!' the young woman agreed. 'That's it precisely! Spending the best years of your life serving the needs of undeveloped human juveniles . . . I hope you're not going to lecture me on morals and try to persuade me to change my mind and have a huge brood of kiddies.'

'No, I'm not. I believe you. I'm quite certain you'll remain childless to the end of your life.'

The boy and his mother walked past: the child was slightly calmer now or, more likely, he had simply resigned himself to the fact that the flight was going to happen. The mother was speaking to her son in a low voice – they heard something about a warm sea, a good hotel and bullfights.

'Oh God!' the young woman exclaimed. 'They're flying to Spain . . . It looks like we're on the same flight. Can you imagine it, listening to that little tub of lard's hysterical squealing for three hours?'

'Not three, I think,' said the man. 'One hour and ten or fifteen minutes . . .'

A slightly scornful expression appeared on the young woman's face. The man appeared perfectly capable and competent. But then how could he not know the most ordinary things . . . 'The flight to Barcelona lasts three hours.'

'Three hours and twenty minutes. But suppose—'

'So where are you flying to?' asked the young woman, rapidly losing interest in him.

'Nowhere. I was seeing off a friend. Then I sat down to drink a mug of beer.'

The girl hesitated. 'Tamara. My name's Tamara.'

'I'm Anton.'

'You probably don't have children, do you, Anton?' asked Tamara, still unwilling to abandon her favourite subject.

'Why do you think that? I have a daughter. Nadenka. The same age as that . . . tub of lard.'

'So you didn't want to let your wife remain a free, healthy woman?' Tamara laughed. 'What does she do?'

'My wife?'

'Well, not your daughter . . .'

'By training, she's a doctor. But in herself . . . she's an enchantress.'

'That's just what I dislike so much about you men,' Tamara declared, getting up, 'that vulgar affectation. "An enchantress"! And no doubt you're quite happy for her to slave away at the cooker, wash the nappies, get no sleep for nights on end . . .'

'I am, although no one washes nappies any more – disposables have been in fashion for a long time.'

At that the young woman's face contorted as if she had been offered a handful of cockroaches to eat. She grabbed her handbag and walked over to the check-in desk without even saying goodbye.

The man shrugged. He picked up his phone and raised it to his ear – and it rang immediately.

'Gorodetsky . . . Completely? No, third-level won't do at all. A full charter flight to Barcelona. You can accept it as second-level . . . Can't you?'

He paused for a while, then said: 'Then one seventh-level for me. No, that's wrong. The boy has a First- or Second-Level gift of clairvoyance. The Dark Ones will dig their heels in . . . A single fifth-level intervention – a change in the fate of one human and one Other . . . All right, put it down to me.'

He stood up, leaving his unfinished mug of beer on the table, and set off towards the check-in desk, where the fat boy was standing in the queue beside his mother with a stony look on his face, shifting nervously from one foot to the other.

The man walked straight past the checkpoint (for some reason no one even tried to stop him) and approached the woman. He cleared his throat politely. Caught her eye. Nodded.

'Olga Yurievna . . . You forgot to turn off the iron when you were ironing Kesha's shorts this morning . . .'

A look of panic appeared on the woman's face.

'You can fly on the evening charter,' the man continued. 'But right now you'd better go home.'

The woman tugged at her son's hand and then went dashing towards the exit. But the boy, whom she suddenly seemed to have forgotten completely, gazed at the man wide-eyed.

'You want to ask who I am and why your mum believed me?' the man asked.

The boy's eyes misted over as if he were looking inside himself, or at something far, far away on the outside – something in a place where well-brought-up children weren't supposed to look (and where badly-brought-up adults shouldn't look either, unless they really had to).

'You are Anton Gorodetsky, Higher White Magician,' said the boy. 'You are Nadka's father. Because of you . . . all of us . . .'

'Well?' the man asked keenly 'Well, well?'

'Kesha!' the woman howled, suddenly remembering her son. The boy shuddered and the mist in his eyes dispersed. He said: 'Only I don't know what all that means . . . Thank you!'

'Because of me . . . all of you . . .' the man murmured pensively, watching as the woman and her child rushed along the glass wall of the terminal building towards the taxi rank. 'Because of me . . . all of you will live lives of luxury . . . All of you are doomed. All of you have been bankrupted . . . All of you are, will, have been – what?'

He swung round and walked unhurriedly towards the exit. By the entrance to the 'green corridor' he stopped and looked back at the queue that had formed at the check-in desk for Barcelona. It was a large, noisy queue. People going away for a holiday at the seaside. There were lots of women and children in it, lots of men and even one child-free young woman.

'God help you,' said the man. 'I can't.'

* * *

Dima Pastukhov had just taken out his lighter to give his partner Bisat Iskenderov a light, even though Bisat had his own lighter – it was simply a routine they'd got into. If Dima took out a cigarette, Bisat reached for his lighter. When the Azerbaijani decided to smoke, Dima offered him a light. If Pastukhov had been inclined to intellectual reflection, he might have said this was their way of demonstrating their mutual respect for each other, despite their differences of opinion on many things – from problems of nationality to which car was classier: the Mercedes ML or the BMW X3.

But Dima wasn't inclined to reflections of this kind – he and Bisat both drove Fords, preferred German beer to Russian vodka or Azerbaijani cognac and had quite friendly feelings for each other. So Dima clicked on the button, summoning up the little tongue of flame, glanced briefly at the exit from the airport terminal building – and dropped the lighter just as his friend's cigarette was reaching for it.

There was a 'dog' walking out through the doors of the departure lounge. A middle-aged man who didn't look frightening at all – quite cultured, in fact. Pastukhov was used to seeing people like this, but this one wasn't simply a 'dog', he was *the* 'dog' . . . from the Exhibition of Economic Achievements district, from way back in the distant past. Only he didn't look drunk now, more as if he had a bit of a hangover.

Pastukhov turned away and started slowly groping for the lighter on the ground. The man with watchdog's eyes walked past without taking the slightest notice of him.

'A drop too much yesterday?' Bisat asked sympathetically.

'Who?' muttered Pastukhov. 'Ah . . . no, it's just that the lighter's slippery . . .'

'Your hands are shaking and you've turned as white as a sheet,' his partner remarked.

Pastukhov finally gave him a light, checked out of the corner of his eye that the man was walking away towards the car park, took out a cigarette and lit up himself – without waiting for Bisat's lighter.

'You're acting kind of funny . . .' said Bisat.

'Yes, I was drinking yesterday,' Pastukhov muttered. He looked at the terminal building again.

This time there was a 'wolf' coming out of it. With a self-confident, predatory gaze and determined stride. Pastukhov turned away.

'You should eat *khash* the morning after,' Bisat admonished him. 'But only the right *khash* – ours. That Armenian *khash* is poison!'

'Ah, come on, they're absolutely identical,' Pastukhov replied in his usual manner.

Bisat spat disdainfully and shook his head.

'They may look the same. But in essence they're completely different!'

'They might be different in essence, but in reality they're absolutely identical!' Dima replied, watching the 'wolf', who had walked past and was also going towards the car park.

Bisat took offence and stopped talking.

Pastukhov finished off his cigarette in a few quick drags and looked at the door of the terminal again.

His first thought was angry, even resentful: Are they holding some kind of grand get-together in there today?'

And then the fear hit him.

The individual who had walked out of the doors when they slid open and was now standing there, gazing round thoughtfully, wasn't a 'dog'. But he wasn't a 'wolf', either. He was someone else. A third kind.

A kind that ate wolves for breakfast and dogs for lunch. And left the tastiest parts for supper.

The classification that immediately occurred to Pastukhov was 'tiger'. He said: 'I've got stomach cramps . . . I'm off to the can.'

'Go on, I'll have a smoke,' replied his partner, still offended.

To have asked Bisat to go to the toilet with him would have been strange. There wasn't any time to explain anything or invent anything. Pastukhov turned round and walked away quickly, leaving Iskenderov in the path of the 'tiger'. 'He won't do anything to him . . . He'll just walk straight past, that's all . . .' Pastukhov reassured himself.

Pastukhov only looked round as he was already walking into the departure hall.

Just in time to see Bisat salute casually and stop the 'tiger'. Of course, his partner couldn't spot them – there wasn't any incident in his past like the one Pastukhov had experienced. But this time even he had sensed something – with that policeman's intuition that sometimes helped you pull an entirely unremarkable-looking man out of a crowd and discover that he had a rod stashed in a secret holster or a knife in his pocket.

Pastukhov suddenly realised that his stomach cramps were genuine now. And he sprinted into the airport's safe, noisy interior, full of people and suitcases.

Since he was a good *polizei*, he felt very ashamed. But he felt even more afraid.

CHAPTER 1

'GORODETSKY WILL REPORT on the situation regarding this morning's incident,' said Gesar, without looking up from his papers.

I stood up. Caught Semyon's glance of sympathy. Started talking.

'Two hours ago I saw Mr Warnes off on the flight to New York. After our colleague had checked in and was buying vodka in the duty-free . . .'

'You mean you went through passport control with him, Gorodetsky?' Gesar enquired, again without raising his eyes.

'Well, yes.'

'What for?'

'To make sure that he was all right . . .' I cleared my throat. 'Well, and to buy something for myself in the duty-free . . .'

'What, exactly?'

'A couple of bottles of whisky.'

'What kind?' Gesar looked up from the desk.

'Scotch. Single malt. Glenlivet twelve-year-old and Glenmorangie eighteen-year-old . . . but that was for a present, I personally think drinking eighteen-year-old whisky is rather flashy . . .'

'What the hell!' barked Gesar. 'Of all the petty selfish indulgences . . .'

'Pardon me, Boris Ignatievich,' I said, 'but Mr Warnes drinks like a fish. And he prefers decent single malts, not White Horse. My bar's completely empty. Tomorrow some other guest will arrive and you'll assign me to look after him. But I can't buy alcohol in the fancy "A-Z of Taste" supermarkets on my salary.'

'Go on,' Gesar said in an icy voice.

'After that I sat down in the bar to drink a mug of beer.'

'How long have you been drinking beer in the mornings, Gorodetsky?'

'Four days now. Since Warnes arrived.'

Semyon giggled. Gesar half-rose to his feet and glanced round everyone sitting at the table – ten Others, all at least Third-Level or, as the veterans said, 'third-rank'.

'We'll discuss the specifics of entertaining visitors later. So, you were drinking beer for your hangover. Then what happened?'

'A woman came in with a child. A fat little boy about ten years old, bawling and howling. He was begging his mother not to get on the plane, said it was going to crash. Well . . . naturally, I scanned his aura. The kid turned out to be an uninitiated Other, High-Level, at least First or Second. From all the indications – a clairvoyant. Possibly even a Prophet.'

A light stir ran round the room.

'Why such bold conclusions?' asked Gesar.

'The colour. The intensity. The glimmering . . .' I strained slightly and broadcast what I had seen into space. Naturally, I didn't create any real image, but the mind will always oblige and find some point in mid-air for a picture.

'Possibly,' Gesar said, with a nod. 'But even so, a Prophet . . .'

'As a rule, a clairvoyant doesn't have the ability to foretell his own future. But the boy was frightened of his own death. That's an argument in favour of a Prophet . . .' Olga said in a quiet voice.

Gesar nodded reluctantly.

'I enquired if we had the right to a first- or second-level intervention – to save the entire plane. Unfortunately, we didn't have that right. Then I personally took the right to a fifth-level and removed the boy and his mother from the flight.'

'Reasonable,' said Gesar, apparently a bit calmer now. 'Reasonable. Is the boy being monitored?'

I shrugged.

Semyon cleared his throat delicately. 'We're working on it, Boris Ignatievich.'

Gesar nodded and looked at me again: 'Is there anything else?'

I hesitated. 'He made another prediction. To me personally.'

'To a Higher Other?' Gesar asked, to make quite sure.

'A Prophet!' said Olga, sounding almost jolly. 'Definitely a Prophet!'

'Can you repeat it for us, Anton?' Gesar asked in a voice that was perfectly calm and friendly now.

'By all means. "You are Anton Gorodetsky, Higher White Magician. You are Nadka's father. Because of you . . . all of us . . ."'

'What came after that?'

'At that point he was interrupted.'

Gesar muttered something and started drumming his fingers on the table. I waited. Everybody else was waiting too.

'Anton, I wouldn't like to seem impolite . . . but are you certain it was your own decision to drink beer?'

I was flabbergasted. Not even offended, just flabbergasted. To ask an Other if he has fallen under someone else's influence is quite a serious matter. It's like . . . well, it's like one man enquiring about the success of another man's intimate life. Between close friends, of course, that kind of question is possible. But between a boss and his subordinate . . . and in the presence of other colleagues . . . naturally, if an inexperienced Other commits some kind of inept blunder, then the question 'Were you thinking with your own head?' is quite appropriate, although even so it's rhetorical. But asking a Higher Other a question like that . . .

'Boris Ignatievich,' I said, furiously tearing away all my layers of mental defence. 'I must have given you some reason to say that. I honestly can't think exactly what. In my view, I acted entirely of my own free will. But if you have any doubts, scan me – I don't object.'

Of course, that was another rhetorical phrase. Absolutely rhetorical. The kind of thing a man who has fallen under some absurd suspicion would say – for instance, when he's a guest in someone's house and is accused of stealing the silver spoons off the table . . .

'Thank you, Anton. I accept your suggestion,' Gesar replied, getting up.

The next moment I blanked out.

And then I opened my eyes.

Between those two points, of course, some time had passed – five or ten minutes. Only I didn't remember it. I was in Gesar's office, lying on the small divan referred to ironically by everyone as 'the brainstorm launch pad'. Olga was holding my head – and she was very, very angry. Gesar was sitting on a chair opposite me – and he was very, very embarrassed. There was no one else in the office.

'Well, then, am I a trembling wretch or am I justified?' I asked, quoting Dostoevsky's famous phrase.

'Anton, I offer you my very humblest apologies,' said Gesar.

'He's already apologised to all the others,' Olga added. 'Anton, forgive the old fool.'

I sat up and rubbed my temples. My head didn't actually hurt – it just felt incredibly empty and it was ringing.

'Who am I? Where am I? Who are you, I don't know you!' I muttered.

'Anton, please accept my apologies . . .' Gesar repeated.

'Boss, what made you think I was under some kind of influence?'

'Doesn't it seem strange to you that after seeing off our guest you sat down to drink beer in a lousy, expensive little cafe, even though you knew you were going to drive?'

'It does, but that's the way the day went.'

'And that, at the precise moment when you suddenly decided to linger at the airport, a clairvoyant boy threw a hysterical fit right in front of your eyes?'

'Life is made up of coincidences,' I said philosophically.

'And that the plane reached Barcelona safely?'

That really knocked me back. 'How?'

'The usual way. Engines roaring and wings swaying. It got there, offloaded all the people and set off on the way back an hour ago.'

I shook my head from side to side. 'Boris Ignatievich . . . of course, I'm no clairvoyant. But when I specifically check the probability of one event or another . . . The boy started howling about a catastrophe. I glanced at his aura – an uninitiated Other in a spontaneous outburst of Power. I started checking through the reality lines – the plane crashed. With a probability of ninety-eight per cent. Maybe . . . well, there are no absolutely certain predictions . . . maybe those two per cent came up?'

'Possibly. But how else can you interpret what happened?'

'A deliberate provocation,' I said reluctantly. 'Someone pumped the boy full of Power and hung a false aura on him. It's a well-known move – you yourself . . . Hmm. Well, then the boy has a fit of hysterics, I hear him howling and start calculating the probabilities . . . let's assume they've been distorted, too.'

'With what intent?'

'To make us use our right to a first-level intervention for nothing. The plane was never going to crash, the kid is of no interest. And we, like idiots, have wasted our bullet.'

Gesar raised his finger didactically.

'But we didn't have the right to intervene in any case!' I exclaimed.

'We did,' Gesar muttered gruffly. 'We did and we do. But reserved exclusively for me. If you had come directly to me . . . I would have allowed you to intervene.'

'So that's how it is . . .' I said. 'Well . . . that really does make it look like a trick. But what about the kid?'

'A Prophet . . .' Gesar said reluctantly. 'A very powerful one. And you bear no signs of having been influenced. So you're probably right.'

'But the plane didn't crash,' Olga said quietly.

We stopped talking for a moment.

'Prophets don't make mistakes. The boy is a Prophet, since he made predictions about his own fate and the fate of a Higher Other. But the plane didn't crash. You didn't interfere in events . . .' Gesar said quietly.

That was when it hit me. 'You weren't checking if I was under some kind of influence or not,' I said. 'You were checking if I saved the plane without permission.'

'That too,' said Gesar, not even embarrassed now. 'But I didn't want to state a reason like that in front of our colleagues.'

'Well, thanks a million.' I got up and walked towards the door.

Gesar waited until I opened it before he spoke. 'I must say, Anton, I'm very pleased for you. Pleased and proud.'

'Why, exactly?'

'Because you didn't intervene without permission. And you didn't even come up with any human nonsense like phone calls about a bomb on the plane . . .'

I walked out and closed the door behind me.

I felt like screaming out loud or smashing my fist against the wall.

But I held out. I was imperturbable and cool.

I really hadn't come up with any 'human nonsense'! The thought had never even entered my head. I was convinced that we had no legal right to save two hundred people – and I had saved one Other and his mother.

I must have learned all my lessons well – I had behaved entirely correctly for a Higher Other.

And that made me feel lousy.

'Anton!'

Looking round, I saw Semyon hurrying to catch up with me. He seemed slightly embarrassed, like an old friend who has just witnessed an awkward and ugly scene. But we had been close friends for a long time already, and Semyon didn't have to pretend that he had been detained by chance.

'I thought I'd have to wait longer,' Semyon explained. 'Well, that was a freaky move by the boss – very, very freaky . . .'

'He's right,' I admitted reluctantly. 'It really was a strange situation.'

'I've been assigned to talk to the boy, initiate him and explain to the mother why he should study in our school . . . basic standard procedure. Why don't we go together?'

'You mean you've already found him?' I asked. 'I only read the names, I didn't take any more trouble . . .'

'Of course we've found him! This is the twenty-first century, Antokha! We called our information centre and asked them who didn't show up for such-and-such a flight to Barcelona. A minute later Tolik called back and gave me the names and addresses. Innokentii Grigorievich Tolkov, ten and a half years old. Lives with his mum . . . well, you know that Others are statistically more common in single-parent families.'

'It's the effect of social deprivation,' I muttered gruffly.

'The explanation I heard is that dads subconsciously sense

when a child is an Other and leave the family,' said Semyon. 'In other words, they're afraid . . . The Tolkovs live not far from here, near the Water Stadium metro station – why don't we mosey over?'

'No, Semyon, I won't go,' I said, shaking my head. 'You'll manage just fine on your own.'

Semyon gave me a quizzical look.

'Everything's cool!' I said firmly. 'Don't worry, I'm not having a fit of hysterics, I'm not going on a binge and I'm not hatching plans to quit the Watch. I'll take a trip to the airport and wander about there for a while. This whole thing's wrong somehow, can't you see? A boy-Prophet mouthing vague prophecies, a plane that should have crashed and didn't . . . it's not right!'

'Gesar's already sent someone to inspect Sheremetyevo,' Semyon told me.

His voice had a sly kind of note to it . . .

'Who did he send?'

'Las.'

'I see,' I said with a nod, stopping in front of the lifts and pressing the call button. 'In other words, Gesar's not expecting anything interesting.'

Las was an untypical Other. He didn't have any Other abilities at all to begin with, and he shouldn't have developed any. But several years earlier he had managed to get in the way of the spell of an ancient magical book, the *Fuaran*. The vampire Kostya, who at one time was my neighbour and even my friend, had used Las to demonstrate that the book gave him the power to turn human beings into Others . . .

What had seemed strangest to me was not that Las was transformed into an Other, but that he was transformed into a Light Other. He was no evil villain, but he had a very specific sense of humour . . . and his views on life would have been more suitable for a Dark One too. Working in the Night Watch hadn't changed him all that much – he seemed to regard it as just one more joke.

But he was a weak Other. Seventh-Level, the very lowest, with only vague prospects of ever reaching the Fifth or Sixth (and Las wasn't desperately keen on the idea anyway).

'I wouldn't say that,' Semyon disagreed amiably. 'Gesar simply isn't expecting anything interesting in the line of magic. You were there, after all, you didn't spot anything. And you're a Higher Magician . . .'

I winced.

'Yes, you are, you are,' Semyon said in a friendly tone. 'You don't have much experience, but you have all the abilities. So digging in that direction is pointless. But Las – he'll look at the situation differently. Practically from a human point of view. His head works in a rather paradoxical fashion . . . what if he spots something?'

'Then the two of us should definitely go together,' I said. 'And you can boldly proceed with initiating the Prophet.'

'Arise, prophet, and see, and hearken . . .' said Semyon, quoting Pushkin. He walked into the lift first when it finally arrived. He sighed: 'Oh, I don't like Prophets and Clairvoyants! They blurt out something about you, and then you wander around like an idiot, wondering what they meant by it. You can imagine such terrifying things sometimes, but it's all total nonsense really, phooey, not worth bothering about!'

'Thanks,' I said to Semyon. 'Don't worry . . . I'm taking all this very calmly. A Prophet – so what?'

'I remember we had a clairvoyant in Petrograd,' Semyon remarked eagerly. 'So in 1916, on New Year's Eve, we ask him what the prospects are. And then he laid it all on us . . .'

★ ★ ★

I managed to intercept Las in the yard, just as he was getting into his freshly washed Mazda. He was frankly delighted when I showed up.

'Anton, are you really busy?'

'Well . . .'

'Why don't you scoot over to Sheremetyevo with me? Boris Ignatievich told me to follow in your footsteps and look for anything odd. Maybe you could come along?'

'What are we going to do about you?' I asked, clambering into the right-side front seat. 'All right, I'll go. But you'll owe me one, you know that.'

'Goes without saying,' Las said delightedly, turning on the motor. 'I'm a bit pushed for time – I had to change my plans for today.'

'What plans were they?' I asked as we drove out of the car park.

'Well, it's like this . . .' Las was slightly embarrassed. 'I was going to get baptised today.'

'What?' I thought I'd misheard.

'Baptised,' Las repeated, looking at the road. 'All right, isn't it? We can get baptised?'

'Who are "we"?' I asked, just to be on the safe side.

'Others!'

'Of course we can,' I answered. 'That's, like, that's . . . a spiritual matter. Magic's magic, and faith . . .'

Las suddenly started talking nineteen to the dozen.

'I just thought – the devil only knows what they'll make of me practising magic . . . I always used to be an agnostic – a broad-profile ecumenist, that is – but then I thought . . . better get baptised, to make completely sure.'

'There was this character in the Simpsons: to make completely sure, he observed the Sabbath day and performed the Salat too,' I remarked, unable to resist the jibe.

'Don't blaspheme,' Las said strictly. 'I'm serious . . . I found this church especially for it, in the Moscow region. They say all the priests in Moscow are corrupt. But in the provinces they're closer to God. I phoned them yesterday and had a talk – well, some acquaintances recommended me – they promised to baptise me today, but then Gesar gave me this assignment . . .'

'You're moving kind of fast,' I said doubtfully. 'Are you really ready for the sacrament of baptism?'

'Of course,' Las laughed. 'I've bought a cross, and a Bible just in case, and a couple of icons . . .'

'Hang on, hang on,' I said, starting to get interested. We'd just come out onto Leningrad Chaussee and started burning up the road to the airport. Las usually put the 'escort' spell on his car, and people had started hastily making way for us. I don't know which drivers saw what – for some it was an ambulance, for some a police car with its siren wailing, for some a government escort vehicle with blinking lights hung all over it, like some chicken-brain techie with his mobile phones – but they all cleared the road for us pretty smartly.

'And have you learned off the creed?'

'What creed?' Las asked in surprise.

'The Nicene-Constantinopolitan Creed!'

'Do I have to?' Las asked anxiously.

'Never mind, the priest will explain,' I said, beginning to feel really amused. 'Have you bought a baptismal robe?'

'What for?'

'Well, when you climb out of the font . . .'

'They only immerse infants in the font – I'm not going to climb into it! They splash the water on grown-ups!'

'You numbskull,' I said emphatically. 'They have special fonts, for adults. They're called baptisteries.'

'Is that what the Baptists have?'

'It's what they all have.'

Las started pondering – thankfully, driving an automobile with the 'escort' spell on it didn't require truly intense concentration.

'But what if there are dames there?'

'They're not dames any more, they're Sisters in Christ!'

'You're putting me on!' Las exclaimed indignantly. 'That's enough, Anton!'

I took out my mobile, thought for a second and asked: 'Which of our guys do you trust?'

'In spiritual matters?' Las asked. 'Well . . . I'd trust Semyon . . .'

'He'll do,' I said, with a nod. Then I dialled the number and turned on the speaker.

'Yes, Anton?' Semyon responded.

'Listen, are you baptised?'

'At my age, how could a Russian not be baptised?' Semyon answered. 'I was born in the tsar's time . . .'

'And are you still close to the Orthodox Faith?'

'Well . . .' Semyon was clearly embarrassed. 'I go to church. Sometimes.'

'Tell me, how do they baptise adults?'

'The normal way is the same as for children. Off with the clothes and duck them underwater three times, head and all.'

'Thanks,' I said and cut off the call. 'Did you get that? Doubting Thomas . . . prepare for the sacrament.'

'What else will there be?' asked Las.

'You stand facing the west, spit three times and say: "I renounce Satan!"'

Las burst into laughter. 'Come on, Anton . . . Stop telling me fibs. Okay, I accept the baptism, I was a bit too hasty there! A genuine, uncorrupted priest won't be mean with the water. But standing facing the west . . . and spitting . . .'

I dialled Semyon again.

'Yes?' he asked curiously.

'Another question. How does the rite of renouncing Satan go in the baptism?'

'You stand facing the west. The priest asks if you renounce Satan and his works. You renounce him three times and spit towards the west—'

'Thanks.' I cut him off again.

Las said nothing, clutching the wheel and looking straight ahead. We had already passed the Moscow Orbital Highway.

'And what other difficult moments will there be?' he asked almost timidly.

'You take the plunge, you renounce Satan,' I said, counting on my fingers. 'And the third step – you must bear in mind that everything in the church is triune, because God is a trinity – the third step . . . you get out of the font and run round the church three times, against the movement of the sun.'

'Naked?' Las asked, horrified. 'With no trousers?'

'Of course. Like the Old Testament Adam, who was without sin until he did taste the fruit of the Tree of Knowledge!'

The phrase sprang to mind spontaneously, but it sounded very convincing.

'Well . . . if I have to . . .' Las said in a quiet voice.

'You could drop into any church,' I advised him. 'Even a corrupt one. And buy a little book, with explanations.'

'I feel awkward going into a church,' Las admitted. 'Not only am I not baptised, I'm a magician too! Bugger it, maybe I should postpone the baptism? If I have to run round the church naked . . . I'll go to a gym for a while, firm up a bit . . .'

'All right, the part about running round the church isn't true,' I said, taking pity on him. 'But I would advise you to take the matter a bit more seriously.'

'How complicated everything is . . .' Las sighed as we trundled towards the terminal. 'Is it D we want?'

'Yes, the new one,' I confirmed.

'Well, then, let's go for it, with God's help!' said Las.

I realised that the zeal of the neophyte still burned bright within him.

CHAPTER 2

IN THE AIRPORT Las and I separated. He set off to talk to people – his abilities were quite adequate for making them talk frankly and openly about everything. First of all he had to talk to the engineers who had prepared that cursed (or would it be more correct to say 'blessed'?) Boeing for its flight, then with the flight controllers and, if he could manage it, with the crew. And I set off to see the Others on duty at the airport.

As regulations required, there were two of them – a Dark Other and a Light Other. Of course, I knew ours – Andrei, a young lad, Fifth-Level, he didn't appear in the office very often but worked at the airport all the time. I'd seen Arkady, the elderly Dark Other a few times too, when I was flying out or coming back myself.

Naturally, they were up to speed on what had happened. Andrei and the Dark Other were only too glad to discuss the story of the plane with me – but they couldn't tell me anything useful because they didn't know anything. The Dark Others had already ironically dubbed the child 'The Boy Who Wouldn't Fly' – and that was probably the most valuable thing I learned. I also noticed that the relationship between Andrei and Arkady was entirely friendly, and made a mental note to recommend more frequent changes of duty personnel. There's no prohibition in principle on friendly relations between Others. There are cases like that: I myself was friendly with a family of vampires, and in Petersburg there's even a unique family – a Light Magician and a Dark Clairvoyant – although they don't work in the Petersburg Watches . . . But in the case of a young Light One and an experienced Dark One there was a risk of undesirable influence.

Best to play safe.

With this thought in mind I wandered on round the airport for a while, discovered a vampire standing in a check-in queue and out of sheer boredom checked his registration seal – everything was in order. I got the urge to have another beer, but that would have been overdoing it. On the other hand . . . I didn't have to drive . . . I caught myself edging closer and closer to the bar.

Fortunately, Las showed up, brisk and cheerful. I turned away from the little restaurant with a feeling of relief and waved to him.

'Ninety-four per cent!' he informed me cheerfully.

I raised one eyebrow quizzically – well, at least, that was the gesture I tried to imitate.

'I've been interested for a long time in the question of how many people pick their noses when they're sure no one can see them. So I asked exactly a hundred people – and ninety-four of them confessed!'

For a second I thought Las must have gone insane.

'And you asked people about that instead of trying to discover something unusual?'

'Why "instead of"?' asked Las, offended. 'As well as! Just think about it: how can you use the minimal amount of magical influence to make people tell the truth first, and make sure they'll forget the questions as completely as possible! I introduced myself as a sociologist carrying out a survey with the permission of the management. I asked about any strange things they'd seen, about where they spent this morning . . . basically, everything I was supposed to ask. That was all under the influence of "Plato". And at the end I asked the question about picking their noses. Surely you realise that someone who has confessed, even in an anonymous survey, that they pick bogies out of their noses with their finger when they're alone will try to forget the whole business as quickly as possible? It was effective, and I got an answer to my question too!'

'Why did you want that answer?' I asked. 'When they're left alone, people often do . . . well . . . things that aren't very attractive at all. Picking your nose with your finger is nothing, really.'

'Of course,' agreed Las. 'But it's indicative! The overwhelming majority of people will defend a footling little lie like that to the death. They don't deny that they peep at immature nymphets, avoid paying their taxes or scheme against their colleagues at work, but they do deny something banal and funny that does no one any harm – picking their nose with their finger! That tells you a lot about people.'

'Next time ask about them picking a different place with their finger,' I replied sombrely. 'What about our business?'

Las shrugged.

'The plane was normal. They checked it out, just like they're supposed to, no faults at all. By the way, did you know that planes can be allowed to fly when part of their equipment isn't working? Well, everything was working on this one. And it's a brand new plane, made three years ago, not some old second-hand junk from China.'

'So no way was it going to crash, then?' I asked, to make absolutely sure.

'Everything is in God's hands,' Las said, with a shrug, and then flaunted his brilliant knowledge of the Bible: '"And a bird shall not fall from the sky without the will of the Lord!" And even more so an aeroplane. Well . . . and it didn't fall.'

'But the boy prophesied it,' I said. 'And the lines of probability indicated an inevitable disaster . . . All right. The plane was in good condition, the crew was experienced. Was there anything strange at all?'

'To do with the plane, or in general?' Las asked.

'In general.'

'Well, a local *polizei* shat himself this morning.'

'What?'

'He couldn't get to the toilet in time. Dumped in his trousers. They found him an old uniform in the duty office and he washed himself off in the shower . . .'

'Las, what is it that attracts you to all sorts of low crudity?' I asked indignantly. 'Even if an employee of the Ministry of the Interior did suffer an attack of dysentery, it's not a fit subject for discussion – let alone for irony! You're a Light One! A Light Other!'

'Well, I feel sorry for both the *polizei*,' Las remarked casually.

My heart skipped half a beat.

'Both? Did they eat the meat pies at the local cafe?'

'Oh no, the other one's digestion is fine,' Las reassured me. 'The other one went insane.'

I waited. In anticipation of more specific questions, Las was clearly doling out the information in small doses quite deliberately – to heighten the drama.

'Aren't you interested?' asked Las.

'Report in due form,' I told him.

Las sighed and scratched the back of his head.

'Well, it's nothing special, really. But it does kind of fall outside the everyday routine. This morning, about the same time you left the airport, something unpleasant happened to this police patrol and inspection unit. One *polizei*, Dmitry Pastukhov, went off to the privy but he didn't move fast enough. And the other one . . . a little while later the other one walked into the duty office and put his holster, ID and walkie-talkie on the desk. Said he'd lost interest in working for the forces of law and order and left. His bosses haven't even informed anyone yet. They're hoping he'll change his mind and come back.'

'Let's go,' I said

'Which one first?'

'The one who didn't run fast enough.'

'No need to go anywhere, then. I told you – he got washed and changed and went back to his post.'

At first glance there was no way of telling that this morning police officer Dmitry Pastukhov had found himself in such a delicate and – why pretend otherwise? – embarrassing situation. Except that his uniform trousers, if you looked closely, were a little too big for him, and they were a slightly different shade of grey from his tunic.

He himself, however, was looking quite magnificent. Inspired, you might say. Like a militiaman in a children's story who has detained a bandit at the scene of his crime and is now being presented with a watch engraved 'For conspicuous valour in the line of duty' by a general. Like a test pilot who has managed to get his plane back to the airfield after its engine failed, and can feel the wheels gently touching the ground. Like a man taking a cigarette out of the pack and smiling awkwardly as he looks round at the gigantic icicle that has just crashed into the pavement at the very spot where he was walking only a moment ago . . .

Like a man who has survived deadly danger and realises that he is still alive, but doesn't really understand why.

Dmitry Pastukhov was sauntering about in front of the entrance to the airport building with his hands clasped behind his back in non-regulation style, gazing around with a good-natured, friendly air.

But as Las and I came closer a quite different expression appeared on the policeman's face.

Like the expression on the militiaman's face when the general tells him: 'Well done . . . well done . . . I suppose you knew whose nephew it was that you were arresting – but that didn't frighten you? You're a real hero . . .' Like the expression on the pilot's face when his plane is already taxiing over the concrete and the fuel tank explodes in a ferocious ball of flame. Or the expression on the face of the man on the pavement, kneading his cigarette to soften it before lighting up, with his stare fixed on the shattered icicle, when he hears a sudden shout above his head: 'Look out!'

He was afraid of me.

He knew who I was. Not exactly, perhaps . . . but there was no point in introducing myself as an inspector, a journalist or an environmental health officer.

He knew that I wasn't human.

'Wait here, Las,' I said. 'I'd better handle this . . .'

Pastukhov waited without trying to walk away or pretend that he hadn't noticed me approaching. He didn't reach for his weapon, as I had been slightly afraid that he might (I didn't want to start the conversation as dynamically as that). And when I stopped two steps away, he heaved a sigh, smiled awkwardly and asked: 'Permission to smoke?'

'What?' I asked, perplexed. 'Oh, of course . . .'

Pastukhov took out a cigarette and lit up greedily. Then he said: 'One thing I really want to ask you: don't make me get drunk any more. They'll chuck me out of the service! We've got another campaign on now, they sack you if you just show up for work with a hangover.'

I looked at him for a few seconds, then something came together in my head and I saw a grey Moscow winter, dirty snow on the verge of Peace Prospect, trading kiosks clustered round the Exhibition of Economic Achievements metro station, two militiamen walking towards me – one a bit older, the other still very young.

'I'm sorry,' I said. 'Did you really get it in the neck that time?'

The policeman shrugged indefinitely. Then he said: 'You haven't changed at all. Thirteen years have gone by – and you haven't even aged.'

'We age slowly,' I said.

'Uh-huh.' Pastukhov nodded and tossed his cigarette away. 'I'm not stupid. I understand everything. So . . . tell me straight away what you want. Or do what you want to do.'

He was afraid of me. Well, who wouldn't be frightened of someone who can make you do anything at all with a single word?

I lowered my eyes, reaching for my shadow. I stepped into it – and I was in the Twilight. There wasn't any particular necessity for it, but an aura can be scanned more thoroughly from there.

The policeman was human. Not the slightest indication of an Other. A man, and by no means the worst of them.

'Can you tell me what happened this morning?' I asked him as I returned to the everyday world. Pastukhov blinked – he'd probably caught a whiff of the Twilight. He couldn't have noticed my disappearing for such a short time.

'Bisat and me were standing here,' he said. 'Just shooting the breeze. Today was a good day . . .' From the way he said it, he clearly didn't think it was any more. 'Then you walked past . . .'

'Did you recognise me, Dmitry?' I asked. There was no point in putting a truth spell on him – he was being quite honest with me.

'Well, at first I just realised that you were one of those . . .' The policeman waved his hand vaguely through the air. 'And then I recognised you, yes . . .'

'How did you realise?'

Pastukhov looked at me in amazement. 'Why . . . I recognise your kind at a glance.'

'How?'

It suddenly dawned on him. 'What, is that so unusual?' he asked, obviously pondering something.

'More than unusual,' I said, deciding not to hide anything from him. 'Usually it's only Others like ourselves who can see us. They recognise us from the aura.'

'An aura – that's like a kind of glow round the head, right?' asked Pastukhov, wrinkling up his forehead. 'I thought all kinds of psychos saw it. And villains.'

'Not just round the head, and not just psychos and villains. But what do you see?'

'Why, I recognise you from your eyes! Ever since the first time we met,' Pastukhov said abruptly. 'You've got eyes like a guard dog's.'

If I hadn't just scanned his aura, I would have felt certain that I was dealing with some strange kind of weak Other who perceived auras in a highly original way. After all, the aura is strongest round the head and the eyes radiate the brightest glow on the face, so maybe that was how he spotted Others?

But no, he wasn't an Other, he was a human being . . .

'That's curious,' I admitted. 'Like a dog's eyes, you say?'

'No offence intended,' Pastukhov said, shrugging. He was gradually recovering his wits.

'None taken. I'm very fond of dogs.'

'And then there are the others, with eyes like a wolf's,' said Pastukhov.

I nodded. It was clear enough. That was how he saw Dark Ones.

'Please, go on.'

'This morning you walked past,' said Pastukhov. 'Well . . . I got the shakes, of course. Like a fool, I thought you'd remember me too, like I did you. But then, why would you? You probably play tricks like that with people every day.'

'No,' I said. 'It's not allowed. That was a critical situation. And I . . . I was young and inexperienced. I just did the first thing that came into my head. Go on.'

Pastukhov wiped the sweat off his forehead and shrugged. 'Then a wolf walked past . . . well . . . that's nothing unusual. I see dogs and wolves at the airport every day. And then this other one came out . . . that was when I really freaked.'

'Another "wolf"?' I asked.

'No . . .' Pastukhov hesitated and started shuffling his feet. 'I've never come across any like him before. To myself I called him a "tiger". That look in his eyes – as if he could gobble up anyone he wanted on the spot . . . And I . . . somehow I thought he'd see right through me, realise I could see who he was and kill me on the spot. That very second. So I decided to beat it. I told my partner I had stomach cramps and I was going to the toilet. I thought, what could happen to Bisat? He can't see your kind! But as I was walking away I saw Bisat . . . stopping that tiger!'

'Can you describe him? The tiger?'

Pastukhov shook his head.

'I only saw him from a distance. Male, middle-aged, average height, dark hair . . .'

'I really hate people who fit that description,' I said, frowning. 'How could you make out the look in his eyes from so far away?'

'I can see the eyes from any distance,' Pastukhov replied seriously. 'I don't know why.'

'Nationality?'

Dmitry thought about that. 'Standard, probably. Native European Russian.'

'So not from the Caucasus, or Asia or Scandinavia . . .'

'No, and not black, either.'

'Anything else?'

Pastukhov closed his eyes and frowned. He was making a genuine effort. 'He didn't have any luggage. When he was standing beside Bisat, I noticed his hands were empty. He probably wouldn't have flown in like that, would he?'

'Thank you, that's interesting,' I said. Of course, the luggage could actually have been invisible. I once lugged an invisible suitcase onto a plane to avoid the excess-baggage charge . . .

The policeman sighed and said: 'Probably I should have gone back, only my stomach really did cramp up. It was so bad, I was afraid I wouldn't reach the toilet in time, even at a run—' He broke off and then went on: 'And I didn't make it. But you probably know that already.'

'Yes,' I said and nodded.

'I shat myself,' Pastukhov said miserably. 'Well, if it had been some kind of digestive trouble, dysentery – anyone can get that, right? But this came straight out of the blue. Anyway, I cleaned myself up as best I could, and then called in to the duty office – I took a change of trousers from an old uniform there. The duty sergeant was roaring with laughter, naturally – by evening everyone will know about it . . . Then I came back to my post.'

'And then?' I was much more interested in this than in Pastukhov's health problems and concern about his good name.

'Well, nothing – or that's how it seemed at first. Bisat just stood there, smiling. I asked him what happened with the guy he stopped. Bisat just waved his hand and said: "Everything's in order, there was no point in detaining him." Well, I thought, the danger's over . . . And then Bisat suddenly takes off his tunic and tears the shoulder straps off, really careful-like! And he tears off his badge! Then he takes out his documents. And his pistol and his walkie-talkie . . . And he hands it all to me! I ask what's wrong with him. And he answers: "None of this makes any sense, there's no need for the job I do." And he walks off to the train! I shouted after him, but he just waved and carried on anyway! He's probably home by now.'

'I heard that he went to the duty office himself,' I remarked.

'Roman told you that, I suppose?' Pastukhov asked me. 'I asked him to say that, when I took the things in. After all, it's one thing if a man just dumps everything in the street, but it's a different matter if he hands it in at the duty office. Maybe he'll change his mind and come back. In any case, he's in for a whole heap of trouble – although they'll probably run him through the funny farm and discharge him on health grounds . . .'

'Do you really think he'll come back?' I asked.

Pastukhov shook his head.

'No, I don't. It's the tiger. He did something to him. Maybe he ordered him to do it – the way you ordered me to get drunk that time . . . Or maybe something else. Bisat won't come back.'

'Thank you,' I said sincerely. 'You seem like a good man to me. I'm sorry about what happened that other time.'

Pastukhov hesitated, then went ahead and asked anyway: 'So what's going to happen to me now? Will you order me to forget everything?'

I looked at him thoughtfully. I didn't want to use even the very simplest of spells on Pastukhov. He was a rather strange man, but a good one.

'Do you swear on your word of honour not to tell anyone anything about our conversation?' I asked. 'Or to mention us at all?'

'What kind of fool do you take me for?' the policeman asked indignantly. 'Who'd ever believe me? I won't tell anyone!'

'Then just one last question. When you're alone and there's no one else there, do you pick your nose with your finger?'

Pastukhov opened his mouth and closed it again, blushed unexpectedly and said: 'Well . . . if I need to . . . occasionally.'

'I'll drop round to see you sometime – we'll need to chat again,' I said. 'But don't you worry about it. It's just a little heart-to-heart talk, that's all.'

'Aha . . .' Pastukhov said awkwardly. 'Thanks . . .'

'Don't you want to ask me any questions?'

Pastukhov shook his head slowly. 'I do. But I won't. The less you know, the sounder you sleep.'

I was already walking back to Las when he called to me: 'Will you help Bisat?'

'What makes you think I'll help him?' I asked.

'Well . . .' The policeman faltered, and then suddenly smiled: 'Because a dog is a man's best friend. Right?'

I wagged my finger at him and walked on to join Las.

'He picks his nose too,' I said acidly. 'Did you note down the details of the *polizei* who left his post? Call the information section, we need his address urgently. No, you drive and I'll call while we're on our way out.'

CHAPTER 3

POLICE OFFICER BISAT Iskenderov lived not far from the airport, in Kurkino. A good district, one that many even considered elite. But Iskenderov lived in a municipal apartment, so he wasn't going to be one of those prosperous policemen who spend all their life pounding the beat but somehow manage to live in luxury accommodation and drive to work in an executive-class Mercedes.

While we were on our way to this policeman who had resigned from the service so suddenly and in such an unusual manner, I told Las about my conversation with Pastukhov.

'Dogs, are we?' Las said thoughtfully. 'That's pushing it a bit . . . But listen, why did you just talk to him? If you'd used Plato, he'd have been delighted to tell you everything. Or just got inside his head – you can do that . . .'

I detected a hint of envy in those last words. Las was a weak Other, with no chance of improving his level. Some spells would always be beyond his reach.

'Las, have you often met people who can see Others?' I asked instead of answering.

'No.'

'Me neither. I've never even heard of such a thing. It seems like he developed this ability after his encounter with me. In that case, there's a chance it could be a consequence of the spell I put on him.'

'And you're afraid that a new spell will take away his ability . . .' Las said, with a nod. 'I get it. Well, you're the Higher One, it's for you to decide.'

'It's for Gesar to decide,' I said. 'But I don't want to hurry things. Pastukhov won't tell anyone. And if he does, he'll end up in an asylum.'

'And that "tiger"?'

'What about the tiger?'

'Who do you think he is? A Higher Magician?'

'Pastukhov didn't call me a tiger . . .'

'Logical . . . But who is he, then? An Inquisitor?'

'No,' I said regretfully. 'I don't think so. Inquisitors remain Light Ones or Dark Ones – whichever they were before.'

'But their aura turns grey.'

I sighed, wondering if I ought to reveal the real facts.

'Actually it doesn't. Their aura is just covered over with grey. A powerful magician can look through the disguise – underneath it's the same as it was before. Either Light or Dark. They don't change their essential nature.'

'So that's the way of it,' said Las, raising one eyebrow. 'So why couldn't it be an Inquisitor, then?'

'An Other with a grey, obscure aura – a tiger? Just doesn't tally, does it? Bearing in mind how precisely Pastukhov characterised us.'

'Then who is he?' asked Las, bemused.

'Gesar can decide that one too,' I replied. 'He's got a big brain in his head. He's lived in this world for a long time. Let him think about it.'

'Yes, that's the right approach, definitely!' Las said approvingly. 'Listen, I was just thinking . . . this *polizei* lied to his partner about wanting to go to the can . . .'

'Right . . .' I agreed, nodding. We'd just driven into the yard of a tall building and Las was looking for a parking place.

'He lied about it first. And then he really did mess himself.'

'Out of fright,' I concluded.

'All the same, it's an unusual coincidence.'

I didn't say anything. There was a grain of good sense in what Las had said. When there are strange things going on all around, every coincidence should be considered very carefully.

'Let's go,' I said, climbing out of the car. 'We'll have a word with this Bisat – and then we'll do some thinking.'

More out of habit than in the expectation of seeing anything unusual, in the entrance hall I shifted into the Twilight. The policeman lived on the first floor – public-service accommodation isn't often allocated on the prestigious upper floors. There was nothing unusual on the ground floor here. Blue moss, the parasite of the Twilight, covered all the walls in an even layer, flourishing especially thickly in the corner beside the radiator and in front of the door of the lift. It was all predictable: young couples kiss beside the radiator before the girl straightens out her clothes and runs back home to mum and dad . . . or to her husband and children. And people swear in front of the lift doors when they discover that the lift's broken and they have to walk up to the twelfth floor, or they rejoice quietly in anticipation of getting back home . . . I cast fire in all directions with habitual gestures, incinerating the parasite. It can't be exterminated completely, of course, but for any Other this is the same as wiping his feet when he walks into someone's home.

The first floor gave me something to think about, though. The blue moss was everywhere except around one door, from which it seemed to have crept away. And quite recently too, only a few hours ago. Fine blue threads were slowly retracting into the dense blue carpet – the same way an amoeba shrinks back when it runs into a grain of salt.

'He lives here,' I said, coming back to reality.

'Did you see something?' Las asked.

'No, nothing really.'

I rang the bell.

Almost half a minute went by before the door opened. Without any questions being asked and also, it seemed to me, without even the glance through the peephole that is an obligatory ritual for anyone who lives in Moscow.

The woman in the doorway was short and plump. A Muscovite's image of 'a typical middle-aged eastern type of woman' – obviously a beauty when she was young but not so lovely now, with a really calm-looking face, as if she was very self-absorbed.

'Hello,' I said, edging forward slightly. 'We're from the department. Is Bisat at home?'

'The department' is a very handy little phrase. Somehow no one ever asks which particular department it is that you're from. The woman didn't bother to check either.

'Come in,' she said, moving aside. 'He's in the bedroom . . .'

We seemed to be expected. Well, it wasn't us, but they were expecting someone.

As I walked in, I glanced at her aura. Nothing special, of course. A human being.

The flat had three rooms, but it was small, and the hallway was really narrow and cramped. Loud rock music – something unfamiliar – was pouring out through the sitting-room door.

I was a player and I could have challenged
The inventor of cards at his game.
My luck always in, I followed my star,
It would never fail me, I would go far,
But disaster struck all the same . . .
This precious life crushes the weak like moths,
You have to choose which you trust the most –
The Holy Bible or a trusty Colt!

Las pricked up his ears – he adored little-known rock bands – then shook his head regretfully and clicked his tongue.

Without speaking, the woman gave me slippers, choosing one of the larger pairs out of a drove of them loitering around the door. Las didn't bother to take his shoes off – and she didn't react to that either.

Strange. Such simple habits are usually the most stable of all. She should either have asked both of us to change our shoes or not bothered to offer me any slippers, in keeping with the fashionable European traditions that are so slow to take hold in Moscow, with its wet climate and its mud.

There was a skinny kid sitting on the sofa in the sitting room with a laptop on his knees. From the laptop a wire snaked across the floor to a pair of speakers. The young lad looked at us and turned down the volume of the speakers but he didn't even say hello, which was really strange for an eastern boy. I scanned his aura too. Human.

'This way . . .'

We followed the woman through to the bedroom. She opened the door to let us go on in and, without speaking, closed it behind us, staying out in the hallway.

Oh, something bad was going on around here . . .

Bisat Iskenderov was lying on the made-up bed in just his

shorts and singlet, watching the TV hanging on the wall facing the bed. Everything in the place was in average Moscow style, with almost no national character at all, absolutely no personal touch: furniture from IKEA, a carpet at the head of the bed (I thought they didn't hang them up like that any longer, that the tradition had died out with the old, stagnant Brezhnev days), a women's magazine on one of the night tables, an anthology of detective stories on the other. A bedroom like that could have been in any Russian town or city. The man lying on the bed could have been Ivan the manager or Rinat the builder.

I don't like flats that don't bear the stamp of their owner.

'Hello, Bisat,' I said. 'We're from the department. What happened to you? Are you ill?'

Bisat looked at me and shifted his gaze back to the screen. It was showing a popular programme – a young female doctor with kind eyes was telling people about periproctitis. 'And now we'll ask someone wearing a T-shirt or a shirt without a collar to come up on stage from the audience . . .'

'Hello,' Bisat replied. 'Nothing happened. I'm fine.'

'But you abandoned your watch . . .' I said.

And I looked at him through the Twilight.

At first I thought there must be something wrong with me.

Then I realised it wasn't me. But that wasn't reassuring at all.

'Las, take a peek at his aura . . .' I said quietly.

Las wrinkled up his forehead and answered: 'I can't seem to see it . . .'

'That's because it isn't there,' I confirmed.

Bisat waited patiently while we talked. Then he answered: 'I abandoned the watch because there was no point in staying on duty.'

'Tell me about the man you talked to before you left,' I said.

'I don't get this,' Las said thoughtfully. 'Are there really people who don't have any aura?'

'Now, imagine that the neck of the T-shirt is really . . .' the female presenter told us from the screen.

'Before I left I talked to Dima Pastukhov,' said Bisat. 'He's a decent man . . .'

'Before that!' I told him. 'Before Dima!'

'Before Dima I talked to the woman in the tobacco kiosk,' said Bisat. 'She's quite an attractive woman, but very thin . . .'

'No, wait,' I told him. 'Bisat, when Pastukhov got stomach cramps and he went into the airport building – remember? You stopped a man coming out of the arrivals hall . . .'

'But he wasn't a man,' Bisat objected very calmly.

'Then who was he?' I exclaimed.

'I don't know,' Bisat said as imperturbably as ever. 'But not a man. There aren't any people like that.'

'All right, tell me what this not-man looked like,' I told him. 'And what you talked about.'

'He . . .' For the first time Bisat thought about his answer. He even displayed a certain degree of animation, reaching out his hand and scratching his stomach. 'He had light hair. Very tall. A short beard. Blue eyes. I asked him for his ID. He said there was no need for that. He put his hand on my shoulder and looked into my eyes. I . . . I was going to ask him what he thought he was doing. But I didn't.'

'Why not?'

'What difference does it make?'

'Your partner Dima described this . . . not-man . . . differently.'

'I don't know how he described him,' Bisat replied calmly.

I sighed, gathered together a little Power in my hand and cast the Socrates spell – a temporary but irresistible desire to tell the truth, and nothing but the truth – in the policeman's direction.

Hurtling through the Twilight, the hazy blob of the spell passed straight through Bisat and carried on through the wall out into the street. Oh-oh, now someone was in for it . . .

'Try the "Dominant",' suggested Las.

I shook my head, looking at the man lying on the bed. A normal man, who couldn't care less about anything now. He had no aura. And spells passed clean through him.

'That won't help. Let's go, Las.'

'But . . .'

'Let's go,' I said.

Bisat turned back to the screen again. The presenter was happily explaining: 'And so, in these delicate folds and wrinkles . . .'

The policeman's wife was waiting for us in the hallway. The music was still playing, only more quietly now.

> Howl if you like, it won't change a thing,
> You must pay the price for your luck.
> Water won't save a shrivelled-up garden
> And money won't buy my life back.

'We'll be going,' I said awkwardly. 'You know . . . you'll probably get more phone calls. And people will call round . . . from work.'

'I want to take him away,' the woman said suddenly.

'Where to?'

'Home . . . To Azerbaijan. There's an *otachi* there – Yusuf. He cures people with herbs. He cures everything. He's not just a herb doctor, he's a *gam*.'

'A wizard?' I asked.

The woman nodded and pursed her lips tightly.

'Take him,' I said. 'Only first show him to our healer, all right?'

The woman looked at me suspiciously.

'He'll come to see you today,' I said. 'A good healer. Believe me.'

'What's wrong with him?' the woman asked.

'I don't know,' I admitted.

'It's like he's lost his soul,' said the woman.

'Wait for the healer,' I told her.

We walked out of the flat. I looked into the Twilight – the blue moss had crept even further away from the door. It didn't like what was going on in there.

'Come on, Las,' I said. 'We've got to see Gesar, and quick.'

But we had to stop for a minute outside the building. Standing in front of the entrance was a young couple – a girl with an expression of simultaneous fury and bewilderment on her face and a young man who was declaring enthusiastically: 'And I only kissed your sister, and that was when I was drunk. But I slept with Lenka once, she came round when you were out . . .'

'We have to tidy things up here,' I decided. 'I'll deal with the girl, and you remove the Socrates from the guy and make him forget everything.'

'Do we really have to?' Las asked pensively. 'It's his own fault – let him take the consequences.'

'Mistakes have to be corrected,' I said. 'At least, those that *can* be corrected.'

Las obviously thinks that I already understand something and the reason we're in such a rush to get back to Gesar is because *he* definitely understands everything – who this tiger is, why a living man has no aura (and at the same time has lost all interest in life), why spells aimed at him pass straight through him. But in actual fact, I don't understand a thing. And I expect Gesar will be just as dumbfounded as I am.

Just what is an aura, if you think about it?

It's Power. The same Power that people produce all the time, but can't use. The Power flows out of them into space and blankets the whole Earth. We Others produce far less of it – which means we can absorb it from the ambient environment. (The blue moss does pretty much the same thing, only we're far more efficient – and we can think too!) If there's no aura, it means there's no Power . . . no life energy . . . the man or Other is already dead.

No, what kind of nonsense is this I'm thinking? No aura? Vampires are dead, they're in a state of 'afterlife', but they have an aura. Their own special vampire aura, but they have it. And my Nadiushka – an absolute enchantress with a 'zero magical temperature' – she has an aura, too, and boy, what an aura that is!

I wiped my forehead. I'd never really attempted to come to grips with all the fine details of our existence. I'd always preferred to let the research team rack their brains over that . . . All these theories are infinitely distant from real life in any case.

So . . . why do beings who are dead have an aura? And those who don't radiate any 'life energy' at all? And why are they alive . . . horrifying as it was to put vampires and Nadya in the same category, I forced myself to do it and tried to view the question in the abstract. Without life energy, it's impossible to live . . . but the dead and 'zero-temperature magicians' don't produce it . . .

Stop! It's all very elementary. They don't radiate it, but they consume it. Other beings' Power is what allows vampires to exist after death. So it turns out that's what keeps Nadya alive too. To refine the analogy . . . my daughter is like a person whose body doesn't produce blood. And she lives on constant, continuous transfusions . . .

I winced and squirmed in my seat. Even just thinking about it was unpleasant. Maybe that was why I'd never gone into the details of how Power, aura and life were interconnected?

Okay, that was all idle conjecture. So Nadya lived on other people's life energy. She was alive and she was just fine. But how was it possible to take away a man's Power and still leave him alive? Not kill him, not turn him into a vampire – but transform him into a strange kind of talking puppet?

I didn't know

'You're lost in thought,' said Las.

'Uh-huh,' I confirmed.

'Listen, I've got a question . . . Higher Others – can they see the soul fly out of the body?'

'The soul?' I asked, mystified. 'Fly out?'

'Well, yeah. The aura's the soul, right? So when someone dies, can you see where the aura flies off to? What I'm getting at is that you could figure out where heaven and hell are. If you take two people dying simultaneously at opposite ends of the globe and pinpoint the direction the souls fly off in, then you could triangulate—'

'Las, the aura is not the soul!' I objected. 'The aura is life energy.'

'Ah, and I thought it was the soul,' said Las, upset. 'So the soul can't be seen?'

'No,' I replied. 'And when someone dies, the aura doesn't go flying off anywhere, it just stops glowing.'

But there was something to all of this. Las's question, my answer . . .

But I couldn't understand what it was, and I ran out of time. We drove under the boom that had risen obligingly to allow us into our car park – and stopped right in front of Gesar.

That's the difference between a real magician and a beginner like me – experience. And the ability to do a whole heap of things all at the same time. If I'd sent someone off to do a job, and then been keeping close tabs on the action, I could probably have sensed that he was hurrying back with something important to report. Only I would have had to do that deliberately. But Gesar seemed simply to have sensed my approach in between doing everything else – and he felt so concerned that he'd come out to meet me.

'Tell me,' he ordered curtly as I started clambering out of the car. 'And quick!'

All right, then, quick it is . . . I looked into his eyes and played back the conversation with Pastukhov and the visit to Iskenderov.

'Let's go to my office,' said Gesar and swung round. Putting up a portal from that distance would simply have looked flashy. 'Call Svetlana.'

'What for?' I asked, taking out my mobile.

'I'll open a portal to your flat. Tell her to come here and bring Nadya.'

A repulsive, chilly tremor of fear ran down my spine.

'No, I don't see any immediate threat,' said Gesar, without turning round. 'But I don't like what's happening one little bit. And I need all the Higher Ones in Moscow.'

As he walked along, Gesar seemed to falter every now and then, not stopping completely but slowing down for an instant. It looked to me as if he was communicating with the other Higher Ones.

But then – what others? I was calling Svetlana . . . why wasn't she answering? . . . there was Olga, too . . . and that was the entire complement of the Night Watch's 'Magicians Beyond Classification'. The Day Watch only had Zabulon on active service now – they had lots of First- and Second-Level Magicians, but recently things hadn't gone so well for them with Higher Ones . . .

'And what shall I do?' Las shouted after us resentfully.

'Call into the science department and have them send Innokentii to me!' Gesar told him. He liked everyone around him to have some task to perform.

Svetlana finally answered.

'Anton?'

'Sveta, Gesar's going to put up a portal to our flat . . .'

'It's already up,' Svetlana answered calmly.

'Grab Nadka and get over here, quick.'

'Is there some kind of rush?' asked Sveta.

'Say they can bring things for a day or two,' Gesar responded briskly. 'But they mustn't dawdle.'

I didn't like that comment at all. Gesar was acting as if Sveta and Nadya were going to be under siege. But we were talking about a Higher Enchantress here (Svetlana might specialise in healing, but everyone knows that any healing spell can be used just as effectively for attack) and an Absolute Enchantress as well. (The fact that she was only ten years old didn't make Nadya defenceless. She could set up a perfectly standard Sphere of Negation, but pack so much Power into it that you couldn't breach it with a cannon.)

'I heard,' said Sveta. 'Right now I'm throwing clean underclothes into a bag . . . Shall I bring anything for you?'

'Er . . .' I hesitated. 'Well, a pair of socks, a couple of pairs of shorts . . .'

'I'll take a risk and grab a clean shirt as well,' Svetlana decided.

When we had almost reached Gesar's office I decided to speak up after all – the boss wasn't faltering as he walked along any more, he'd obviously contacted everyone he needed to . . .

'Boris Ignatievich, I can see you already understand what's going on . . .'

'I don't understand a damn thing, Anton,' answered Gesar. 'Not a damn thing. I've never even heard of anything like this. And it . . .' He chewed on his lips, trying to choose the right words. 'It frightens me.'

He swung the door open and we walked into his office.

CHAPTER 4

THE FIRST THING I noticed were the portals hanging in the air. The Higher Others summoned by Gesar certainly weren't wasting any time.

Then I counted the portals. One of them, with a thin, glittering frame, was waiting for my girls to pass through it. And three portals were already slowly fading away.

Three?

I gazed at the people sitting there at the table.

Olga. Clear enough. I nodded to her automatically.

And this quiet little old man with the tousled grey hair, wearing a threadbare suit and wide, old-fashioned tie, looking like an aged professor or doctor?

And this sturdy man with a beard, whose face seemed familiar to me somehow – not from the life of the Watch, but from human life? I'd seen his face on TV, or maybe in the newspapers . . .

We didn't have anyone like these two in the Watch.

'Thank you for not delaying,' said Gesar, walking over to his chair. 'Let me introduce you. This is Anton Gorodetsky. You must have heard of him.'

'Who doesn't know Anton Gorodetsky?' the little old man said, with a smile.

'This is Mark Emmanuilovich Jermenson,' said Gesar. 'Higher Light One and Battle Magician.'

'Sergei,' said the second man, introducing himself. 'Sergei Glyba. Higher Light One.'

'I know you,' I said, finally remembering. 'You're . . . you're that—'

'Clairvoyant!' he confirmed delightedly.

He really was a clairvoyant. One of those who are published regularly in the yellow press and equally yellow magazines, who appear on TV and sit among 'the invited guests' in the front row at countless talk shows. He had forecast the financial crisis, when it was almost over already; the strengthening of the rouble, just before it fell; the replacement of dollars in the US by some weird kind of 'ameros'; an asteroid shower; a landing by aliens from space; an epidemic of goat flu; unprecedented growth in the Russian economy; typhoons and earthquakes.

If it had always been the exact opposite of what he forecast that happened, his prophecies would have made some kind of sense. But it was the usual clairvoyant's babble, a matter of random sensationalism. Sometimes he was mocked in the press, but his imposing appearance and slick tongue made him a favourite with the readers (especially the women) and he was never out of work.

'You're a clairvoyant?' I enquired dubiously.

'Anton, surely you don't think I would do serious forecasts for humans?' Sergei replied, smiling.

'I've never seen you in the Watch,' I said.

'They aren't in the Watch,' Gesar said morosely. 'You could say that Mark Emmanuilovich is retired.'

'Following injury,' Jermenson added with a jolly smile.

'And Sergei simply doesn't want to serve,' said Gesar.

'It's my right,' replied Glyba. 'I want to live like a human being.'

Sveta emerged from the final portal, holding Nadya by the hand. The portal immediately faded away.

'Hello,' Nadya said very politely. 'Hello, Uncle Gesar and Aunty Olya.'

Seeing Mark and Sergei gazing at my daughter with undisguised curiosity, I laughed.

'So everyone's here – excellent,' said Gesar. 'Let's get down to work. You are all aware of what Anton has found out . . .'

Oho – he'd moved really fast. Not only summoned them, but briefed them too.

'We have an emergency situation,' Gesar went on.

'An extreme emergency, is it?' Mark Emmanuilovich enquired.

'Quite extreme,' Glyba said unexpectedly, leaning his head back and closing his eyes. 'Gesar . . . thank you for getting everyone together.'

'What do you see?' Gesar asked, without looking at the clairvoyant.

'Nothing.'

'Then why such a panic?'

'I don't see *anything*, Gesar.' Sergei mopped his forehead and gave a crooked smile. 'That's why the panic. You know that I can always see something . . .'

'Usually foul abominations of some kind,' Gesar muttered.

'Well, that's the way life is. But right now – there's nothing.'

'Are you forecasting the end of the world, then?' Jermenson asked him. 'Is there really nothing afterwards?'

'No, not necessarily,' Glyba said, with a frown. 'With your experience, Emmanuilovich, you ought to be familiar with the basics of divination. A diviner's "blindness" results from a situation in which the immediate future is being affected by forces that surpass the diviner's powers by at least one order of magnitude. That is, for the second rank it would have to be a First-Level Magician, for the first level – a Higher Magician . . .'

'And that leaves us with a quite remarkable conclusion: a force has appeared in Moscow that surpasses the powers of a Higher Magician by an entire order of magnitude,' Gesar summed up. 'I don't know about you, but to me that seems pretty close to the apocalypse . . .'

'Uncle Gesar.' Nadya raised her hand down at the far end of the table, where she was sitting with Svetlana. 'The powers of Higher Ones can't differ by an order of magnitude, they taught us that in school . . .'

Gesar frowned. 'Nadya, let's do without the "Uncle". You're . . . er . . .'

'A big girl now,' Nadya said amenably. 'Well, they taught us that the Power possessed by Higher Magicians is practically identical: minor fluctuations measured in the course of direct confrontations of strength like the "press" are of no significance and are not stable. One day one Higher Other has more pure Power, the next day another one does. The most significant factors in confrontations between Higher Ones are experience and the tactics applied in combat.'

'The exception to the rule?' Gesar asked curiously.

'So-called "Zero-Order Magicians" like me,' Nadya replied without any superfluous modesty. 'We infinitely surpass the Power of any other magicians, including Higher Magicians, because theoretically we can create a spell with any degree of Power.'

'With any degree of Power, within the limits of the magical energy that exists on Earth,' Gesar added. 'Be more precise in your formulation!'

'Yes, I just didn't have time to finish,' said Nadya.

She wormed her way out of that neatly!

'All right. A-minus,' said Gesar. 'So what did you want to say?'

'How can there be a magician who surpasses a Higher Clairvoyant by an order of magnitude? He's either a Zero-Order Magician, or a . . .'

'Well, well?' Gesar encouraged her.

'Or not a magician at all.' Nadya suddenly felt embarrassed and snuggled up against her mother. Svetlana put her arm round her shoulders. I caught my daughter's eye and nodded approvingly.

'We cannot entirely exclude the existence of another Zero-Order Magician,' said Gesar. 'But none of the prerequisites exist.'

'And that includes any prophecies concerning it,' remarked Glyba. 'But Nadya was foretold.'

'Let's examine the other possibilities,' said Gesar. 'A magician, even a Zero-Order one, is only a magician.'

'A Mirror?' Svetlana asked quietly.

There was a tense silence.

A Mirror is bad news. He's very bad news, because it's practically impossible to fight against him. A mirror is generated by the Twilight – that is, no one really knows why any particular, ordinary, uninitiated Other with an indeterminate aura, who is inclined equally towards the Light and the Darkness, becomes transformed into a Mirror Magician, and how it happens. But we do know in general why the Mirror appears and what happens after that. The Mirror shows up at a place where the balance between the Light and the Darkness has been seriously disrupted, and then joins the losing side. He eliminates the gap. And in the most direct fashion possible – either by killing magicians or by taking away their power. Eleven years earlier Svetlana had lost most of her power – and we were very lucky that she had been able to restore herself so quickly.

'It can't be a Mirror,' said Gesar, shaking his head. 'A Mirror Magician only rises up the levels in the course of combat with normal magicians. Have any of our Higher Magicians fought a Mirror?'

'How about the Dark Ones?' suggested Mark Emmanuilovich.

'They only have one Higher Other in their Watch: Zabulon himself.'

'What about Yury and Nikolai?' asked Jermenson, raising his eyebrows in surprise.

'Yury moved to Minsk seven years ago – his career prospects are better there,' Gesar laughed. 'And Nikolai is in the reserve, like you. For more than four years now. I don't think he does anything very much, except go fishing on the Akhtuba . . .'

'He still writes romance novels, under a female pseudonym,' Olga put in.

'Does he?' asked Glyba, suddenly interested. 'And what are they like?'

'Quite readable,' Olga said eagerly. 'Especially—'

'Quiet!' said Gesar, tapping his finger on the table. The sound was surprisingly loud. He closed his eyes and sat for a few moments without speaking. 'I've asked Zabulon to check on his Higher Ones in the reserve. But I'm assuming that none of them has fought with anyone. And why would a Mirror be killing Dark Ones? With the present balance of power, he should be killing us again!'

'Then who?' Jermenson asked, with a shrug. 'If not a Mirror . . . one of the ancient magicians? There were Zero-Order Magicians among them . . . well . . . close to it, at least . . .'

'Who and why?' Gesar asked. 'Most importantly – why? Why appear in Moscow in secret, do God only knows what to someone who just happens to cross your path . . . No, let's consider other possibilities!'

'Not a Mirror, and not a High . . . er, Zero-Order Magician that we don't know about?' asked Glyba.

'What other possibilities can there be?' said Svetlana, asking her first question. 'I'm sorry, Boris Ignatievich, my borsch has been left half-cooked on the stove, Nadya was just doing her homework, then you dragged us over here . . . and, as far as I can see, you're not even sure why!'

Gesar looked at me and said: 'You have a go, Anton. What frightens you in all this?'

I thought for a minute before starting to answer.

'A plane . . . a plane that should have crashed, but didn't. A boy-Prophet who turned up so fortuitously right in front of my eyes. What he said . . . about me in the first instance. A policeman I ran into many years ago and who can now see Others, although he himself isn't an Other. His partner, whose aura has disappeared and who couldn't give a damn about anything any more. Some unknown individual, whom the policeman called a "tiger". The fact that the two policemen described this unknown individual quite differently. The fact that a clairvoyant Higher Magician is unable to foresee events.'

'But how can all that be interconnected?'

'I don't know,' I said honestly.

'And what exactly is it that frightens you? Surely not what was said about a "tiger"? This policeman of yours calls us "dogs" and the Dark Ones "wolves".'

'What frightens me is the intense concentration of strange elements,' I said. 'It all started this morning. Only eight and a half hours ago. There's so much, and all at once!'

Gesar nodded. He seemed satisfied with what I'd said.

'That's right. Too many strange things. It can't be a coincidence, so there must be a common reason. Can you suggest any possibilities?'

'You're just like Dr House, Boris Ignatievich,' Svetlana said ironically.

'What?' asked Gesar – it was one of the rare occasions when I'd seen the boss bewildered. I don't believe he ever had any interest in the cinema and all he watched on TV was the news and the figure skating, which he found attractive for some reason.

'It doesn't matter,' said Svetlana. 'Just this . . . famous doctor. He used to propose crazy theories to his junior colleagues, and then choose the correct one himself.'

Gesar gave Svetlana a rather dubious look. Then he nodded and said: 'I hope he had more enterprising colleagues than mine. I haven't heard a single theory so far.'

'A divine being,' Jermenson said unexpectedly. 'No, I'm not talking about God or a Messiah, but perhaps we're dealing here with a manifestation of some sacral, mystical entity . . .'

'Retirement's having a bad effect on you, Mark,' Gesar said irritably. 'The only mystical entity in our world is us – the Others. All the rest is human folklore.'

'Well, some Others don't think so . . .' Jermenson muttered, but without any real conviction.

'So this is Other folklore, then!' Gesar snapped. 'Are there any serious theories?'

'An emanation of primal Power,' suggested Glyba. 'The Light or the Darkness . . .'

'That's the same "divine entity" again, only in different words,' said Gesar.

'But the Light and the Darkness exist,' said Glyba, with a shrug. 'When we swear on the Light, it confirms our words.'

Gesar frowned. 'Sophistry. We don't know how or why it happens. Do you know? I don't. Possibly one of the Great Magicians of ancient times created a spell that's still working now. To suspect the Light and the Darkness of conscious action is—'

'It's just like expecting the Twilight to create a Mirror and send it to the side that's losing . . .' Olga said in a gentle voice.

Gesar shut up.

He didn't simply stop talking, he shut up. He sat there for a while, gazing at the tabletop, and then said: 'The theory is accepted. It's absurd. I don't like it – because I'm afraid of something of the kind. But as a theory, it's accepted. Anything else?'

Nadya raised her hand again. 'Boris Ignatievich, I don't think we should be trying to guess right now,' she said. 'What difference does it make to us who has appeared? After all, we already know that he's very powerful and he does strange things. So all right. We need to understand what he wants.'

'And?' asked Gesar.

'Da— Anton . . .' Nadya blushed.

'It's all right, we know that he's your daddy,' Gesar said in a surprisingly gentle voice. 'Go on.'

'It all started when daddy saw the boy-Prophet who was afraid to fly in the aeroplane because the aeroplane was going to crash,' said Nadya, clearly embarrassed. 'Well, he saved the boy and his mummy, didn't he? But what if someone else wanted to save him too, only he did it a simpler way: he saved the whole aeroplane all at once? And that's why the aeroplane didn't crash. And then, when he realised the boy wasn't on it any more, he set out to look for him . . .'

'That business with the policeman? Why did he give himself away like that? He left witnesses and a trail as well.'

'He didn't give himself away. He . . . he introduced himself,' Nadya said quietly.

'He left his visiting card,' exclaimed Olga, snapping her fingers. 'That's right. He realised that one of the policemen had recognised him as an Other and deliberately affected his partner. But what made him think we'd find those policemen, and so quickly?'

'If that policeman is an ordinary person, but he can see Others, it could be the result of his contact with daddy,' said Nadya. 'They taught us that a spell can leave a side effect, a trace . . . and that trace is usually connected with the magician who cast the spell. What if someone saw the trace on the policeman and realised he was connected with my daddy? For him it was . . . well, like kicking a dog to make it whine so that its master would look round.'

'A fine comparison,' Olga said drily.

'Sorry,' Nadya answered, 'I was judging from the point of view . . .'

I noticed that Gesar had been sitting with his eyes closed for about half a minute. And slowly turning crimson. Then he opened his eyes and stood up.

'Right. I can't hear Semyon. And I can't contact him. Someone else try!'

Olga closed her eyes too.

Glyba applied his palm to his forehead picturesquely.

Jermenson chewed on his lips.

Svetlana frowned intensely.

But I took out my mobile and pressed one of the 'hot keys'.

'Yes, Antokha?' Semyon answered cheerfully.

'Where are you?'

'Me? I'm at Olya and Kesha's place. Drinking tea. Telling them all about our wonderful school for artistically gifted children.'

'Gesar can't make contact with you,' I said

There was a brief pause, and then Semyon said: 'You know, I can't make contact either. With anyone. It's like . . . everything's gone blank . . .'

'Tell him we're on our way,' ordered Gesar, walking rapidly towards the door. 'Anton, Mark, Olga, you're with me! Svetlana, Sergei, you're in charge of the Watch.'

'I'm not on the staff!' Svetlana exclaimed indignantly.

'Consider yourself drafted,' Gesar flung out without looking round.

'Sveta, if we start arguing now, the child might be killed,' Olga said gently as she got up to follow Gesar. 'And Semyon too. Do you understand?'

And Svetlana, who I could remember beating off Gesar's attempts to get her involved in the Watch's business at least a hundred times, backed down immediately. She just asked as we left: 'What exactly do I have to do?'

'Kill everything strange that tries to get into the office,' Gesar replied.

'I'm a doctor, not a killer!' Sveta exclaimed indignantly.

'Every good doctor has his own graveyard,' snapped Gesar.

When we ran out into the yard, the boom across the entrance was already raised and Alisher and Garik were getting into the patrol van – a battered old Japanese SUV. They were obviously on duty-call today.

'Mark Emmanuilovich, please join the two young watchmen, if you would be so kind,' Gesar said briskly.

Apparently he seriously believed that we needed to have at least one Higher Other in each vehicle.

We got into the old BMW that Gesar had been riding around in for as long as I could remember. I sat in the front, Olga was on the back seat and Gesar was at the wheel. He didn't usually sit there, I wasn't even sure that the Great One knew how to drive a car.

But it turned out that he did – and how! We went flying out into the street and roared straight off up the oncoming lane, which apparently seemed less crowded with traffic to Gesar. We were spared the choruses of loud curses from drivers about wild, irresponsible Duma deputies and bureaucrats by just one thing.

The car was invisible.

And moreover, Gesar didn't use an ordinary spell like the Sphere of Negation or other similar ones. We were entirely invisible. We were an empty space, hurtling along the road like a draught, a void as far as any other driver could see.

To be quite honest, this is pretty stressful, even when the driver at the wheel is a Higher Magician who could well have more than a hundred years of driving experience.

But it turned out that Gesar had no intention of playing tag with the motorists of Moscow. A moment later the car slipped into the Twilight.

Any Other can enter the Twilight. And taking someone else with you, or carrying something in, is a simple technical matter.

But to drag an entire car into the Twilight!

'Remember the way we rode into the Twilight on a battle elephant?' Olga suddenly asked with a laugh.

Was she joking or serious? Who could tell . . .

Now we were hurtling along through Twilight Moscow. The first layer is the one closest to reality. Here there are even buildings, cars and people. Everything is grey, dull and slow – but still real. Almost real, that is. Except that blue moss has been added to the roads and the walls of the buildings . . .

Our car had changed radically too. The old but sturdy German automobile seemed to melt: its dimensions shifted, the interior became far more old-fashioned, the wheel in Gesar's hands shrank and became slimmer, with a glittering nickel rim on the inside and a rampant-deer emblem in the centre. A similar figure of a deer sprang up out of the bonnet. The instrument panel bulged out, thrusting towards Gesar a semicircular speedometer with four tiny square dial-plates lurking under it. At its centre the basic on-board computer was replaced by an absolutely primitive two-band radio receiver and in front of me a primeval mechanical clock appeared.

'Yes,' said Gesar, 'I prefer Russian cars. A Series 2 Volga. My faithful old warhorse. Please don't tell anyone about it – I know what you humorists are like . . .'

It wasn't just a facade – I could smell the leather upholstery and I started slipping about on the shiny seat. Well, would you believe it . . . I didn't even know the Soviet automotive industry had ever made a Volga with a leather interior and automatic transmission . . . maybe it even had airbags in it . . . they could certainly come in useful!

That boss of ours! Riding around in an ancient Volga and disguising it as a decent old 'Beemer'! I wouldn't have expected that kind of secretive patriotism from him, to be honest . . . or maybe it wasn't patriotism, just conservatism?

But then, as a general rule, patriotism and conservatism are inseparable.

Gesar swung the wheel, swerving away from a Range Rover standing in the middle of the road. It was a strange-looking kind of vehicle – hung all over with advertising slogans and rotted right through, with its engine falling out of the chassis. This informational phantom probably hadn't existed in the real world for a long time already, but it was still decaying here in the Twilight – that's what happens with objects when they've been a focus of human attention for a long time, for whatever reason. The result of some kind of road accident, maybe?

'No, we need to go deeper,' Gesar suddenly decided.

This time he really did amaze me. He groaned – and the world around us turned completely colourless.

We were on the second level of the Twilight.

All the buildings became wooden – I must say that wooden buildings nine or ten storeys high look really strange. The road turned into a winding country track covered in tussocky grass. The people almost disappeared: here on the second level they were barely even visible. Everything was grey. Instead of cars there were little clouds of steam hanging above the road – as if someone had breathed out, emptying his lungs on a cold day . . .

Well, and of course, it turned very cold.

And the car changed again.

Very noticeably and for the better.

The deer, arched over in its leap on the bonnet, was transformed into a young woman with wings.

I gazed for a while at the emblem of two intertwined Rs, then asked:

'So you prefer Russian automobiles, then, Boris Ignatievich?'

Gesar dove the Rolls-Royce Phantom hard over the empty roads, hurtling nonchalantly straight through the clumps of steam and the human shadows. Most people wouldn't notice anything. Some would sense a chill on their skin and feel a blank, hopeless yearning for something glorious and enthralling – some experience that life had never granted them. In cases like that Americans say: 'Someone just walked over my grave.'

But the reality is actually even more chilling – at that instant an Other has just walked or driven straight through you.

'Everyone lies, Anton,' Gesar said suddenly. 'Everyone lies.'

So apparently he did watch TV after all.

And his conservatism wasn't equivalent to patriotism either.

'A really fine car,' he admitted. 'That's just between the two of us, of course.'

We travelled through the second level at the same speed as in the ordinary world. Except, of course, that there weren't any traffic jams blocking our way. But that wasn't what interested Gesar. The important thing was that time passed far more slowly here than in the real world – we would reach Semyon literally a minute after the phone call.

But then, whoever was on his way to him could also move through the Twilight. And even go a layer or two deeper.

If there *was* anyone on the way to him, of course.

Suddenly Gesar swore out loud. Technically speaking, I didn't know the language that he switched into – probably it was the one they spoke in Tibet when he was a child there. But the intonation left no doubt: the boss was swearing.

'Shame on you, Gesar,' said Olga, confirming my hunch.

'Don't you notice anything unusual?' asked Gesar.

I looked around and said: 'The Twilight. Blue moss. The usual.'

'We're on the second level,' Olga said thoughtfully. 'What's blue moss doing here?'

To be quite honest, there wasn't a lot of moss. A few patches here and there on the road. Here and there on the walls. They were barely noticeable, because there are no colours on the second level, but they were definitely there.

Blue moss on the second level of the Twilight!

'I've never seen anything like it,' I admitted.

'The point is that I've never seen anything like it either,' Gesar declared. 'Except perhaps—'

He wasn't given a chance to finish – because a fireball flared into life dead ahead of the Rolls-Royce's windscreen.

CHAPTER 5

IF YOU WISHED to divide all known magic into two parts, the easiest way would be to divide it into battle magic and everyday magic. Despite the opinion common among novice Others, there would be two or even three times as much of the 'everyday' variety. This is painstakingly hammered into the heads of the beginners at the very first classes in the Night Watch – magic is not intended for doing harm, for war or killing . . . for every Fireball or Viper's Kiss you can find five peaceful spells: the Crusher for breaking down refuse, the Iron for ironing clothes, the Awl and the Drill Bit for making holes in domestic conditions, Prometheus for lighting a campfire or barbecue easily and conveniently . . .

Fairly quickly, however, the beginners realise that almost all the domestic spells work in battle conditions too. Their only shortcomings are basically that they are slower or that they consume more Power than specialised battle magic. In the time that it takes a beginner to create and adjust a Drill Bit or apply an Iron to his adversary's face, you can fling the Triple Blade ten times over.

That's why, after a brief period of interest in the non-standard applications of the Crusher or the Vent Valve, most Others stop experimenting and begin using everyday magic in everyday life and battle magic in battle.

Apart, that is, from certain Others who will sooner or later earn the legitimate title of Battle Magician.

They are the ones who eventually fathom a most important truth – it's easy enough to put on an impressive show, battering each other with fireballs or trying to crush each other with the Press. And it also carries on for a very long time. Because that's what your adversary is expecting from you. And he protects himself with the Barrier of Will, the Sphere of Negation, the Magician's Shield . . . There they stand, facing each other – a Light Other and a Dark Other, hammering at each other with spells, defending themselves against spells, sometimes even finding time to abuse each other verbally in the process. Maybe this is a good thing. After all, the majority of magical duels are not fought to the death but until one of the adversaries surrenders or withdraws from the field of battle. Otherwise we would have wiped ourselves out ages ago.

But if a genuine Battle Magician enters the fray – then everything goes very differently. He employs the good old healing spell Willow Bark or its jolly Dark variant, Aspirin. And the unsuspecting enemy suddenly finds that his body temperature has fallen to that of the ambient environment. A Battle Magician doesn't fling the Triple Blade, he applies the simple little Grater, which Svetlana uses when she makes vitamin salads for Nadya out of apples and carrots, and I use to clean off the saucepans if something gets burnt on . . . And his adversary suddenly becomes a millimetre or two slimmer. Instantly, from all sides. Usually no one can continue the battle after that.

I, of course, am very far from being a genuine Battle Magician. But it was still a long time since I'd flung any fireballs.

That said, a fireball like the one hurtling towards us was worthy of the utmost respect. To adopt the jargon of commercial managers, this was a Premium-Class Fireball. Speaking in poetic terms, it was a Tsar-Fireball. A biologist would have said it was an Alpha-Fireball. As a cool, calculating mathematician might have remarked, it was a fireball with a diameter of about three metres.

It was a fireball fearsome enough to make you shit yourself!

'Fuck your fucking mother!' Gesar howled, twisting the wheel round. In a moment of genuine terror only the Russian language could convey the true depths of his feelings. It made me feel proud of our great Russian culture!

The Rolls-Royce jerked to the left – like any driver, Gesar automatically turned so as to place the person beside him in the line of fire instead of himself. Nothing personal, just a pure reflex response.

I produced one too – I struck the windscreen with both hands, surprising myself by knocking it out completely, and held my open palms out towards the blazing sphere flying at us. I didn't even have time to think what I was going to use – the Sphere of Negation or the Magician's Shield. Because it turned out that I was already instinctively using the Press – striking at the bundle of flame with pure Power.

And the instinctive response worked. Whether or not a Shield could have withstood the impact of such a prodigious fireball is open to question. Whether Gesar could have dodged out of the way in time was not clear either. A good fireball vectors in on its target, like a modern missile.

But the pure Power strike did the trick. The fireball burst, splashing in all directions like hot oil. Some small gobbets of flame even hit the car, but Olga had her wits about her too and we were covered with the semi-transparent scales of some cunning form of defence. The car itself was clearly pretty much pumped full of spells too. The flames streamed downwards, under the wheels, and we bounded straight through the roaring, raging firestorm.

Just in time to catch sight of our adversary.

To me he didn't look anything like the descriptions that the policemen had given.

Very young, a little over twenty years old.

Slim, with blond hair.

A pleasant face, very genial, almost noble-looking somehow.

Light-coloured clothes (you can't make out more than that on the second level of the Twilight) and a cloak. Honestly, I swear, a cloak! A genuine one, fluttering behind his shoulders, as if he was some kind of comic-book Superman!

The young man stood there and gazed at the car thoughtfully. Not exactly looking disappointed, but certainly rather surprised.

'Come on,' said Gesar, switching off the ignition and slipping out from behind the steering wheel. Olga and I followed him. Outside the car the cold of the Twilight seized us in its vicelike grip. There was a steady, freezing wind blowing, the eternal wind of the second level.

'Who are you and what do you want?' shouted Gesar.

The young man didn't answer. He seemed to be pondering something.

'Night Watch! Leave the Twilight!' I said, not quite raising my voice to a shout but in a loud, impressive tone.

'Otherwise we shall use force,' Olga put in, backing me up.

The young man started to smile. And Gesar said in a low voice:

'Now, I wouldn't have said that. What if he—'

And then he did. I don't know what Gesar was about to say, but the young stranger certainly needed no prompting. He spread his hands – I thought he was moulding another fireball out of the air, a little bit smaller than the first one, but there wasn't any bright glow, although Power of some kind was glimmering in the palms of his hands, something was being prepared . . .

'Freeze!' shouted Olga, and I responded to the word as if it were a command – I struck at the stranger, with all the Power I had, with a localised time halt.

And why not? If you think about it, it's humane and it's reliable. The enemy is immobilised but entirely unharmed. We have time to figure out what to do, he has no time of any kind.

Only Olga wasn't asking me to use a freeze: she was warning me what the stranger was about to do.

Gesar suddenly disappeared – it looked as if he'd skipped down or up a level in the Twilight. Olga flew off about ten metres to one side with a gigantic leap that an Olympic champion, or even a hungry vampire, would have envied. But I stayed standing there like a fool, right in the path of the freeze that was advancing towards me . . .

Only I wasn't fated to end up suspended in the Twilight, stuck like a fly in the amber of halted time. My own freeze – far, far weaker than my adversary's – crashed into the spell hurtling towards it. And, as often happens with spells, they immediately interacted.

A faceted form like a precious stone suddenly appeared, suspended above the middle of the sombre grey road that was hemmed in by the grotesque wooden buildings. It rotated slowly, sinking down into the ground. Looking through it, I saw our adversary fragmented into a host of tiny little figures.

'Old fool!' bellowed Gesar, appearing beside me. He waved his arms – and there was a flash of green flame beyond the transparent crystal.

'You shouldn't be so hard on yourself, boss,' I told him, unable to resist.

I caught Gesar's baffled glance.

'I'm glad you're still able to joke, but I meant him,' said Gesar, nodding in the direction of the green fire. 'And you, Anton, have clearly used up all your reserves of good luck for today. Shooting down a Freeze with a Freeze is no easy task.'

'You meant him?' I asked, nodding in the direction of the young man. I looked at the green fire that was gradually fading away. 'What is that?'

'It will slow him down,' Gesar said evasively, but very confidently.

The green fire went out.

The young man shook some strange, sticky green sparks off his cloak and looked at us. This time his expression was far from friendly.

'Oho,' said Olga, coming back to us. 'So we couldn't give a damn for Gesar's Taiga . . .'

'Something terrible's about to happen,' Gesar declared, and then he took off his jacket and threw it down on the ground.

Had he decided to have a fist fight, then?

The young man didn't seem to have anything against fisticuffs – he moved along an arc, avoiding the section of space frozen in time by the spells. And despite his likeable, attractive appearance, somehow I was reminded only too clearly of what Pastukhov had called him.

A tiger . . .

Just at that moment I heard an engine roaring. Battle Magician Jermenson and the team had finally caught up with us. He leapt out of the SUV before it had even stopped, I think. Garik put up a Magician's Shield on the run, and to judge from its power he must have used one of the Watch's amulets. Jermenson moved out in front, Alisher fell in behind him with his head inclined and his hand pressed to his heart – it looked as if he was preparing to work as a reserve power source, pumping Jermenson full of energy.

The blond young man stopped, assessing the disposition of forces. To be quite honest, it wasn't clear what move he was thinking of making in a situation like that – he was facing four

Higher Magicians, as well as a couple of field operatives who might be less powerful but had pretty good battle experience.

Jermenson moved his hand up through the air, as if he was lifting an invisible load. The ground bulged up between him and the stranger, sprouting into a pillar three metres high. The pillar shuddered, taking on the features of a grotesque human figure, beside which the boxer Nikolai Valuev would have looked like a slim, handsome but rather undersized fashion model.

I had come across golems before. Rather more often, perhaps, than I would have liked purely for educational purposes. But this was the first time I had seen a golem created – and so quickly, without any runes embedded in the clay, without any obvious programming.

'Oh, these sly Jewish tricks!' said Olga.

The young man was clearly disconcerted by the golem. He made some elusive kind of movement – and a monstrous weight seemed to crash down onto the golem, crumpling it and driving it back into the ground. Only that didn't bother the golem. It soaked into the ground and immediately oozed out of it at another point, much closer to the stranger, reaching out a massive hand for him.

A rapid flickering of fingers, a brief fluttering of lips – and the arm reaching out to the stranger started falling to pieces, collapsing onto the ground in lumps of clay, as if some invisible meat-slicer was chopping it off as it advanced.

The golem paid no attention to this and simply carried on reaching out its arm. The falling clay wriggled on the ground and was absorbed back into its feet, so it didn't lose any mass at all.

'She ilekh adonia nekhbad mi a makom a ze!' shouted Jermenson.

The young man took a step back. Cast a quick glance in our direction. Then at Jermenson.

And at that precise moment the darkness behind the stranger

thickened and condensed into a black ink blot dangling in the air. A spiked leg that looked like a limb of a gigantic praying mantis stepped out of the blot, to be followed by its owner – a demon every bit as large as the golem.

Unfortunately, the cavalry arrived too late for the fight. The young man cast a quick glance at the demon, spread his arms – and disappeared. Without any flashes, glimmers or sparks. Without opening any portals, dissolving into the air or sinking down through the ground. He simply disappeared.

It was only reasonable from his point of view. If the heads of the Night Watch and the Day Watch both attack you, and they have a few Higher Others tagging along – the best thing to do is beat it, and quick.

The golem hesitated for a moment and then soaked back into the ground. Golems created to carry out a single assignment usually crumble into dust. But this one didn't crumble – it didn't seem to think that its assignment had been completed.

'Hello, Zabulon,' said Gesar.

The demon metamorphosed into a man – an ordinary, rather short man of indeterminate age with an undistinguished face. It had always amazed me that the Dark Others moved through the lower layers of the Twilight in such horrifying forms. I used to think there were dangers that I didn't know about lurking down there, but it was a long time now since I'd been an inexperienced novice magician. I'd walked the Twilight through and through, on all its levels, and I knew there weren't any bloodthirsty beasts in it.

Or was I wrong after all? Maybe the Dark Ones followed their own paths, unlike ours?

'And hello to you, Gesar,' Zabulon said with a nod. 'What kind of loathsome beast was that?'

I laughed. And I kept on laughing until understanding dawned on Gesar's face.

'Did you see a repulsive, malicious demon, Zabulon?' he asked.

The Dark One frowned. And nodded.

'I saw a cunning, elderly man,' said Gesar. 'Anton, I surmise, saw some pleasant, straightforward young guy. Jermenson saw a wise old Jew. Olga saw a wily, guileful woman.'

'You forgot to add that you didn't just see a cunning, elderly man, but a very modest, cunning, elderly man,' said Olga.

'Yes, and one with a very high opinion of himself,' snorted Zabulon. 'But, as it happens, he only disappeared when I showed up.'

'Maybe he just has a well-developed aesthetic sensibility . . .' Alisher muttered, but in a low voice. It's not really a good idea for an ordinary Light Magician to quarrel with Higher Dark Ones.

The three of us – Gesar, Zabulon and I – went up to the flat where the small Tolkov family lived. Zabulon had politely confirmed in advance that the Day Watch did not claim any right to initiate the boy-Prophet, but said that he would be interested in taking a look at the child. Simply out of general interest, because a genuine Prophet only turns up once or twice in a generation, and he had never met a Prophet with a 'tiger' hot on his trail.

'Do you have any ideas about all this?' Gesar asked him as we were riding up in the lift.

'Yes, Gesar. I do. That it's a good thing you met this boy first and he's not our headache.'

'Well, well, the Day Watch forgoes a Prophet,' Gesar muttered. 'I suppose you wouldn't have fought the "tiger" for him?'

'I would have,' Zabulon confessed regretfully. 'Greed would have forced me to. But I certainly didn't like to see that four Higher Light Ones couldn't even frighten a single stranger, let alone defeat him.'

'And who is he, this stranger?' I asked.

Zabulon looked at me and something very hostile flickered in his eyes. No, there wasn't any personal vendetta between us at the moment. But we'd done each other plenty of bad turns in our time. It had just happened that when I was a rank-and-file member of the Watch I'd managed to foul things up for Zabulon . . . and become his personal enemy. Right now, though, we had a quasi-truce.

But Dark Ones don't become Higher Others because they know how to forgive and forget. They simply know how to wait.

'I don't know, Anton, I don't know,' Zabulon answered, with a sigh. 'At first I thought we were dealing with a Mirror Magician after all. But a Mirror only reflects Others' power, not their appearance, and the way he behaved . . .' Zabulon stopped short.

'Finish what you were saying,' Gesar said amicably. 'You might as well.'

'By the way, you haven't already forgotten that I helped you out just now, have you?' asked Zabulon.

We walked out of the lift onto the eleventh floor.

'I haven't forgotten,' said Gesar. 'And I'm ready to help you . . .'

'The Day Watch,' Zabulon corrected him.

'The Day Watch of Moscow,' Gesar agreed, 'in a situation where to do so will clearly not be detrimental to the goals and interests of the Night Watch or human beings.'

'Evasive, but acceptable,' Zabulon said, with a nod. 'My dear enemy, I even sympathise with you slightly. I have a distinct feeling that this "tiger" of yours is not a person at all.'

'Why ours?' I asked.

'Why not a person?' asked Gesar.

'I'm prepared to answer one question,' Zabulon declared gleefully. 'You choose which.'

Gesar snorted contemptuously and said: 'Basically, the answers to both questions are elementary. He didn't have any aura at all. He could hardly have concealed it from several Higher Others.

And he appeared differently to each of us. That means he's not a material entity, but merely reflected in our consciousness. And he's "ours" because he's interested in the boy who is now under our protection.'

'Oh, so there's no need for any answers, then?' Zabulon asked delightedly.

It sometimes seems to me that they could go on sparring like that for ever.

'Answer Anton's question,' said Gesar. 'Why the "tiger" is our problem.'

Zabulon nodded: 'By all means. In my view, the real issue is not that he's hunting the boy. Perhaps he merely wanted to pat him on the head and wish him luck in his fight for the cause of the Light? What is far more interesting is that the "tiger" left after I made my appearance.'

'He didn't want to fight on two fronts,' said Gesar, growing more sombre with every second.

Zabulon burst into laughter.

'Too hopeful by far! I suspect that he didn't wish to harm me.'

'A kindred spirit?' I asked.

'Oh, don't be so childish, Anton!' Zabulon rebuked me. 'When has that ever been a hindrance to Dark Ones? At the present moment the Day Watch is less powerful than you are. If he had annihilated all of us the Night Watch would simply have been exsanguinated, but the Day Watch would have been left practically dead.'

'Maintaining the balance is the Inquisition's job,' said Gesar. 'Is that what you're hinting at?'

'No, Gesar. What I'm hinting at is that the balance is also maintained by the Twilight. This is a Twilight Creature. You may not believe in them, but . . .'

For a few seconds Gesar and Zabulon stared daggers at each

other. I felt like saying: 'Don't bother – you're not going to fight anyway!' – but I wasn't sure that I would be right.

The situation was defused by the door of one of the flats opening. An old granny stuck her head out of the door slowly and solemnly, like a tortoise poking its head out of its shell. Actually, she wasn't even fifty yet, but she looked like a genuine old woman, the caricature Russian 'babushka' of the American and European imaginations – flabby and shapeless, wearing a sloppy housecoat, slippers over thick stockings, a headscarf. Incredible! You usually only see that kind of thing outside a church.

'What are you doing standing there?' the granny asked. 'Get off my doormat, you pervert.'

Zabulon glanced down at his feet in surprise. He really was standing on the corner of the mat that the granny had set out in front of the door of her flat. The mat had clearly seen better times. It had once been part of a big, bright carpet of synthetic fibre, the kind that people used to queue up for in Soviet times. And then, when even the polyvinyl chloride had faded with age, was covered in stains and worn right down to the bare threads, it had done time lying on an open balcony. The rain had drenched it. The insane city moths had tried to gnaw on it. A tin of paint had been spilled on it.

And now this putrid, semi-decayed floor covering had been hacked into crooked pieces and set out in front of the door as a doormat.

Zabulon gave an emphatically polite nod and stepped off the mat.

'Come up here to drink, have you?' asked the granny. 'The ninth floor, that's where the winos live! But we're decent people here!'

The most surprising thing was that Zabulon wasn't even slightly angry with the granny. He studied her with the intensely keen interest of an entomologist gazing at a cockroach and attempting to establish contact with it. Gesar was the one who was fuming.

'We've come to see your neighbours,' he said. 'Everything's all right, don't worry.'

'To see Olka?' the granny exclaimed delightedly. 'Police, are you? Not paying her loans, isn't she? I warned her not to get carried away! Lives without a husband, raising that little dumpling all on her own, but she keeps on doing it, always having the place decorated or flitting off abroad somewhere' – at this point her words rang with the genuine hatred of someone who has never travelled anywhere – 'or buying a flat TV, or taking that dumpling of hers to clubs and classes . . .'

'Anton, do something,' Gesar begged me. 'I'm . . . afraid I might overdo it.'

'Yes, do a bit of work,' Zabulon said, with a nod. 'Remoralise her if you like. I promise not to count it against your allowance for intervention.'

I probably could have tried to exert a positive influence on the granny. After all, she hadn't always been like this, had she? People aren't born like that. Something bad happens to them . . . or maybe it's some special spitefulness virus, as yet unknown to science.

'I won't remoralise her, I'm afraid I might rupture myself in the process,' I said. 'Go to bed, grandma!'

I didn't even want to read her name, as if I was afraid of soiling myself on her thoughts.

'To bed?' the granny echoed in amazement.

'You'll sleep for exactly ten hours,' I said. 'And when you wake up, you'll forget about us.'

The granny nodded and closed the door, pulling her head back in through the crack at the very last moment.

'The brilliant solutions are always the simplest,' said Gesar. And he rang the bell at the next door.

Olga Yurievna answered it. Her eyes were slightly hazy, like the eyes of any person who has come under the gentle but irresistible influence of an Other.

'Come in!' she said in the tone of a hospitable housewife and stepped aside.

I spotted Semyon immediately – he was standing in the middle of the room, pressing the boy Kesha up against himself with one hand and 'holding' a very, very unpleasant spell, cocked and ready to fire, in the other. Semyon is a very experienced and proficient field agent. But after seeing the 'tiger' with my own eyes, I knew that no amount of experience and skill would have helped him.

When we appeared Semyon let out a deep sigh of relief and fluttered his hand through the air, dispersing the spell. Then he said: 'They're friends, Kesha, everything's fine . . .'

And then he spoke to us, with far more feeling.

'Thank you. You've no idea how glad I am to see you. Even you . . . Zabulon.'

CHAPTER 6

IN THE FAIRY-TALE books, young magicians' parents are always honestly informed that their child is being taken away to be taught magic. In the Watches they never do that. Firstly, we don't have any special school. Others are taught at the Watch, and it's rare for more than a third of them to be children, since the abilities of an Other can manifest themselves at any age. For Others, as for chess players, there are no 'adult' and 'child' ratings. Secondly, it's something that the parents simply don't need to know. And the point is not just that they might give something away – that's easy enough to prevent with simple spells. The problem is actually something quite different . . .

Over the many centuries before humankind finally lost its belief in magic and the wizards and sorcerers set up the Watches and were divided into Light Ones and Dark Ones, we acquired substantial experience in dealing with human beings. Imagine you have been told that your child is a wizard or a sorceress. At first, you'll probably be glad to find out (or distressed, if it contradicts your ardently held faith or no less ardent atheistic convictions). But later . . . later you'll feel resentful. Of course, all parents want the best possible future for their children. But one so much better than the norm? To accept that you will live the short life of an ordinary human being, while your child will be able to work miracles and will live for hundreds of years – that's not easy! Very many people come completely unglued and start taking their irritation out on the child in various ways, which may be more or less explicit. And that, by the way, can lead to very serious unpleasantness – children have far less self-control than adults do.

But even that's not the most important thing.

People may be glad that their child is an Other.

They may genuinely love the child and not allow even a single drop of envy into their hearts.

This usually means that we're dealing with a good, loving family.

But then the most difficult part starts.

'Daughter, your grandmother's seriously ill . . . but you could help her, couldn't you?'

She could. A seventh-level intervention. A trifling matter, of course . . . but it disrupts the balance between the Watches.

'Son, life's getting really hard nowadays . . . Could you drop into my office? There's a man there, and it depends on him whether they give me a raise or not . . . could you have a word with him?'

He could. It's only a sixth- or seventh-level intervention. And it undermines the morals of a young Other.

'What the hell are the bastards doing now! This law will destroy our entire education system!'

There isn't even any need to say anything. The good, honest Other child gazes at the glistening features of the functionary on the TV screen. And involuntarily wishes him ill.

An inferno vortex swells up above the wise bureaucratic head. And not the kind that they accumulate every day from ordinary human curses – they can answer for those themselves, with their drug-addict children, booby-trapped automobiles, spy cameras in the bathhouse – but a genuine, really serious vortex. One that will stir up such a stink that the Inquisition will intervene to make peace between the Watches and determine who's to blame and what one side owes the other.

Therefore the best, in fact the only way is to explain to someone, no matter how big or little they might be: 'You are not human. You are an Other. It's not better or worse . . . it's different. The misfortunes and problems of ordinary people are nothing to do with you any longer, and you have nothing to do with them. You'll have plenty of misfortunes and problems of your own.'

Sometimes it takes a while, but eventually everyone understands.

And as for the parents . . . they learn that their talented child is now going to study in a special school in addition to the ordinary one. A special school for physics and chemistry, or for art. Or else attend a macramé club five times a week. It doesn't matter in the slightest what they think, because they will accept any lie and never try to discover the truth. There was a time when I thought that even this was cruel. Then I realised that it wasn't cruelty, but firmness. Benign firmness.

. . . What is genuinely cruel is to initiate an Other who is in love, or who is loved with all the ardour of human passion. And to explain that, no, he probably will not be able to rejuvenate or extend the life of the object of his love . . . that he must never tell her anything . . . That must be like living as a spy who has been planted in an enemy country. Except that Others are not spies, and the lovers generally separate. Even if the Other is content to love a human being and can reconcile himself to remaining silent and watching as old age stealthily advances – even so, day after day, year after year, life itself pulls them further and further apart. Interests, tastes and habits change. And love dies.

That's why those people who decline the chance to be initiated, and so remain human, probably act wisely. Stupidly, but wisely . . .

'I won't be able to tell mummy anything?' asked Kesha.

'Not a thing,' Gesar confirmed.

'But Hermione . . .' said Kesha, glancing at Gesar from under his eyebrows, '. . . that's Harry Potter's friend . . .'

'I know,' Gesar said approvingly.

'She told her parents.'

'But afterwards, remember, she had to erase their memories,' Gesar remarked gently. 'Believe me, it's best not to say anything at all.'

Yes, after J. K. Rowling's books the job has become much easier. Children grasp the basic idea without even a blink now, only the absence of Hogwart's is a serious disappointment for them. Gesar claims that Rowling was commissioned to write her books by the London Watch or, rather, both Watches, and the decision to let her have a strictly controlled amount of information was taken by the Inquisition. Maybe it's true. Or maybe he's just joking. For Light Others the ability to joke easily compensates for the impossibility of lying.

'But I'll still go to ordinary school?' Kesha asked, just to make sure, and clearly hoping to hear the answer 'no'.

'Of course,' said Gesar. 'Ignorant magicians are no good to anyone. You'll go to our school after your lessons in the ordinary one. But right now . . . right now you'll have to live with us for a little while, in the Night Watch. There are rooms there for the staff, they'll give you one, with a big TV, a games console . . .'

'The Internet,' Olga added.

Kesha turned slightly pale – at ten years old, fright at the prospect of finding yourself somewhere without mummy is far stronger than any joy at the ability to cast spells. But he asked quite firmly: 'And mummy will let me?'

'Of course,' said Olga, nodding. 'We'll persuade her. And it's not for long. A few days . . . perhaps a week. Then you'll come back home.'

Zabulon smiled sarcastically, but didn't say anything. Somehow he didn't seem in any hurry to leave – apparently he couldn't get enough of the sight of a genuine Prophet. He and I were standing off to one side, but Gesar and Olga were sitting on the sofa, one on each side of Kesha, singing a duet in praise of the advantages of life as an Other. After the serious fright that Semyon had suffered before we arrived, he was drinking tea in the kitchen with Olga Yurievna. Nothing so very terrible had actually happened to him while we were on our way there. He simply discovered that he'd lost the ability to communicate with anyone by magical means, that he couldn't probe the surrounding space or divine the future for even a minute ahead. And there was also the sense of impending danger that had been growing with every second. Semyon didn't know anything about the 'tiger' but he had realised that this was no ordinary skirmish between the Watches, that it was something far more serious than that. So he had been standing there with some kind of spell cocked and ready to fire, waiting to see who would reach him first . . .

'It's interesting that I'm a wizard,' Kesha said indecisively. 'But . . . do I *have* to be one? Can't I stay human?'

Gesar and Olga exchanged glances over the boy's head. Zabulon cleared his throat.

'Yes, you can,' Gesar admitted, 'if you want to. Do you want to?'

'No,' Kesha said firmly. 'I just wondered.'

When the catty neighbour had called the boy a dumpling, she'd been pretty close to the truth. He was flabby and round-faced, like Doughnut in the book about Dunno. The skin on his face was lumpy, the way it usually is in older people but only very rarely in children. Parents who have children like that usually say in an apologetic tone: 'You know, he's very clever and good-natured.'

As for being good-natured, I didn't know, although the boy's aura was good, unambiguously Light. There was nothing there for Zabulon. But as for him being bright – that seemed to be true enough.

'Is it all because of the plane?' Kesha continued with his questioning. 'Because I got frightened?'

'Yes,' Gesar said, with a nod. 'The plane really could have crashed. And Anton' – Gesar nodded in my direction – 'realised that you're a Prophet.'

'And he saved the plane?' the boy asked.

'As you can see, the plane didn't crash,' said Gesar, avoiding a direct answer.

'So I can only predict things? Is that all?' Kesha asked with evident disappointment.

'No, certainly not. That's just the thing that you'll be best at,' said Olga, joining in the conversation. 'It's like with music. Everybody's taught to play the piano, even the violinists and the flautists. As a basic training. So you'll be able to throw fireballs, stop time, make yourself invisible . . .'

I suddenly felt a keen desire to smoke. I'd only been smoking very rarely just recently, but I still felt calmer with a pack of cigarettes in my pocket. I looked at Zabulon. He was languishing, kneading a long, dark cigarette in his fingers. We glanced at each other and headed for the balcony without saying a word.

This balcony was just the way small balconies in small flats are supposed to be – thoroughly cluttered. There was a sledge and an old child's bicycle, a collection of empty jam and pickle jars, a large cardboard box full of all sorts of junk and a small plastic case of tools. The box was open and I could see that the hammer and the pliers had a light coating of rust. Well, who stores tools on an open balcony? Ah, these women . . .

Or maybe I should say: Ah, these men? It's tough being a single mother. Especially in Russia.

We smoked – Zabulon obligingly held up a little tongue of flame for me, pinched between his thumb and forefinger, and I lit up, accepting his offer quite naturally. I took a deep drag and said: 'I suppose we'll have to send his mum off to some holiday resort. Why should she hang about here, if the child's going to be with us? And that way . . . she might pick someone up, have a bit of fun . . .'

'Send her,' Zabulon agreed. 'The Day Watch has no objections.'

'You're all heart today,' I said. 'And that makes me wonder.'

'I can afford to be tender-hearted,' Zabulon laughed. 'But you, Anton, are embarrassed by your own goodness.'

'Why so?'

'Why else would you use those words? "Mum", "pick someone up", "a bit of fun" . . . You vulgarise your own kind suggestion. You feel embarrassed.'

I thought about it and agreed. 'Yes. I feel embarrassed. These days even good magicians try to appear wicked. Zabulon . . . tell me, what does that mean – a Twilight Creature?'

'Purely theoretical,' laughed Zabulon. 'Don't bother your head about it.'

'No one lives in the Twilight,' I said.

'If no one lives there, then they don't,' the Dark One agreed simply, and I realised I wouldn't get any more information out of him.

'So okay,' I said, launching my cigarette end into flight from the balcony with a flick of my finger and incinerating it in mid-air with a second flick. 'Thanks at least for helping. And for not laying claim to the kid.'

'If he'd been a Battle Magician, I would have laid claim to him all right,' Zabulon chuckled. 'The boy isn't ours, of course, but there are always opportunities . . . And if he'd been a Clairvoyant, I'd have fought for him then. But a prophet? No, thank you.'

'You value a Clairvoyant more than a Prophet?' I asked, amazed.

'Of course. A Clairvoyant speaks of what might happen – and the future can be changed. A Prophet pronounces the Truth. That which is inevitable. Why would we want to know the inevitable, Anton? If the inevitable is bad, there's no point in upsetting yourself sooner than necessary. And if it's good – then let it come as a pleasant surprise. With great wisdom comes great sorrow.' Zabulon looked at the cigarette in his hand. 'Be seeing you, Light One . . .'

The cigarette flared up in his fingers with a sombre crimson flame. The fire leapt onto his fingers, ran up his arm and engulfed his entire body. Zabulon smiled at me through the flames – and disappeared.

The smouldering cigarette fell at my feet.

'Poser,' I said. 'Cheap ham . . . swell-headed freak!'

Zabulon's demonstrative refusal to fight for the boy-Prophet frightened me. Maybe he was just trying to put a good face on things, but something told me that the Dark One meant exactly what he had said.

But no way had he told me everything he knew.

Had he really had so little contact with Prophets, did he understand so little about who this tiger was?

And what was a 'Twilight Creature' anyway?

Zabulon had spoken as if Gesar ought to understand him perfectly well. Which meant that Gesar knew too . . .

But, naturally, I didn't ask the boss about it. Boris Ignatievich has his own opinion about what he ought to let his subordinates know so that they can discharge their obligations successfully.

Our visit to the Tolkovs' flat ended exactly as I had assumed it would. The boy's mother was put in the SUV and sent off to the airport, accompanied by Igor, Alisher and Jermenson – to board a regular flight to Barcelona and enjoy a holiday at a seaside resort.

She was clearly a good mother, judging from the fact that Semyon had had to use two sixth-level suggestions to persuade her to leave her child in our charge while she relaxed on the beaches of Catalonia. And for us Gesar opened a portal directly to the office of the Watch.

And he even initiated the boy in person there and then, as we were traversing the Twilight. You could have said that was a great honour, if not for the fact that the boy was a genuine Prophet.

The rooms for overnight stays were located on the semi-basement level of the office. It's the right place for them. In reality hardly anyone ever stays there – usually it's only the duty staff or Others from out of town who are here on business.

There are other levels below that, starting with the artefacts repository and archives and ending with the holding cells. But that's a whole different story: there's a different staircase for accessing those levels and it's not that easy to get down there.

Kesha was allocated a room that was usually occupied by non-smokers. They dragged in a huge flat-screen TV set, two games consoles, a heap of DVDs and two sacks of toys that had been bought in the nearest branch of Children's World. From the look of things, the staff member sent to buy the toys had no children of his own, otherwise the heap wouldn't have been such a jumble of stuffed animals, Lego sets, remote-controlled cars and helicopters, board games that could only be played in a group and wooden toys for developing the skills of kindergarten-age tots. Kesha stood with his hands braced against his well-fed sides, gazing at the chaotic heap in mild fright.

'Semyon, make sure that he's fed by someone with a family, who has children,' I said. 'And preferably with a child less than a hundred years old. Or else they'll bring the boy shish kebabs, beer and smoked sausage.'

'It's too early for him to have beer, that I understand,' Semyon said with a nod. 'But what's wrong with sausage and shish kebabs? I remember one time during the Civil War, I picked up this street kid at the station – he turned out to be a Light Other. You know him, by the way, it's . . . well, never mind that. He was skinny as hell. Anyway, I fed him up with sausage for a month! It happened in the Ukraine, they make good sausage there . . . if you fry it . . .'

'Okay, I get the idea,' I said, also nodding. 'Then definitely ask one of the women to take care of the boy. Okay?'

'I will,' Semyon chuckled. 'Only the boy won't see his supper for a long time yet – the boss wanted to start teaching him the basics of magic immediately.'

I shrugged. What was all the hurry about? The child was under the protection of the entire Night Watch now. We could take our time to work out what he was capable of.

'I'll be off,' I told Semyon. 'I'll collect my family and go home. Svetlana promised me borsch.'

'Borsch – that's great!' said Semyon, breaking into a broad smile. 'I reckon I'll go to the canteen. I'll get something to eat and ask the cook to knock something up for the kid.'

Our cook was a woman about forty years old. As an Other she was pretty weak, but as a cook she was outstanding. The only difference between the food in our canteen and food in Michelin-listed restaurants was the price.

'Now that's a good idea,' I told him approvingly.

In the car Nadka babbled away incessantly. Firstly, she was in raptures over the portal that Gesar had opened. She knew how to open portals herself all right, but in the first place she was strictly forbidden to do it, and in the second place there was something different about Gesar's portal. Some kind of 'subtle energy structure' and 'personal selectivity'. Basically, Gesar had spent a tenth of the usual energy on opening it, and only those who were allowed could pass through it.

Secondly, Nadya felt very sorry for the little boy-Prophet. Because he lived with his mummy, but without a daddy. Because he hadn't gone to the seaside. Because he was in the boring office without his mummy . . . although they had brought him some interesting toys – could she borrow the little helicopter to play with? Because he was too fat to be good at sports and they probably laughed at him at school.

Thirdly, Nadya was very proud that she'd given Gesar the right advice. No, she didn't boast about it straight out, but she kept coming back to that moment . . .

Svetlana smiled gently as she listened to the chatter from the back seat. Then she said in a low voice: 'I was very worried about you.'

'There was a whole army of us.'

'And what good did that do you? I don't like these magical mystery thingamajigs.'

'That's pure human atavism,' I sighed. 'Others are supposed to love magic in all its manifestations. By the way, do you know what a Twilight Creature is?'

'It's the first time I ever heard of it,' said Svetlana, shaking her head.

'Me too . . .'

'But I know!' Nadya exclaimed from behind us – that incredible ability children have to hear everything interesting, even if they never shut their own mouths for a second!

'Well?' I asked, pricking up my ears.

'If there are plants in the Twilight . . .'

'What plants?'

'Blue moss! Then there must be someone who eats it.'

'And who generally eats moss?' asked Sveta.

'Deer,' I replied automatically. 'But this guy . . . he wasn't anything like a deer. A bit of a maggot, maybe, but not a deer, no way . . .'

'Anton!'

'Now what have I said?' I growled. Nadya started giggling. 'We've got a critical situation here,' I went on.

'It's not critical any longer! Someone's hunting the boy-prophet. Well, so what? No one can stand up against the entire Watch, especially if the Dark Ones help too. Gesar will contact the Inquisition now, if he hasn't done it already. They'll scour the archives and find out what's going on. It might possibly be some kind of sect. Like the Regina Brothers, remember? You'd better decide what you'd rather do – finish cooking the borsch or do Nadya's maths with her,' said Sveta.

'I choose the maths,' I replied. 'I don't know how to cook borsch.'

A sect . . . Maybe it really could be. One that had been sitting quietly, doing nothing for a couple of centuries, waiting for a prophet. Maybe they wanted him to reveal the meaning of life to them. Sitting there, waiting . . . Pumping artefacts full of energy, training a hunter . . .

A good theory. Exotic, but coherent. I'd have liked to hope that was the way it really was.

CHAPTER 7

NADYA AND MATHS didn't get along. Languages were fine, and she did the work herself on principle, without using magic. History was excellent: she found it all very interesting, both human history and Other history. She also read a lot and enjoyed it.

But she had trouble with maths.

We just about scraped through the quadratic equations (you can call me a sadist and bring in the children's ombudsman, but she went to a school where the programme differed from the one approved by the ministry of education). My daughter closed her exercise book with a sigh of relief and climbed onto the bed with a book. I glanced quickly at the cover and decided it must be some kind of Harry Potter clone – it showed an inspired-looking boy working spells (well, that is, with his hands wreathed in blue glowing mist and his forehead wrinkled up grimly). And I went into the sitting room, picked out a Terry Pratchett book and lay down on the sofa with it.

What more could a middle-aged magician with a family want for perfect contentment at the end of a hectic day? Read about invented magicians while his wife cooks the borsch and his daughter's doing something quiet and peaceful . . .

'Daddy, so there really are Twilight Creatures after all?'

I looked at Nadya. What was stopping her from reading?

'Probably. I don't know.'

'And they chase after Prophets?'

'Don't believe everything it says in fairy tales,' I replied, turning a page. The magician Rincewind had just got himself into yet another scrape, which he would wriggle his way out of, of course. Heroes always wriggle their way out of scrapes, if the author loves them . . . and if he's not sick of them.

'But they're not fairy tales!'

'What?' I took the book out of my daughter's hands and opened it at the publisher's imprint page. Aha . . . they certainly weren't fairy tales. The Other Word publishing house. They publish books and various printed materials for Others. For Light Ones and Dark Ones, indiscriminately. Of course, they don't produce anything really serious: genuine spells are either too secret to be printed, or they can't survive the mechanical application of the text to paper. Some things can only be conveyed by the spoken word and by example. They print the very basics – secrecy isn't particularly important here: if a book like this finds its way into an ordinary shop (as sometimes happens), people will think it's a children's book or a fantasy penned by some graphomaniac. The book was called *The Childhood of Remarkable Others*.

'Is this some kind of textbook?'

'For reading out of class. Stories about the childhood of great magicians.'

I didn't get to study in the magician's classes. In those years they didn't find so many Others, and setting up special classes for them was regarded as impractical. So I did my learning on the job . . .

I leafed through the chapters about Merlin, Karl Cemius, Michel Lefroid and Pan Chang. I stumbled across a chapter about Gesar and smiled when I read the first lines: 'When the Great Gesar was a little boy, he lived in the mountains of Tibet. He was an unattractive, sickly child, he often caught cold and was even given the offensive name Djoru, or "snotty". No one knew that Gesar was really an Other, one of the most powerful magicians in the world. The only one who did know was a Dark Other, Soton, who dreamed of making Gesar a Dark One . . .'

'Look further on,' Nadya begged me impatiently. 'About Erasmus . . .'

'Was Erasmus of Rotterdam really a Prophet?' I asked in surprise, opening the book at the page that had been marked. The bookmark was pink, with little fairies out of some Disney cartoon on it. 'Ah, Erasmus Darwin . . .'

The author certainly didn't make a great effort to vary the introductions for his young readers. But that actually lent the narrative a certain epic quality.

'When the great prophet Erasmus Darwin was a little boy, he lived in the small village of Elton in Ireland. He was always a dreamy and romantic child. He often used to run out of the house and lie in a field of blossoming clover, examining the little flowers. Erasmus was convinced that plants could love like people, that they even had their own sex life. He wrote his remarkable poem *The Love of Plants* about this. But that was later . . .'

I closed the book and looked at the title page. *A textbook of extracurricular reading for middle and senior school age.* I snorted.

'Daddy, do you really think I don't know anything about sex life?' asked Nadya.

I looked at her. 'Nadya, you're ten years old. Yes, I think you don't know anything about it.'

Nadya blushed slightly and murmured: 'But I watch television. I know that grown-ups like to kiss and hug . . .'

'Stop!' I exclaimed in panic. 'Stop. Let's agree that you'll talk about this with mummy, okay?'

'All right,' Nadya said and nodded.

I tried to hand her book back to her.

'So is it true about the Twilight?' Nadya asked again.

'About the Twilight? Ah, yes . . .' I started looking through what came next. Erasmus had learned how to enter the Twilight . . . Others had decided to take him into the Watch . . . well, well, into the Day Watch . . . What?

I sat down on the edge of the bed and stared at the text.

'. . . Prophets and Clairvoyants are always highly valued in the Watches, because their gift is only found rarely – especially the gift of a genuine Prophet. And if a Prophet starts working for one of the two forces, it can lead to great disasters. Therefore the Twilight itself tries to prevent this. If a Prophet might say something very, very important that Others ought not to know, a Twilight Creature comes to him. The Twilight Creature is created by the depths of the Twilight and the power of the Twilight Creature is infinite. None of the Others can stop it or defeat it. And either the Watches leave the Prophet alone, or the Twilight Creature kills him – to prevent a great disaster . . . Little Erasmus was lucky. When he realised that the Twilight Creature was on his trail, he went to his favourite tree – an old hollow ash – and shouted out the prophecy into the hollow. When a Prophet utters the most important prophecy of his life, he doesn't remember exactly what he has said. The Twilight Creature realised that no one would find out about the prophecy and left Erasmus in peace . . .'

After that the narrative continued, talking about how the artful Erasmus also persuaded the Watches to leave him in peace and lived a happy life, amusing himself by creating golems and bringing corpses to life, often uttering ordinary predictions for the Others – and sometimes shocking the people around him in the eighteenth century by telling them about the Big Bang or jet engines fuelled by oxygen and hydrogen, or the spontaneous appearance of life in the oceans. There was also a little bit about his grandson Charles, who was far more famous among human beings. In time, Erasmus had retired from any kind of work and staged his own death as Others are in the habit of doing, and now he lived somewhere in Great Britain, not wishing to see anyone . . .

I quickly leafed through the chapter to the end. And what exactly was so remarkable about this Prophet that I personally had never heard of? Ah . . . there it was . . .

'You will probably ask why Erasmus Darwin is remarkable. Well, it is because he managed to outwit the Twilight Creature. Prophets are usually only able to make their most important prophecy if they utter it immediately after being initiated – even the Twilight Creature needs time to find its prey. But Erasmus guessed how to evade his pursuer when the beast was already dogging his heels. Under the gaze of its eyes, blazing so brightly in the darkness, people seemed little different from the plants that Erasmus loved so much . . . Never despair, never give up, even an overwhelmingly superior force can be outwitted – that is what the life of the remarkable little Other Erasmus teaches us . . .'

'Burning so bright in the darkness . . .' I said and rubbed the bridge of my nose. 'Tiger, tiger . . .'

'Quoting poetry now, are you?' asked Svetlana, glancing out of the kitchen.

'What do you mean?'

'"Tiger, tiger, burning bright, in the forests of the night. What immortal hand or eye could frame thy fearful symmetry? In what distant deeps or skies burnt the fire of thine eyes?" Blake. William Blake. His poem *The Tiger*.'

'You wouldn't know if he happened to be acquainted with Charles Darwin's grandfather, would you?' I asked.

'Erasmus?' Svetlana asked brightly. 'The one who was an Other?'

I nodded and got up off the sofa.

'He was more than a mere chance acquaintance. Blake even illustrated his books. Something about the love of plants.'

'So Blake didn't just write poetry?'

'Well, actually he illustrated heaps of books and is just as famous as an artist as he is as a poet. And, by the way, he wasn't an Other in the literal sense of the word, but he did possess the rare ability—' Svetlana suddenly stopped dead.

'Well?' I asked wearily, opening the cupboard that Nadya was strictly forbidden to touch. Locks would be useless against her, unfortunately, but Nadya's a bright girl and she keeps her word.

'He could see Others. Dark Ones and Light Ones.'

'Like my *polizei* acquaintance,' I said. 'Svetlana, I've got to go to work.'

'Are you going to have some borsch?' my wife asked.

I just sighed as I stuck all sorts of magical trinkets into my various pockets. I was a hundred per cent certain that none of these amulets would actually be any use to me, but the habit was too strong.

'Anton . . .' Svetlana called to me when I was already in the doorway.

'What?'

'I once left the Watch, so that we could be together.'

'I remember.'

'I've been wanting to ask you for a long time . . .'

I looked at her. Svetlana paused for a moment, then lowered her eyes.

'Take care.'

I raced up to Gesar's office on the third floor like a lunatic. Considering that I was waving a book on the childhood of outstanding Others in the air, I must have looked like someone who has discovered a coded prophecy for the next two hundred years in *Pinocchio*, together with a report of an encounter with aliens from another planet, the formula of a cure for the common cold and an obscene acrostic at the beginning of chapter two.

'Where's the fire?' asked Gesar.

He was sitting on the edge of the desk, and the boy-Prophet was lounging in his office chair. The chair was rather spacious for the boy, to put it mildly. Judging from the fact that Kesha was sitting in a clumsy imitation of the simplest meditation pose, Gesar must have been trying to teach him to control his gift. There was no one else there.

'The Tiger!' I exclaimed wildly.

'He's far away,' Gesar replied calmly. 'I believe we'll be okay until the morning.'

I cited Blake's poem:

'Tiger, tiger, burning bright
In the forests of the night,
What immortal hand or eye
Could frame thy fearful symmetry?

In what distant deeps or skies
Burnt the fire of thine eyes?
On what wings dare he aspire?
What the hand dare seize the fire?

And what shoulder and what art
Could twist the sinews of thy heart?
And when thy heart began to beat,
What dread hand and what dread feet?'

'You could at least quote the entire poem,' Gesar replied, and continued:

'What the hammer? What the chain?
In what furnace was thy brain?
What the anvil? What dread grasp
Dare its deadly terrors clasp?

When the stars threw down their spears,
And water'd heaven with their tears,
Did He smile His work to see?
Did He who made the lamb make thee?

Tiger, tiger, burning bright
In the forests of the night,
What immortal hand or eye
Dare frame thy fearful symmetry?'

Kesha gaped at us wide-eyed. Nowadays you don't often see two grown men suddenly start reciting verse. Then he closed his eyes again. Such diligence – incredible!

'Is the full version any more help to us?' I asked sullenly.

'I just think it suggests that we have time until the morning,' Gesar explained.

'You know everything already,' I said. 'The Prophet Erasmus Darwin. The only Prophet who ever got away from the Twilight Creature.'

'I don't know,' Gesar replied simply. 'That's one version of the story. But I regard it as poetic licence in an account of one of the standard squabbles between the Light Ones and Dark Ones of Ireland.'

'Is the Tiger something like a Mirror?' I asked.

'No. By no means is every Prophet pursued by Twilight Creatures. And they're not concerned in the least about the balance between the Watches. If . . . if the legends are to be believed . . .

they try to prevent the utterance of prophecies that foretell unprecedented disasters and catastrophes. And they eliminate anyone who stands in their way . . .'

'You knew,' I said. 'You knew everything, Boris Ignatievich . . .'

'I didn't know!' Gesar retorted gruffly. 'Do you think I'm some kind of computer that remembers everything? Zabulon hinted at Twilight Creatures. I'd never heard of anything of the kind, but I put on a brave face – as if I understood what he was talking about. I set the analysts onto it, they combed the databases and half an hour ago they came up with the same book you have there . . . plus two hundred pages of analysis and theories. Was it Tolik who tipped you off? I'll strip him of his bonuses until the end of the century!'

'No one leaked any information to me,' I said, leaping to my friend's defence. 'The book's on Nadya's extracurricular reading list and she came to me with a question. I read it. And after that . . . after that we guessed the whole thing as a family. About Erasmus, about Blake and the Tiger . . .'

'Apparently the Twilight Creature didn't come to Erasmus in human form,' Gesar laughed. 'And afterwards he said something about it to someone he knew, who wasn't an Other, but could see . . .'

'Boris Ignatievich, we have to ask the Inquisition for help,' I said. 'If all this about the Tiger is true, then how can we—'

Gesar didn't let me finish. 'They refused, Anton.'

'What?' I asked, bewildered.

'The recommendation of the Inquisition is not to get involved in a conflict and let the Tiger take the boy.'

That was the first time he pronounced the word 'Tiger' so that it sounded like a name.

'But he . . .' I said, glancing sideways at Kesha.

'Yes, the Tiger will kill him,' Gesar said with a nod.

'Boris Ignatievich!'

'The boy can't hear us,' my boss reassured me. 'I've put up a screen. Just so that our voices won't disturb him.'

'Gesar, then who is he, this Tiger?'

'No one knows, Anton. He's far too rare a beast. Either the Prophet manages to utter his main prophecy and the Tiger backs off. Or . . . or he kills the Prophet and leaves. I presume that's why Prophets are such a rare breed too. He usually finds them before we do.'

'What's a main prophecy?'

Gesar sighed and glanced ostentatiously at his watch. Then he pointed to one of the chairs and sat down in the one beside it. He glanced round at Kesha and wagged his finger at him. The boy closed his eyes again.

'The very first prophecy that a Prophet makes when his powers become effective is called his main prophecy. It can be extremely important or absolutely insignificant. But according to one theory – one theory – we're getting into very uncertain territory here, Anton.'

'Don't drag it out.'

'This theory says that the first prophecy doesn't just predict reality, but changes it. But there's another theory that says . . . of course a Prophet can't change reality. But he selects one of the possible courses that reality can follow . . . develops it and fixes it. To use old photographers' terminology.'

'There aren't any photographers left who develop images and fix them,' I muttered. 'So the Tiger tries to stop the first prophecy because, if it's terrible, it will come true?'

'That's right. If the kid predicts World War Three, then it'll happen. If he predicts a hit by an asteroid a couple of kilometres long, then one will fall on us . . .'

'But what he told me in the airport—'

'That's not a prophecy. Just a harbinger. He has to make his prophecy now, after initiation. Usually during the first few days. Sometimes in the first few hours.'

I looked at the fat little lad squirming in the large, threadbare chair and asked: 'What do you want to do, boss?'

'Shake the boy up a bit so that he utters his main prophecy. It's by no means certain that it *will* be something terrible. Anton. I really don't feel like capitulating to some weird Twilight Creature that won't even talk to us!'

'And don't you feel sorry for the boy?'

'You can't feel sorry for everyone. If dozens of Others have to spill their blood to prevent a child shedding a single teardrop, then let him bawl. But I don't want to just hand him over for slaughter without at least trying to do something.'

'So, if the Tiger comes . . .'

'Then the Night Watch will not do battle with him.'

'That's contemptible.'

'It's honest. If the Inquisition came to back us up, we'd have some kind of chance. Maybe. But they've refused. Now everything depends on how much time we have until the Tiger shows up. If it's not before morning, I'll probably have got the boy to speak out by then. Let him utter his prophecy . . . I won't even listen to him. He can mutter it into the toilet bowl. Or into a hollow in a tree, like Erasmus . . . I can grow a tree with a hollow, especially for the occasion. But if the Tiger comes at night . . .'

'But Boris Ignatievich, where in Blake's poem does it say anything about him coming in the morning?'

Gesar paused for a few seconds, and then quoted it again.

> 'When the stars threw down their spears,
> And water'd heaven with their tears . . .'

'That's a fat lot of help.'

'Well, I just hope it means what I think it means,' said Gesar.

'Well maybe it really does mean the morning,' I said. 'You know how . . . poetical . . . all these poets are.'

'The analysts tell me that it's actually an allusion to Milton's *Paradise Lost*, a reference to the fallen angels who were defeated, fell from heaven and were lamented by the other angels . . . You're right, Anton, poets are so poetical. How can you tell what it is they really mean?'

I walked over to the window and looked out at the sky over Moscow. The usual low Moscow sky. No stars to be seen, although it was dark already and they should have appeared by now. Rain . . . rain was possible . . . perfectly possible . . .

'Anton, you won't be able to do a thing,' Gesar said gently. 'Even I won't. Or the entire Watch, all together. You go. I'm going to work with the boy. I just hope I'll get it done in time.'

The boss is a dyed-in-the-wool pragmatist, of course. And his pragmatism would allow him to hand the boy over to a creature from the Twilight, or even to a real tiger in the zoo, if he decided that was the lesser of two evils. But he would try everything he could to save him, out of sheer stubbornness . . .

I knew that.

'I'll be in the office for a while. Call me if anything happens, Boris Ignatievich . . .'

Gesar nodded.

'Is our conversation confidential?' I asked, just to make sure, as I walked over to the door.

'As you think best,' Gesar replied unexpectedly.

I hesitated and looked at my boss.

Then I walked out, closing the door firmly behind me.

There were three people sitting in the duty room – Las, Semyon and Alisher. What they were discussing wasn't the boy-Prophet and it wasn't the Tiger. Their topic of conversation was far more exalted.

'And then I suddenly realise,' Las was saying, 'that I have been granted peace and the world of the spirit. So my decision to turn to God was the right one!'

'I should think so, after a bottle of cognac,' Alisher remarked. 'Hi, Anton!'

'Hi,' I replied, perching on the table. The duty watchmen's room is fairly large, but the two sofas, large round table with chairs around it and mini-kitchen along one wall don't leave much free space.

'The cognac's got nothing to do with it!' Las exclaimed indignantly. 'Do you believe in Allah?'

'I do,' Alisher replied. 'But then, I don't drink.'

'What about beer?'

'I drink beer. But the prophet said the first drop of wine kills a man – he didn't say anything about beer.'

'Excuses, excuses' Las snapped. 'So why mock at my faith in God?'

'I'm not mocking,' Alisher said calmly. 'It's very good that you believe. Only you shouldn't confuse a state of intoxication with the touch of God's hand. It's improper.'

Las gestured dismissively. 'A slight intoxication helps a man to cast off the chains of convention and frees his mind.'

'That's no condition of divine revelation, far from it,' Semyon chuckled. 'I like going into churches, it's calm, the smell's good and the aura's benign. But I don't sense God.'

'Your moment will come too!' Las declared solemnly. 'You'll sense God within you. You're a good man, after all.'

'I'm an Other,' Semyon replied. 'A good one, I hope. But an Other. And for us, I'm afraid, there is no God . . .'

'Guys, can I ask a question?' I put in.

'What is it?' asked Las, livening up.

'If you know for certain that it's impossible to win but, if you don't fight, someone's going to be killed . . . what would you do?'

'If it's impossible, why should I die too?' asked Las.

'If you have to fight, it's not important if you're going to win,' Alisher answered.

'Why, are the lad's chances as bad all that?' Semyon asked, with a frown.

I carried on with my own questions. 'Guys, have you ever heard of the Twilight Creature?'

Silence.

'I've only just found out about him too. That's because we don't read children's books. Only I'm not sure if I ought to . . .'

'If you've started, then finish,' said Semyon. 'Either say something straight out, or never mention it. It's not fair otherwise.'

'I think Gesar has left the choice up to us,' I said. 'Guys, tonight the office is going to be stormed. Attacked by a certain creature, that is . . . And we can't possibly defeat it.'

CHAPTER 8

Quite honestly, I'd got the idea that Gesar had given me his unspoken blessing to enlist volunteers. I could see immediately the way it would be – me telling the guys, them telling their friends, the entire Watch gathering in the office, and the Tiger showing up to be met by all the Light Ones in Moscow . . . And together they would see him off. After all, who said that a Twilight Creature couldn't be defeated? Those lousy analysts . . . origins unknown, strength unknown, intentions obscure, impossible to defeat . . .

We would defeat him. We'd all get together – and beat him. It would be more fun all together. How could Semyon, Alisher and Las possibly agree that we ought to hand over a defenceless child to some mysterious, unknown creature?

'If it was one of us that ended up in a mess like that, then I'd get involved,' said Semyon. 'If it was your daughter . . . knock on wood,' said Semyon, tapping the table. 'But for that kid – no way.'

'He is one of us!' I exclaimed indignantly.

'He's a Light Other,' said Semyon, nodding. 'But not one of us. Maybe in a year's time he would have been one of us. Maybe in a month. But not yet. You say yourself there's no way we can beat this thing. Why would it be better if we all died?'

'But how do we know it's impossible?' I asked indignantly.

'Judging from the skirmish this afternoon, it is impossible,' Semyon replied calmly. 'We don't have a chance. And wiping out the Watch for the sake of one Other is stupid.'

'Semyon's right,' said Alisher, nodding. 'I'm not afraid of being killed in battle, if there's a chance of winning. But this – this is a game beyond our level. I saw him . . . and I didn't like what I saw. Let's hope Gesar can teach the kid to prophesy.'

'But you just said that if you have to fight it doesn't matter if you win or not!'

'Right. But we don't have to fight on this one.'

I looked at Las.

'Why does the Prophet have to be an obnoxious little kid and not a beautiful young girl?' Las exclaimed. 'There's no motivation to sacrifice yourself!'

'I thought you were about to get baptised . . .' I reminded him.

'Exactly. I want to be able to do that. You know, even those thick-skulled knights who picked a fight at every chance they got only dashed off to do battle with a dragon if it had carried off a delightful young maiden, not some scruffy brat of a shepherd boy.'

'How egotistical your motivation is,' I said sarcastically.

'Aesthetic,' Las corrected me. 'If I'm going to sacrifice myself, I want the goal to be exalted.'

'And the life of a Prophet isn't an exalted goal?'

'Prophets usually give utterance to predictions that are pretty grim.'

A chilling presentiment stole into my mind as I looked at them.

'Have you already discussed the situation, then?' I asked.

'Of course,' said Semyon. 'We didn't know who it was we were dealing with. But it doesn't take a genius to predict that the attack will be repeated.'

'And what if I dig my heels in and try to defend the lad?' I said, looking Semyon in the eye.

'Then I'll help you,' Semyon said, with a nod. 'And we'll die together. So I ask you not to do it. Think of Svetlana. And Nadya. And tell me honestly – are you prepared to die for some kid you don't even know?'

I looked at my friends.

Thought for a few moments.

Imagined Sveta and Nadya . . .

Then the boy-Prophet.

And I said: 'No, Semyon. I'm not.'

'And you're right,' said Semyon, nodding. 'Exalted feelings, noble impulses, reckless courage, foolhardy self-sacrifice – that's all very fine. But there has to be a reason for it. A real reason. Otherwise all your Light Other aspirations amount to no more than stupidity. The annals of the Watches recall many Others who were noble but stupid. But they're history now. And unfortunately their example is not worth imitating.'

'You'd better go home,' Alisher put in. 'You're not on duty.'

And I realised that when Gesar gave me permission to reveal the information about the Tiger, he'd had a different purpose in mind. To make me see sense.

Well, he'd done just that.

I didn't go home, of course. No, I didn't pester anyone else with questions about whether they would wade into a hopeless battle with a Twilight Creature. And I didn't make the rounds of the office, mentally placing Others in the key defensive positions. I went to the analysts and scrounged a copy of the report for Gesar (before they gave me it, the guys contacted the boss and got his go-ahead). A close reading convinced me that Gesar wasn't lying and in the opinion of the analysts (based on rather poorly documented attempts to fight the Tiger – in the fifteenth and nineteenth centuries) we wouldn't be able to defeat the Twilight Creature.

At night, strangely enough, the Watch office is empty. We're called the 'Night Watch' and we patrol the streets mostly at night (how else can we do it – our main client base are the lower Dark Ones, the vampires and shapeshifters, who find it harder to control themselves) but our work is like an iceberg: most of it's invisible. And that work takes place during the day – paper-shuffling, training, analysing data, studying fresh information. We live among human beings, after all, and it's more convenient for us to live by their rhythm. At least we managed to push an initiative through the human parliament recently to coordinate daylight-saving time across the entire country . . .

I sat at the computer in my office for a while. Went into my e-mail and wrote a couple of letters. For some reason I suddenly remembered the song that the policeman Iskender's son had been playing, searched for the group that performed it and was surprised to discover that it was from Kazakhstan – I hadn't realised before that they played anything but the *dombra* down there! Then I found a pirate site where their other songs were available. I clicked on the title *Obedient Boys*, leaned back in my chair and listened:

> Stabbing sharp asters into the streets,
> The moon rose to greet susceptible youth,
> And sang as she beamed out pagan brightness:
> 'Children, kill your electrical glare,
> Children, before you are all left eyeless,
> I'll point out salvation, show you the way:
> All those who walk the moonlight path
> Reach the magical city some day.
> Where everyone breathes inspiration like air

And all of the architects there are dreams,
And it's not banknotes, but sunlight that warms,
And if you're in love, they won't think you a fool.'
And the young boy sitting there on the stairs
Believed in the moon's fateful songs of deceit.
And when he believed, the stairs started growing
And carried on, reaching right up to the sky.
The boy set off up to climb the ribbed steps,
But his friends and family all came running:
'You have no business up there in the sky!
Stop! Don't go – this fate is for fools!'
And, listening to them, the boy came back down
With a lingering, longing glance at the moon.
But later he hid and hated them all
And wept for what he had seen in the sky.

That made me wince. The wrong choice. The boy-Prophet was nothing like a romantic young hero, but the song was reproaching me for something.

He wept, feeling emptiness filling his breast.
His way had been lit, as he scrambled on high,
By the light of his tremulous, fluttering heart,
But running back, he dropped his lamp in the sky.
And there it hung now, a small star up in space,
Like a bright, shiny little Christmas-tree toy,
Among all the other little toy hearts
Left there by all the obedient boys . . .

What the hell was this? Why couldn't these Kazakhs imitate Russian kitsch pop and sing songs about beautiful girls, expensive resorts and glittering cars, instead of propagating this decadent romanticism! I turned off the computer and walked out of the office.

My feet took me to the basement floors of their own accord. The door of one of the rooms was open and I glanced inside. The two 'old-timers', Jermenson and Glyba, were sitting there, sipping calmly on glasses of cognac. Mark Emmanuilovich was snacking on non-kosher smoked eel, while Glyba, a member of the old Soviet school, was using 'nikolashka' – a sliced lemon, sprinkled with coffee and sugar. There was a sign of the new times, however – the coffee wasn't instant, but natural, and Glyba was crumbling the beans over the lemon with his strong fingers.

They were sitting with their backs to me, but that was no hindrance to them.

'Come on in, Anton!' Jermenson called amiably.

'You'll have a glass of cognac,' Glyba told me no less sociably. Told me, not asked.

Without speaking, I joined them at the table and took a glass. To my surprise, the cognac wasn't French, but Moldavian – a pot-bellied bottle with a label that said *Surprise*.

'To the victory of the forces of good,' said Jermenson, taking a sip from his glass.

'Over the forces of reason,' Glyba continued.

I downed my glass in one and immediately regretted it. The cognac turned out to be surprisingly good. In fact, you could say it was excellent.

'Where do you get this?' I asked.

'You have to know the right place,' Glyba laughed. 'See, Emmanuilich? I told you Anton was a rational person.'

'That's just it, he's a real person, human . . .' Jermenson said gruffly. He took a long leather case from his jacket pocket and held it out to me. 'How about a cigar, young man? I highly recommend it. None of that sacrilege with a lemon, the only thing that goes with a good cognac is a genuine cigar.'

The Great Ones seemed perfectly placid and relaxed. Not at all as if they were preparing for a skirmish with the Tiger. But in that case what were they doing in the office?

'Has Gesar already told you?' I asked.

'About the Tiger?' Jermenson responded. 'Yes, of course. I ought to be ashamed of myself. I've heard about this kind of thing before . . . It was a very long time ago, though.'

'And?' I asked abruptly.

'We're going to sit here until the morning, gabbing the way that old men do,' Jermenson said, shrugging. 'If he comes . . . well, then we'll take a look. We're not going to fight, just take a look . . . There's no charge for looking.'

'You're going to watch the Tiger kill the boy?'

'In a case like this, leaving is even more cowardly,' Jermenson replied coolly. 'Why don't you tell us what he prophesied to you at the airport? Word for word. Maybe Gesar's wrong? Maybe the boy has already uttered his prophecy?'

'But then why would the Tiger bother to carry on chasing him?' Glyba responded. 'No, you tell us, Anton. We're genuinely interested.'

'"You are Anton Gorodetsky, a Higher Light Magician. You are Nadka's father. Because of you . . . all of us . . ."' I shrugged and spread my hands. 'Is that any good as a prophecy?'

'No,' said Glyba, shaking his head. 'Djoru's right: it was a harbinger, induced by stress.'

'But there is something interesting about it!' said Jermenson, raising his finger. 'Right?'

'Right,' said Glyba, splashing more cognac out into the glasses. 'First, the prophecy will be addressed to one particular person. It's linked to Anton. Perhaps because he's the one the boy met?'

'Or because Anton saved him . . .' Jermenson said, with a nod. 'And it's important that he said "Nadka's father". Our little friend doesn't look like one of those children who address all little girls in that familiar fashion. That means . . .'

'That means the prophecy is linked to Nadya as well, and the boy-Prophet has to become friends with her.'

'And it concerns all Others – "all of us" is in there for a reason. But the clinching role will be played by Anton.' It looked as if this wasn't the first time that Jermenson and Glyba had brainstormed together.

'It's very interesting, it really is!' said Glyba, beaming. 'I'd like to hear it. I hope Djoru will be able to explain to the boy how to prophesy.'

'Djoru might have managed it,' said Gesar, walking into the room, 'but I haven't.'

He sat down with us (now that was strange – I thought there were only three chairs at the table before then) and took a glass. (Well, there definitely wasn't a fourth glass on the table before, let alone a full one!) He looked at me, cleared his throat, took a sip of cognac and said: 'The ball keeps going wide of the goalpost. The lad is an Other, the lad really is a Prophet. Only we were mistaken. He's not a Higher Other, only first or second rank.'

'That's not crucial for a Prophet,' said Glyba. 'He'll utter his prophecies less often, that's all.'

'This isn't just a matter of initiation,' Gesar went on. 'Or of understanding the technical details. I've explained all that, he's a bright boy. But there has to be the right state of mind. The readiness to prophesy. And that's harder to induce. All my fiddling and fussing got me nowhere – his head's lost somewhere up in the clouds . . .'

'Probably remembering his mother,' Glyba said sympathetically. 'I ended up in the Watch as a child too, I missed my family terribly . . .'

'Boris Ignatievich, can I have a word with him?' I asked.

'Give it a try,' Gesar agreed willingly. 'I don't think it will help, but try it. Only don't drag it out – it's almost midnight already, the kid can hardly keep his eyes open . . .'

His look as he watched me go was sympathetic and approving, but without any real enthusiasm.

Innokentii Tolkov, ten and a half years old, Prophet of the first level of Power, was not sleeping yet. He was sitting on the floor beside the heap of toys provided out of the Night Watch's largesse and twirling a toy telephone in his hands. When I appeared, he became embarrassed and put the phone back into the multicoloured heap – it was a toy for tiny tots: a few large buttons with numbers that played some kind of jolly Chinese tune when you pressed them, and a button for recording any phrase that you wanted. Nadya had had a 'telephone' like that too, when she was three years old.

I suddenly felt really worried.

'Hi, Kesha,' I said, sitting down on the floor beside him.

'Good evening, Uncle Anton,' said Kesha.

'Well, you've got a real treasure hoard here,' I said awkwardly, dragging a toy helicopter out of the heap. 'My Nadya wanted to play with one of these . . .'

'You take it for her,' Kesha said calmly. 'I don't need it, after all.'

I looked into his eyes – and 'worried' became 'terrified'.

'How do you mean?' I asked in an artificially cheerful voice.

'Uncle Boris told me everything. About the Twilight Creature that's hunting me. And how you won't be able to stop him.'

'Why?' I asked – of course, the question wasn't meant for the boy. 'Why?'

But Kesha answered anyway.

'He said that was his last chance to motivate me. That I have to pluck up my courage and make a prophecy. Then the beast will leave me alone.'

'And so?'

'I can't do it, it doesn't work,' said the boy, lowering his eyes guiltily. 'I tried really hard, honest I did! I'm sorry . . .'

He was even apologising to us . . .

'So what then?' I asked.

'Uncle Boris said that if I couldn't manage it, there was no point in worrying. I ought to go to bed and get some sleep, maybe the creature won't come after all. And then everything will be all right, and in the morning I'll definitely manage it.'

'But you didn't go to bed,' I said.

'I'm afraid,' the boy replied simply.

'Did you really try hard?' I asked.

'Yes – do you think I'm a fool? But Uncle Boris said that if there was no hope I shouldn't waste my time trying any more.'

He looked up at me and said: 'You go now, it's all right. I'll play for a while and go to bed.'

'If there's no hope . . .' I said. 'If there's no hope . . .' I slapped at my pockets. Took out my phone. 'Hang on a moment, Kesha . . .'

Generally speaking, phoning your ten-year-old daughter at midnight is not the most pedagogically correct decision. But before I could even call, the phone jangled in my hands and I raised it to my ear.

'Hello?'

'Daddy, were you going to call me?' Nadya's voice was not even slightly sleepy and it sounded very, very eager.

'Yes.'

'Are you doing battle? With that creature?'

'No, Nadya, we're not going to fight a battle with it. We wouldn't be able to beat it.'

'What if—'

'And you're not going to fight a battle with it either!'

'But you do want me to come, don't you?'

'Yes, only not to fight a battle at all, but to . . .' I began.

There was a breath of cold air. A dark, glowing oval with a belt of white sparks round it appeared in mid-air. Nadya stepped out of it, barefoot and wearing nothing but her pink pyjamas.

'. . . give Kesha some hope,' I finished, gazing at my daughter.

'Daddy, I managed it just like Gesar!' Nadya exclaimed joyfully. 'Oh, hi!'

No, Nadya wasn't embarrassed. But Kesha blushed and lowered his eyes.

'Nadya, I'm afraid we've got almost no time left,' I said. 'Perhaps only a few hours. Kesha has to make his first prophecy. He knows how to do it. But it's not working for him. I think you can help him somehow.'

'Maybe I should give him a kiss?' Nadya asked in an innocent voice. 'To inspire him. That always helps in the cartoons!'

Why, the little . . . the little . . . no, not witch, of course. But she does have a bit of the witch in her. Like every woman.

'I'm afraid kisses won't do it,' I said. 'Nadya, talk to the boy. Try to understand what the problem is. I . . . I won't be far away. I'll be back in five minutes.'

I walked out of the room, closed the door behind me and thought that in just a couple of years' time I would be more wary of leaving my daughter alone with little boys. Would you believe it! 'I'll kiss him!' I ought to throw that TV out . . .

'Anton!'

I walked into the room where Gesar, Alisher and Jermenson were sitting. There seemed to be more cognac in the bottle than before, which roused my suspicions. Glyba had gone off somewhere, but the Kazakh White Magician's replacement by Alisher had not affected the way the group was passing the time.

'There was some kind of . . . movement . . .' said Gesar, gazing at me. 'Tell me, you haven't done anything stupid, have you? Like teleporting the lad away from here?'

'No, it was Nadya,' I said. 'I called her . . . to talk to the boy. She's known all her life that she's an Other. Maybe she can give him some ideas?'

'A truly devoted father,' said Gesar.

'Well, that's what you wanted, isn't it?' I asked him. 'When you told the boy that there was no hope, that he should give up trying?'

Gesar shook his head slowly.

'No, Anton. Thank you for valuing every word I say so highly, but it wasn't a hint. I simply said there was no hope. I wasn't thinking of your daughter . . .'

'But how lovely that would be . . .' Jermenson said thoughtfully. 'A pity . . .'

And then I felt the 'movement' that Gesar had mentioned. As if the Twilight had swayed, splashing out energy, and then frozen.

'I'll go and give Nadya's ears a tweak,' I said.

'It's not good to tweak little girls' ears,' said Gesar, getting up. 'And that's not her.'

'It's the Tiger,' said Jermenson. He got up too.

'Anton, take your daughter and leave,' said Alisher, pulling a bracelet made of three intertwined rings – gold, silver and copper – out of his pocket. He threaded his left hand through it and dangled it in the air, as if he was gauging an invisible load.

'What are you doing?' I asked. 'You said . . .'

'Never mind what we said,' Jermenson replied, with a shrug. 'And anyway . . . if we can spin things out for an hour or two, that could decide everything. He won't come through the Twilight, Gesar?'

'No,' Gesar said firmly.

'Perhaps we should ask the Inquisition after all . . . or Zabulon . . .'

'I asked. A quarter of an hour ago. Help was refused.'

'Then it's up to us,' Jermenson declared cheerfully. 'A very curious experience altogether . . . wouldn't you say so, Ali?'

'For sure,' said Alisher, and shook the hand with the bracelet. His body was enveloped in a white glow. He shook his hand again and the glow faded away.

'Yes indeed,' said Jermenson, beaming. 'I thought there was nothing left that could surprise me, but this Tiger really is a new experience in my life.'

And at that very moment there was a loud crash above us. Rumbling and powerful – as if something had exploded. The magicians raised their heads and listened.

'Semyon,' said Gesar. 'I told him not to interfere . . . It's a pity we don't employ corporal punishment in the Watch.'

'We could introduce it,' Jermenson said brightly.

'He's not overdoing it,' said Alisher. 'But the guys don't want to surrender the office without a fight. Even if it is only symbolic . . .'

Gesar looked at me.

'Anton, your task is simple. After the Tiger comes down the stairs and appears at that end of the corridor, we'll have from three to five minutes. You can do something – to ease your conscience. A spell or two, only try not to nettle him . . . And then grab your daughter and leave. She knows how to open a portal.'

'I can do that too,' I said without any real conviction.

'Good. Then leave. And don't even try to take the young lad

with you. No pointless heroics. You've still got a long life ahead of you.'

'All right,' I said, nodding, disgusted to realise that I really meant it.

'We'll do everything we can to try to delay him, and then leave,' said Gesar, either just for me or for all three of us. 'A few minutes might be some kind of help . . .'

A piercing whistling sound started up overhead, as if steam under high pressure was escaping from a small aperture. What were they doing up there? Or was that the Tiger?

'A beautiful scene,' Jermenson said unexpectedly. 'And very positive . . . international . . . A Tibetan, a Kazakh and two Jews trying to save a little Russian boy . . .'

'I'm Uzbek,' Alisher remarked.

'I'm not Jewish,' I commented.

'With a surname like Gorodetsky?' Jermenson asked dubiously.

'It's an ancient Russian name! From the name of the town on the Volga where my ancestors used to live.'

'That makes it even more beautiful,' Jermenson decided. 'A Tibetan, an Uzbek, a Russian and a Jew . . .'

'It sounds like the beginning of a joke,' Alisher muttered.

Gesar gazed at Jermenson and asked: 'You mean to tell me you're a Jew, Mark?'

'Mock on, mock on,' Jermenson growled.

Overhead something started knocking rapidly – as if someone had turned on a sewing machine. Or started firing a sub-machine gun, which was more probable – it wasn't likely that the Tiger would leave the boy alone for a pair of well-stitched trousers.

'Optimists,' Gesar snorted.

'Well, why not give it a try?' Jermenson said, shrugging. 'You know, when they invented gunpowder I was absolutely delighted. Nothing better against carrion raised from the dead.'

The light bulbs in the corridor suddenly blinked and went out. A moment later they started glowing again, but dimly – the emergency generator had cut in. But a couple of seconds after that they went out and stayed out.

I waved my hand and hung several magical lights along the length of the corridor. Gesar snapped his fingers and extinguished the two closest to us, then growled: 'Will you ever learn . . .'

We distinctly heard footsteps coming down the stairs. Not rapid, but confident. The Tiger stepped down onto the floor and stopped at the far end of the corridor. He looked in our direction – the darkness didn't seem to bother him. He smiled and took a step forward.

There was a crash and the Tiger was enveloped in a frosty white vortex. Like mist or a blizzard . . . The Tiger froze for a second and then, with a certain effort, took another step, heading towards us.

'I told you it wouldn't work,' Gesar called back over his shoulder.

'But it was worth a try!' Jermenson replied resentfully.

The two Higher Ones stepped forward together, shielding Alisher and me. And at that moment the door behind our backs slammed. I looked round and saw Nadya.

My daughter looked thoughtful, but pleased about something. She walked up to me, took my hand and asked: 'Is that him?'

Meanwhile the Tiger had stopped moving. An expression of perplexed confusion appeared on his face, as if a Zero-Level Absolute Enchantress was something that his plans hadn't taken into account.

'Who do you see?' I asked her. 'A little girl?'

'No. A tiger. He's big and stripy and his eyes are blazing.'

'Beautiful,' I sighed.

'Daddy, you shouldn't kill tigers. They're in the Red Book.'

'It's all right to kill this one,' I said. 'Only we can't seem to manage it somehow.'

And suddenly the Tiger spoke. During our previous encounter he hadn't uttered a word and, to be honest, I'd been certain that he didn't know how to talk . . .

'Go away. I don't want you.'

'And we don't want *you*,' Gesar replied. 'Why don't you go away?'

The Tiger shook his head. (I wondered how Nadya saw that. A talking tiger? Shere Khan from the cartoon film about Mowgli?)

'The prophecy must not be heard.'

'He's only a little boy,' said Gesar. 'Leave him alone, give him time. Let the prophecy be uttered into the empty air. Let no one hear it.'

'A risk,' said the Tiger. 'He is a Prophet first and foremost. And then a little boy. Leave.'

'Give him time,' Gesar repeated.

Instead of answering, the Tiger started advancing again. Apparently the time for talking was over.

I didn't understand exactly what it was the Great Ones did. The corridor was suddenly swathed in a multicoloured fiery cobweb, with blue, green and orange threads strung through the air. The Tiger ran into them and his face contorted, as if in pain. But he carried on walking. Slowly, but surely.

'Anton, leave!' Gesar barked.

I looked at Nadya. Squeezed her hand tighter. Nodded.

'Do we have to go, daddy?' she asked very calmly.

I nodded again.

'He only needs just a little bit longer,' said Nadya. 'Why don't I—'

'We're leaving!' I shouted. 'Open the portal. I order you to!'

'Daddy, you can't order me to run away!'

'I'm not ordering you as your daddy, but as a member of the Watch!'

Nadya looked at me, and I wasn't sure if it would work. Since she was little we had taught her to respect the Night Watch. Explained that what members of the Watch said was an order. That magic was not to be played with. But she was a little girl, for her all fairy tales had a happy ending – and I saw an energy that could engulf the whole of Moscow raging in her eyes . . . only no one knew if it would be any use against the Tiger.

'Nadya, please,' I repeated wearily.

Tears glinted in my daughter's eyes. She pressed her lips together and nodded – and a portal opened up beside us. I glanced at the Tiger – he had already walked halfway along the corridor. He wasn't attacking, we weren't his enemies . . . We were no hindrance to him, he was on his way to kill the Prophet.

I took hold of Nadya's hand and tugged her towards the portal . . .

And at that instant the Tiger stopped. He raised his hand and rubbed his forehead in a perfectly human gesture. And smiled.

The door behind our backs opened and the little Prophet Kesha came out into the corridor. He was soaking wet, like some fat man who has been forced to train in the gym. His eyes looked slightly drowsy and dopey, he gazed at us perplexedly, barely even recognising us. His nose was bleeding.

'Everything is all right,' said the Tiger. 'I am leaving.'

Apparently he was simply going to walk away – along the corridor. But the floor under his feet suddenly shattered, spraying planks and small chunks of concrete in all directions. The golem that Jermenson had set in motion during the first skirmish had caught up with its adversary after all.

With an expression of extreme surprise on his face, the Tiger tumbled down into a pit, where the earth was heaving like boiling porridge. I caught a glimpse of the golem's hands, the Tiger's leg . . . For a second, I thought I could see a long, stripy tail sticking up out of the ground like a giant worm . . .

Then it all disappeared.

'I'm afraid the golem hasn't killed him,' said Jermenson. 'I'm afraid the Tiger simply didn't think it necessary to fight . . .'

The coloured cobweb faded away. Gesar and Jermenson looked at each other, slowly breaking into smiles.

I leaned down to Nadya and asked in a quiet voice: 'How did you help him?'

Glancing round at Kesha, Nadya went up on tiptoe and whispered in my ear.

'I said that if he didn't speak out his stupid prophecy right now, I was going to give him a thrashing and tell everyone that he'd been beaten by a little girl.'

'And he believed you?' I asked.

'I punched him in the nose.'

I took my handkerchief out of my pocket and walked over to the boy. Handing him the handkerchief, I said: 'Tilt your head back and press this against your nose. Now we'll call a . . . doctor.'

And as he tilted back his head in confusion, I parted his fingers, took the toy that was clenched in them and stuck it in my pocket.

'We were lucky,' said Gesar, coming up to us. 'The prophecy hasn't been revealed, the Tiger has gone. Congratulations, my lad, all your troubles are behind you!'

'We were lucky,' I said, echoing Gesar.

The toy phone I had taken from Kesha was burning a hole in my pocket. I didn't know if I would risk pressing the button to play back what was recorded on it. Or whether there really was anything recorded on it at all.

But it was certainly a good thing that the Twilight Creature didn't understand anything about modern children's toys.

Part Two

DUBIOUS TIMES

PROLOGUE

'I'LL BE TAKING the lesson today,' said Gorodetsky. 'Anna Tikhonovna is ill.'

'What's wrong with her?' Pavel asked anxiously. 'Something magical?'

'Cholecystitis,' Anton replied.

'That can be cured with a spell,' said Pavel. He was not much older than twenty, from the generation that had grown up on computer role-playing games and Harry Potter.

'It can,' Anton agreed. 'But why bother, when you can take a medicine to expel the bile?'

'Magic's quicker,' Pavel persisted.

'And more complicated. Strangely enough, the illnesses that respond best to magical treatment are the deadly ones. Plain ordinary colds, gallstones, colic and haemorrhoids are easier to cure by ordinary means. And anyway, it's always best to economise your Power and your capacity for magical intervention.'

'What for?' asked Pavel, glancing round at the other students, as if looking for support. 'We're much stronger than the Day Watch.'

'That's exactly what we're going to talk about,' Anton said, nodding. He walked round the classroom, running his eye over the students: ten Others, ten future magicians and enchantresses. Six adults, four children and juveniles. The usual balance – the age at which a person is identified as an Other can vary greatly. The youngest student, the Prophet Innokentii Tolkov, was ten and a half, and the oldest, the enchantress Galina Stanislavovna, was fifty-two. Some of them would join the Watch, and some would decide to carry on living a human life . . . or almost human.

'How many students do you think there are in the Day Watch?'

'Ten,' said Pavel.

'Afraid not,' said Gorodetsky, shaking his head.

'A hundred,' answered Nadya.

'That answer doesn't count. You heard about it at home.'

'So what?' Nadya asked indignantly. 'What difference does it make where I heard it?'

'Well, you got it wrong anyway,' said Anton, shrugging. 'That was a long time ago.'

'A hundred and fifty-three,' muttered Innokentii.

'That answer's acceptable,' said Gorodetsky, nodding. 'Although I thought they had a hundred and fifty-one students, but I won't argue with a Prophet. What does this imbalance tell us?'

'That there are more bad people in the world than good ones?' Galina asked in a quiet voice. Before being initiated she had been a teacher of Russian language and literature for senior-school classes in a small town outside Moscow. So Anton supposed she had a right to an assumption like that.

'Not people, Others!' Denis corrected her. He was thirty-something, a former soldier who had been discharged from the army during the reforms. Strangely enough, his human profession and his specialisation as an Other coincided – he promised to make a rather good Battle Magician.

'Sorry, Denis, but people is right,' Galina Stanislavovna said quietly, but firmly. 'Others aren't born bad or good . . . and neither are people, by the way. Others take the side of the Light or the Darkness depending on their state of mind at the time of initiation . . .'

'One comment,' said Anton. 'Who wants to correct that?'

Several students raised their hands. Anton nodded at Farhad, a former manager from an oil company in Kazan. A self-made man with a successful career in business – people like that didn't often become Light Others.

'The terms Light Ones and Dark Ones don't mean good and bad, or good and evil,' said Farhad. 'If we divide them using human yardsticks, they are altruists and egotists. Those who want the best for everyone around them and those who want the best for themselves.'

'And occasionally, for their own personal benefit, Dark Others are capable of doing good for the people around them, while Light Others can occasionally cause them harm,' said Anton, nodding again. 'That's right. Although I am surprised that you're still poring over the basics . . . What does the Day Watch's fifteen-fold advantage over us signify?'

'There are more egotists among people,' said Galina Stanislavovna.

'The Night Watch isn't as good at looking for future Others,' suggested Denis.

'Both explanations are good,' said Anton. 'We won't try to determine how correct they are just yet. Tell me, in that case, why is the balance between the Watches maintained?'

'Because you're a Higher Other,' said Denis. 'So is Gesar, and Svetlana . . . and Nadenka's an Absolute Enchantress!'

Gorodetsky nodded.

'That's right. The Night Watch has significantly fewer members, but at the same time we have a greater number of powerful magicians. And to get back to the previous question, this has been the normal situation over many centuries. There really are more Dark Ones. The Light Ones really are more powerful. Overall, there's parity. And that, Pavel, is why you shouldn't use magic for every tiny little thing. Where you can put your trust in science, that's what you should do.'

Pavel nodded, although, to judge from his expression, Gorodetsky hadn't convinced him completely.

'Anton, have there ever been any attempts to alter the balance of power?' asked Galina Stanislavovna.

'Of course there have,' said Anton, nodding. 'The most far-reaching of them was called the Great October Revolution. Communist ideology was based on altruism and the experiment by the Russian Watches was officially sanctioned. Essentially, it was the greatest intervention by Others in human life after the Renaissance, the Great Plague and the independence of the North American states.'

'And the Dark Ones allowed it?' Galina asked in amazement.

'Of course. In the first place, they were in our debt . . .'

'For the independence of the USA?' Denis chuckled.

'No, for the Renaissance. And in the second place, the Dark Ones were of the opinion that the dissemination of communist ideology among people was bound to produce an increase in egotism and dark emotions.'

'And were they proved right?' Galina asked indignantly.

'No. We were all wrong. It didn't change the balance of egotists and altruists at all, in the world at large or in Russia. After that the tacitly accepted general opinion was that the ratio of "one to fifteen" or, more precisely, "one to sixteen", is a constant that expresses the balance of altruists and egotists among human beings.'

'But what is it in the USA, for instance?' enquired David Saakyan. The seventeen-year-old school pupil had been initiated only a month earlier, and he was interested in absolutely everything.

'In the USA, Sweden, Zimbabwe, North Korea, Estonia, Brazil . . . anywhere you like – the ratio is exactly the same. Unfortunately it has turned out that neither the social system, nor the standard of living, nor the dominant ideology have the slightest influence on the ratio of potential Light Ones and Dark Ones. Therefore it's a constant. Of course, powerful social upheavals bring about shifts in one direction or the other – but sooner or later they are smoothed out. And whether people belong to the Christian or Muslim faith, or any other, doesn't change the ratio.'

'Daddy, but that can't be right,' Nadya objected indignantly. 'People act differently everywhere!'

'Yes,' Anton said, with a nod. 'Of course they do er . . . Nadezhda Antonovna. The way people behave depends on the basic moral tenets and norms in a society. Naturally, the Khmer Rouge, Al-Qaeda terrorists, respectable middle-class Europeans and, say, members of the Komsomol in the 1930s, would behave quite differently in identical situations. But that wouldn't change the essential point. The ratio of altruists and egotists, even among Benedictine monks and members of the Gestapo, is the same. It's just that their altruism and egotism are expressed differently.'

'But that's the whole point!' protested Nadya, refusing to give in.

'For human beings. For them, of course, the difference is very great. But unfortunately not for us.'

'Why? We're supposed to make people's lives better, aren't we?'

'How? The Light Others created a society that professed altruism and universal brotherhood. The result was that they bred monstrous egotists who gleefully betrayed everything that was sacred.'

'We didn't betray anything!' exclaimed Galina Stanislavovna, jumping up off her chair. Her lips were trembling. 'It wasn't us. We were betrayed!'

'Really?' Anton asked gently. 'Remember yourself during those years, please. When leaders betray their people and the people don't overthrow them, it's not just the leaders who should be blamed.'

'All power corrupts,' said Denis. 'The Light Others should take power into their own hands . . .'

'And drive people to happiness with the whip?' laughed Anton. 'Never mind the fact that people understand this happiness differently? And are you certain that the Light Others won't be corrupted by power? Think about it. And please, for the next lesson, write an essay on the subject: "What would the human world be like if the Light Ones decided to take power?"'

'Then what is the point of our existence?' Galina Stanislavovna asked bitterly. 'If you think that we can't influence human life and change it for the better?'

'Oh, right,' Anton said with a nod. 'That's another essay: "What is the meaning of an Other's life?"'

The class groaned.

'But if we . . .' Galina Stanislavovna began

'In the name of all that's holy, keep quiet!' Denis implored her. 'The last thing we need now is a third essay!'

CHAPTER 1

ANNA TIKHONOVNA WAS drinking tea in Gesar's office. There was a cup standing in front of the boss, too, but he seemed to be entirely absorbed in the document that was open on his computer.

'How did the lesson go?' the old woman asked curiously.

'Fine.' I sat down facing her, taking advantage of Gesar's silence to pour myself a cup of tea. 'I told them you had cholecystitis.'

'Good,' said Anna Tikhonovna, nodding. 'I hope you're not too tired, Anton?'

'No, no, of course not,' I said and took a sip of tea. Anna Tikhonovna was a woman of the old school. They said that, when there was no one there to see, our one and only teacher even drank her tea out of the saucer. She refused to acknowledge green teas and despised even more the herbal infusions that were called 'teas' through some misunderstanding. As she conceived it, tea had to be as black as tar and as strong as a sinner's conscience.

Or the other way round. As black as that conscience and as strong as tar.

And sweet.

Under the old woman's watchful eye, I gave in and put three lumps of sugar into my cup. Stirred it. Took a swallow.

Strangely enough, it tasted good. Although at home I would never even have thought of drinking tea with sugar. I wouldn't even have been able to swallow it.

'Why do you dislike this lesson so much, Anna Tikhonovna?' I asked. 'I recall that in my time you didn't take it either – you had flu. Tiger Cub took us for it . . .'

We fell silent for a moment.

'Anton, do you feel comfortable taking that lesson?' the teacher asked.

'Well . . . not really,' I said, wincing. 'Explaining to young people that all their grandiose plans to ennoble humanity or their own country will never be anything more than so much dust, that all we can do is work with the minor details and stand up to the Day Watch . . . Yes, it's not very enjoyable.'

'But it has to be done,' said Gesar, without looking up from the computer. 'Anton, how do you cancel a marked list in Pages?'

'Go into "view", call up the "inspector" window and there'll be a bookmark in it . . .' I looked at Gesar in surprise. 'Have you decided to master the Mac now, then?'

'It's interesting to learn something new,' said Gesar, sliding the mouse around the desk. 'Or do you think I'm already too old for that?'

'Oh, come now, boss,' I answered, sipping at my tea. 'You're still a very robust old man.'

'Moving from an abacus to an arithmometer was hard for me. But moving from an arithmometer to a calculator was easy. And I never did like typewriters, I even used to have a shorthand typist before . . .' He paused and smiled at some memory or other. Anna Tikhonovna smiled slightly as well. 'But I liked computers straight away. There's something right about them . . . magical!'

'I wholeheartedly approve,' I said, with a nod. 'No, really. It's useful to master a new skill.'

'And how is our little Prophet doing?' Gesar asked out of the blue.

'He's learning his lessons.'

'Has he made friends with anyone?'

'With Nadya,' I said. 'But I assume you know that.'

'I do,' Gesar admitted. 'At that age, if a girl thumps a boy on the nose it marks the start of a long and firm friendship. A pity everything's so much more complicated for grown-ups.'

'Uh-huh,' I muttered. The boss had not started talking about Innokentii simply out of idle curiosity – I was sure of that.

'Rather annoying that no one heard his prophecy,' the boss went on.

'Yes,' I agreed, pricking up my ears.

'And Nadya definitely didn't hear anything?'

'Definitely. She just thumped the kid to motivate him and walked out.'

'And there weren't any security cameras in that room,' Gesar carried on lamenting. 'Or were there?'

'There were. Only Nadya . . . er . . . switched them off.'

'Burnt them out,' Gesar corrected me. 'Why, by the way?'

'So that no one would hear the prophecy.'

'Logical, logical . . .' Gesar sighed.

Anna Tikhonovna and I exchanged glances. Of course, I had known the boss for a hundred years less than our teacher had. But it wasn't hard to understand that he was steering the conversation round to some subject that only he was aware of.

'You know what's bothering me, though?' asked Gesar, suddenly leaning back in his chair and pushing the keyboard away.

'The universal problems of all creation,' I growled.

'Yes, you're right, Anton. Precisely that, the universal problems of all creation. I've realised that I don't know what the Twilight is.'

'A parallel reality with a stratiform structure,' said Anna

Tikhonovna. 'Passing from one level of the Twilight to another requires the expenditure of Power – on both the transition itself and the maintenance of one's own vital functions. Each successive layer of the Twilight differs more and more from our world, although it is possible to pass from the sixth level directly to our world, which is thus also the seventh level of the Twilight.'

'An absolutely comprehensive explanation – for an Other in his first month of instruction,' said Gesar. 'Allow me to remark that only ten years ago, young Others were absolutely certain that the Twilight had three levels . . . and I myself knew nothing about the transition from the sixth layer back to our world. But still, what is the Twilight?'

'Parallel worlds,' I said, with a shrug. 'Of course, that's an explanation on the level of science fiction, but any other would be from the realm of fantasy. We can even surmise that it is certain variations on our world, the way that it might have been . . . alternative worlds that separated off at some time from ours . . .'

'Or was it our world that separated off from some other?' said Gesar. 'All right, let's accept that. Our science team can't say anything that makes better sense in any case. And the Inquisition's research centres wouldn't have anything much to add . . . they'd only cloud the whole issue with their "subtle structures", "dark matter" and "quantum fluctuations". But still, what is the Twilight? Just six worlds that humankind hasn't managed to foul up?'

'You can't get that Tiger out of your head,' I said, realising where he was leading.

'Of course,' Gesar said, nodding. 'As long as we swear on the Light and the Darkness and receive a certain response that was defined ages ago' – Gesar waved his hand through the air and for an instant a small sphere of blinding white fire flared up on his palm – 'we can regard it as some kind of law of physics. But the

Tiger – he was alive. He spoke. He modelled his behaviour according to ours. When an avalanche engulfs a skier, that's a law of nature. But when the avalanche starts pursuing one single boy, who's messing about in the snow at the foot of the mountain, and it actually carefully tosses everyone else aside or goes around them . . . that's not just wet snow plus the force of gravity any longer. That's intelligence.'

'The laws of nature are not intelligent,' I replied. 'The force of gravity is not intelligent. Electricity is not intelligent. A savage looking at a television might assume that it's a sapient being, but we—'

'A sapient being? Looking at a television these days, the only possible assumption is that it's a loud-mouthed, hysterical madman suffering from progressive mental debility,' Anna Tikhonovna said derisively.

'What I mean is that the Tiger's intelligence is by no means proof that the Twilight is intelligent,' I said stubbornly. 'Was the Mirror – Vitalii Rogoza – intelligent? Of course. But at the same time he was spawned by the Twilight in order to maintain the balance.'

'The Twilight merely influenced an indeterminate Other, Vitalii Rogoza,' said Gesar. 'And Rogoza acted intuitively, without really understanding what was going on. The Tiger's a different matter.'

'All right,' I sighed. 'I won't argue. You're not running me through all this just for the fun of it, boss. Or for the sake of my education.'

'Of course not,' Gesar said, nodding in agreement. 'And Anna Tikhonovna's not here by chance either. Oddly enough, she's our greatest specialist on the living and quasi-rational manifestations of the Twilight. In other words – on folklore.'

I looked at our teacher in amazement. She was a bright old woman, of course, but there was the science section . . .

'It's my hobby,' Anna Tikhonovna said modestly. 'I don't have the strength to go chasing bloodsuckers through the streets, my health won't allow it. And I don't think I'm any kind of genius. But I do have a lot of free time, so I spend it on things that our men of science don't take into account . . .'

'I have only myself to blame that I didn't know about this any sooner,' said Gesar. 'I expect things would have been a lot simpler with the Tiger.'

'I study Mirrors, Shades, the Transparent Other, Tigers, the Clapper, the Clay Man . . .' Anna Tikhonovna continued.

'The Transparent Other? The Clapper? The Clay Man?' To say I was surprised would have been putting it mildly.

'Oh, Anton, they are such interesting phenomena!' Anna Tikhonovna exclaimed, warming to her subject. 'The Clapper, for instance, only appears on the second level of the Twilight. In the whole of history, only five cases have been recorded. When an Other—'

'Anna Tikhonovna, I'm prepared to concede that there is something to this item of folklore too,' said Gesar. 'But let's get back to the Tiger.'

'You ferreted out everything about the Tiger yourself,' the teacher sighed. 'It's a pity, of course, that you didn't come to me, I could have saved you heaps of time. The only thing I have is – I know Erasmus's address.'

'Erasmus Darwin?' I exclaimed in delight.

'Anton, don't even ask me how I got hold of it,' said Anna Tikhonovna, lowering her eyes modestly. 'You know that according to the law, no one has the right to disturb an Other who has deliberately withdrawn from active involvement with the Watches . . .'

'I would have needed permission from the head of the local Night Watch and a clear statement from the head of the Day Watch that he didn't object, simply in order to apply to the local branch of the Inquisition for the address to be released,' said Gesar. 'And even then they could easily not have given me it . . .'

'But I went about it more simply,' said Anna Tikhonovna, unable to resist, and started telling her story, despite that 'don't even ask me how I got hold of it' business. 'I read Erasmus's *Sexual Life of Plants* and wrote a critical treatise on it. Well . . . partly laudatory and partly critical. Just critical enough to pique Erasmus slightly. I published it in an English journal – and a week later I received a rejoinder.'

She smiled. I couldn't help smiling too.

'So our dendrophile took the bait . . . What happened then?'

'We wrote to each other for a while. For the sake of appearances I argued at first, then I admitted that my criticism was entirely wrong – basically, I repented, and Erasmus changed his attitude towards me. It's not very often these days that anyone shows any interest in his beloved scientific work. We got along famously for a while, he even started flirting with me and invited me to visit him. But then I made a mistake. I was really only interested in the story of the Tiger, Anton . . . and I mentioned him. Erasmus evidently realised where my interest lay. And he took offence.'

'Why?'

'Surely it's obvious? His beloved botany, which was the reason why he associated with me in the first place, turned out to be nothing more than an excuse for getting to know him . . .' I could hear the note of embarrassment in the old woman's voice.

'Imagine that you have an interest, a fanatical interest in something slightly crazy,' Gesar put in. 'And suddenly you meet an Other who shares your passion – for collecting moths, for instance. Or for studying the medicinal properties of kefir. And you communicate with them, you feel glad to know them . . . perhaps you even fall in love. And then suddenly you discover it's all just an excuse to get close to you and find out about the Chalk of Fate, which you once held in your hands.'

'I get it,' I said with a nod. 'Erasmus hasn't changed his address, has he?'

'Not as far as we've been able to find out,' said Gesar, shaking his head.

'And where does he live? Somewhere in the back of beyond, obviously. Amid boundless, grassy expanses and centuries-old trees? The heather-clad wilds of Scotland, the bleak cliffs of Wales . . .'

'He lives in London,' Gesar snorted. 'As the years pass by, you start to appreciate comfort, believe me.'

'A work trip to London . . . not bad,' I mused wistfully.

'Well, that's where you're going.'

'Well, I won't argue with that,' I replied quickly. 'Who with?'

'On your own. No combat situations are anticipated. We don't have anybody who's acquainted with Erasmus – apart from Anna Tikhonovna, but in view of the circumstances under which their contact was broken off . . .'

'But don't you know him?' I asked hopefully.

Gesar shook his head.

'No, I don't. And Foma Lermont doesn't, either. We could dig up some contact at the fourth or fifth remove, but that's not likely to be any help.'

'I've just had a thought,' Anna Tikhonovna put in almost timidly. 'What if Anton took Kesha with him?'

'You think Erasmus might be moved by a boy whose fate is so much like his own?' asked Gesar, rubbing the bridge of his nose. 'What do you think, Anton?'

'I don't think a four-hundred-years-old Other is likely to be very sentimental,' I replied. 'I'd rather take Svetlana with me.'

'Just as soon as she comes back to the Watch,' Gesar chuckled.

'Go to London, Anton. Have a talk with Erasmus. Perhaps he might tell you something important. If not . . . it'll blow your cobwebs away for you. I've signed off on your trip, the tickets are ready, pick them up in the accounts office. You fly tomorrow morning.'

'Business class, I hope?' I joked.

'Yes,' said Gesar.

That put a damper on my urge to be witty. Of course, the Night Watch wasn't a poor organisation, and we didn't make all that many business trips . . . But why had Gesar suddenly turned generous enough to send me business class?

'And what's the per diem?' I asked.

'A hundred and twenty pounds a day. And the hotel's paid.'

Was he being serious, then?

'Will I be staying in the Radisson or the Sheraton?' I asked, testing the water further.

'No chance,' Gesar laughed. 'A small, traditional English hotel – what better way to get to know a strange country?'

'Boris Ignatievich, where's the catch?' I asked, giving up.

'There isn't one. It's simply that you really have been doing a pretty good job just recently. Let's say I've invented a holiday on the house for you. If you don't achieve anything, I won't criticise you for it, and if you really do find out something – I'll send you on your next mission in the corporate plane.'

'Uh-huh, if only we had one,' I chortled as I got up.

'I'm just about to buy one,' said Gesar. 'Which do you think is best – a Gulfstream or an Embraer?'

'A Yak-40,' I answered and walked out of the office.

What bothered me most of all was that Gesar didn't seem to be joking.

What would the Night Watch of the city of Moscow want with a corporate jet plane?

It would be better if they changed the air conditioners in the office – in summer the heat was so bad that you could hardly breathe!

If there was one thing I was certain of after fifteen years in the Watch, it was that Gesar never did anything without a good reason. He didn't set any assignments on a purely functional basis, or in sudden fits of altruism.

For instance, take that old business with the boy Egor, the indeterminate Other who was being hunted by vampires. Why did Gesar suddenly decide to send me out 'into the field' to catch bloodsuckers who broke the rules? Simply to shift me from office work to the front line? No – or rather, not just for that. It was also to create a thicker smokescreen around the boy and teach me a lesson about the 'goodness' of the Night Watch – and the 'wickedness' of the Day Watch. And very probably he was also nudging me in the direction of Svetlana, tying our relations together in the knot that would lead to Nadya being born. And perhaps even with the intention of explaining – to me and the other watchmen – what a Mirror is. Could the boss have been expecting a Mirror to appear, suspecting it was Egor and not that poor devil Rogoza, who was fated to turn into it? And incidentally, the Russian boy's first name and the young Ukrainian's family name even sounded vaguely similar – Egor and Rogoza . . .

Damn it! Now I was really going over the top! Inventing my own conspiracy theories. Gesar's an arch-intriguer, of course, and all his actions have double and triple agendas, but latching onto the fact that two names have similar sounds – that's a sure step down the path to paranoia.

What did Gesar really have in mind, sending me to London like this, and on such sensationally good conditions – a paid trip, a business-class flight and a safe, hassle-free assignment? We had plenty of less powerful but highly professional members of the

Watch, male and female, who could have met Erasmus and tried to find out something from him.

Either Gesar suspected that the assignment could turn out more dangerous than it seemed . . .

Or he saw some special qualities in me that would allow me to handle the assignment better than the others . . .

Or the whole deal was phoney, to distract someone's attention from the real business. Say, Gesar believed that Zabulon was following me and would now go dashing off to London to see Erasmus too.

I sighed. I could carry on thinking up any number of theories. But somehow I had the feeling that I was missing something very simple and very logical – and therefore missing the most logical explanation.

'I wouldn't bother my head about it if I were you,' Svetlana said as she packed a little suitcase for me. 'Gesar's being devious, of course. But he needs you, and in general I think he's very fond of you. He had to send someone to London to see Erasmus for form's sake – so why not you?'

'But he clearly thinks this business with the Tiger case isn't over yet,' I said pensively. We were in the bedroom. Nadya was watching TV in the sitting room and we could talk frankly.

'I don't think it's over, either . . .' Svetlana froze over the suitcase for a moment, with a pile of clean shorts in her hands. 'Anton, is there anything you're hiding from me?'

'How do you mean?'

'Anything to do with the Tiger and the prophecy?'

'I told you everything I knew,' I said, prevaricating slightly. I really didn't know what had been dictated into the toy telephone. I wasn't even sure that anything had been dictated into it at all . . . 'Sveta, how many days are you packing my suitcase for?'

'Three . . . five . . . seven. For a week.'

'What for? I've got a return ticket after just two days.'

'Obviously for some reason I felt it was right to put in seven sets of underclothes for you,' Svetlana said thoughtfully. 'And I've put in five shirts . . . and two warm sweaters as well . . .'

'London's sweltering, just like Moscow,' I remarked.

'I know,' Svetlana sighed. 'Unfortunately, I'm an intuitive clairvoyant.'

I nodded. Most Others, even when they feel a need to act in one particular way and not any other, can't explain the reason why. And Svetlana didn't know why she was packing me a bag for a week. That boy Innokentii would be able to explain it – when he learned to manage his gift.

'And I'll put in a raincoat for you,' Svetlana said unexpectedly. 'And an umbrella.'

'Will it fit?' I asked doubtfully, looking at the suitcase.

'I'll stretch it on the inside.'

The funny thing was that the spell which made it possible to pack a whole heap of junk into a small volume had only appeared fairly recently. It had simply never occurred to a single Other that it could be done – until people started describing magical bags and suitcases in books of fantasy and fairy tales. Naturally, the path from concept to realisation was not long. But even at that time not every magician was capable of casting the 'handbag' – aka 'nosebag' – spell.

Svetlana could, of course.

'I'll expand your suitcase for two weeks,' said Svetlana. 'You never know . . . if you really did get delayed, there'd be shorts and shirts spraying out in the middle of the airport.'

'Thanks,' I said. 'What can I bring you from London?'

Svetlana brushed that aside.

'Don't you try choosing any clothes for me . . . London has the oldest toyshop in the world: Hamleys. Drop in there and buy something for Nadya.'

'Clothes?' I asked.

'Toys.'

I harrumphed. I reckoned our daughter was pretty much indifferent to toys already. If I'd had a son, everything would have been simple enough. Buy him some radio-controlled helicopter, or some fancy kind of construction set.

'Barbie?' I asked, straining my imagination.

Svetlana sighed, smiled and explained. 'Look what girls her age are buying and get that.'

'I'll do that,' I said happily. 'Still, what shall I bring you?'

There was a moment's awkward silence, with just some dialogue in squeaky cartoon voices from the TV in the sitting room: 'I want to know what the meaning of life is!' – 'Then you need Cusinatra, who gives meaning!'

'We need a food processor for the kitchen,' said Svetlana, laughing at something. 'But you don't have to drag it all the way from Great Britain. Bring what the English do best of all.'

'A global language or an empire?'

'Good whisky.'

'In the first place, whisky is either Scotch or Irish, and not English. And in the second place, when did you start drinking?'

'I'll try it,' said Svetlana, smiling again. 'And you'll have a drink with your friends. And your conscience will be clear, because you've brought me a present.'

Gesar was feeling so benevolent that I didn't even have to book a taxi – Semyon called round for me at seven.

'There's your present for Erasmus,' he said, waving one hand towards a tightly packed plastic bag, crudely sealed with sticky tape, that was lying on the boot of the car.

'What's in it?'

'I don't know. What kind of presents do people take from Russia? Vodka, caviar . . .'

'A matryoshka doll and a balalaika,' I said in the same tone. I opened the suitcase and stuffed the plastic bag into it. In defiance of all common sense it fitted easily into the tightly packed case.

'Did Sveta put a "nosebag" on it?' Semyon asked.

'Uh-huh. She has the strange idea my trip's going to last a whole week.'

'I'd trust what Svetlana says,' Semyon said seriously.

'I do.'

Along the way, after we'd made the turn onto Leningrad Chaussee, Semyon unexpectedly asked: 'Anton, do you mind if I ask you a personal question?'

'Go ahead.'

'How are things with you and Svetlana?'

'In what sense?'

'The most direct sense possible. How's the relationship?'

'Just fine,' I said. 'Best friends and comrades. Complete mutual understanding.'

'That's not exactly what's required in family relationships,' Semyon said didactically. 'You and I are the ones who should be best friends and comrades – we fight together. But in bed and at the family table comradeship is inappropriate.'

I said nothing for a moment, then lowered the window on my side of the car, took out a cigarette and lit up. Leningrad Chaussee was already packed with cars, but Semyon was driving easily and quickly.

'What made you suddenly bring this up?' I asked. 'You lousy psychotherapist . . .'

'I want to help you,' Semyon explained. 'I've lived in this world for a long time, after all, and I've seen a lot. It was hard to make everything fit together at first, right? You and Sveta are both strong individuals, it's hard for you to adjust to suit someone else, even if you want to. And then somehow it all came together after all. You had a daughter and everything was really good, right? But afterwards, when she grew up a bit – everything got a bit messy again. Comradely.'

'So?' I asked, taking a greedy drag.

'You need shaking up a bit,' Semyon said imperturbably. 'For instance, you need a good row about something, the real thing, with smashed plates, or a fight. Separate for a while, get really miffed with each other. But that's hard for you, because of your daughter . . . And it would be good if you were unfaithful to her. You've never been unfaithful to Svetlana, have you?'

'Listen, you, sod off . . .' I said, starting to get really wound up. 'When you were a kid, didn't your mum tell you not to poke your nose into other people's family business?'

'No, my mum just loved sticking her nose into other people's squabbles,' Semyon replied. 'Anton, don't go taking offence, there's no one else who'll tell you this. But I love you and Sveta very much. And I really want everything to be fine for you.'

'So you advise us to have a fight or be unfaithful to each other!'

'Well, I'm a simple soul and my methods are simple,' Semyon chuckled. 'You could turn to a therapist for help instead, go to sessions for a year or two, spend a bit of time on the couch, talk about life . . .'

'Screw you,' I said crudely, flicking my cigarette out of the window.

'Anton, there's something big brewing,' said Semyon. 'Trust my intuition on that. Hard times are on the way and it would be good if we can all be in good shape to meet them. With no discord in our hearts or our families . . .'

'You get married then, set up a durable social unit of your own . . .'

'My love was a human being. She died,' Semyon replied simply.

'I told you about that. And it seems like I'm the one-woman kind. Like yourself. Okay, don't go getting upset, don't make a big thing of it.'

'Oh, sure, first you lay all this on me, then it's "don't make a big thing of it",' I muttered. 'Shall I bring you something from London? Whisky . . .'

'I can buy whisky here,' Semyon said dismissively. 'You know what, drop into Fortnum and Mason's, that's on Piccadilly. Buy me a jar of Yorkshire honey, I really love it and you can't get it here.'

'The world's gone crazy,' I said. 'I asked Sveta, she told me to bring whisky. And a healthy drinking man like you wants a jar of English honey!'

'I like tea with honey,' Semyon said impassively. 'And an intelligent, loving man like you should think of a present for your wife yourself, and not ask what you should bring. Even a jar of honey would do.'

CHAPTER 2

It was a bad landing at Heathrow. No, there was nothing wrong with the plane, we were on schedule, we touched down on the runway gently, docked with the bridge quickly . . .

But a flight from somewhere in South-East Asia had arrived at Terminal Four just ahead of us – maybe from Bangladesh, maybe from Indonesia. And a hundred and fifty Russian passengers found themselves queuing up for passport control behind two hundred swarthy Asians.

Each one of them was carrying a whole heap of documents. It looked from the papers as if they were all planning to study at Oxford or Cambridge, invest hundreds of thousands of pounds in the economy or collect a multimillion-pound inheritance. Basically, the Bangladeshi-Indonesians had so many grounds for entering the country, it was immediately obvious that most of them would end up working in the restaurants or on the construction sites and farms of Britain. The officers at passport control – also, for the most part, not native Anglo-Saxons – understood this perfectly well, and they checked the documents with exacting precision. Every now and then a check ended with a passenger being led aside – for further investigation . . .

The stream of passengers from our flight who had British citizenship dribbled rapidly past a separate set of desks. Not such a very thin stream, though – it seemed to me that about twenty per cent of the people who had flown to England with me were 'servants of two masters'. The others lined up sombrely between the queue guides. Men dreaming of a smoke after the flight fidgeted miserably. Children who had sat still for too long in the aeroplane were acting up. Women dreaming of 'strolling along Piccadilly' and storming the shops of Oxford Street sent text messages and rummaged in handbags.

Of course, I could have jumped the queue altogether. One way or another. If it came to that, I could simply enter the Twilight and bypass passport control altogether – a young guy did that before my very eyes, although on the plane I hadn't even suspected that he was an Other. In fact, if I hadn't had a visa in my passport, I'd have done the same without the slightest hesitation.

But I felt uncomfortable. A woman patiently joined the back of the queue with two little infants, feeding both of them simultaneously, 'Macedonian-style'. Admittedly, after a while she was sent to a short queue for those who didn't have to stand in line with everyone else. There were children and old people standing in front of me too. But there was nothing to be done – we'd arrived at a bad moment, and for Europe the endangered species of Russians is made up of the same kind of suspect 'third-world' folk as the denizens of any overpopulated Asian country. Maybe even more suspect – although Russia might have accepted its role as a third-world country, but from time to time it still demonstrates certain ambitions and is reluctant to acknowledge its colonial status openly.

Anyway, positively overflowing with noble feelings, I decided to wait out the queue together with my compatriots. And for the first half-hour I felt genuinely proud of the way I was acting.

I held out for a second half-hour from sheer stubbornness, realising that to pronounce a spell and bypass passport control now would be as good as admitting my own stupidity.

No special questions arose when my turn came. The officer, who was a Sikh to judge from his turban, glanced at the visa, asked how long I had come to Britain for, was told that it was two or three days, nodded and slapped his stamp down on my passport.

I passed through the checkpoint manned by a Dark Other and a Light Other without any delay at all – my Higher Other aura inspired respect.

I felt so worn out after the queue that I didn't take the express train, even though it went to Paddington, which would have been very convenient for me. I walked out of the airport terminal and turned left, towards the spot where smokers were ruining their health at an appropriate distance from decent people. A little glass isolation cell had been set up outside for the victims of nicotine dependence. But the exhausted passengers and uniformed airport workers still disregarded the rules and smoked in the open air.

I lit up too. Beside me a beautiful young miss with long legs and an expensive aluminium suitcase was slavering over a thin cigarette and swearing on the phone at someone called Peter, who hadn't arrived in time to meet her. The girl happened to be Russian, but she was speaking English and swearing like a real virtuoso. When she finished talking she shook her head helplessly, then immediately phoned Moscow and started discussing the difference in mentality between Russian and English men with a girlfriend.

I chuckled and set off towards the taxi stand. A long line of tall cabs, including some antiques and some ultra-modern specimens, was waiting patiently for customers.

The hotel Gesar had sent me to was a perfectly ordinary little

London hotel, located in Bayswater – a district famous for hotels like that. Or perhaps it was the opposite – infamous for its abundance of cheap tourist accommodation. The hotel didn't have any signs that were visible only in the Twilight, like the 'yin-yang' symbol which traditionally means 'Others welcome'. I was beginning to suspect that although Gesar had given me a business-class flight, he had economised on the accommodation.

Or was there actually some point in staying in the three-star Darling Hotel that occupied two houses in an old Victorian terrace (white walls, columns at the entrance, single-glazed windows with wooden frames)?

My room was typical for that kind of hotel – that is, small, with narrow doors, a low ceiling and a tiny bathroom. But the bathroom fittings were new, in the European style, and there was a flat-screen TV with a hundred satellite channels, including a couple of Russian channels squeezed in between the Arab and Chinese ones, and a minibar, and an airconditioner. The bed was also surprisingly large and comfortable.

It would do. I hadn't come here to loiter in my room.

Exactly what I did now was entirely up to me. I could take a stroll round the shops, buy souvenirs and sit over a pint of beer in a pub, putting business off until tomorrow. I could go to visit Erasmus – unceremoniously, without an invitation. I could ride or walk through Hyde Park to Belgravia, where the office of the London Night Watch was located, and ask for their cooperation.

Or I could just phone Erasmus.

I took out my phone. Disdaining all subtlety and cunning, Mr Erasmus Darwin now styled himself in the French manner – as Monsieur Erasme de Arvin. And, when I heard his voice in the handset, I even realised why: he spoke with a slight accent, which any modern person would have identified as French.

In actual fact it was an echo of times gone by. An eighteenth-century accent.

The speech of old Others usually doesn't differ much from modern speech. A language changes gradually, the new words enter the Others' vocabulary, they pick up new intonations and only a few individual old-fashioned words or expressions are left. The more an Other associates with people, the more active he is in the Watch, the harder it is to tell his age by listening to him.

But if an Other has kept his association with his fellows and with humans to the minimum . . .

There was the accent. And the old-fashioned turns of phrase. And particular words . . . If I had studied English the way normal people do, and not absorbed it magically, I would hardly have understood a thing . . .

'Erasme on the line, I heed you.'

'This is Anton here. I've come from Moscow and I really need to see you, Mr Darwin. I'd like to have a word with you . . . about tigers . . .'

There was a brief pause. Then Erasmus said: 'Long have I awaited your call, Antoine. I thought not that you would come from Muscovy, as a Gaul I saw you . . .'

'You saw?' I asked, confused.

'It is known to you that I am a Prophet,' Erasmus told me. 'Come you to me – I shall not seek to thwart fate, but shall receive you.'

'Thank you very much,' I said, rather taken aback by such frank benevolence.

'Nonsense is it to thank me, Antoine. The address is known to you. Take a cab and come without delay.'

Monsieur Erasme de Arvin, retired Prophet of the Day Watch and connoisseur of the intimate life of plants, lived beside a park.

Properly speaking, the hotel where I was staying was also located beside a park, but there's a big difference between Hyde Park and Regent's Park. They may both belong to the Queen, but the former is noisier and simpler, more popular – as in 'of the people'. You can find absolutely anything close by – from hugely expensive mansions and luxurious shops (that's on the Thames side) to cheap hotels and ethnic neighbourhoods inhabited by Chinese, Albanians and Russians (that's on the railway-station side, where that most likeable of English immigrants, Paddington Bear, once arrived).

Regent's Park, however, is surrounded by expensive houses standing on land that also belongs to the Queen – and they can't be bought, only rented, even though it may be for a hundred or two hundred years, so none of the residents in these luxurious mansions and apartments that cost millions can truly say 'my home is my castle'. But that didn't seem to bother anyone very much – at any rate, as I walked along the side of the park I spotted a parked Bentley with a number plate that read ARMANI and a couple of people with faces that I'd seen in films, or on the front pages of the newspapers.

Well, anyway, if you've lived in this world for three hundred years and have still not accumulated enough money to settle anywhere you fancy – then you're a total idiot. Of course, there are people like that to be found even among Prophets, but Erasmus was clearly not one of them. So of course he could afford a little mansion close to Regent's Park.

However, the reality exceeded all my expectations.

Rather than using schematic tourist maps or the more detailed police variety, I relied on my phone with its built-in GPS system. I didn't want to gape at the little screen like some crazy gadget-fanatic, so I simply clipped on the earphone and walked along, following the commands dictated by the pleasant female voice. As everyone knows, apart from the standard voices you can find hundreds of patches for GPS systems on the Internet: if you prefer, you can have your route indicated to you by a grandiloquent Gorbachev or a punch-drunk Yeltsin or a fussy Medvedev, and for the true connoisseur there is even Lenin – 'You are on the right road, comrades!' and Stalin – 'Deviate to the right!' My soundtrack imitated some old film: 'To the left, milord,' 'To the right, milord,' and I liked that – somehow it seemed to fit well with Erasmus.

Well, first I walked along Albany Street, glancing curiously at the expensive mansions and old buildings, either of red brick with little towers and bay windows, or with white walls and columns. It was a very touristy district, so I also came across the famous red telephone booths (strangely enough, in this age of digital mobile phones, people were still using them) and the impressive cylindrical forms of the Royal Mail's postboxes (and people dropped letters into them in front of my very eyes). All this retro that the tourists go dewy-eyed for really did look quite natural, not at all affected, and yet again I was stung by sad thoughts of Moscow. What could my city have been like if it had not been demolished, reconstructed and torn to pieces in order to squeeze profit out of every single clod of earth? Completely different from this, of course, but also alive and interesting – not the present soulless agglomeration of bleak new developments and dilapidated Stalin-era blocks with only rare, usually completely reconstructed old buildings.

The GPS whispered: 'To the left, milord.' Obediently walking in through one of the entrances to Regent's Park, I found myself in a kingdom of mighty trees, fragrant flowers and people strolling along paths. Probably less than a third of them were actual Londoners – most were tourists with cameras.

I wondered where Erasmus actually lived. In a little shack surrounded by his beloved plants?

I suppressed an urge to glance at the screen. It was more

interesting to follow the commands. The system's memory included even the narrowest little paths, and I followed them deeper and deeper into the park. There wasn't any real wilderness here, of course, there couldn't possibly be, but I encountered fewer and fewer tourists.

Then I saw a huge building that seemed to me to stand in the park itself, or right on its very edge. In actual fact, there was an avenue running along the boundary of the park, and a house had been built on it. It reminded me most of all of the finest examples of architecture from the Stalinist period – there were even statues on the cornice under the roof, only I couldn't make out who exactly they represented: mythological characters, maybe, or important British cultural or political figures, or representatives of the various peoples of Britain. To judge from the cars parked by the building it was inhabited by people with millions in their bank accounts.

But the GPS led me further along the avenue.

So did he really live in a little shack, then?

'Straight ahead, milord,' said the GPS. 'We're arriving now, milord.'

I halted in bewilderment. There in front of me was an old church. Well, maybe not a church, but something ecclesiastical – an abbey, or a monastic building, constructed in a strange architectural style, with two wings, like a country-estate house but quite clearly some kind of religious edifice.

'To the right, milord.'

The right wing of the building looked rather different. Well, there were the same moss-covered walls, stained-glass windows and tall, carved wooden doors. But it was a dwelling house. Or, rather, the residential section of the abbey or church.

Well, and why not, if I thought about it? Especially in England. If there'd been a church here it would have had a house for a priest – or, rather, a vicar. Let God have the church and the people have the house. No services would have been held here for a long, long time, and the vicar's descendants – stop, could he have had any descendants? Probably he could, vicars weren't celibate like Catholic priests – they had chosen a different path. And, sooner or later, someone had sold the house to Erasmus. Or perhaps the house had belonged to the Darwin family and he had inherited it.

The door opened just as I walked up to it and stopped, wondering what to do – press the button of the bell, or knock with the heavy bronze knocker. An elderly, fat, grey-haired gentleman in an old-fashioned tweed suit looked at me curiously.

'Mr Darwin?' I asked.

'Monsieur Antoine?' He had either completely assimilated his image as a Frenchman or he couldn't quite get used to the idea that I wasn't a Gaul. But the archaisms had almost completely disappeared from his speech. 'Come in. I've been waiting for you for ages.'

'I'm sorry I'm late,' I replied automatically.

A historical film could have been shot in Erasmus Darwin's residence. Several, in fact. The kitchen into which I followed my host was equipped according to the very latest word in 1970s technology. Or, more precisely, the American 1970s, with lots of chrome and glass and touchingly naive design work. Darwin prepared coffee in a huge machine with a glass container for coffee beans on top of it. As it ground the beans, the machine rumbled like an airliner taking off. Standing on one of the tables under the colourful stained-glass windows was a bright, gleaming antique food processor, with CUISINART written on its side. The fridge was also a brand that I didn't know.

Carrying a tray, on which he had placed coffee cups, a cream jug and a sugar bowl, Erasmus led me into the sitting room. Here the 1970s capitulated ingloriously to the 1920s or 1930s – superbly polished leather furniture and dark wood everywhere – in the wall panels as well as the furniture – a marble fireplace . . . in which, to my amazement, genuine logs were burning! As far as I was aware, that was strictly forbidden – at one time, to combat the famous London smog, all the fireplaces in the city had been converted for gas. There was no TV, of course, but there was a valve radio, housed in a substantial wooden cabinet that looked like a small cupboard.

'Are you not feeling cold, Antoine?' Erasmus asked. 'Perhaps a drop of porto with cognac?'

'But it's summer outside,' I said, amazed. I don't always grasp certain elementary things straight away. 'Ah . . . but then . . . it's so cool in here. Thick walls, right? Thanks, I'll gladly take a drop of porto with cognac.'

A look of relief appeared on Erasmus's face.

'Why, of course, you're from Musco . . . Russia!' he said delightedly. 'Drinking in the morning wouldn't bother you!'

'It's almost lunchtime already,' I said diplomatically, making myself comfortable in the deep leather armchair.

'Damn the porto!' Erasmus exclaimed. 'Fine, old, warm-hearted Irish whiskey!'

Well, after all, three centuries is quite long enough, not only to acquire part of an abbey in the centre of London, but also to become an alcoholic.

From out of a wide sideboard with shelves concealed by little doors of cloudy matt-glass, Erasmus took several bottles. He examined them fastidiously and selected one that had no label at all.

'A hundred and fifty years old,' he told me. 'I have whisky older than that, but that's not really important. What matters is that in those days petrol engines had not yet polluted nature with their stench, rye was rye, malt was malt and peat was peat . . . Would you like ice, Antoine?'

'No,' I said, mostly out of politeness, in order not to make Erasmus go to the kitchen.

'Quite right!' Erasmus said approvingly. 'Ice is for the uncouth yokels in the colonies. If required, I have pure Irish water . . .'

He splashed out a tiny drop of whisky for each of us. I touched my lips to the dark, almost black potation.

It tasted as if I had taken a sip from a peat bog.

And then it felt as if I had drunk liquid fire.

Erasmus watched me, chuckling quietly.

'It takes a bit of getting used to,' I said, putting down my glass. 'It's very . . . very unusual.'

'Do you like it?'

'I can't say yet,' I admitted honestly. 'But I can say one thing for certain – it's a unique drink. Lagavulin doesn't even come close.'

'Ha!' Erasmus snorted. 'Lagavulin, Laphroaig – all that's for pampered modern folk . . . But you're forthright, Antoine. I like that.'

'What point is there in lying to a Prophet?' I asked, shrugging.

'Well, what kind of Prophet am I . . .' Erasmus said and sipped on his powerful drink, suddenly embarrassed. 'Just a petty Clairvoyant . . . Yes, I'll try to talk in a way that you can understand, but I don't see people very often – if I seem excessively old-fashioned, please tell me straight away.'

'All right.' I picked up the plastic bag I had brought and held it out to Erasmus. 'The head of the Moscow Night Watch asked me to give you this.'

'His Eminence Gesar?' Erasmus asked curiously. 'And what's in it?'

'I don't know,' I said.

Erasmus took a small paperknife off the mantelshelf and started opening the bag with the enthusiasm of a five-year-old child who has found his long-awaited present on Christmas morning.

'How have I merited the attention of the great warrior of the Light . . .' Erasmus muttered. 'And why have I been favoured with a present . . .'

I realised that the retired Dark Other was playing the fool. But for someone who lived practically locked away from the world in the centre of London, that was an entirely forgivable weakness.

Eventually the package was torn open and its contents displayed on the low coffee table. As I had anticipated, the plastic bag had contained far more than could have fitted into it naturally. There was a litre bottle of vodka – and old vodka at that: the spelling on the label was pre-revolutionary. And there was also a three-litre glass jar, filled with grainy black caviar. Illegal, poached goods – no doubt about it. But then, that was hardly likely to bother Gesar, and it would bother Erasmus even less. And, finally, there was the flower pot that I was used to seeing on the windowsill in the boss's office. Growing in the pot was a terribly ugly, crooked little tree that any bonsai master would have grubbed up out of pity. I recalled with some embarrassment that during a certain meeting that had dragged on for a long time, when Gesar had said that anyone who wanted to smoke could do so, I'd stubbed my cigarette ends out in the tree's pot, for lack of an ashtray. And I wasn't the only one.

Erasmus set the vodka and caviar on the floor without a second glance. Then he placed the pot with the little tree in it at the centre of the small table and sat down on the floor to gaze at this botanical misunderstanding.

The tree stood about fifteen centimetres high. As gnarled as an ancient olive and almost completely bare – there were only two little leaves protruding optimistically from one branch.

Erasmus sat there, looking at the little tree.

I waited patiently.

'Astounding,' said Erasmus. He reached for his glass and took a sip of whiskey. He turned the pot slightly and looked at it from a different angle. Then he screwed up his eyes – and I could tell that the old Other was looking at the little tree through the Twilight.

'You're not aware of the essential significance of this gift, are you?' Erasmus asked, without looking at me.

'No, sir,' I answered, with a sigh. And suddenly it occurred to me that Erasmus was probably a Sir in the original meaning of the word.

Erasmus stood up, walked round the plant pot and muttered: 'Well, damn me . . . Anton, please step back or protect yourself . . . I'm going to use my powers a bit.'

I thought it best to move back and also put up a Magician's Shield, taking the glass of whiskey with me, just to be on the safe side. This proved to be the correct decision – it was a quarter of an hour before I moved back to the little table. Erasmus spent all that time tussling with the bonsai. He plunged search spells into the plant, observed it through the Twilight, even withdrawing as far as the third level. He crumbled a pinch of soil from the pot between his fingers and ate it, sniffed at the leaves for a long time – and actually seemed delighted at that: his face lit up, but then he gestured in annoyance and poured himself another whiskey. He spent the last minute standing there, toying with a fireball on the palm of his hand as if he was struggling against the temptation to incinerate the pot and the bonsai, together with the table.

But he restrained himself.

'I give up,' Erasmus growled. 'Your Gesar is truly great . . . I can't work out the meaning of his message. Are you sure he didn't ask you to communicate anything in words?'

'I'm afraid not.'

Erasmus took off his jacket and threw it across an empty armchair. He sat down in another chair, rubbed his face with his hands and muttered: 'I'm getting old . . . Well then, you wished to talk about tigers, Antoine?'

'Yes, and you were expecting me, Erasmus?'

'It's all interconnected . . .' he said, still unable to take his staring eyes off the bonsai. Then he said: 'Antoine, move the plant to the mantelshelf. I'll deal with it later, try everything I possibly can . . . I'm sure I'll be able to solve Gesar's riddle eventually. But meanwhile I can't bear to look at it, it annoys me. Tell me, how did you find me?'

'The story of your childhood is no secret, esteemed Erasmus,' I said.

'But it is not so very widely known . . .'

'It's described in a little book that my daughter was reading.'

'Oh!' exclaimed Erasmus, keenly interested. 'Did you think to bring it with you?'

'Damn,' I said, embarrassed. 'You know, somehow it never occurred to me – I could send it to you.'

'If it's not too much trouble,' Erasmus said, with a nod. 'Forgive an old man's vanity, I enjoy collecting every reminder of the human period of my life . . . But how did you discover my address? I didn't think the Night Watch of London had that information.'

'It wasn't the Watch,' I admitted. 'I acquired the address from private sources . . .'

Erasmus waited.

'Anna Tikhonovna works in our Watch . . .'

'Anna!' Erasmus exclaimed. 'What a fool I am – I should have guessed . . .' He gave me a sideways glance. 'Well, does she still laugh when she remembers how she caught me?'

'Pride and Prejudice . . .' I said pensively.

'What?'

'She doesn't find it amusing at all. She's still distressed that your relations were severed so abruptly. Of course, she was interested in the story of the Tiger – she collects all sorts of oddities that are ignored by official science, but she enjoyed being in touch with you.'

Erasmus shrugged. Then he muttered: 'I found it interesting too . . . she was so delicate in the way she made it clear that she was an Other, and she knew who I was . . . but at the same time she displayed such a deep knowledge of botany. The article she published in that journal was most interesting . . . a most agreeable lady, it was quite surprising that she was from Musco . . . I beg your pardon, of course, Antoine, but I didn't really like Russian women before that.'

'That's quite all right, I'm not very taken by the English ones,' I replied vengefully.

'We really ought to have met,' Erasmus went on. 'We could have looked into each other's eyes and understood each other better.'

'Yes, the Internet doesn't allow for genuine contact,' I said profoundly.

'What Internet, Antoine?' Erasmus laughed. 'It was more than thirty years ago! The USSR still existed then! Letters on paper – with just a little spell, so that the censor wouldn't examine them and they would arrive more quickly . . .'

Yes, I'd really put my foot in it. Sometimes I forget just how recently all these mobile phones and computers appeared.

'So the publication was in a real journal, then?' I said, taking the point. 'A scholarly one, on paper? And I thought it was a "live" journal . . .'

Erasmus laughed until he cried, and then he said: 'There you are, Antoine. Even you will start feeling like a dinosaur soon, decorating your home with Soviet posters and red banners! Never mind, one can get accustomed to the way time flies . . . Well then, let me tell you about the Tiger. About my Tiger. And then you can explain to me what you're so agitated about.'

CHAPTER 3

THE EIGHTEENTH CENTURY was not an age well equipped to ensure a happy childhood. But then, it wasn't all that great for an active prime of life and a peaceful old age either. It was easy to die, in fact it was very easy. Life was merely the prelude to death and the life after death – the existence of which only very few doubted.

Sometimes this prelude was a long one, but far more often it was short.

Both for humans and for Others.

'Are you listening to me or sleeping, boy?'

Erasmus Darwin was fourteen years old, and in the twentieth century he would have been offended to be addressed as 'boy'. But in the eighteenth century it was quite normal. As a matter of fact, someone from the twentieth or twenty-first century would have taken Erasmus for a child of ten or eleven. He might also have been perplexed by the fact that Erasmus's trousers and jerkin were in no way different from those of his adult companion, but that was also a part of that time. Children were not special creatures, requiring different treatment, food and clothing. They were simply little human beings who might possibly be fortunate enough to become full-fledged adults. Even in the paintings of the finest artists of that time the bodies and faces of children were indistinguishable from the bodies and faces of adults – if the artist's eye did detect the difference in proportions, his mind rejected the distinction. A boy was simply a little man. A girl was simply a little woman . . . indeed, girls changed their status and became women very quickly, and no one found that disconcerting. Leavened with the first yeast of civilisation, the human dough was seething and expanding. Humankind had to grow. And for that, there had to be as many births as possible, because it was beyond human power to reduce the number of deaths.

'I'm not sleeping!' Erasmus protested indignantly.

'Then where is your spirit wandering?' asked Erasmus's companion, giving the boy a furious look. The man looked about thirty years old – a substantial age. If he had been human, that is. But he was an Other and only he knew how old he really was.

'I was thinking . . . about this . . .' said Erasmus, spreading his arms out self-consciously.

'About this?' Erasmus's companion looked at the blossoming meadow in disgust. 'Tell me, boy, are you a bee that gathers nectar?'

'No . . .'

'Then perhaps a witch who brews potions?'

Erasmus shuddered slightly. He was afraid of witches, although as things had turned out he didn't need to fear them any more.

'No, teacher . . .'

'Or are you a peasant, who is going to pasture his cows here?'

Erasmus didn't answer.

'You are an Other,' his companion said firmly. 'You possess the great power of clairvoyance and prophecy. You have been granted a different fate from on high, and mundane matters should be of no concern to you.'

'But is it truly from on high?' Erasmus muttered to himself.

His companion heard but, contrary to his usual habit, did not fly into a rage. He shrugged and sat down on the ground, crushing the grass and the flowers. And he replied: 'I have seen Others who shout that their power is from God: they observe the fasts, follow the Gospel and go to church often. I don't know what they say at confession – perhaps they have their own priests . . . I have seen Others who believe that it was Lucifer, the luminiferous Prince of Darkness, who granted them their mighty power. At night they burn black candles made from the fat of corpses – you should see how they smoke and stink! They kiss a severed goat's head and commit obscenities too abominable for me to speak of. But one thing I can tell you for certain – I have not seen God, or his servants, and I have not met Satan, or his vassals. Perhaps they are simply not concerned with us. Perhaps our Power is simply a power, like a bird's ability to soar through the sky or a fish's ability to breathe water.'

'I don't want to burn black candles or commit obscenities,' Erasmus said, just to be on the safe side.

'Then do not do either,' his companion replied indifferently.

'But I feel bored in church, teacher,' Erasmus confessed. 'And . . . and I once stole a penny . . . and in the evenings, when Betty brings the warming-pan to my bed, I ask her to lie down beside me . . .'

'Maidservants are created to gladden their masters' hearts,' Erasmus's companion replied magnanimously. 'And you are more than just her master. You are an Other. Take your pleasure with Betty as you desire.'

The boy didn't say anything. The man narrowed his eyes and peered at him. Erasmus moved his hand slowly above the crushed stalks of grass, and they straightened up, reaching for his fingers.

'You have an affinity for the kingdom of plants,' the man admitted reluctantly. 'That is more fitting for a witch than a magician, but the Power always finds unexpected ways to manifest itself . . . Only do not forget that you are a Prophet. Who will be victorious in the battle on the hill?'

'The king,' Erasmus replied instantly. He blinked in bewilderment and looked up. 'On what hill?'

'It matters not. You foretell the future, even though with little skill as yet. But tell me: in three or four hundred years, who will rule on the Capitol Hill?'

'A black man will ascend the throne and all will glorify him as a peacemaker. But he will send iron birds across the ocean to seize the treasures of the Libyans and the Persians, and by that shall be caused a great war and convulsions in the world . . .' the boy intoned slowly, as if he was sleepy.

'Hmm,' said Erasmus's companion, scratching the tip of his nose. 'No, you are still far from your main prophecy. Too many errors. The Italians are always fighting the Arabs, but how can a black man rule in Rome? Persia – well and good . . . but there are no treasures in Libya, it is all desert that engenders nothing but a useless black oil. And even if there are iron birds in the world at that time – what ocean is this? Italy is separated from Libya by only a sea. No, too many errors – you are not yet ready. There is still time.'

'Time for what?'

'To prepare for the coming of the Executioner.'

. . . I poured myself another finger of whiskey and asked: 'So you called him the Executioner, Erasmus?'

'Yes, it was Blake who called him the Tiger – you know what poets are like . . .' Erasmus gazed pensively at the crimson coals glowing in the smoke-black opening of the hearth. 'At that time my teacher called him the Executioner . . . or the Silent Executioner . . . or the Executioner of Prophets. The last title is probably the most correct one. He only comes to Prophets. To those who are preparing to make their main prophecy.'

'What for? What is so important about the main prophecy?'

'It's global, that's all,' Erasmus chuckled. 'A forecast of a war in Libya or a flight to the moon concerns only a particular incident. Despite the significance of the events involved. The first prophecy must concern the whole of humankind.'

I pondered that for a moment or two, trying to decide exactly what it was in Erasmus's words that had bothered me most. Then I realised.

'Humankind?'

'Yes, of course. The first prophecy is too global to be concerned only with us Others. The prophecy always speaks of human beings. Of humankind.'

'What kind of event could it be that affects the whole of humankind?' I wondered out loud. 'A world war?'

'For example,' Erasmus said, nodding. 'Of course, not even World Wars One and Two affected the whole of humankind directly. But, generally speaking, their impact was global.'

'Were the World Wars foretold?' I asked.

'Of course. Not merely foretold, but prophesied. World Wars One and Two. The Socialist Revolution in Russia . . .'

'The communists can be proud of themselves,' I remarked. '"An event of world-historical significance" – that's what the revolution was called in the USSR.'

Erasmus laughed.

'And what else have Prophets prophesied?

'Drawing on my own informal sources of information,' Erasmus said modestly, 'other events honoured to be the subject of a first prophecy were the creation of nuclear weapons, the discovery of penicillin, the appearance of rock music . . .'

I looked at Erasmus incredulously, but he nodded confidently.

'Yes, yes, the appearance of rock music. And also the publication of Edgar Allan Poe's poem *The Bells*, the fashion for miniskirts, the release of the film *The Greek Fig Tree*, the birth of Alistair Maxwell . . .'

'Who is Alistair Maxwell?' I asked, bemused.

'He died in Australia in the 1960s,' said Erasmus. 'As an infant. He lived for less than a month.'

'What of it?'

'I don't know. But then, did the film *The Greek Fig Tree* really have a powerful effect on people? Or miniskirts?'

'Miniskirts certainly did!' I said firmly.

'Let's assume so. Then Alistair probably had an influence too.'

'How?'

Erasmus shrugged and spread his hands.

'Sometimes prophecies are not clear straight away. The effect of Maxwell's birth on humankind evidently has yet to be clarified.'

'Half a century after his death in infancy?'

'"There are more things in heaven and earth, Horatio . . ." There have been a few other strange prophecies, but it was never possible to prove that they were prophecies and not just predictions. Well, and naturally, there are some things we've never heard. Because of the Tiger, or for other reasons.'

'Including your prophecy,' I said.

Erasmus was embarrassed. 'Including mine . . . But, you know, I really wanted to live.'

'It's hard to blame you for that,' I agreed.

The teacher woke Erasmus as morning was approaching. He acknowledged no difference between the night and the day and, naturally, people could not hinder his movements in any way.

'Get up!' said the teacher, pressing his hand over the boy's mouth. 'Be quiet and do not make a sound!'

Erasmus crawled off the bed. The teacher threw him his clothes – stockings, trousers, shirt, jerkin . . .

'He is close,' said the teacher, pale-faced and with his lips trembling faintly. 'I managed to get away . . . he was distracted by the village . . .'

'By the village?' Erasmus asked uncomprehendingly as he dressed hastily.

'Yes, I made the people attack him . . . that will win us nothing except time – the Executioner is always thorough, he will finish with the people first.'

Someone stirred sleepily in Erasmus's bed, someone buried under the eiderdown. The teacher looked at Erasmus's crimson face and said: 'Don't wake Betty! She'll give us another minute or two . . .'

Erasmus only hesitated for a moment. Then he nodded and clambered out through the window after his teacher.

The garden was fragrant with the cool freshness of the imminent dawn. Erasmus trudged after his teacher, who muttered quietly as he walked:

'How could I . . . what a mistake . . . you've been ready to make the prophecy for a long time . . . I missed the harbingers . . .'

'If I speak the prophecy, will the Executioner go away?' asked Erasmus.

'Yes, but only if no one hears the prophecy. Or if humans hear it.'

'And if you hear it . . .'

'The prophecy is for people!' his teacher snapped. 'It will come true if humans hear it! It will not come true if no one hears it. You will not remember what you have said – he won't touch you after that – but if I hear it . . . he will kill me! So that I don't tell the people!'

'Then . . .' Erasmus grabbed his teacher by the flap of his jerkin.

'Then leave me. I remember what you taught me, I'll do everything – and I'll speak out the prophecy!'

'You won't manage it,' replied the teacher. 'You're not fully prepared yet. You need a listener. You're too inexperienced to prophesy into empty space . . . I didn't prepare you in time . . .'

He groaned suddenly and grabbed hold of his head.

'What's happened?' Erasmus exclaimed.

'I'm a fool, boy. I should have defended the house . . . and you could have spoken the prophecy to your stupid girl . . . The Executioner would have left.'

'And the prophecy would have come true?'

'Yes. That is bad, all prophecies are bad . . . but you would have remained alive.'

The teacher suddenly laughed bitterly. 'It seems that I have become attached to you, boy . . .'

'And Betty . . . Will he kill her?'

'The Executioner does not kill people. He will drink her soul,' the teacher replied. 'She will become indifferent to everything, like a straw doll.'

'She's not so very passionate as it is . . .' the boy muttered.

They had run almost a mile away from the manor house when they were overtaken by the sound of a woman's piercing scream that broke off almost immediately.

'We didn't know that the prophecy had to be heard by a human, not an Other,' I said. 'Gesar tried to persuade Kesha to prophesy in his presence . . .'

'Kesha?' Erasmus asked, baffled.

'Yes, a boy-Prophet – he was discovered in Moscow just recently. Actually, that's what prompted us to disturb you . . .'

Erasmus shook his head. 'Your Great One is taking a great risk. If only he hears the prophecy, then the Tiger will switch from the boy to him . . . and the Tiger is more powerful than any of us. What is the situation now? Is the Tiger on the trail?'

'No, we've already dealt with the situation.'

'And what was the prophecy?'

'We don't know. Nobody heard it. The boy was alone in a room in our offices. We managed to delay the Tiger, and the boy spoke his prophecy.'

'When he was entirely alone in a room?' said Erasmus, shaking his head incredulously. 'That's strange. Very strange. It is very rare indeed for a Prophet to be so well prepared that he can prophesy into empty space. It's difficult – usually the Tiger gets there first, or the prophecy reaches human ears . . .'

'But you managed it!'

'I'm a special case. For me there has never been any great difference between a man, a dog and . . . an oak, for instance,' Erasmus said, with a smile.

The Executioner overtook them at the edge of the forest. He seemed to be walking at an unhurried pace, but the distance between his dark silhouette and the Others who were running as fast as their legs could carry them narrowed with every second.

'Run, boy!' said the teacher, halting in the dust of the country road that ran along the edge of the forest. 'Run . . . try to find someone and say what you have to say . . . Run!'

There was no hope in his voice. He was simply doing what he believed had to be done. Not out of high moral principles – he was a Dark One. Perhaps he would have found it abhorrent to live in a world where he had allowed the Executioner to take his pupil. Or perhaps he was simply not used to losing.

The motivations of Dark Ones could be very hard to understand sometimes.

'Hey, Twilight Creature!' he called out. 'I am a Higher Magician of the Darkness! You shall not pass me! Go back!'

The Executioner didn't even slow his stride. Erasmus saw rustling vines of blue fire sprout from his teacher's hands and settle on the ground. The vines shuddered, as if preparing to pounce at the enemy.

The Executioner still didn't slow his stride.

Erasmus realised that there was nothing his teacher could do. That he would struggle for a minute or two, or three, that the vines of dark fire would tear at the ground and the air, lash impotently at the Executioner's body. And then the moment would come when the Executioner would grab his teacher, crush him, toss him aside – and carry on walking. To reach the Prophet.

He didn't just understand this. He *saw* it, almost as if it was real.

Erasmus already knew what this was. It was not simply a prediction that might not happen. It was a harbinger of the prophecy . . . he was seeing the fate of an Other, which meant that was how it would be . . . for certain . . . almost for certain – if he did not utter a prophecy, his genuine First Prophecy, which would change the world and alter fate . . .

He swallowed hard to force down the lump in his throat and looked round. There was an old hollow oak growing only three paces away from him. Erasmus dashed to the tree, stood on tiptoe and pulled himself up – the hole in the trunk was a bit too high for him. He thrust his head into the shadowy opening that smelled of mouldy leaves and rotten wood. Something inside it rustled – a woodmouse that was settling down inside the hollow oak went darting into a dark crevice in a panic.

That didn't bother Erasmus at all. He really didn't believe that people, animals and plants were different from each other in any way.

He closed his eyes. He would have stopped his ears, but he had to cling on to the edge of the hole. And so he simply tried not to hear anything – not his teacher's voice, nor the whistling of the fiery lashes, nor the menacing sound made by the Executioner, which sounded like a tiger growling. (Erasmus had never seen any tigers, but he assumed that they must growl exactly like that.)

Get away from everything.

From the past.

From the present.

From the future.

The past is not important. The present is inconsequential. The future is indeterminate.

He was not just some common clairvoyant, he was a Prophet. He was the voice of fate. What he uttered would become the truth.

Only someone had to hear him. They absolutely had to.

Then why not this old oak?

The boy imagined his shadow, lying on the bottom of the hollow. And he lowered his head towards it.

. . . Erasmus opened his eyes. His teacher was sitting beside him, cradling his limp left arm. The arm looked crumpled, almost chewed.

'The Executioner . . .' Erasmus whispered.

'You managed it, boy,' the teacher said with bewilderment in his voice. 'I can't imagine how, but you spoke your prophecy into empty space. And the Executioner has gone. In another moment he would have killed me.'

'I didn't speak into empty space,' Erasmus replied. 'I . . . I told the oak tree.'

A faint smile appeared on his teacher's face.

'Ah, so that's it . . . Well then, there is probably some purpose to your love of trees. Probably it is a part of your gift. A prevision of the fact that you would only escape if you loved oaks and aspen trees.'

He started chuckling and laughed for a long time, until he cried. Then he got up and shook the dust and mud off his clothes. Dark patches remained on them, but that did not worry the teacher.

'It is time for us to say goodbye, young Erasmus. You know your own abilities, you will be able to stand up for yourself. If you wish for power – you will achieve it. On your own, or in the Day Watch.'

'In Dublin?'

'In Dublin, Edinburgh, London. In any city of the world that is now or shall be.'

He even slapped Erasmus on the shoulder before turning and walking off along the road into the distance. He probably was truly fond of this pupil. But, of course, he didn't look round.

Erasmus sat there in the dust for a while, thinking. His strange enemy had disappeared. It was getting light.

Life promised a multitude of interesting things, and Erasmus had always had a zest for life.

He decided to go back to the manor house and see what had happened to Betty. Perhaps it wouldn't be so bad if she had become indifferent to everything. Perhaps now she would allow him to do certain things that she had previously rejected with a giggle.

I said nothing for a while. Then I remarked: 'In the book it said it was an elm tree.'

'An oak,' Erasmus responded immediately. 'I'm not very fond of elms. Oaks are far more profound and substantial.'

'And what was your teacher called?'

'I assumed that you knew,' Erasmus said briefly.

'I think I have a good idea already, but . . .'

'His name was Zabulon. We have never met again, but I know he has been the head of the Day Watch in Moscow for a long time already. You two are acquainted, I believe?'

'The creep, he could have told us everything straight away!' I exclaimed angrily. 'He had already dealt with a Tiger!'

'Zabulon never tells everything,' Erasmus replied.

'And how about you, Erasmus?'

'Neither do I,' Erasmus chuckled. 'I don't play the Watches' games, thank you very kindly! But only idiots tell everything. Information is both a weapon and a commodity.'

'If it's a commodity . . . it seems to me that you owe us something,' I threw out tentatively and looked at the absurd bonsai standing above the fireplace.

Erasmus frowned and also gazed at the gift from Gesar.

'I do,' he admitted reluctantly. 'Only I can't tell exactly how much . . . All right, ask. I'll answer a few more questions. Let's say three. Three questions, three answers.'

Oh, these old magicians, with their old-style formalities! Three questions, three answers . . .

'You said you were waiting for me,' I said. 'That you'd been waiting for a long time, thinking that I was French . . .'

'Perhaps it's for the best that you are Russian,' said Erasmus. 'I haven't really liked you Russians very much, begging your pardon, since the Sebastopol campaign. But I like the French even less.'

'Ever since the Hundred Years' War . . .' I murmured.

'Just about. But you Russians are past history now. You're a dead enemy, and a dead enemy can be respected and pitied.'

I wouldn't have expected myself to respond like that. The glass cracked in my hand, scattering splinters and the remaining drops of whiskey across the floor, and something very unpleasant must have appeared in my glance. Erasmus instantly raised his hands in a reassuring gesture.

'Stop, stop, stop . . . This is only my opinion, the opinion of an old clairvoyant who has withdrawn from the affairs of the world. I . . . I did not take into account that you are still so very young, Antoine. And I was overly brusque.'

'To put it mildly,' I said under my breath.

'None of the Great Ones links himself with the nation from which he has emerged,' Erasmus said in a conciliatory tone. 'But you are young, and I forgot that. I offer my apologies, An . . . Anton.'

'Accepted,' I replied sullenly.

'I really had been expecting you,' said Erasmus. 'The point being that one of my prophecies referred to myself. It was nothing really special – just a few words: "And at the end there shall come to me Antoine, who shall learn the meaning of the first and be witness to the last."'

I frowned.

'What is that about?'

'It's about me,' Erasmus explained. 'Quite possibly your visit means that I shall die soon. And you will learn the meaning of my first prophecy and witness my last one.'

'What is your first prophecy about?' I asked.

'Is that the second question?' Erasmus asked, to make sure.

'Yes!'

'I don't know,' the old prophet said, smiling. 'I told you, I shouted the prophecy into the hollow of an old oak.'

I had to think for about half a minute before I asked the third question. There was no point in arguing about the second one that had been wasted so lamely.

'Can you explain to me, clearly and distinctly, in what way can I hear your first prophecy?'

Before replying, Erasmus poured himself some more whiskey. Then he asked: 'Are sure you want that? Two hundred and fifty years have gone by, but what if that prophecy has not yet been fulfilled? If so, the moment you hear it, you will trigger the mystical mechanism of prophecy . . . First, it can come about, if you tell a human being about it. And second, as long you alone know the prophecy, the Tiger will hunt you.'

'Yes, I want it,' I replied. And I thought about the toy phone lying in my pocket, with the boy Kesha's prophecy (possibly) recorded on it.

'Perhaps you are right,' said Erasmus. 'Knowledge is a great temptation that is hard to resist . . .'

He stood up and walked over to the sideboard, opened it and took something dark and dusty out of the deepest corner. He held it in his hands for a second, examining it, then walked back to me.

'Take it, Anton.'

I took the small, dark bowl – or, rather, chalice: it had a wide top, but there was also a small base, covered with simple, unpretentious carving. The chalice proved to be surprisingly light.

'Wood,' I decided.

'Oak,' Erasmus stated.

'Is this . . .'

'Well, it's not the Holy Grail, of course,' Erasmus chuckled. 'I carved it myself out of that oak tree.'

I looked questioningly at the old Prophet.

'I don't know,' said Erasmus. 'I don't know *exactly* how to hear the prophecy. But plants have a memory too. And it's there somewhere . . . my first prophecy.'

After a moment's thought, I raised the chalice to my ear and listened intently to the sound of my own blood. Alas, no voices . . .

'Perhaps I should fill it with wine and drink it?' I asked.

'In that case, whiskey,' Erasmus chuckled. 'If you drink enough of it, there's nothing in the world you won't hear.'

He had a satisfied look, as if he had just cracked a good joke.

'I think you're being cunning with me,' I said. 'You either know . . . or you can at least surmise exactly how to extract the information.'

'Perhaps,' said Erasmus, not arguing. 'But then Gesar didn't explain his present, did he now? And I don't really want you to hear the prophecy.'

'I can hardly blame you for that . . .' I agreed. 'Although you seem to take the prediction of your own death rather calmly.'

'Prophecy,' Erasmus corrected me, turning his back to me and reaching out his hands towards the fireplace. 'But you don't know just how vague prophecies are. "At the end" – whose end? Mine? Or the whole of humanity's? Or does it simply mean the time – at the end of the day?'

'It can hardly be the time,' I said. 'It's morning now.'

'I ought to have asked you to come round in the evening,' said Erasmus, throwing his hands up in the air. 'Although, there is one other possibility! "At the end there shall come to me Antoine . . ."'

I said nothing.

'Perhaps it was about you?' the prophet suggested amiably, giving me a sideways glance. 'And you have come to me at your end . . . and, after all, if the Tiger starts hunting you . . .'

'That's what I don't like about you Dark Ones,' I said, getting up. 'Thank you for the chalice.'

'Don't be offended, Anton.' Erasmus was either embarrassed, or he was pretending to be. 'I only wanted to forewarn you and indicate all the possible meanings of the prophecy . . .'

'How long is it since you were last in contact with Zabulon? I asked abruptly.

'Permit me not to answer that question . . .' Erasmus said, with a sigh.

'Consider that you already have,' I said. 'Give my greetings to your teacher.'

Since we were in London I felt justified in taking my leave in the English style, and did not say goodbye.

CHAPTER 4

THAT EVENING I was sitting and drinking beer in a pub called The Swan, not far from my hotel.

I liked English beer, although I was rather baffled by its numerous different sorts. The one I was drinking this time was light and smelled of honey (perhaps even Yorkshire honey) – and that suited me fine.

The pub itself was very presentable, although it was a thoroughgoing tourist trap. (What else can a pub be, if it's on a busy street right beside the famous Hyde Park and a dozen hotels?) An inscription on the wall proudly stated that the inn could trace its history back to the early seventeenth century, and at one time it had been the place where criminals on their way to the scaffold drank their final mug of beer.

The English ability to pride themselves on what other nations would prefer to forget is a remarkable trait . . .

As I drank my beer, surrounded by noisy tourists and scurrying young waitresses, I gazed at the park and wondered what to do now.

I had delivered Gesar's mysterious gift to Erasmus. I had obtained information from him – all that he was willing to impart, at least.

And I had also acquired an oak chalice in which Erasmus's prophecy was supposedly stored.

After I'd left the old Other's home I had travelled as far as the shop Fortnum and Mason that Semyon had told me about and had bought him the honey he was lusting after. Surrendering to the herd instinct, I got some for myself as well. Then I set out for the toyshop Hamleys (if the shop sign could be believed, the oldest shop for children in the world) and, after jostling my way through five storeys of clamouring children and their parents, I chose a present for my daughter. At first I tried, like an honest spy, to make out what girls of her age were buying, but then I realised that all those beads, stickers and glittery things wouldn't bring her any joy at all. And then I went down into the basement, where I found something like a toy maze with two tiny electronic beetles that were supposed to run through it. The toy was so astoundingly absurd that I bought it without a second thought, and at the checkout I picked up a teddy bear as well.

The true horror of the situation was that I had carried out the entire programme for my visit to London in a single day! Whisky and other alcoholic souvenirs could be bought more easily in the airport. I could devote the whole of the next day and half of the one after that to tourist pastimes – museums, parks, pubs, bridges . . . and shops too, of course.

But somehow I didn't fancy any of it. Neither the gloomy severity of the Tower, nor the magnificence of the royal parks, nor the glitter of London's shops. I had already been on Piccadilly. I had gazed at the Thames and tossed a two-pence piece into the murky water. I wanted to go home!

I was probably insane.

I finished up my mug of beer and fell into thought for a brief moment. I didn't want to go to the hotel: the only entertainments there were the tiny bar and the TV in my room. Basically, there was nothing to prevent me having another pint . . . I started rising to my feet from the wooden bench that is traditional for all self-respecting pubs.

'I've already got it in.' A full mug of beer appeared on the table in front of me.

First I lowered myself back down onto the bench. And then I looked into the face of the woman who had shown such unexpected solicitude for me.

Although there really wasn't any need for that. I had recognised Arina from her voice.

The former witch and present Light Other had another mug of beer in her hands. The old woman preferred Guinness.

But then, the old woman also preferred to look like a woman 'under thirty': full-figured, beautiful and dressed in haute couture. Elegant grey skirt and jacket, high-heeled shoes, a pink blouse so simple in style that it had clearly cost a monstrous amount of money, a little Louis Vuitton handbag and a silk scarf round her neck. And in all this she didn't look like a spoiled rich bitch whose purchases are funded by her husband, but more like a serious businesswoman, a top manager in some major corporation or bank.

'Glad to see you,' Arina said with a smile. 'You've . . . matured, Anton.'

One thing I had always liked about her was her precise way of expressing herself. Not 'you've aged' – what question could there be of age? Not 'you've grown up' – from the extreme vantage point of her long years I was a veritable infant, but for Arina to say that would have been to admit her own age. Not 'you've changed' – experienced Others know that very few individuals are capable of genuinely changing.

Although Arina had done it.

'Are you aware of the fact that the Inquisition is looking for you?' I asked. 'And that all members of the Night Watch and the

Day Watch in every country of the world, regardless of their level of Power and specialisation, are obliged to summon the Inquisition when you show up and take measures to detain you?'

'Yes, I am,' Arina confirmed. She thought for a second and decided not to provoke me. 'I hope we can manage without that?'

'We can,' I agreed.

For a minute or so we drank our beer and looked at each other. She was a strange Other. Once she was a Dark One who often committed good deeds. Then she contrived to change her colour and become a Light One – but in the process she caused worse grief and disaster than some werewolves or vampires. I even had a sneaking suspicion that fundamentally it was all the same to Arina what she was called and how she was regarded – at any moment she was capable of abominable meanness or noble generosity. And it was entirely possible that in working evil she would appear to be a hundred-per-cent Light One, and in doing good would look every inch a Dark One, from her head to her feet.

I even suspected that, contrary to the general opinion, Arina was capable of changing her colour over and over again.

It wasn't exactly that for her there was no difference – she could see the difference all right. It was just that she regarded the path from the Darkness to the Light as a well-beaten track, not a narrow little path that crumbled away behind you.

'Strangely enough, I'm glad that you got away that time,' I said. 'Despite all the mischief you got up to.'

'I had to help the departed to find rest,' Arina said, with a shrug. 'And I think the outcome justified that. And Saushkin the elder ended his . . . activities. And Edgar found rest too. The world became a better place. Your nerves suffered a bit, I admit that, but it all turned out well in the end . . . Peace?'

'Peace,' I said after a brief pause. 'That's all in the past now. I'll mention in my report that I met you, but I won't do anything rash.'

'Thank you,' said Arina. 'That's precisely the right decision! And anyway . . . I came looking for you for a reason.'

I said nothing. I didn't ask how she had found me and what she wanted me for. She wouldn't tell me how, in any case: a witch has her own cunning methods. And she was going to tell me what for without being asked.

'Have you already met Erasmus?' Arina asked.

I smiled and didn't answer. Arina's sources are pretty good, but not omniscient.

'I assume you have,' Arina went on. 'Are you going to share the news?'

'What for?' I asked.

Arina sighed. 'Now that's the right question. Anton, how do you intend to deal with the Tiger?'

'I don't. He's gone.'

'And when he comes back for you?'

'Why would he do that?'

'You've always tried to avoid actions with irrevocable consequences, Anton. I don't believe the boy's prophecy was simply lost in the void.'

I shrugged.

'Arina, if I had heard the prophecy, the Tiger would have come after me, right? That's the first thing. The second is that I was physically nowhere near him. The boy was egged on by Nadya. And then she left him too. Surely you don't think I would have left my daughter unsupervised if I had even the slightest suspicion that she had heard the prophecy . . . and was therefore in danger?'

A shadow of doubt flickered across Arina's face.

'Yes, that's true . . . that's right. I understand that. But something doesn't fit! You must have tried to save the information and keep it for yourself. You wouldn't be you if you hadn't!'

I laughed.

'Well, Arina, that's all fine and dandy, but how could I have done it?'

'A tape recorder?' Arina suggested.

'A tape recorder is an ancient device for recording and reproducing music . . .' I said pensively. 'Yes, yes, I remember . . . when I was a kid I had one: you put these cassettes into it, they had this tape coated in iron oxide . . .'

'Anton, don't play with words. Tape recorder, cassette deck, dictaphone – it doesn't matter what it was! The older generation may underestimate technology, but at least I have enough wits to understand that. You're young, you used to work with technology. You could have thought of something. Any telephone can record sounds nowadays. Tell me honestly: has the information been preserved?'

'I think you should be the first to show a bit of frankness,' I said.

'Why?'

'Because I hold all the trump cards.'

Arina nodded. She looked at a young waitress running past, carrying food to some table. The girl nodded, offloaded her plates and went dashing to the bar counter.

'Agreed,' said Arina. 'All right, listen.'

'Are you sure this is the right place for a private conversation?' I asked. 'There are plenty of Russian tourists in here.'

'The waitress is from Riga, and she has excellent Russian too,' Arina answered. 'Don't worry, no one will hear us.'

I hadn't noticed anything like a Sphere of Negation or any other privacy spell, but I believed Arina. Witches, even ex-witches, have their own magic.

'Then tell me,' I said.

'Anton, the main prophecies must be fulfilled. They absolutely must. The Twilight demands it . . . life itself demands it.'

'Is that so?' I asked in surprise. 'And I thought the Twilight tried to obstruct the Prophets.'

'That's a mistake,' said Arina, shaking her head. 'Does it not surprise you that, for all his omnipotence, the Tiger moves so slowly?'

'Well . . .'

'The Tiger is the spur, the lash urging the Prophet on. The Tiger hurries him along, trying to make him pronounce his main prophecy as quickly as possible.'

'A bold conclusion,' I said.

The waitress brought us two more beers. She looked slightly bewildered – first, in pubs you're supposed to buy beer at the bar yourself, and second, Arina hadn't bothered to pay. I handed the girl a tenner without saying anything.

'I think we'd better start from the basics. Who is a Prophet?' Arina asked me. Then she answered her own question: 'He's not just an Other who is capable of forecasting the lines of probability, so that he can "look into the future". At that level all of us can "foresee the future", to a greater or lesser degree. In the right set of circumstances, even ordinary human beings are capable of similar prescience.'

'A Prophet is qualitatively different,' I said. 'Another kind of Other, pardon the pun.'

'Ah, but he isn't,' Arina laughed. 'The difference is quantitative. A Prophet reads the lines of probability for the whole world, not only his own or the lines of people close to him. A Prophet informs us which direction humankind will move in, only not in the form of a learned treatise but with just one single fact that at first glance seems insignificant. Take the year 1956, for instance. At the age of sixty-two, the French Prophet André Lafleur utters his first prophecy, his main one – it happened that way because he was initiated late in life . . . The prophecy is absolutely crazy: "Soon shall the girl Mary shorten skirts and the world shall be adorned with naked legs."'

I snorted.

'There, exactly,' said Arina. 'Those who heard the prophecy quite reasonably suspected that André had gone senile and lapsed into lascivious fantasies in his old age. And note – only a year later the first Sputnik was launched into space! But here was a Frenchman muttering something about Mary, who would clip skirts shorter . . . But then in 1963 Mary Quant – a Londoner, by the way – showed her collection of miniskirts. They shook the world. And the result? The sexual revolution, emancipation, a significant increase in the birth rate in the Old World. So what was more important, the Sputnik or the miniskirt?'

'The Sputnik,' I said resentfully, although I myself had defended the importance of miniskirts to Gesar.

Arina laughed.

'It was all important. The Sputnik was prophesied too, but space flight was a generally anticipated important development. No one foresaw those twenty centimetres of cloth being snipped off, and they could only appreciate how important they were many years later. That's the way a Prophet works – he foresees great upheavals and forewarns us of them through small events.'

'Then perhaps you know what was so remarkable about an Australian who died as an infant . . .'

'Alistair Maxwell? Yes, I know. The boy's death broke up his parents' marriage. In the late 1970s his mother had another child, by another man. That boy lives a perfectly ordinary life . . . but at the age of fifteen he pulled a little girl who was drowning out of the water. The situation didn't seem like an emergency, he didn't even realise that he had actually saved someone's life. But now that little girl is one of the most powerful enchantresses in the

Australian Day Watch. They forecast a great career for her. But if that infant hadn't died . . .'

'I get it,' I said. 'It's just like in the joke.'

'What joke?' asked Arina.

'Well, this guy has died and he asks God: "What was the meaning of my life?" And God answers: "Remember, in 1972 you were travelling in a train and you passed the salt to someone in the restaurant car? Well then . . ."'

Arina laughed.

'Yes, right. Sometimes it can be just like that. But if you really go into them thoroughly, all those strange prophecies can be explained.'

'And you've gone into them.'

'Yes. It's important.'

'All right, prophecies are important,' I said, nodding. 'No one's arguing with that. But does a Prophet really create the future? Does whether he is heard or not really determine the way the world will be? I've heard various different theories.'

'To be honest, I don't know,' Arina admitted reluctantly. 'Maybe the prophecy shouted into the hollow of an old elm tree was fulfilled anyway. And maybe not.'

'Oak,' I said. 'Erasmus entrusted his prophecy to an oak tree. He doesn't really like elms.'

'Ah, what a finicky druid . . .' Arina laughed. 'So oak trees are dearer to his heart, are they? I don't know if a prophecy works without listeners or not, Anton. That's like the question about whether a tree falling in a remote forest makes any sound or not. Probably not – that's what most researchers agree. But one thing that's quite definite is that a prophecy can be changed.'

'Well now, that's a real turn-up,' I said wryly. 'Everyone's convinced that prophecies are the ultimate instance of truth, that they're unchangeable, unlike mere predictions. And only you know the truth.'

'Yes, only I know it,' Arina replied perfectly calmly. 'Because I have already changed prophecies.'

'Right, from this point on, let me have more detail,' I told her. I thought for a second and got up. 'And, you know what . . . let's go somewhere else.'

'Are you going to invite me to a hotel?' Arina laughed.

'I don't think I ought to do that. Let's sit in the park.'

'They're just about to close it for the night,' replied Arina. 'But then, what difference does that make to us?'

Drinking beer in a children's playground is an old Soviet tradition. Where else could young people go when they wanted to drink . . . let's say, beer? They had no money for restaurants in the USSR, there weren't any pubs and bars, the tiny apartments were all packed with mum, dad, granny, brothers, sisters and relatives from the country who had come to town to buy salami . . . no way you could get it on there. So the over-aged children, who not so long ago were scrabbling about in the sandpits, sat on the children's benches and swings in their own courtyards to drink their beer . . .

The USSR passed on, RIP, but the apartments didn't get any bigger and young people didn't get any more prosperous. Where the children's playgrounds survived, they still served two shifts – infants during the day and senior-school pupils and students in the evening. The more stupid evening gatherings were rowdy, they dropped litter, played loud music and were aggressive with people walking by – for which they were dispersed by old grannies, who knew no greater joy than to ring the militia. The more cultured gatherings sat there quietly, concealed their alcohol, greeted passers-by politely and cleared up their own litter. I used to sit in one of those gatherings too.

Well, at least it seems to me that our gathering was cultured and polite, and it didn't get on anyone's nerves. But, of course, it's quite possible that the inhabitants of the houses round about might have had a completely different opinion.

Anyway, one thing I could never have imagined, neither as a young dosser, nor even after I became a Light Other, was that late one evening I would find myself sitting in Princess Diana's playground in Kensington Gardens, London, drinking beer with an ancient witch!

'Luckily for me the prophecy was pretty clear,' said Arina. 'Masha was a diligent girl and she prophesied like that too – neatly. Only she tried to rhyme everything. She had it fixed in her head that a prophecy had to be in verse. So there I am, sitting in front of this nitwit and wondering what I should do. If I hadn't understood who it was all about, I wouldn't have taken any notice. What's the point of complaining about what can't be changed . . . right? But I did understand. It was 1915 – everything was quite transparent: "With the loss of his heir, the tsar is deranged, Bolsheviks are hanged in the cells. War lasts nine years, Moscow is consumed by flames and the country partitioned as well. Little Russia is German land, Siberia comes under the Japanese hand, a third of the people die of starvation, the world absorbs the rest of the nation."'

'A genuine apocalypse,' I said sarcastically.

'I think that's what it would have been,' said Arina. 'The death of the Tsarevich Alexei could have affected Nicholas in an unexpected manner. He could have crushed the revolution . . . and then lost the First World War. And Russia would effectively have ceased to exist. The Japanese in the Far East, the Germans in the West.'

'It's kind of hard to believe,' I remarked.

'It was a prophecy, Anton. It ought to have come true, people had heard it. But I intervened.'

'You cured the tsarevich?'

'Well, I didn't cure him . . . let's just say I prolonged his life. Nicholas dawdled and lost his nerve, the Bolsheviks took power. Blood was spilt, of course . . . but it could have been worse.'

'So we could call you the salvatrix of Russia,' I said acidly. 'And a Hero of the Soviet Union into the bargain, since you helped the revolution to happen.'

'Well, yes, pretty much,' Arina said modestly.

The children's playground that we had unashamedly occupied was luxurious. Standing at the centre was a wooden ship that looked as if it had sailed here from Never-Never Land and been abandoned by Peter Pan. During the day there was no space to draw breath on the ship, with squalling hordes of children clambering up the masts and the rope ladders, but now the two of us were sitting there, a Magician and a Witch, each clutching a bottle of beer that we hadn't touched in ages.

'Let's suppose I believe you,' I said. 'Let's even suppose that you're not wrong and it was a prophecy and you managed to change it. Then what?'

'The Watches have been messing about with petty nonsense for ages,' said Arina. 'Stewing in their own juice. Even their conflicts are basically make-believe.'

'Would you like a war?' I taunted her. 'Which team are you playing for this season, the Light Ones? And what about the Treaty – do we honour it?'

'I don't want war,' Arina replied seriously. 'We Witches are a peaceful crowd. And Light Witches especially . . . Remind me of the Great Treaty, will you, Anton?'

I shrugged and recited what everyone is taught in their first lesson as an Other – no matter if it's in the Night Watch or the Day Watch.

We are Others
We serve different powers
But in the Twilight there is no difference between the absence of darkness and the absence of light
Our struggle is capable of destroying the world
We conclude the Great Treaty of truce
Each side shall live according to its own laws
Each side shall have its own right
We limit our rights and our laws
We are Others
We create the Night Watch
So that the forces of Light might monitor the forces of Darkness
We are Others
We create the Day Watch
So that the forces of Darkness might monitor the forces of Light
Time will decide for us

'Excellent,' said Arina. 'The Treaty, you will observe, does not prohibit intervention in human life. It only limits the struggle between Light Ones and Dark Ones.'

'So what?' I was beginning to get fed up. 'The Dark Ones have intervened, the Light Ones have intervened . . . who should know better than you? And what came of it? How many wars have been unleashed by experiments to create the ideal society? Communism, fascism, democracy, autocracy, glasnost, globalisation, nationalism, multiculturalism – how much of all this is human, and how much is ours? We prod people in one direction, then in the other. We observe how things have turned out. Then we cross out the result and start all over again. Ah, it doesn't work . . . well, let's try it in a different country, in a different culture, with different social attitudes . . . What, communism was hopeless? I don't think so. But we got tired of that toy. What, democracy is false through and through? Hardly. But we've given up playing with that, too. But you know, it's all the same to people what they die of – the building of communism or the introduction of democracy or the struggle for rights and freedoms. And I reckon the best thing we could do for human beings is leave them in peace! Let them live their own lives, think up their own rules, learn from their own mistakes!'

'Do you think I shouldn't have intervened in the fate of Russia?' Arina asked.

'Yes! No! I don't know . . .' I said, and shrugged. 'But what if after all those upheavals the outcome had been better? If there hadn't been any World War Two, for instance?'

'I couldn't just sit there and do nothing,' said Arina. 'And I couldn't ask anyone for advice. Not Gesar, not Zabulon – they would both have tried to turn the situation to their own advantage. But you're different, I can talk things over with you. You're normal. You're still human.'

'I'm not so sure any more . . .' I said, glancing at the black-skinned security guard walking along the edge of the children's playground. He looked attentively at the roundabouts and the swings, then his glance slid over us without seeing and he walked away.

'We are all human, Anton. Some more so, some less so. Yes, there are situations that aren't clear, when you don't know if you ought to intervene. But there others that are absolutely clear, unequivocal!'

'What do you want from me?' I asked.

'Anton, Prophets only appear rarely. Eight instances in the whole of the twentieth century. And it's even rarer for their first prophecy to be documented before it becomes known to people and comes into force. If you know the boy's prophecy . . .'

'No, I don't know it. I swear.'

'But can you find out what it is?' Arina asked specifically.

'Yes, probably. What's more, it's possible that I can find out what Erasmus's first prophecy was. Although, after all these years, it has probably been realised already.'

'That's not certain,' said Arina. 'Gagarin's flight into space was prophesied in the seventeenth century . . . Anton, you really astound me, in the best sense of the word.'

'Since you changed colour, you're simply itching to do good,' I said.

'Maybe so. But aren't you? Anton, no one in the Watch would dare to do anything like this. I'm prepared to try. And I swear to you that if the prophecy turns out to be good, or unclear – then we won't do anything. Let it come true. But what if we've suddenly been given a chance to steer people's lives in a better direction?'

'"We",' I snorted. 'The last time you said "we" was when you were with Edgar and Saushkin. They came to a bad end.'

'You don't trust me, and that's right,' Arina said, nodding. 'But with you I'll have the chance to do something genuinely important, not just drudge away aimlessly in a Watch.'

'I'm almost certain you told Edgar the same thing,' I replied sombrely.

'Think, Anton,' said Arina, opening her handbag and taking out a little sphere. 'For the time being, I'll go back to . . . my place. Pardon me for not inviting you – the Minoan sphere only transports one.'

'I thought it was a single-use item,' I said.

'No, it's a single-charge unit,' Arina said, with a smile. 'And I know how to recharge it. I'll come to visit you in the morning, if you don't mind?'

I shrugged. Arina smiled, grasped the sphere tightly in her fist – and disappeared.

I sighed, picked up the empty beer bottles and started climbing down off the little wooden ship. Unlike the witch, I would have to make my way to the hotel on foot.

On the way into the playground Arina had opened the gate with some method of her own, by crumbling dry grass in her fingers and sprinkling it on the lock, but I'd never liked fiddling about with the spell 'Bilbo' and I decided to bypass the fence in the Twilight. To my surprise the playground was locked on the first level of the Twilight too, and on the second it was surrounded by something like a line of wizened trees, with prickly branches protruding out towards the park. I examined this apparently dead hedge curiously. Dry tree trunks like that were more often encountered on the third level, but there they were scattered about chaotically, while these looked as if they had been planted deliberately. Or perhaps fixed into the ground. Fortunately, there was no need to go any deeper – this barrier was only a hindrance if you were trying to get into the playground, not get out of it. Whoever the Other was who had worked on the playground, he had certainly done a thorough job. I squeezed through the branches, walked away a bit and returned to the real world. After the cold and silence of the Twilight, the London park seemed warm and full of sounds. Somewhere in the distance I heard the subtle song of a reed pipe. I set off through the park, intending to leave it at some point closer to my hotel. On the way I came across a rubbish bin that had considerately been emptied before the park's evening closing, and I lowered the two empty beer bottles into it.

What could be more delightful than an evening stroll through a deserted park?

The artless melody sounded closer and closer. And suddenly I saw the musician. Sitting there on the crooked trunk of an immense tree that had been bent over by the wind a long time ago and had carried on growing like that, almost parallel to the ground, was a little boy dressed in some kind of fanciful rags. The boy was playing his reed pipe, completely absorbed. Huge fireflies circled round him, as if they were dancing.

'Hey!' I called out to the young musician. I was so disconcerted that I asked in Russian: 'Isn't it late for you to be out here?'

The boy turned sharply in my direction. His milk teeth glinted snow-white, either in the glimmer of the fireflies or in the distant glow of street lamps on the Bayswater Road. The boy jumped down off the tree – and disappeared. The fireflies fluttered after him, with a jingling sound.

'Hell's fucking bells!' I swore. 'This is bullshit! I don't believe in . . .'

But I didn't actually finish the phrase.

Of course I don't believe in fairies. It's ages now since I even believed in Santa Claus.

But even so, I preferred not to say it.

CHAPTER 5

THE MUSIC ROARED. Harsh, unfamiliar and, to my ear, totally discordant. But the people around me seemed to like it. The discotheque was packed solid – the young people weren't dancing so much as swaying, twitching on the spot and brushing against each other, periodically grabbing each other by the hands and starting to move in a strange, grotesque, tangled roundelay. The ceiling glowed, and it wasn't just beams of light from projectors or disco lamps, it was as if the panels of the ceiling were themselves radiating light. Streaks of different colours were replaced by an even orange light, then the ceiling started glowing cerulean blue – and then it became a single, continuous screen. Above us was the sky, with white, feathery clouds drifting across it.

'What's this?' I asked, dodging away from a chain of teenagers that had just meshed together.

'A discotheque,' they told me.

I turned my head. Standing beside me was a youth of about eighteen, short and chubby. He looked familiar somehow.

'Kesha?' I asked, suddenly recognising him.

'What, Anton Sergeevich?'

What?

I didn't know 'what'. I didn't understand where I was and how I'd got here. But I had to ask something.

'Where's Nadya?' I said, suddenly realising that was the right question.

'Here,' Innokentii Tolkov replied with a shrug. 'Somewhere here . . .'

I tried to spot her in the crowed. Then I realised I was involuntarily looking too low, at the level where a ten-year-old girl's head would be. I should be looking higher . . .

And I saw Nadiushka almost immediately. I wasn't sure how I recognised her . . . she had grown, just like Kesha. But she had changed far more – her head was completely shaved, with just two clumps of white-bleached hair left above her ears. A long narrow skirt, with slits that reached almost right up to her waist, boots that reached halfway up her calves . . . and an absolutely plain white blouse. Nadya looked grotesque and pitiful, even hideous, dressed like that, but this was my Nadya. And I felt my heart contract painfully in my chest.

I took a step forward, elbowing my way through the jostling youngsters, grabbed my daughter by the arm and dragged her out of the chain of 'dancers'. The bright-coloured metal bracelets that covered her entire wrist jangled.

'Dad?' Nadya asked in surprise. 'What are you doing here?'

'What are you doing here?' I asked at the same time.

Nadya shrugged.

'Relaxing.'

The boy and girl between whom Nadya had been swaying in the chain pushed their way through to us. They looked . . . well, appropriate. The boy was wearing a glittering thong and a fluffy shirt (yes, it was a shirt, and it was fluffy), the girl had the same kind of plain blouse and long skirt with slits that Nadya was wearing.

Clearly, that was fashionable.

It was a long time since I'd attended any teenage gatherings.

'Nadya, what does this ersatz want?' the boy asked. Not actually threateningly, but defiantly.

'Pull on back,' Nadya replied incomprehensibly. 'This is my abu.'

The boy gave me a look that was unfriendly, but a bit softer. And he asked: 'Any problems, honourable sir?'

'No problems,' I said. 'And if you disappear straight away, none will arise.'

The boy grinned crookedly. Apparently I hadn't scared him. The little fool. I could soon have him on his way home to do his homework and wash the floors . . .

'Everything's smooth, Vovik,' said Nadya. 'Lighten a bit.'

'Tap me if anything comes up,' Vovik answered, and flashed another glance at me. Then he disappeared into the crowd with his girlfriend.

'What idiot kind of slang's that?' I asked.

'The usual,' Nadya replied and sniffed. Her eyes were red. 'What did you come here for, dad?'

'Nadya, let's go home,' I said.

'What for?'

'Nadya, your mum will be worried,' I said, appealing to the argument that had worked unfailingly when she was ten.

'What have you and mum got to do with anything?' asked Nadya.

I got a terrible cold feeling in my chest.

'Nadya, I don't understand what's happening,' I said. The music was hammering in my ears, dark storm clouds were covering over the sky on the ceiling screen. 'Let's talk somewhere else.'

'What's wrong with here?'

'This is no place for a Higher Other!' I exclaimed in exasperation.

Nadya laughed. And if at first it was simply quiet laughter, as if she'd heard a good joke, an instant later it had become loud, hysterical giggling.

I hate women's hysterics! It's a totally dishonest trick to use in the relations between men and women!

The only thing worse than women's hysterics is men's hysterics.

'For a Higher Other?' Nadya repeated. 'For an Other? Dad . . . daddy, you've really lost it! Dad, after what you did to us, how can you even say the word "Other"?'

And she went off into the crowd, still laughing and running her hand over her face, as if she was brushing away tears.

And I stood and watched her go.

Then I shifted my gaze to Kesha.

'"You are Anton Gorodetsky . . ."' I said. '"Because of you . . . all of us . . ." Just what have I done to "all of you"?'

'I don't know,' replied Kesha.

'Why didn't Nadya say anything to you?'

'She didn't see me.'

Thunder rumbled above my head, and heavy raindrops started pattering down. I held out my hand to them . . . a drop fell onto my palm and disappeared. There was rain, but it was an illusion – like the clouds above me.

Like everything here.

'Why didn't she see you, Kesha?'

'Because this is your vision, Anton Sergeevich,' the young man replied. 'And your dream.'

He swung round and disappeared into the crowd too – still as plump, awkward and unattractive as he had been as a child.

And apparently still as lonely and unhappy.

'It's not true!' I shouted.

And I woke up.

In silence.

The low ceiling of a cheap London hotel. In general the English live in tiny houses the size of postage stamps. Probably so that it's easier to defend them – after all, 'my home is my castle'.

Sunlight splashing in through the small window. Morning, although it's still early . . .

I glanced at the clock – only seven a.m., local time.

Then I looked at Sir Erasmus's wooden chalice standing on the bedside table. Maybe it was the beer that was to blame, or maybe it was the glass of cognac I added to it while I was watching the television before I went to bed, but when I wanted a drink of water I had unpacked the gift and drunk the water out of it. And not casually either, but in the profound conviction that I would then hear Darwin's first prophecy.

It didn't work, as far as Darwin's prophecy was concerned. But now I'd got one of my own.

Or had I?

What was it – a very vivid and realistic dream produced by a mixture of alcohol, fatigue and a host of new impressions?

A prophecy?

I can foresee the future, like any Other – like any human being, if it comes to that. Even better than many Others – at one time Gesar quite seriously recommended that I should specialise in predictions. But I have dreams that are simply stupid too, like anybody else.

Mulling this over, I went to the toilet and took a shower. (Everything was squeezed very compactly into two square metres – and these people reproached the Soviet Union for the 'Khrushchev slums'?) I got dressed and walked pensively downstairs into the semi-basement, where the hotel's small restaurant was located. The waitress who was bustling about there, pouring the guests coffee and clearing away the dirty plates, had such an everyday face that I greeted her in Russian. And I guessed right.

'Oh, hello,' she said, embarrassed for some reason. 'Will you have tea or coffee?'

'Coffee,' I said with a nod, casting an eye over the food laid out on the table.

'The coffee's not great,' the girl whispered quietly, leaning towards me.

'Even so,' I replied just as quietly. 'I have to wake up.'

'I'd better make you some instant,' the girl suggested and disappeared into the kitchen.

I took a yogurt, a piece of bread, a hermetically sealed plastic briquette of cheese (Cheddar is Cheddar) and scrambled eggs, which is the most outrageous insult to eggs that Europe has been able to invent.

But at least they were hot.

I sat down at a table in the corner and picked up a lump of the crumbling eggy mass with my fork, examined it cautiously and popped it into my mouth. It tasted better than it looked . . .

At that moment I smelled coffee. Good, genuine coffee, not chemicalised instant. And then a huge cup of this delightful coffee appeared in front of me.

'Thank you,' I said, looking up.

Smiling, Arina took my plate with the scrambled eggs and left it on an empty table. She said: 'Don't eat that garbage. I tell you that as a Witch.'

She held out another plate, with fried eggs, cooked just right, so that the yolks had thickened but were still liquid, sprinkled with finely chopped spring onions and with pieces of fried fatty bacon just visible in the congealed whites. Arina set down another cup of coffee in front of herself.

'"Eat the hare's dung, it makes you feel young"?' I declared. Since Arina's only response to Filatov's poem was simply to raise an eyebrow in surprise, I sighed and said, 'You're not a Witch any more, you're a Light One.'

'There's no such thing as a former Witch. How did you sleep, Higher One?'

First I dispatched a piece of fried egg into my mouth and followed it with a large gulp of coffee. Then I said: 'Your doing, was it?'

'What, exactly?' Arina asked in surprise.

'My dream.'

'I've no idea what you dreamed about,' she said, shaking her head and frowning. 'Something unpleasant, was it? Prophetic? I don't interfere in your dreams.'

'It's nothing – nonsense, really,' I said, with a dismissive wave of my hand. I downed the rest of the coffee. 'Listen, do you earn a bit on the side as a waitress in London?'

'Unfortunately I don't have a work permit,' Arina laughed. 'It's all charity work. You're looking a bit crumpled.'

'I had a nightmare,' I admitted reluctantly. 'Nothing very informative. Just Nadka, grown up already and . . . kind of strange . . . like all teenagers, I suppose . . . Not very nice, to be honest. And she accused me of doing something to the Others.'

Arina's expression turned serious. And what she said only convinced me that she took this dream seriously.

'It's nonsense, Anton. Some dreams are just dreams. Can you tell me about it in a bit more detail?'

'No,' I said, shaking my head. 'Okay, let's drop it. Do you happen to know if fairies really exist?'

'Er . . .' Arina hesitated. 'I don't know. Probably not, of course, but it seems kind of rude to say that right beside Kensington Gardens.'

'Yesterday, as I was walking to the hotel, I saw a little boy on a fallen tree. He was playing a reed pipe and glowing insects were swarming around him. He saw me, grinned and ran off.'

'Ran off or flew off?'

'That I don't know.'

'And you decided you'd run into Peter Pan?'

'God only knows what I thought!'

'Inversion. And projection.'

'What?'

'A vapour trail. How many people have read the story of Peter Pan? How many children have watched a cartoon or a film? How many of them have imagined Kensington Gardens and Peter? How many of those were overt or potential Others?'

'We can't create people.'

'Any woman can do that,' Arina laughed. 'But we're talking about something different here. An image – one that has been adequately visualised – is projected onto a point at which there is already an immense concentration of Power. The Power at the various levels of the Twilight starts to get agitated. The energy is stabilised at a higher level. You can calculate it using the Boltzmann Distribution, the whole process is almost identical to thermodynamic equations, you can even use Planck's Constant – only for the twilight it's called the Canterbury Constant.'

I suddenly realised that I was sitting there with my mouth wide open, holding a fork with a piece of fried egg suspended on it. I hurriedly clamped my mouth shut, biting the fork painfully, and swore in a whisper.

'It's the standard process for the appearance of ghosts,' Arina continued. 'Don't the Light Ones teach that these days?'

'No,' I admitted. 'And the Dark Ones don't, either . . . probably.'

'Well, they should,' said Arina. 'It's no practical use at all, but surely you must be interested in where phantoms come from, the life of the Twilight, which spells will be most effective at what point in space?'

'I didn't even know it was possible . . .' – I hesitated – '. . . to reduce it all to formulas.'

'But Witches have always known that,' Arina told me. 'Surely you don't think that Witches are dirty old women who boil up unappetising substances in cauldrons and mutter "by the pricking of my thumbs . . ."?'

I thought it best not to say anything. Arina drank her coffee, clearly savouring the situation.

'Well, what have you decided?' she asked insistently.

'The mere fact that I'm talking to you without trying to arrest you is official misconduct,' I said gruffly.

Arina snorted.

'Swear on the Light and the Darkness,' I said.

Arina raised her eyes to look at me.

'Swear that you had nothing to do with the dream I had last night,' I went on.

'So things are that bad, are they?' Arina said, with an understanding nod. 'All right . . .'

She said nothing for a few seconds, as if she was trying to recall something. Then she reached her hands out across the table and turned them palms upwards.

I was scalded by a chilly breath of wind.

The few other hotel guests all turned away and diligently stopped noticing us.

'I, Arina, swear on the primordial Powers. I, a Dark One Beyond Classification, swear on the Darkness – and may the eternal Darkness bear witness to my words. I, a Light One and Healer Beyond Classification, swear on the Light – and may the eternal Light bear witness to my words. I, the thirteenth and final Head of the Supreme Conclave of Witches, do swear on the earth from which I came, the water that is within me, the air that surrounds me, the fire into which I shall depart. I have not exerted any influence on you, your powers, your prophecies, your thoughts, your visions, your desires, your fears, your love, your hate, your joy and your sorrow. All that I have said to you is true or I believe it to be true.'

A white flame started dancing on her left palm, a spot of darkness condensed on her right. Arina brought her palms close together – and a small sphere started spinning furiously between them. It was white and black at the same time, it glowed brightly and consumed light simultaneously. It wasn't grey, like the Inquisitors had, but dual, simultaneously Light and Dark.

'I believe you and accept your oath,' I said.

The small sphere shrank to a blindingly black point and disappeared.

'So, Head of the Supreme Conclave,' I mused. 'And the Watches tried so hard to guess who that was and where she had disappeared to . . .'

Arina shrugged.

'I'm simply choosing the lesser evil,' I added.

'Even when choosing the lesser evil, never forget that you're still choosing evil,' Arina said seriously.

'But in choosing nothing, we choose both the greater and the lesser evil at once,' I replied.

'Then we understand each other,' she said, nodding – the final Supreme Witch of the Conclave that had been disbanded a hundred years earlier.

'But that still leaves one little problem,' I said. 'The Tiger. As I understand it, the prophecies are not active at the moment.'

'They're sleeping,' said Arina.

'If we learn what they are – the Tiger will come for us.'

'But if we reveal them to humans – the Tiger will leave us in peace.'

'And what if the prophecies are bad? Are you suggesting we

should die a heroic death? Or open Pandora's box, and to hell with human beings?'

'No and no again. Witches have always preferred to choose a third way.'

I looked at her questioningly.

'We have tried to understand the nature of the Tiger,' said Arina. 'As you have no doubt already realised, in certain areas the Conclave possessed knowledge that equalled the knowledge of the Watches. We did not succeed, but . . .' She paused. 'We did find an Other who knows how to defeat the Tiger. He is still alive. I suggest that we meet him, to obtain this information – and open the prophecies after that.'

I sat there for a while, digesting what I'd just heard. Then I asked: 'Where is he? Somehow I get the feeling it's not London and not Moscow.'

'Formosa,' Arina said, nodding.

It took me a few seconds to recall what used to be called Formosa in Arina's time.

'Taiwan?' The globe that I had given Nadya a year earlier to further her general education appeared in front of my eyes. 'That's . . . How far is that?'

'Almost ten thousand kilometres. Fourteen hours. Fortunately, there's a direct flight,' said Arina, looking at her watch, an elegant timepiece of pink gold – probably with a diamond mechanism, I thought. 'It's half past seven now. The flight's in one hour and forty minutes. Do you need long to pack?

'Do you mean to say that you already have tickets?' I asked.

'I mean to say that I checked us into the flight yesterday evening. The lack of a visa won't bother you too much, will it? You can buy clean underclothes at the airport, if we have time, and if not – in Taipei.'

'I suppose the taxi's already waiting?' I asked.

'Yes,' Arina said. 'The meter's running. Well, how about it? What's your decision?'

I spread some butter on a slice of bread and put a piece of cheese on top. I took a bite and chewed it before I said: 'I don't need to buy any underclothes. I don't even need socks. Sveta packed my bag for a week.'

I watched London slipping away beneath the plane and thought about what I was doing now.

Our entire life is an endless sequence of choices. Stay home or go out for a walk. Go to the cinema or watch TV. Drink tea or water.

Even these insignificant decisions can change a life completely, let alone the more serious alternatives! Get married or wait a while. Change your job or stay in the old one. Move to a different city or country.

I had had to make choices too, and I still didn't know if I had always made the right one. But the action I had just taken could well be the most serious choice in my life. Not, of course, because I hadn't rushed in to arrest Arina, as demanded by the regulations of the Night Watch and the circulars from the Inquisition. As a Magician Beyond Classification, even if my rank was rather doubtful and reflected my potential rather than the experience and wisdom that still had to be added to my Power, I had sufficient freedom of action.

I could, for instance, state that I did not consider myself capable of detaining Arina (which was the truth!) and had decided to play for time.

Or – and this would also not have required me to offend against veracity – I could justify my actions by the need to acquire additional information and clarify who was capable of resisting the Tiger, and how. After all, recent events at our office had demonstrated that this was a matter of priority!

And then the very existence of the two prophecies and my own strange dream positively demanded further investigation.

Of course, to be fair, I ought to have told people what was happening . . . at least Gesar. But even here I had a convincing excuse – a Higher Witch, let alone the former Head of the Conclave, was quite capable of intercepting practically any kind of message, even a pupil's communications with his mentor.

So, from the official point of view, I was more or less in the clear. I could find a wagonload of excuses for my actions.

And I wasn't really concerned about my own safety, either. I hadn't required Arina to swear an oath not to harm me, but I had no grounds for suspecting her of anything bad. If I'd been able to work with Zabulon, I should be able to get along with a former Witch who was now a Light One.

So what was bothering me?

A pretty Chinese hostess was handing out glasses of champagne. Arina had lashed out on first-class tickets – but then, why would an experienced Witch be short of funds? Arina, in the seat beside me, took a glass. I declined and, after a moment's hesitation, asked for a cognac. A fourteen-hour flight – there would be plenty time to have a drink and then sober up.

The morning was starting to come together.

'Will you show me the chalice?' Arina asked.

I got my bag down without any objections and took out the artefact that Erasmus had made. Arina held it in her hands for a while, then shook her head.

'I can't sense any magic.'

'Neither can I, but not everything can be sensed.'

'That's true.'

Arina poured her champagne into the chalice and drank it. She shrugged. She raised the vessel to her ear and listened to it, as if it was a seashell.

'I've tried that,' I said. 'I drank out of it, and listened to it. It seemed to me that Erasmus knew how to awaken the prophecy – but he didn't think it necessary to explain.'

'How did you manage to persuade him to part with the chalice?' Arina asked curiously.

'A present from Gesar helped,' I said and told her about our office bonsai tree that had found a new home with Darwin.

'Riddle upon riddle,' Arina said, and shrugged. 'Everyone knows Gesar is a sly old fox, but I have no idea what he's thought up this time . . .'

'Information for information,' I said. 'Tell me about this Other we're going to see.'

'He's called Fan Wen-yan,' Arina replied. 'Actually, he has plenty of different names, but that's the one he uses now for living among human beings. He's about three hundred years old. A Light Other, but he has never been a member of any Watches.'

'What rank is he?' I asked.

'Fourth.'

'Is that all?' I asked, amazed.

Of course, fourth rank is pretty serious, not just the ability to perform petty magic tricks, like seventh rank. But in three hundred years even a weak Other hauls himself up two or three levels from his original level. Did that mean Fan had been a total weakling when he was initiated?

'Why so snobbish?' Arina snorted. 'Weren't you a fourth-ranker once upon a time?'

'Fifteen years ago,' I admitted. 'But I was initiated as a Fourth-Level Other.'

'Well, he started right at the very bottom,' said Arina, confirming my surmise. 'From the Seventh-Level. And he climbed patiently . . . In 1925 he was appointed curator of the Gugun Palace Museum in Beijing. Great Others were not required there, the Chinese respect the authorities, no one attempted to steal the treasures. Even when the Xinhai Revolution took place' – Arina gave me a glance and took pity on me – 'and that was in 1911, the imperial treasures weren't plundered seriously . . . Fan Wen-yan would have had a quiet life, but in 1930 something strange happened. Fan Wen-yan had a friend, a Prophet. A weak one, but a Prophet nonetheless. I don't know the details – maybe he was more than just his friend . . .' Arina laughed. 'Anyway, the young man prophesied something or other, and the only witness to it was Fan. For some reason he didn't like the prophecy and he didn't want to reveal it to the human population. And so the Tiger came for Fan and his friend. That wasn't what they called him but, from all the descriptions, it was the Tiger.'

I waited.

'His friend was killed. But Fan managed to do something . . . either he destroyed the Tiger . . .'

'How could he have destroyed him?' I exclaimed in surprise. 'The Tiger has only just been in Moscow . . .'

'But are you sure that there's only one Tiger?' Arina asked with a smile. 'Anyway, Fan managed to do something. Killed it, drove it away, frightened it off, bought it off – I don't know what. But the prophecy wasn't proclaimed, and later, under interrogation in the Night Watch, Fan said that he "would rather cut himself into pieces and feed them to the tigers in the Beijing zoo than utter what had been revealed to him". When we put everything together and realised that a weak Chinese magician had managed to drive away the Tiger, it was decided to find him and clarify the details. Not for any specific requirement . . . but additional knowledge never does any harm.'

'So what stopped you?'

'Infighting, Anton. For us Russian Witches the World War and the Revolution were far greater calamities than they were for Others in general . . .'

'Why?'

'We Witches are closer to the earth. To the country where we grew up, where we acquired our powers. In 1914 it was already difficult for us to gather in the Conclave – for a Russian Witch to sit beside a German one, an English Witch beside an Austrian one – and then after the Revolution, with the USSR on one side and everyone else on the other, reaching an agreement about anything at all became quite impossible. Then I went to sleep, hid away from my friends, left the Conclave . . . and it fell apart anyway: its time had obviously come. So we didn't do anything about this. It's a pity . . . I didn't have Fan's fortitude when my friend prophesied in 1915 – I told people everything.'

'But you did it your own way,' I said, nodding.

'Yes, I managed to get around the prophecy and save the country. Her prophecy became inaccurate, it became just one more false prediction. It seemed like I'd done well . . . but then I heard about Fan, and I couldn't get his story out of my mind. So when I came back to the world, I started looking for him. And I found him.'

'What's he doing in Taiwan? Did he flee from the communists?'

'Of course not. He's indifferent to human ideology, just as we are. But he was the curator of an imperial museum, you understand? And when the Chinese who weren't communists started withdrawing to Taiwan in 1948, they took the museum treasures along. And they took Fan with them . . . what else could he do? So now he works in the Gugun National Imperial Museum.'

'But that's in Beijing.'

'No, that's just the Gugun Imperial Museum. This is the National one.'

'But will he tell us everything?' I asked.

Arina shrugged.

'Any pressure or force is out of the question,' I said, just to be quite clear. 'I'm not going to quarrel with the Chinese Others.'

'I haven't gone insane either,' Arina said with a nod. 'Only better say "Taiwanese", and not "Chinese". It's more polite and more correct.'

'Any other pieces of advice?'

'Perfectly elementary ones. Never raise the subject of the two Chinas in conversation. Praise Taiwan, but don't abuse China! Even if the subject does come up, avoid offering any opinions. It's their internal problem and foreigners shouldn't interfere in it. By the way, you should behave the same way in mainland China, if you end up there.'

'I get it,' I said.

'Refrain from any bodily contact. I don't mean sex, simply try not to invade their personal space, don't touch anyone when you talk to them, don't slap them on the shoulders, don't hug them. It's impolite.'

'You've done all your homework,' I said.

'What else does an old-age pensioner have to do?' Arina said, smiling. 'On the other hand, you can feel quite safe on the streets, the crime rate there is very low. And you can eat anything at all anywhere at all, no matter what the food's made of. The Taiwanese are very strict when it comes to hygiene. A chef whose hygiene certificate is out of date, or who breaks certain rules, goes to jail for several years. Regardless of whether anyone was poisoned by his cooking or not.'

'I like that,' I said, recalling the Moscow kebab stalls where 'chefs' in filthy overall coats sliced meat of unknown origin off a revolving grill. 'How did they manage it?'

'Harsh dictatorship,' Arina laughed. 'You're a big boy, you ought to understand that punctual transport, public order and safe streets, polite people and good medical services are all the achievements of dictatorship.'

'Oh, sure. London's a good example,' I said sarcastically.

'Of course. It's just that in England the period of dictatorship is over already. They don't enclose the land and drive peasants out of their homes any longer, and they don't hang children for stealing pocket handkerchiefs. They don't sell opium to China, using gunboat diplomacy, and get a quarter of the country's population addicted to it. They don't loot the colonies for treasures any more. The Brits worked hard for their dictatorship and they earned the right to democracy, tolerance and pluralism.'

'An interesting view of the world,' I said.

'An honest one,' Arina parried. 'You know yourself that "a gentleman to the west of Suez is not answerable for what a gentleman does to the east of Suez . . ." And the Brits aren't so special. Tell me what you can feel proud of in the history of our own country. Military victories? The annexation of territory? Space flights? Factories and power stations? A mighty army and a world-famous culture? All of it was created under tyrants and dictators, Antoshka! St Petersburg and Baikonur. Tchaikovsky and Tolstoy, nuclear weapons and the Bolshoi Theatre, the Dnieper Hydroelectric Power Plant and the Baikal-Amur Railway.'

'Haven't become a communist in your old age, have you?' I growled.

'What for?' Arina snorted. 'I'm talking about firm-handed power, harsh power, if necessary. I'm not interested in political posturing.'

'Then what's the point of all these achievements, if St Petersburg was built on bones and you couldn't buy toilet paper in the Soviet Union?'

Arina smiled.

'It's the same as with the European colonies in Africa and Asia, the English enclosures that ruined the peasants, the American slaves in the cotton fields . . . and the never-ending bloody wars all around the planet. First a country gets fat and flourishes – don't confuse that with the people, it's the country we're talking about! Then the rulers mellow a bit, the people relax – and life gets free and easy. The Roman legions no longer march on the orders of Rome, but stagnate somewhere like Judea. The aristocracy devotes itself to its vices, the people to theirs . . . the only differences are the price of the whores and the types of gastronomical delicacies. And somewhere not far away the numbers of resentful, hungry people bound together by a single, inflexible will are already multiplying, and they regard the former mighty power as a tasty lunch. And then there are two possibilities – either the country will rouse itself and start to live again, even though that will be really tough on the people . . . or the country will die. And the people with it, of course. It will become a part of the dictatorship that it had left behind and to which it didn't wish to return. The eternal cycle of strength and weakness, harshness and flabbiness, fanaticism and tolerance. People are lucky if they're born at the beginning of an age of peace, when an aristocrat can no longer hunt down a commoner with his dogs and the commoner doesn't yet insist on his right to be an idle drone. That's what they call a golden age . . . only it doesn't last long, not even a century.'

'And can a society where this balance has been achieved be happy?' I asked.

'Of course,' Arina said. 'Only the balance can't be achieved for long. I once argued about that with a student in St Petersburg – he was a bright young man. I explained to him that society balances on a razor's edge. On one side there is inertia, apathy and death, on the other there is harshness, severity and life, and it would be good to walk the path through the middle – but you can't balance on a razor for long. He didn't agree, though: he was stubborn and he believed strongly in communism.'

'Yes, as far as I know, he never did agree,' I said thoughtfully. 'All right, Arina, I'm not willing to argue.'

'You don't agree either,' she said, nodding. 'I understand. It's youth, Anton. Don't worry. It'll pass.'

CHAPTER 6

I HALF-SAT, HALF-LAY on the spacious seat, looking through the plane's window at the white mantle of clouds and listening to music. I used to have a minidisc player that I crammed all my favourite songs onto. Unfortunately, minidiscs died the death . . . or rather, they're in the process of dying out now, having become the exclusive preference of retro types, romantics, skinflints and conservative journalists. Their place has been taken by MP3s, simply files without any external medium. Download what you like from the freebooting piratical expanses of the Internet and listen to your heart's content . . .

So there I was, listening, as usual, in random-selection mode. The electronics selected the group Orgy of the Righteous. Sometimes it seems to me that I affect the choice involuntarily: the songs are simply too much in tune with my own thoughts . . .

My heartbeats insist that I have not died
Dawn peeps through my eyelids scorched by the flames
And standing right there when I open my eyes
I see the Great Horror that has no name.

We were all overwhelmed, trampled into the ground
They swept us aside like a raging black flood.
Our standards and banners thrust into the sand –
They smashed every one, drowned us in our own blood . . .

I looked at Arina. The witch was sleeping: she'd either crashed out after the complimentary glass of champagne, or she was tired after some mysterious nocturnal exploits that I knew nothing about . . . or it was simply out of habit. She still looked just as young and beautiful, only her mouth had come half-open like an old woman's and a slim thread of saliva was trickling out onto her chin.

Through the burnt crops I could creep to the river,
Cut loose a boat and then leave, safe and free,
To be this war's one and only survivor.
But I spit in their faces, tell myself: 'On your feet!'

My heartbeats insist that I have not died
Dawn peeps through my eyelids scorched by the flames
And standing right there when I open my eyes
I see the Great Horror that has no name.

And I see the Shadow, dead ashes and stones,
I see there is nothing more left here to guard.
But raising my battered shield high once again,
I reach for my scabbard and wrench out my sword.

The last warrior of a dead land . . .

But what I know dies not with me this day,
Even though victory can never now be mine:

They have no right to see the dawn's bright ray,
They have no right even to be alive.

And through my cracked war horn I trumpet out loud,
Sounding the charge for all our lost men.
'Follow me!' I bellow. 'Forward!' I shout.
When none are alive, the dead must rise again.

Sergei Kalugin's voice fell silent. I set the player on pause and adjusted the seat to a more comfortable position. I glanced sideways at Arina. Fortunately, she had closed her mouth, but now her chin and cheeks seemed to have turned flabby. When she slept, the illusion seemed to dissolve – although it didn't really, it wasn't the crude 'yashmak' that all witches use, it was something far closer to being real. But that made it all the harder for the witch to maintain it.

How strangely life works out sometimes. There I am sitting in Moscow, delighted at the idea of a short work trip to London – and suddenly I get caught up in a swirl of events and dragged off to the other side of the world, to a place I don't really know anything about . . . even though half the computer hardware I can remember was produced in Taiwan.

And who with? A former witch who is now a Light Other. Someone I once fought a deadly duel with . . .

I felt a sudden ache in my chest. It wasn't a physical pain, but a clear, piercing realisation that my duel with Arina wasn't just a thing of the past, it was waiting for me in the future too.

It wasn't a vision of the future, no. Something else. As if subconsciously I had already understood everything that hadn't yet come together, that was still stuck in my conscious memory in the form of separate, scattered splinters. All these Prophets, dreams, visions, Tigers, Witches, Gesar and Zabulon – it had all merged together to produce a result that I didn't like at all.

And the main reason I didn't like it was because I would have to kill. Or be killed.

What the hell was going on! What rotten damned impulse had made me pay attention to some bawling kid at an airport – I could have just walked on by . . .

I winced painfully. I could have just walked on by. And allowed him to die? And another hundred and fifty people with him?

Of course I couldn't.

That's the way things are arranged in this world – one person's life is always another person's death.

The pretty air hostess walked by quietly, smiling. Catching my eye, she inclined her head slightly and glanced inquiringly at the empty glass on the broad armrest of the seat. I nodded. I waited for her to bring the cognac, took a sip – and stayed there, half-lying in the seat. I could have done with a bit of sleep . . . but sleep wouldn't come now. My biological clock would go completely haywire. First from Moscow to London, then from London to Taipei . . .

Why was I certain that I would have to fight with Arina?

And not simply fight, but fight to the death?

Yes, she had become a Light One, but she was still a dark schemer . . . as bad as Gesar.

Yes, she had revealed a certain amount of information to me, but she was concealing even more.

Yes, somehow she knew things that she ought not to know. I had the feeling that she had a source in one of the Watches . . . I made a mental note to investigate the idea. Of course, she said that she hated Zabulon, and she really had changed her colour – but where was the real truth in all of this?

All of us, even in relationships with our friends, leave some things unsaid and hide others. Not necessarily with any bad intention. Sometimes it's simpler and quicker not to say something than to try to explain and persuade.

What was it that had disconcerted me?

Arina had sworn that she hadn't influenced me. I believed her, and it wasn't just a matter of the oath – with her persuasive abilities she had no need to resort to direct magical influence on a person's mind.

But her oath had referred to the past. She hadn't said that she wouldn't do me any harm. That she wouldn't ever try to deceive me or fight against me. A mere detail, of course . . . but if she hadn't been keeping that possibility in mind, she would definitely have tried to intensify her oath, make it more convincing.

What else?

I took a sip of the pungent cognac and tried to summon up Arina's face in my memory. Strange, in my mind's eye, even though she was still young, her eyes were old and faded . . . wise . . . and sad.

Those eyes were already gazing into the future.

She knew that our alliance was a brief one.

Or, at least, she took the possibility seriously.

Arina looked at me as if I were someone she liked, but who would inevitably become an enemy – and soon, very soon.

Well, then . . . two could play at that game.

For the time being our interests coincided.

We'd have to see how things went.

Of course, I didn't feel like sleeping. I switched on the entertainment centre built into the seat, leafed through the film listing, watched some movie about vampire hunters for about ten minutes, chuckling. On the one hand, it was very funny. It was like the way Russians watch Hollywood movies about Russia, the way a real doctor laughs when he watches *House* or *Doc Martin*. But then, really, it was all just wrong! In recent times the classic poppycock about vampires being afraid of holy water, garlic and crosses has disappeared without trace. But that doesn't mean the screenplays have got any more intelligent. It's just that the old, unfashionable clichés have been replaced by new nonsense – by vampires who are glamorous, mysterious, elegant . . . Various pseudoscientific explanations have appeared – either vampirism is caused by a virus, or a vampire's blood has a low haemoglobin content, or it's a mutation (movie directors are happy to put absolutely anything down to a mutation).

In actual fact, it's all much simpler than that. The first vampires were obviously beings who assumed that form in the Twilight. It was some kind of sadomasochistic complex, very probably a perfectly banal disorder of sexual appetence, but manifested in an Other rather than in a human being. I think that initially there was nothing to it except the sexual excitement that the Other derived from biting pretty girls and being able to do this with impunity, thanks to his special abilities. What else could he do? It was the Middle Ages, social manners were simple, back then there weren't any of our modern, specialised clubs for people who like to bite each other – in those days that led straight to the stake and the fire. One of the first vampires – perhaps this is secret knowledge that they preserve in their legends – experimented with the composition of the toxin that vampires inject into their victim. After all, a standard vampire bite doesn't kill, it plunges the victim into a blissful and helpless condition. By injecting slightly more poison, the vampire induces retrograde amnesia in the victim. And with just a little more – the person dies. Not even from loss of blood – most vampires only need two or three hundred millilitres a month – but simply from poisoning . . .

But one day a vampire dragged his victim into the Twilight. Some version of the toxin developed by one of the first vampires killed the victim – but the death occurred in the Twilight, which has its own laws. And the human being ceased living, but did not completely die. He was transformed into something capable of existing for an infinitely long time, while retaining his reason, acquiring an absolutely incredible regenerative capacity and also, in part, the abilities of an Other – even if he had not possessed them initially.

The crucial point was that this version of the toxin did not kill human cells: it deprived them of the ability to renew themselves naturally by dividing, but it endowed them with a quite fantastic capacity for intra-cellular regeneration. A large dose of the toxin 'preserved' a human being almost instantly – young vampires remained young for ever, any injuries regenerated within minutes. A smaller dose transformed a human being into a vampire gradually – children grew up, young people aged . . . until the toxin triumphed completely and the vampire 'froze' in its final form, like a fly in amber. Without the abilities of an Other, without the Twilight, this would not have been of any great advantage to the vampires – theoretically speaking, a vampire would not have been able to regenerate a severed limb, any totally destroyed cell would have died for ever, there would have been nothing to replace it with . . . But the vampires were helped out here by their magical abilities. On entering the Twilight, they created something like a map of their organism, a Twilight matrix – and so they were able to control their bodies perfectly in the Twilight, by checking against this matrix: they could grow younger or older as they wished, change their appearance, regrow lost limbs . . . and the most experienced and powerful of them could even shift into non-human form.

So far, even in all this, there was nothing truly horrible: it was more an expression of the human dream of immortality. Although in consummate vampires the reproductive function disappeared, those who had not been completely transformed were even capable of producing offspring . . .

There was only one problem. The vampires were no longer

alive. Growth and the multiplication of cells – these are the very essence of life. The 'preserved' cells were no longer alive, but they were not dead. They did not radiate energy into the Twilight, did not make any contribution to the Power on which all Others draw. And consequently they could not receive energy. In order to remain a full-fledged vampire, consume Power and not fall apart owing to the creeping, inevitable death of individual cells, vampires require living cells. Even if they are not their own.

Blood provided these cells. It was the easiest form of all to maintain alive within the vampire organism. By the way, novice vampires prefer to drink blood of their own group, it's easier for them to work with. And the thirst for this blood, the organism's desperate striving not to die completely, developed into the vampire Hunger that is the source of so many problems. Experienced vampires can cope with it, but not all new converts can – that's why vampires' victims die so often from being drunk dry, although in reality the vampire has no need to do this, and he will vomit up the excess blood a few minutes later in any case . . . Blood from blood banks offers a solution, but not a complete one – the vampire's subconscious still demands fresh, hot blood, flowing into his mouth straight from the arteries . . .

There were plenty of other interesting things concerning vampires. Some of them, strangely enough, have filtered through into the human sphere and been incorporated into folklore. For instance, the Master of Vampires. If a human being is turning into a vampire gradually – and that, after all, is the route followed in most cases – the level of toxin in his organism dwindles and it has to be constantly topped up by further bites. And the bites have to be from the same vampire who initiated him. The alternative is death. A fully formed vampire no longer requires this, but for reasons that are obvious to any politician, old and experienced vampires try not to spawn fully formed vampires. It is far better to keep your brood on a short leash and maintain genuinely absolute power over at least a small handful of the undead . . .

By the way, the biology of werewolves and shape-shifters is extremely complicated. However, they don't drink blood, they eat raw flesh. The Light shape-shifters, who prefer to call themselves simply shifters, eat animal flesh. Dark shape-shifters eat human flesh. As far as I can see, here again the problem is mental rather than physiological – Bear told me that he couldn't sense any difference in the influx of Power . . .

At the time I didn't happen to ask about the circumstances in which he had tried human flesh. There were rumours that he used to be a Dark One. And there were rumours that he had fought in a human army and had been a Russian partisan during World War Two, although it could have been another war. There were even rumours that our scientific section had spent a long time studying him, and you could expect them to carry out any kind of experiment . . .

I'm not convinced that knowledge makes people happier: as a general rule, those who are unaware of the truth are far more carefree.

So had Zabulon been right when he quoted that biblical truth to me: 'With great knowledge comes great sorrow'?

No, that way of thinking wasn't right, either. Absolutely no truths are absolute.

I smiled at my sophistical turn of thought, but then decided that it wasn't sophistry after all, more of an aporia or, perhaps, a case of Eubulides' 'paradox of the liar'.

I carried on for a while pondering the binary, ternary and quaternary logic that had been encouraged so vigorously by the cognac. Then I turned the film on again. The hero was killing a vampire. The vampire was screeching malignly, mouthing vague curses and stubbornly refusing to accept the inevitable.

What am I thinking of? Who needs all this – the paradox of the liar and the ancient Greek philosopher Eubulides, whose intellectual games once reduced Greek sages to suicide? Who needs logic, anyway – apart from a handful of armchair scholars, who will reduce it to a well-chewed pap of logical schemas, which more practical scholars will take as the basis for programming languages and mathematical models, which will eventually allow even more practical programmers to write programs making it possible for entirely business-minded directors to film in convincing detail all this stupid shit that is shown in cinemas and broadcast on TV all around the world?

'Having fun?'

I turned my head. Looked at Arina. Nodded.

'Yes, kind of. It's really such incredible nonsense, all this fantasy.'

The witch was looking enchanting again.

'I laughed for a long time at *The Blair Witch Project*,' Arina admitted. 'But you know . . . for two days afterwards I slept with the light on.'

'You did?' I asked, astounded.

'What are you so surprised at? When you live alone in the forest, in a little hut, and you watch horrors like that at night . . .'

I just shook my head. I hadn't seen that film, but maybe there really was something horrific about it.

'I liked *The Lord of the Rings*, though,' said Arina, continuing to share her impressions. 'Nonsense, of course, but what a wonderful fairy tale!'

I didn't try to argue with that. In our duty office *The Lord of the Rings* was shown non-stop: it had become a kind of ritual, like the Russian cosmonauts watching *The White Sun of the Desert*, and the entire population of Russia tuning in to *A Twist of Fate* on New Year's Eve. They didn't really watch the film, it just played along in the background, but from time to time heated arguments would break out about what kind of spell you could use to set your adversary spinning like that and whirl him up to the top of a high tower . . . or whether it was really possible to create an amulet that would imitate the One Ring of Power – so that it would influence its wearer, and be almost impossible to destroy, and make it possible to enter the Twilight effortlessly. Strangely enough, the film had actually contributed something new to practical magic – after all, there's always someone who's simply too stubborn to believe that 'it can't be done' and will come up with a way to do it.

'I suppose everything seemed very strange when you woke up?' I asked.

'Of course,' Arina snorted. 'Well . . . television and computers – they're just human toys. But the medicines really did surprise me, yes . . . They almost put witches completely out of business.'

'They almost did?' I asked.

'Well, yes. Although it was even worse in the 1930s – there was so much the doctors didn't know how to do, but hardly anyone believed in folk healers. The young people would just laugh in your face. Nowadays it's not too bad, in fact it's all right. The first person anyone goes running to is a psychic or a healer,' Arina declared derisively. 'The X-ray or the blood analysis comes after that. It all helps the young witches, they have someone to practise on and the money's good. The charlatans have multiplied too, of course: put the crystal ball on the table, pull the curtains, and away they go, intoning in an otherworldly voice: "I, Eleonora, hereditary White Witch, healer and diviner, mistress of the Tarot, ancient Tibetan magic and sacred incantations, do hereby remove the diadem of singlehood, casting the spell of good fortune . . ." And the doleful music plays, and the little lamps glow in different colours. But if you look closely, it's just that old slut, Tanya Petrova, forty-two years old but looks fifty-five, who suffers from angina pectoris, thrush and an ingrown toenail – she used to be a Young Communist activist at the railway-carriage repair shop, and now she's gone in for being a witch . . .'

Arina gave a very lifelike imitation of the charlatan and I smiled and said: 'We leave people like that alone. They distract attention from the Others.'

'Yes, I know, I know,' Arina sighed. 'I leave them alone, too . . . more or less. I might hex them with eczema on a tender spot . . . sometimes, if I get angry – just to teach them a lesson. And sometimes when I can't take any more I feel like teaching them a serious lesson. But then I think: just what am I doing? We could end up boiling in cauldrons next to each other in hell – me because I deserve it, and her for sheer stupidity and greed!'

I scratched the tip of my nose. The conversation was getting interesting.

'Do you seriously believe in hell?'

'How can you believe in God and not believe in the devil?' Arina asked. And the way she said it immediately made it clear that for her 'God' was written with a capital letter and 'devil' with a small one.

'You believe in the cauldrons and griddles?' I continued. 'Forgive me if that's a personal question . . .'

'Not at all, what's personal about it?' Arina exclaimed in surprise. 'I don't believe in the cauldrons, of course, that's a figure of speech . . .'

'And the griddles?' I asked, unable to resist.

Arina smiled.

'Those too. But the system has to have a feedback loop, there has to be a reward for a righteous life and a punishment for a sinful one.'

'What system?'

'The relationship between the Creator and his creatures. Humans and Others, that is. And while humans have a choice, unfortunately we don't – we're all guilty and doomed to the torments of hell.'

This was getting more and more interesting.

'Okay, so you believe in God, that's your personal business,' I said. 'In actual fact, that's not so very rare for an Other – but usually their view of God is more . . . er . . . humane.'

'What has being humane got to do with God?' Arina asked in surprise. 'Humane attitudes are for human beings. That's obvious even from the name.'

'Okay, let's accept that, but . . . You know, the usual idea is that God values people's good deeds, their behaviour! You can be a magician, an Other, but still do good deeds . . .'

'That contradicts the rules,' Arina said strictly. 'The Bible is quite clear, no ambiguous interpretations are possible – sorcery is evil. "Regard not them that have familiar spirits, neither seek out wizards, to be defiled by them . . ." or, more specifically: "There shall not be found among you any one that maketh his son or his daughter to pass through fire, or that useth divination, or an observer of times, or an enchanter or a witch, or a charmer, or a consulter with familiar spirits, or a wizard, or a necromancer. For all that do these things are an abomination unto the Lord and because of these abominations the Lord thy God doth drive them out from before thee . . ."'

'Have you always been so smart?' I asked. 'So why did you go in for being a witch?'

'What choice does a little peasant girl have?' Arina asked, with a shrug. 'Master Jacob didn't ask me – not when he pulled my skirt up, and not when he shoved me into the Twilight. And once I'd become a witch, I had to live as a witch – there's no way that can be fixed by praying.'

'No way?' I protested. 'It seems to me that you underestimate the mercy of God.'

Arina shrugged again.

'Perhaps you're right,' she agreed with surprising readiness. 'Only I've done more than just work magic. There have been times when I've tormented people to death – starting with Jacob, my teacher. And that's really bad – to kill teachers . . .'

'But he raped you!' I cried indignantly. 'An underage girl!'

'Phooey,' said Arina, with a wave of her hand. 'Big deal. He didn't rape me, anyway, he seduced me. He gave me a sugarplum, as it happens. He hardly beat me at all. And as for me still being a little girl – times were different then, they didn't check your passport, just looked to see if you had any boobs or not. If it hadn't been Jacob the sorcerer, it would have been Vanka the shepherd or Yevgraf Matveevich the master who deflowered me . . .'

She thought for a second and added: 'Most likely Vanka, I wasn't really comely enough for the lord to summon me.'

'And I was sure you killed your teacher for the rape,' I said. 'Remember what you wrote in your statement? "Lascivious brute" – I think that was it.'

'Lascivious brute!' Arina agreed. 'And so he was. I washed for him and cooked for him, and in bed I tried with all my young girl's might! But every month he went to the whorehouse, or seduced some society lady . . . I wept and wailed and hammered at him with my fists, but he just spread his arms and said: "*Meine liebe* Arina – you must understand that man is by his nature a licentious beast, disposed to seek conquests in the field of love. I sleep with you because it is useful for your instruction and training, but you have neither the body nor the experience to lay claim to my full attention." Of course, I realised that he was right. Only I thought I'd filled out really well on my pupil's rations, with my breasts way out here, and a backside like that! And I already knew how to satisfy a man in any way at all. But he still kept going off to others on the side! It was my birthday, I was thirteen, and he spent the day in the brothel! Well . . . I just couldn't stand it. I challenged him to a duel, all fair and square. I hoped he would surrender and ask for forgiveness – I would have forgiven him. But he obviously couldn't believe that I'd grown stronger than him, he fought to the death . . . and so . . .'

Arina sighed.

'You're not making fun of me, are you?' I asked.

'No, why would I?' Arina replied. 'You have to understand, Light One, that life is complicated, it's not black-and-white, but coloured, in fine speckles. Of course, there are some who are villains to the depths of their soul, and some who are righteous through and through. But their kind don't live long. And most are a mixture. Everything's jumbled up together in people, and we came from people, and there's no getting away from that . . .' Arina turned to a hostess who was passing by and said, smiling: 'Dearie, bring us something to eat, will you? Champagne for me and cognac for my beau.'

'I don't want it,' I muttered.

'Then champagne for him too,' Arina said imperturbably.

CHAPTER 7

I WAS CERTAIN they would start to check us out at the airport. Naturally, we passed through passport control without any problems – the vigilant Taiwanese border guards saw non-existent Taiwanese visas in our passports, and the smart Taiwanese computers docilely swallowed their non-existent numbers. Arina dealt with it – to be honest, I would have preferred simply to pass through the control point while invisible, or walk in through the Twilight. But the Witch preferred to create the fake entry documents, muttering: 'Just to keep my hand in . . .' We hadn't got any sleep in the plane after all, but we had drunk plenty of champagne and cognac, and our eyes were tired from watching films, so we were looking in really fine shape. All I personally wanted was to get to the hotel and collapse into sleep.

After passport control we passed through the control point for Others, and once again it all looked remarkably friendly. No one blocked our way: as we approached passport control we simply saw a poster that was only visible to our kind, politely inviting all Others to 'visit the check room'. For humans, the poster had a far more frightening message – it declared that in Taiwan the penalty for importing narcotics was capital punishment, and if you had anything suspicious that had been left in your pockets by oversight, it would be best to drop it into the rubbish bin thoughtfully placed below the poster . . .

'What remarkable trust,' I said as we made our way towards the 'check room'. 'And what if we simply decided not to go? The way out's wide open.'

'Don't be a dunce, charm-caster. I'm sure we've been followed from the moment we left the plane – or rather, from when we were still on the plane.'

'What makes you think that?' I asked in amazement

'Our hostess was a Light Other. Weak, only Seventh-Level. But we weren't concealing ourselves – and I think we did right not to.'

The check room was tucked away closer to the exit, between the toilets and a souvenir stall. (I can't imagine who would buy souvenirs when they've only just got off the plane, but there were a couple of strange individuals like that standing at the stall.) We walked through the door into a perfectly cosy little area with soft furniture, a tiny bar counter, its own toilet and a supervisor's desk. In this case the term 'reception desk' would have been rather more appropriate. I really didn't want to think of the two pretty girls behind the desk as supervisors. In Russian the word carries far too many bureaucratic associations. The girls were twenty at the outside, and they looked even younger than that: they both had pretty, smiling faces – but one was Light and the other was Dark.

That applied in the literal sense too – one of them had very thoroughly bleached hair.

In fact, no one tried to conceal the fact that we had been watched. As we walked in, the light-haired girl was just pouring a second glass of champagne. Arina laughed and directed my glance to the bottle with her eyes – I looked closer and realised it was the same sort that we had been served in the plane.

'Welcome to the land of Taiwan,' the dark-haired girl said, leaning towards us in a half-bow. 'Have you chosen the hotel in which you will stay, venerable Great Ones?'

'The Shangri-La,' Arina replied, accepting a glass.

'Here is a card with the address, which you should show to your driver,' said the dark-haired girl, holding out a small rectangle of cardboard to the witch. 'Unfortunately, not all our drivers here know English . . .'

'We are Others, and we can—' I began, astounded at the absurdity of the situation – after all, we were speaking Chinese.

'If you begin talking in Guoyu or Taiwanese, the driver will feel very awkward. The card indicates the approximate cost of the journey to the hotel in new Taiwanese dollars. If the driver demands a greater amount, pay him, and then call the phone number on the card to let us know.'

'And then what will happen?' I asked out of curiosity.

'He will be sacked,' the girl twittered. 'And your money will be returned. May your stay in Taiwan be calm and joyful.'

'Do we have to fill in any forms?' I asked.

'There is no need for that, Mr Gorodetsky,' the girl replied in Russian – and not just in Russian acquired by magical means. Her speaking voice had the very slightest hint of an accent – just enough to add a little piquancy – and perfectly clear Moscow pronunciation.

I wondered whether, if I had been from St Petersburg, I would have been met by a girl who had studied or worked there.

Feeling slightly embarrassed, I finished my champagne, took the card, bowed briefly to the girl (now where did I get manners like that?) and then Arina and I left.

'They do their job well,' Arina said approvingly.

'I like their approach to money-grabbing taxi drivers,' I said, nodding in agreement.

'Certainly. Although I should point out that frequently one taxi driver working here in Taipei feeds half of his mountain village. The temptation to rip off a tourist is very great . . . But I agree, it's not good to abuse tourists. Especially if those tourists are us.'

'And did you notice that their level of Power was screened?' I asked. 'Of course, I didn't scan them actively . . .'

'The Light One's Third-Level,' Arina replied as she watched out for a car. 'But the Dark One's a smart girl: she covered herself well. She had an interesting kind of amulet made of seaweed and fish skin . . . I didn't get through her defences either. Come on, there's the taxi stand.'

I'd been wrong about the airport. The serious talk was waiting for us at the hotel.

We took adjacent rooms. (Arina had enough delicacy not to suggest moving in together.) I looked over my room and stood for a minute at the immense French window that covered an entire wall, gazing out at Taipei as it was flooded by the lights of evening. The sight was astounding. And not at all because of the skyscrapers, although right in front of the hotel there was one that simultaneously resembled a Chinese pagoda and some exotic fruit, thrusting its pinnacle up into the sky. There are bigger skyscrapers in New York, Shanghai and Hong Kong.

The astounding thing here was the contrast. Taipei was not such a very tall city: on all sides there were entire neighbourhoods of buildings no more than three or four storeys high. The isolated high-rise structures should have looked alien here.

But the contrast was astonishingly harmonious. The old city, huddling down against the ground, looked like undergrowth, with the skyscrapers sprouting up through it. The low, far-from-modern buildings were not in the least ashamed of their appearance – on the contrary, they actually seemed to take pride in the glittering modern structures rising up from among them.

I involuntarily recalled the vociferous protest campaigns that had raged in St Petersburg when there were plans to construct a skyscraper there. All that hysterical howling about the destruction of the cultural environment, the disfigurement of the glorious line of the horizon, the possibility that unique seventeenth-century ruins, or even the camps of primeval human beings, might be buried under the skyscraper . . .

Yes, of course the mentality in St Petersburg is special, cultivated on the swamps by the damp, piercing wind. But I would quite happily have sent all the protesters to live for a month or two in an old Petersburg communal apartment block, with mouldy walls and narrow little windows. And then I would have asked them to vote on whether it was necessary and possible to erect modern buildings in an old city.

After all, love of one's country doesn't simply mean that you want to preserve as many tottering old ruins as possible. Otherwise the whole of North America would live in Indian wigwams and the log huts of the first settlers; London would consist entirely of the Victorian and Edwardian buildings so dear to the heart of the tourist, but not so very comfortable on the inside; and as for Africa and Asia – well, enough said . . .

I looked at the soaring skyscrapers and thought that I was beginning to understand the Chinese a little bit better. The ones living on the mainland and the ones on this island.

And I even envied them a little.

I opened my suitcase, took out some clean underclothes and walked into the bathroom. Everything was very stylish. There was even a little television set standing on a shelf beside the sink. An expensive business: all these televisions for bathrooms require insulation against damp and they cost big money. I once wanted to put one like that in our bathroom at home, to watch the news while I was getting washed, shaving and brushing my teeth, but the price put me right off the idea.

I picked up the television – it was absolutely tiny, only twelve inches wide. I could easily lift it with one hand. I turned it round. At the back I saw microcircuits glittering behind the holes in a standard plastic cover. How come? The guests get washed, splash water about, take hot showers, fill the bathroom with clouds of steam – and there's a TV set standing here, with no insulation? It'll blow a circuit! It might last a year, but that circuit will still blow! Why hadn't they put in an expensive one, a proper one?

Well, for the same reason that they don't demolish old buildings until they fall down on their own, an inner voice whispered to me. A special TV would cost two thousand dollars. One like this barely costs a hundred. Surely it's far simpler to change it once every year or so than invest money in technology that rapidly becomes obsolete?

I put the television back down, switched on the BBC and stepped into the shower, realising that, for all my lack of sophistication, I had managed to grasp an intriguing point that was very far from our Russian mentality. Back home there either wouldn't be a TV in the bathroom or there would be an insanely expensive one, and the price of the room would rocket by fifty per cent. We don't like disposable items. We can still remember how to mend nylon tights, wash plastic bags and go to fetch the milk in a can. We can find a multitude of uses for an empty yogurt carton – from growing seedlings to storing small change.

To some extent Russia has unexpectedly found itself marching in step with the countries of the West and their obsession with ecology, economising resources and recycling. Not because the green movement is popular here, but because of this centuries-old habit of economising. Only, as often happens in Russia, we take everything to absurd extremes – in both directions: the same people who darn their tights also buy hugely expensive cars and domestic appliances . . .

I wonder if that's a plus or a minus for us, I thought as I sluiced myself down under the shower head. Take this shower, for instance. The head's not cheap, probably quite expensive, in fact, with its tiny little holes for the water and valve for sucking in air. Self-indulgence? Not exactly. A shower like this uses about half as much water as mine in Moscow does. But we've only just realised that water costs money – and a lot of it! No one really appreciates what they have in abundance, so we Russians have never really valued or cared for our forests, rivers and natural environment – or even ourselves, basically. The attitude in that old one-liner 'Shall we wash these children or have new ones?' is still around, only nowadays we Russians take care of the children . . . but not of ourselves. What has to happen to us before we understand that we have to take good care of everything we have, of every tree in our boundless forests, every little stream that isn't even marked on the maps, every village with only five households, every soldier drafted into the army, every man in the street toiling under his dreary daily burden? What will it take to change us? Communism didn't change us – it valued people in words, but even then not all of them, and only as cogwheels in a single, integrated mechanism. Democracy didn't change us: on the contrary, it gave us all the freedom to hate each other. What is it that we want? Maybe, like the Jews thousands of years ago, only pain and death, to lose our state and be scattered throughout the world, despised and oppressed by other nations – maybe only that will allow the Russian nation to come to its senses and recover its unity. To unite, but not as it has united in the past – without counting the losses or acknowledging the cost of victory – but on some other level? All great peoples have to suffer catastrophes sooner or later, to pass through their own national holocausts: this is a lesson known by China, which was once dying of opium addiction and has been torn apart, and by Germany, which suffered defeat in two wars and the disgrace of Nazism. And it should also be remembered by Russia, which has suffered fratricidal revolutions and bloody wars . . .

But for some reason it isn't.

I turned off the water and looked at the murmuring television.

One inclination we Russians are always ready to indulge at the slightest nonsensical excuse – such as a cheap TV or a shower head – is to meditate on the fate and fortunes of our Homeland and the Universe. We're always good at that.

I towelled myself down, put on a bathrobe and walked out of the bathroom. And that was when the doorbell rang quietly.

Somehow I was certain it wasn't Arina.

And I had no intention of playing the fool and asking who had come visiting.

'Come on in, gentlemen.'

There were two gentlemen – a young one and an elderly one. And there was also a middle-aged lady.

All three of them were Others, and all Light Ones. They had politely not masked their auras. The elderly man was a Fourth-Level Magician. The young man was a Second-Level Magician. The woman was a First-Level Clairvoyant. Oho. I didn't think the Taiwan Watch could exactly be packed full of First- and Second-Level Power. So my unofficial visit had been taken with all due seriousness and appropriate respect.

'Will you allow us to enter, Anton Sergeevich?' the young man enquired politely. And then, without waiting for my permission, he continued: 'You may call my male companion Esteemed Mr Pasha, my female companion Esteemed Miss Lena and me – simply Petya.'

'Come in, Pasha, come in, Lena, and you come in too, Petya,' I replied and stepped aside. Naturally the Russian names were a gesture of traditional Chinese courtesy – they would have introduced themselves to an American as John, Jim and Jill, for example. 'Please forgive my bathrobe. I took a shower after the journey.'

'That is very good,' Petya said approvingly while his companions came in and seated themselves in the armchairs. It was only then that I realised there were obviously too many chairs in the room – four of them. I could even see that two of them were a slightly different colour from the others and were standing in rather inconvenient spots in the passage. 'A healthy mind in a healthy body,' Petya concluded.

'As they say in Russian: "You have to choose one or the other",' I joked sourly.

'They are mistaken,' said Petya, waiting for me to sit down. I sat down and swore under my breath – I felt like striking an affectedly casual pose by crossing my legs, but in the bathrobe that was impossible.

Which was what they had been counting on.

Okay, I'd have to put up with it. No point in getting fancy and changing the bathrobe into a suit, or teleporting my own clothes onto myself. That would just be too affected altogether.

Once he was sure we were all seated, Petya himself perched on the edge of an armchair, looked at Pasha and asked me: 'Did you have a good flight? Did you have any problems on the way? Did you like our airport? Have you had a chance to enjoy the architecture and atmosphere of Taipei?'

'Yes, no, yes, no,' I replied. 'Are my respected visitors in good health? Have the consequences of the latest typhoon been liquidated?' (To be honest, I didn't know when there had last been a typhoon here and how strong it was, but they happen all the time in Taiwan.) 'Are the Dark Ones up to their mischief?'

The elderly man suddenly smiled.

'And the views of the rice and tea harvest are good here, too,' he said, with a nod. 'All right, Anton, let's stop the fencing. A visit by such a powerful member of the Russian Watch is a conspicuous event on our quiet little island. We would like to enquire what has brought you here – and with such a surprising companion.'

I didn't reply immediately.

For some reason Arina and I had never discussed this situation at all, even though we realised that our arrival would not go unnoticed.

'This isn't a business trip,' I said. 'It's a private visit.'

The elderly man nodded and looked at me, waiting.

'Certain events took place in Moscow . . . some time ago . . .' I went on cautiously.

'We know,' said the woman. But she didn't clarify.

'Since I was personally involved in the events, I took what happened very much to heart,' I continued, finding myself constructing the phrase in an almost Asian style. 'When the esteemed Witch Arina and I met in London, I was informed by her that, as often happens, the same thing had already happened somewhere else . . . and that the highly esteemed Mr Fan Wen-yan, who works in the Gugun Imperial Museum – the Gugun National Imperial Museum' – I corrected myself – 'can cast some light on that old story . . .'

The Taiwanese exchanged glances.

'Your companion is wanted by the Inquisition and by your own Watch,' said Pasha. 'Does that not perturb you?'

'As a Higher Other of the Night Watch I have the right to choose my own tactics and decide how to act,' I said cautiously. 'And in addition, at the present moment her interests and my own coincide. And as for the Inquisition . . . unfortunately, I am not able to guarantee the detention of the Witch Arina. She is in possession of a Minoan Sphere and at any moment she can disappear to absolutely anywhere at all. Teleportation with the assistance of this artefact cannot be intercepted or traced,' I added, to make things perfectly clear.

'We are aware of that,' Pasha said, nodding. 'We acknowledge your right to make this visit.'

'And your right to choose your own tactics,' added Lena.

'And to speak to Mr Fan Wen-yan,' said Petya, putting in his own kopeck's worth.

'But any unsanctioned use of magic against the Others and people of Taiwan will be punished with the full severity of the law,' Pasha continued.

'Even if you are provoked, in danger or only indirectly responsible,' Lena advised me.

'Mr Fan Wen-yan will decide for himself whether or not to have dealings with you. You must not badger him,' added Petya.

All right, fair enough. Honesty had proved better than politics.

I paused and then nodded: 'Thank you, dear colleagues. I had not dared to hope for or expect such a cordial reception and magnanimous conditions. Naturally, it is not our intention either to violate your customs and traditions or to inconvenience in any way the Others and ordinary citizens of Taiwan.'

Pasha smiled.

'We are all citizens of Taiwan, Mr Gorodetsky, including the Others, both Light and Dark. Allow me once again to welcome you to our island and . . . I can sense several artefacts in your bag, and I find one of them especially interesting. May I take a look at it?'

Especially interesting?

There was nothing magical in my suitcase, apart from the suitcase itself being enchanted. And in my bag . . . there was the comb that Svetlana had given me for my birthday, nothing special, simply so that my hair would grow well and the style would hold . . . a few small bottles of healing potions, also from her – the magical equivalent of painkillers and antacids . . . a perfectly ordinary silver ring with a piece of amber in which a small amount of Power had been accumulated, also a present, but Olga had given me it after a certain Watch operation – nothing unusual, every second Other wears a ring like that . . .

'What artefact do you mean?' I asked.

'It has the form of a chalice,' Petya clarified politely.

So that was it . . .

I walked over to the bag, took out Erasmus's chalice and held it out to Petya. He hid his hands behind his back.

The chalice was taken by Pasha, who politely pretended not to have noticed my gaffe. Or perhaps it wasn't a gaffe? Who was I supposed to hand the artefact to – the most powerful of them, as a sign of respect, or the weakest, so that he could check to see if it was dangerous before handing it on to his boss?

These Chinese rules of courtesy are so complicated!

Pasha took the chalice and turned it round in his hands. Then he looked at me.

'Do you know how to use this, Gorodetsky?'

'No.'

'And are you sure you want to find out?'

'Yes,' I replied without hesitation.

But Pasha didn't explain anything to me. He looked at the chalice, stroking it with his dry, tenacious fingers as if he was making conversation. Perhaps he was a tale-ender – a rare specialisation that involved the use of objects to extract information from the past . . .

Pasha looked at Lena. She shrugged. Then he looked at Petya. He nodded.

'This vessel contains grief and sadness, Gorodetsky,' said Pasha. 'You should know that if you wish to drink from it.'

'We know how to awaken the prophecy,' Lena confirmed. 'It is simple.'

'But we will not tell you that,' Petya said in conclusion. 'We do not wish to be responsible for the possible consequences.'

They all got up together and moved towards the door. Petya went out first and stood in the corridor, holding the door open, then Lena followed. Pasha lingered for a moment and gave me a look of either fellow feeling or compassion.

'In Europe it is usually thought that always and everywhere there are at least two paths to follow, and one of them is good. In Asia we know that there might not be any paths at all, or there might be a countless number. But that does not mean that even one of them will prove to be good.'

'I live in Russia, I replied. 'That is not Europe, and it is not Asia. We have no paths at all, only directions, but that has never disconcerted us.'

Pasha raised one eyebrow, pondering my words. Then he smiled, nodded and went out.

Petya closed the door behind him.

I slipped off the bathrobe and dressed hurriedly, and a minute later I was knocking at the door of the adjacent room. It opened with a click, although Arina was standing at the window, looking out at Taipei.

'Did you have any visitors?' I asked.

'They just left,' Arina answered, without turning round. 'Pasha, Lena and Petya. Fourth-, First- and Second-Level. Light Ones.'

'How amusing – they were in my room as well,' I said. 'And they just left, too.'

'Childish tricks,' Arina remarked scornfully, 'I expect we even had identical conversations.'

'Probably,' I agreed. 'Didn't they try to arrest you?'

'I explained that it was pointless,' Arina replied. 'But they could see that for themselves, anyway. Well, then – shall we go to see Fan?'

'"I'll take you to the museum, my sister told me,"' I murmured, quoting Mayakovsky. 'Why be in such a hurry? I'd rather have a decent meal, catch up on my sleep and have the meeting tomorrow.'

'All right,' Arina agreed readily. 'There are several good restaurants right here in the hotel. Or we could go out into town. I told you that you won't get poisoned here, didn't I?

'Yes, you did,' I replied. 'Are you feeling sad about something?'

Arina looked at me and then turned back to the window.

'Time, Anton, time . . . I look at how the city has changed, and I realise how I've changed myself. An old crone who looks young – strong, healthy, immortal – but an old crone.'

'I'm sorry,' I said. 'Why is it like that for you witches? If an Other is even Fifth-Level, he can keep his body young . . .'

'We're witches,' Arina replied, as if that was an explanation. She paused for a moment and then added anyway: 'The way we absorb our Power is a bit different. We draw it from the earth, the wind, the rivers . . . nature doesn't know how to be eternally young, Anton. Nature was ancient when people were still no different from animals. Mountains grow old and crumble, rivers change their courses, earth is carried away by the wind . . . We're the same. Theoretically probably immortal – like all Others. But we grow old, although slowly. It's very hard to take, charm-weaver . . . I can recall drinking sweet plum wine and kissing my lover – one of the thousands I've had – in this city. But I was still young then. And the city was different. And life seemed brighter.'

'But has the city really got worse?'

'Not even Moscow has got worse, although it's been trying hard enough in recent years,' Arina snorted. 'No, it's not worse, just unfamiliar. And that's what makes my old heart ache.'

I felt awkward, as if I'd glanced through a keyhole and seen something that wasn't intended for my eyes at all.

'Come on, let's go and try those Chinese delicacies,' Arina said, rousing herself and turning away from the window. 'After that I intend to visit the spa, but I don't suppose you'll be keeping me company?'

'I think not,' I agreed.

'Quite sure? They offer a discount for a party of two,' Arina laughed. 'A jacuzzi with a view of the city at night, a massage, aromatic oils . . .'

'"Be gone, you libertine, your caress is repugnant,"' I declaimed, modifying Kozma Prutkov's verse slightly. And immediately I realised just how inappropriate it was in this case.

'That's not it, Anton:

> "Be gone, you toothless hag! Your caress is repugnant!
> From out your countless wrinkles artificial pigment
> Crumbles like plaster, dropping on your breast.
> Be mindful of the Styx and bid these passions rest!"'

'I'm sorry,' I muttered.

'It's all right,' Arina laughed. 'I'm not some old Greek woman, I'm a genuine Russian. An old woman, yes, but with my own teeth – note that for the record! And I won't argue with the conclusion either:

> "You should be lying now – long overdue the day! –
> Calcined to crumbling dust, within an urn of clay"'

'Arina, please accept my apologies.'

Arina chuckled again.

'Forget it. And thanks for reminding me of Volodya . . .'

'What Volodya?'

'Well, not Putin, obviously. Volodya Zhemchuzhnikov, the poet . . .'

'One of the four authors who were "Kozma Prutkov"?' I asked, gazing at Arina's dreamy smile. 'Did you have an affair with him, then?'

'I don't tell anecdotes about famous and historical individuals,' Arina snapped. 'I was brought up better than that. I could tell you about a certain count, without giving you his name – what a joker he was! He once came to visit me in a carriage, absolutely naked and carrying an absolutely immense bouquet of white roses. Well, he wasn't shy of his own driver, naturally enough, and I lived in a secluded spot. He walked straight in without being announced – and his wife was sitting there with me: she'd come to complain about her husband's debauchery . . .'

'I'm certain that could not have been a pure coincidence,' I remarked in a quiet voice.

'Well then, what did the joker come up with, once he grasped just how embarrassing the situation was?' Arina went on. 'He threw the bouquet down at his wife's feet and, without so much as a glance at me, flung himself on her like some wild beast. And he shouted: "What have you done to me? You have bewitched me! At the mere thought of you, I tore my clothes off in the carriage!" And the stupid fool believed him. She pulled a ring with a magnificent ruby off her finger, put it in my hand and whispered: "Thank you, enchantress!" Then she bundled her husband up in the tablecloth and dragged him off home. And wouldn't you know, the next day he sent me a matching bracelet to go with the ring . . . he didn't show up himself, the great stud.'

Arina stopped talking, pleased with her story.

'You've convinced me yet again that Witches view the world from a highly original perspective,' I said.

'Not Witches, but women, and not the world, but men,' Arina laughed. 'All right, let's go. I won't try to seduce you, especially since you have a spell on you that your wife put there . . .'

'You already admitted that was a lie,' I remarked.

'I did? I'm really getting old,' Arina sighed.

CHAPTER 8

When I found my swimming trunks in among the clean underclothes in the suitcase, I examined them thoughtfully for a while.

I'd never really thought of Taiwan as a seaside resort. But it was an island, after all. And it was in the south.

Could Sveta really have sensed that I would end up by the sea? I wondered what it was called here – Yellow Sea, Sea of China, Sea of Japan . . . So far the only ones I had swum in were the Black Sea and the Mediterranean.

But somehow I doubted that fate would hand me such a pleasant surprise. The only amusements for me would be the hotel and the museum . . .

The hotel! But of course. It was a five-star hotel, and that meant—

A couple of minutes later I was standing in the lift, wearing the bathrobe over my trunks and a pair of hotel slippers. And a couple of minutes after that I was lying in cool water and looking up at the sky.

The hotel swimming pool was on the roof. Huge, deep and almost completely deserted – either because it was so early or because all the other guests were busy with other things. Apart from me, the only person there was a fat man of European appearance, lounging in the round bowl of the jacuzzi that projected into one corner of the pool and gazing at me benignly. Probably the right thing to do would have been to start dashing across the smooth surface of the water, tearing it open with a lively crawl, a stubborn breaststroke or an energetic butterfly. Maybe my example would have inspired the chubby hotel guest to take up sport and develop a wonderful physique – and could eventually have led to him changing his life completely.

But I myself could only swim in one style, the one that we used to call 'frog paddling' when I was a kid, which is basically the most primitive possible variety of breaststroke, known to mankind ever since Neolithic times.

And, apart from that, I felt too lazy.

I splashed about in the pool for a while, gazing at the clear blue sky. Early September in Taiwan is quite a hot period, and it rains frequently too. But this morning it was remarkably cool and sunny at the same time.

It would be good to stay on here for a few days . . . No, it would be better to come here with my wife and daughter. To take a look at a different natural setting and culture, try the local cuisine and really go swimming in the sea. It was a shame Svetlana didn't want to come back to the Watch. With her abilities . . .

I sighed and climbed out of the water. It was time to have breakfast and look for Arina – the Witch wasn't likely to be in the mood to sleep until midday.

We set out for the museum in a taxi, although I had suggested getting to know the Taiwan underground system. The museum was located outside the city, and we drove past new and old neighbourhoods along a rapid-transit highway. I gazed out of the window curiously.

'You should travel more, Gorodetsky,' Arina said, glancing round at me. 'Otherwise when you're away on business external appearances will distract you from the essence of things.'

'Everything just doesn't add up, somehow,' I admitted.

'Take your example from your bosses,' Arina continued. 'Gesar, for example. Born in Tibet. Worked in territory that is now modern China and India. And then in Europe – in Holland.'

'Really?' I asked in surprise.

'Of course. Although that was a long time ago. Then he moved to Russia. St Petersburg, Moscow . . . Settled in Central Asia. And now he's back in Moscow again. I wonder where he'll end up next?'

'I think at this stage Gesar's lost interest in shifting about.'

Arina laughed.

'Oh, come on Anton. As long as the work's still interesting, Gesar stays put. But after that – he leaves.'

'He has no time to get bored in Moscow,' I muttered. The very idea that Gesar could leave Moscow and go to France or China, call himself Antoine Guésare or Ge Sa-ro seemed like total and absolute balderdash.

'Maybe so,' Arina agreed easily. 'Maybe so . . .'

Our taxi, driven by a taciturn Taiwanese who kept turning round constantly to give us a friendly smile, went through some kind of tunnel and turned right. We drove up to the museum or, rather, a parking lot, beyond which a park began, and further off, against a background of hills, we could see buildings – modern buildings, but in the traditional Chinese style, yellow and turquoise, with pagoda roofs.

Arina settled up with the driver and spoke to him briefly, provoking approving laughter. We bought two tickets and set off along the broad avenue through the park. There were plenty of visitors: European and Asian tourists, Taiwanese as well – represented primarily by school excursions.

'I hope Mr Fan is working today,' I said. 'And that we won't have to walk round the whole museum looking for him . . . although I really wouldn't mind taking a look at the precious exhibits. Do you know if there are many magical artefacts among them?'

'Not many,' said Arina, shaking her head. 'The Chinese have traditionally kept the applied arts and magic separate. Their most interesting magical artefacts look entirely banal: a pair of chopsticks, for example, a plain-looking fan or a scroll made of strips of bamboo . . .'

I suddenly noticed a young Chinese moving purposefully towards us. The main stream of people was flowing into the museum, but there were some people coming out, and this guy was definitely heading towards us.

'Is that Fan?' I asked.

Arina didn't get a chance to reply. The young guy stopped in front of us and bowed his head slightly.

'Mr Anton, Miss Arina. Mr Fan Wen-yan asks you to wait for him in the Zhishan Garden, in the Orchid Pavilion. Mr Fan Wen-yan believes that the beauty of that spot is salutary and inspiring for a meeting that flatters him so greatly. Mr Fan Wen-yan asks you to follow me.'

The young man was speaking Chinese, and he was not an Other. Bowing once again, he set off along the avenue, without even looking to see if we were following him.

Arina and I exchanged glances.

'And Mr Fan Wen-yan also believes that if any unforeseen situations should arise, it is better for this to happen in the park, and not in the building among the precious exhibits,' Arina laughed. 'Well, anyway, it would be impolite to reject his invitation . . .'

Turning off the avenue to the right, we walked into the park, which, in fact, was every bit as interesting as the buildings – it was laid out around a number of pools according to all the rules of art (I don't know if that hackneyed term 'Feng Shui' is appropriate here, but there was clearly a definite structure to the layout). The ponds were covered with flowers, which I recognised (although I was doubtful at first) as lotuses. The pastoral setting was so idyllic that it seemed unnatural, like some picture that had come to life or the virtual reality of fantasy novels.

About twenty metres from a beautiful pavilion, which really was smothered in orchids and built, naturally, in the traditional Chinese style, the young man stopped. He looked at us and said seriously: 'I cannot go any further. I am sorry.'

I realised why he could not continue to accompany us. Hanging over the pavilion was a Sphere of Inattention – one of the simplest of spells, but absolutely effective as far as humans are concerned. In principle, the small building was still visible to people strolling in the park, but no one kept his eyes fixed on it or tried to go any closer. An unpretentious but efficient means of keeping away prying eyes and ears.

'Thank you,' I said and Arina and I walked to the pavilion.

Everything had been prepared for our conversation. Waiting for us on an elegant little table were a teapot, cups, candied fruits and some other kinds of local sweetmeats. Soft red cushions had been thoughtfully arranged on the benches. In addition to the Sphere of Inattention, I detected another five spells to prevent eavesdropping and spying by Others, one more directed against humans – not to distract their attention, but to prevent anyone taking photos or videos – and one with a strange design. At first I suspected that it affected the minds and the vision of people sitting in the pavilion, but having studied it a little I realised it was relatively innocuous. Its entire effect consisted in making the already wonderful view on all sides even more amazing, in addition to awaking in the soul a gentle sadness and sense of peace in the face of nature. I thought for a moment and allowed the spell to affect me. A very elegant and agreeable magic.

'Why, the jokers,' Arina said good-naturedly, looking round the pavilion. She was obviously doing the same as I was – untangling the net of spells. 'How many did you spot?'

'Two against people, five against Others, one for our own enjoyment. A very amusing little spell, so Chinese – woven out of air, water and earth . . .'

'That's right,' Arina agreed, with obvious disappointment, giving me a sideways glance. 'That's what there is. You're a good charm-weaver, Anton . . .'

'Thank you.'

'Don't say thank you when a Witch praises you,' Arina said unexpectedly. 'It's a bad sign.'

I looked at her.

'Feeling nervous?'

Arina nodded.

Just at that moment an elderly Taiwanese man appeared out of the trees and came towards us. Short, stout and smiling, he looked like one of the incarnations of the Buddha. A Light One, of the fourth level of Power, seemingly without a specialisation in any particular aspect of magic – he practised all of them a little bit . . .

'Mr Fan,' I said, getting up and bowing. To my surprise, Arina also stood up and lowered her head quite sincerely.

'Stop it, stop it!' exclaimed Fan, waving his arms. 'Let's have none of this oriental ceremonial! It's quite unnecessary, believe me, we're civilised Others, we live in the twenty-first century . . .'

He walked up into the pavilion, shook me firmly by the hand, touched his lips to Arina's palm and then looked around with undisguised pleasure.

'Ah, how I love this place! And how rarely I am granted the opportunity simply to sit in peace and quiet in pleasant company . . . Will you have tea? We Taiwanese are crazy about green tea. But in Russia you mostly drink black tea, right? With milk? Or is it the English who drink it with milk?'

'We drink green tea and black tea, with milk and with lemon,' I said.

'With milk and with lemon?' asked Fan, wincing. 'At the same time?'

'Oh, no,' I said, feeling myself involuntarily starting to relax. 'Either one or the other. We have lots of different ways.'

'Excellent!' exclaimed Fan, beaming. 'This mutual enrichment of cultures and fusion of customs is a wonderful thing. I like Russia a lot in general, I like reading Dostoevsky and watching Russian films.'

I took the final remark to be an oriental politeness and didn't enquire which Russian films he had seen. We sat down and Mr Fan poured our tea himself.

'What has brought you to Formosa in these delightful days of our autumn?' Fan continued. 'Apart from simple interest in these exotic climes? No, no, don't answer – allow me to guess for myself!'

We allowed him. Fan pondered for a few moments, drinking his tea in tiny sips, then suddenly exclaimed: 'I know! The Tiger! I heard about the skirmish that the Moscow Watch was involved in!'

'The Tiger,' I admitted. In all honesty, the gleeful comedy that Fan had played out was not much better than the comically managed visit to the hotel. But at least it was more upbeat and cheerful to watch.

'A terrible . . . er . . . creature,' said Fan. 'I'm not sure that the word "creature" suits the case, it's unlikely that the Tiger has any essential substance as we understand it. But we have to call him something, do we not?'

'You have already encountered him,' said Arina. It wasn't a question, but Fan nodded.

'Yes, yes, yes. An old, painful story. Eighty-something years ago . . .' He fell silent for a moment and something genuinely heartfelt showed through the affected jollity. 'I had a friend. A very good friend, we were inseparable. These days we would be considered lovers, but then the idea never even occurred to anyone – including us. But on the spiritual level we were very close, closer than married couples or brothers.'

Fan put down his cup and looked at Arina.

'He was a Prophet and I was the only one to hear his first prophecy. Prophets often forget what they prophesy and only remember some time later. But Li remembered his prophecy. So we were able to discuss it . . . and decide what to do. Li was greatly concerned that I too had heard the prophecy and was therefore doomed to become the Tiger's victim.'

'You didn't think of telling the prophecy to humans?'

'No,' said Fan. 'We didn't. Not a single human has heard it . . . and neither has any Other apart from me. When my time comes, I shall take it with me into the Twilight and bury it there.'

'I see,' Arina said, nodding. After a brief pause, she added: 'Those were hard times.'

'There are no easy times,' Fan remarked.

'The very existence of the Celestial Empire as a unitary state was in doubt.'

'The Celestial Empire is now divided,' said Fan.

'But perhaps the outcome could have been worse?' Arina asked insinuatingly.

Fan poured himself some more tea. Then he said: 'We knew that if the prophecy remained with us, the Tiger would come. The legends are preserved in the chronicles – and we could surmise why some prophets had preferred to die without telling anyone what they had foreseen in the future. We did not want to die. And we started searching for a way out . . .'

'The simplest way out is to change the prophecy,' said Arina. 'I had a similar case. It threatened . . . a very bad future for Russia. We told the prophecy to humans, and then I did something to prevent it from being realised.'

'Then it was not a prophecy, but a prediction,' Fan said, with a shrug. 'A prophecy that has been proclaimed to humans cannot be annulled. It will be realised.'

'It was a prophecy and I changed it!' Arina said firmly.

Fan pondered for a moment. Then he looked at Arina in a different way.

'I am very sorry, esteemed Miss Arina. But a prophecy that has reached humans always comes true. The only thing that can be done is to postpone it by destroying the shortest and most obvious route to its realisation. But a prophecy that has not been realised in its own time will only accumulate power and strike again, with even graver consequences. I am very sorry.'

Arina's eyelid twitched. Then red patches appeared on her cheeks.

'That's nonsense!'

'I am afraid not, Miss Arina. As you can understand, I studied this matter very closely at one time. And what's more, I continued studying it later. For eighty years I have been collecting all the information I can find about prophecies, the Tiger, the possibility of changing the outcomes of prophecies . . .'

'You can't know everything!' Arina cried: it was almost the only time I had seen her lose her self-control. 'You don't know my case! The prophecy didn't happen and it won't happen.'

'I do not know what it was that you heard in your time and what you did,' said Fan, bowing his head. 'And I do not dare to ask, although if you share it with me, I shall be grateful. But ask yourself – is what you tried to avert possible today?'

The only sounds in the silence that followed were the chirping of birds and the chattering of insects in the park. I remembered what Arina had told me.

To be honest, the only thing that raised any doubts was the 'tsar'.

But then, prophecies are always allegorical, they are transmitted through the consciousness of the prophet. Arina's friend who liked rhyming her prophecies couldn't have said 'president', could she? Or 'general secretary'?

'But could the prophecy already have come true?' I asked. 'Arina, some things could quite easily be regarded—'

'Shut up!' Arina growled. 'Fan, how can the Tiger be killed?'

'He cannot be killed,' Fan said, shrugging again. 'The Tiger is the embodiment of the Twilight in the real world. Can you kill the Twilight, Witch?'

'I'm an Enchantress!'

'You have changed your colour, but you were, are and always will be a Witch,' Fan replied calmly. 'There is no insult in my words. Let me ask again: can you kill the Twilight?'

'Why does he come, Fan?' I asked quickly, to get in before Arina.

I didn't think he would answer. But Fan did begin to answer, and with obvious enjoyment – he had probably not had such interested listeners very often.

'The Twilight needs Power. This Power is provided by people, ordinary human beings, and the greater their joy or sorrow, the more Power there is. The Twilight is not cruel, but it demands what it needs. Human joy suits it perfectly well, but it rarely happens that there is more joy than sorrow. Far more often people become indifferent and jaded – and, in that case, the

Twilight starts to starve. The blue moss is the Twilight's simplest and weakest instrument: it absorbs Power and can bolster human emotions. But if there are more and more indifferent people in the world, if good and evil give way to quietude and apathy . . . then the Twilight brings forth the Tiger. Prophets are born constantly, but if the Twilight has sufficient nourishment, they can act as they wish – utter good prophecies or bad ones, conceal them, forget them . . . But if humankind calms down, tells itself that it has achieved a state of equilibrium and calm – then the Tiger comes to the Prophets. He makes no distinction between good and bad prophecies. All he wants is for them to be proclaimed. Sooner or later a Prophet opens the door for great upheavals, grief and joy. And the Twilight sates its appetite once again. It is not malicious. It is simply alive . . . and, like everything living, it wants to eat.'

Fan picked up a small piece of something candied and tossed it into his mouth.

'But the Twilight is simply . . . simply . . .' I faltered to a stop.

'Simply what?' Fan laughed. 'Simply another world? Simply another dimension of reality? And we, the Others, who can enter into it, who can simply say 'burn' and spout forth flame, or transform our bodies into those of demons, or see the future? Esteemed Anton, you make use of magic and you take all this absolutely for granted. But exactly how do you make use of magic?'

'I enter the Twilight . . . or simply—' I broke off and vowed to myself not to use that word again. 'Or I reach out to it . . .'

'And then what? Do you grow cannon instead of arms and enema tubes instead of fingers? How do you fight and heal? How can you talk Chinese, when you have never studied it? Where do you think all of this comes from? From the Twilight? In response to your wishes? What is the Twilight to you, then? A computer with a screen that you can just prod with your finger to get what you want? But a computer was invented by someone, someone made it, and someone wrote the programs for it. A computer has no rational mind and you cannot make it brew you coffee or weed the vegetable patch. But the Twilight docilely shares with you the Power that it needs itself and allows you to perform one trick after another . . .'

'But what for, if it is rational?' I exclaimed.

'The blue moss also eats Power as well as gathering it,' Fan laughed. 'The Twilight needs the blue moss for one purpose. The Tiger for another. And the Others for yet another. But all of us together do the same thing – we stir up humankind, we jolt people, make them do something, invent something, strive for something . . . sometimes they achieve success, sometimes they take a beating. We are all part of the Twilight, its symbiotes if you like. Its hands and feet, eyes and ears. The rakes and spades it uses to cultivate its vegetable patch – humankind. Do you wish to rebel against the Tiger? You will be rebelling against the Twilight. And therefore against yourself, against your own nature, your abilities, your life. The Tiger cannot be killed.'

'Then what did you do?' Arina asked. I looked at her and shuddered – she had aged. No, her camouflage hadn't disappeared, but now it was only the mask of a beautiful and confident woman on the face of an unhappy, devastated old one.

'We sacrificed to him. A Tiger has no need to kill a Prophet if the Prophet has already proclaimed his prophecy to human beings and thereby set the mechanism working. And if the Prophet is willing to die in order not to reveal the prophecy . . . if the Tiger realises that really is the case . . . then he leaves. He is not cruel. He does not punish for resistance. All he does is try to achieve a result. If no result is possible – the Tiger loses interest in the Prophet.'

'And you killed your friend to show the Tiger that the prophecy would not reach human ears . . .' Arina whispered.

'No. I was the one who should have died. We had thought it all through . . .' Fan hesitated. 'But Li had thought a little further. He deceived me. He arranged things so that I killed him, I killed him in front of the Tiger, while certain that I would die myself. That convinced the Tiger. He realised that Li was sacrificing himself and that I would never insult his heroic deed by repeating what he had said. The Tiger turned and walked away. New Prophets are born in the world all the time, and each of them on one occasion utters something that can turn the human world upside down. The Tiger walked away.' Fan stopped, but then went on after all: 'After saying that he felt for me. It was moving. I wanted to die too, but Li had asked me to live. So I had to live.'

'Wait,' I whispered. The old magician's words had roused something in my memory. 'Wait, Fan. Something's not right. Something doesn't fit. I . . . I believe you. Or rather, I believe you are saying what you think is the truth, and it looks like the truth, but . . .'

'But?' Fan repeated, obviously intrigued.

'But if the Tiger hunts Prophets simply in order to induce them to speak, not to make them remain silent . . . why did he want to kill the boy-Prophet in Moscow?'

'He did not want to kill him,' Fan said firmly. 'He was trying to urge him on. Make him hurry.'

'When we tried to protect the boy, the Tiger demanded that we leave. And he said . . . he said that the prophecy must not be heard.'

Fan gazed at me unblinkingly. His expression had suddenly shed all its geniality.

'Did he lie?' I asked.

'No, the Tiger cannot lie. You misheard. You didn't catch what he said.'

I reached into the Twilight, shuddering as I remembered Fan's words . . . how was I doing this? How did I control energies that I didn't understand? How did I perform what people called miracles? It wasn't important, just at the moment it didn't matter if Fan was right in what he had said about the Twilight . . .

'Here, catch,' I said, tossing a replica of my memory to Fan.

Fan stared into empty space, watching us standing in the Tiger's path in the basement corridor of the Watch . . .

'Inconceivable,' he said slowly. 'The Tiger does not want the prophecy . . .'

'Has that never happened before?' I asked. 'Not ever?'

'There have been cases . . . but I thought . . . they were a matter of misunderstanding and stubbornness . . .' Fan looked at me again. 'It is good that no one will hear this prophecy.'

'Why?'

'I am frightened by what might have been said.'

'It can still be heard,' murmured Arina. 'Anton, the sly dog . . . Anton has preserved the prophecy, I don't know how, but he kept a recording – I sensed it.'

'Destroy that recording,' Fan said quickly. 'Do not toy with the Primordial Power.'

'The Primordial Powers are the Light and the Darkness.'

'The Primordial Power is the Twilight! All the rest are merely its manifestations! Destroy the recording!' Fan jumped to his feet.

'Don't you dare!' Arina exclaimed, also getting up. 'Don't you dare, Anton! What if . . . if there's something in it capable of annulling a prophecy? Of destroying the Tiger!'

'Back off, will you, both of you!' I shouted. Fan and Arina were closing in on me, with their eyes blazing so brightly that I was frightened. 'I'll decide for myself what to do! Stop it!'

Fan halted, shook his head and put his hand to his forehead.

'Please forgive me . . . that news was simply too strange. Please forgive me.'

But Arina didn't stop. She kept advancing on me with small, mincing steps, until she bumped into me and froze with her face close to mine. Her eyelids were trembling, her eyes were insane.

'Anton . . . Anton, we have to follow this path right to the end. Where's that recording, Anton? Where's the prophecy? If we don't like it, we'll . . . we'll do what Fan and Li did. You'll kill me and the Tiger will calm down . . .'

'He won't calm down,' I said, shoving Arina away. 'Because you're not my best friend and your death won't prove a thing to the Tiger! *You* calm down. There's no need to hurry, no need to do anything hasty and ill-considered.'

'Do you realise what I did?' Arina whined. 'Do you realise that? I destroyed our homeland, Anton! We ought to have died and not let the prophecy out into the world, or let it come true . . . but I put it off! And it turns out that I just stretched the spring tighter! I was blinded by my self-assurance, by my faith in myself . . . I decided to fight. And now everything will be even worse, do you understand that, even worse!'

'Arina, we don't know anything yet,' I said. 'Perhaps your prophecy was actuated in the 1940s. Remember? "Little Russia is German land." That was what it said, right?'

The insanity in Arina's eyes faded for a second.

'Yes . . . no . . . But the rest of it hasn't happened . . . Anton . . .' Her voice became wheedling. 'You know I managed to restore a few things from the *Fuaran* . . . I can increase the powers of Others – that's very important – and there are lots of other things in there that nobody knows about . . .'

Poor Fan Wen-yan's eyebrows climbed up onto his forehead.

He had only just shared with us his own experiences and his opinion of the Twilight, which contradicted all the fundamental theories of the Others.

And in return he had heard a fragment of an old 'postponed' prophecy and learned that the legendary *Fuaran* was in the possession of a Witch, who had even managed to restore it, and that it could increase an Other's Power. (I could imagine how he felt hearing that, when it had taken him three hundred years to reach the Fourth-Level!)

'Anton . . . darling . . . you have no idea of what I can do – I can do things for you that no one else can . . .' Arina's hands were pressed against my chest and she leaned her head to one side, looking into my eyes. 'Anton . . . dearest . . . you did keep the prophecy, didn't you?'

'Yes,' I said, nodding while gazing into Arina's eyes.

'Anton,' Fan said very calmly and politely. 'I'd like to point out that—'

'Anton, how did you keep it?' Arina went on.

'There was this toy there,' I explained. 'A toy phone that you can record a few words on. Kesha was holding it in his hand after he uttered the prophecy. He doesn't remember anything – but there was a recording on the phone. I haven't listened to it, but I recorded it onto a flash stick.'

'And where is that flash stick?' Arina asked.

'In my wallet,' I said.

'I hate to intrude, Anton,' said Fan, taking a step towards us, 'but I'd like to point out that the spell Long Tongue has been cast on you.'

Before he even finished speaking I shoved away Arina, who had already lowered her hand into my jacket pocket. The witch was extremely light. She flew several paces through the air and flopped down onto the pillows.

And I desperately checked all the defences that I had applied to myself.

The Barrier of Will . . . the Rainbow Sphere . . .

Everything was in order, the defences were sound.

The irony of the situation was that it was an extremely complex and well-structured defensive system, which would easily have repulsed a Dominant or any other attacking spell. It would also have fended off the Long Tongue – a spell that novices play with during their first year of training – except that I myself had removed that element of defence! The Long Tongue was woven into the spell for admiring the landscape, which I had thought was a local Taiwanese spell applied to the pavilion by our courteous hosts. It really did look like an ordinary spell for entertainment . . . right up to the moment when it was allowed access. After that it started working, gradually increasing in power.

No, this wasn't Fan's work! The more closely I examined the spell, the more clearly I saw that although the enchantments linked to air, water and earth seemed to have been crafted in the Chinese manner, they were actually slightly different.

More elegant, more feminine.

More witchlike.

This spell had been cast by Arina. She had cast it almost instantaneously, in the few moments it took us to walk to the pavilion, woven it neatly into our hosts' sentry and defensive spells, without disturbing them in the slightest, and she had even disguised it as local work!

It probably wasn't a trap that had been planned in advance just for me. More likely it was for both of us. And probably Arina had deliberately hinted at Fan's homosexuality, so that if anything went wrong I would take her magic, which bore a clearly feminine imprint, for the magic of an effeminate man – which Fan, of course, was not: the shield he had just thrown up was crude, rough and effective.

Arina didn't just think two or three moves ahead, she was ten moves ahead of the game!

Instead of straightening out the old spells, I preferred to cast a new one, the Ice Crust, severing the threads twined around my mind.

'Anton . . .' Arina said plaintively, without even attempting to get up. 'Why?'

'Don't try to creep into my mind, Witch,' I said. 'I'll decide for myself what to do.'

'But Anton, I only wanted—' she began. Fortunately, this time I was ready for her to try to make me talk, and the thrust of the Dominant dissolved harmlessly in the Rainbow Sphere.

'Stop that!' I exclaimed. 'Enough! You lost!'

Fan stood nearby, adding more and more Power to his Magician's Shield. And apparently summoning someone.

'Give it to me!' Arina shouted. She didn't get up, but suddenly somehow she was on her feet, as if the earth itself had tossed her up into the air. Arina's eyes were blazing, her hands were held out towards me – and I could feel the wallet jerking about in my pocket, trying to leap out and fly to the witch.

I struck out with a Press. In any other situation I would have had enough sheer Power to knock the person in Arina's place off her feet.

But she was a Higher Other too. And while the *Fuaran* had made me a Magician Beyond Classification by chance, Arina had obviously worked long and hard on her skills. She brushed aside my Press with a wave of her hand: the flowering orchids behind her seemed to explode and a banister rail went hurtling out of the pavilion. How right Fan had been when he decided not to meet in the museum!

I stood there, bent over slightly, waiting for what would come next.

Strangely enough, it wasn't exactly an attack. Arina used a Triple Key – but one so powerful that my entire mental defence cracked and gave way.

'Understand me!' Arina screamed.

And I really did understand her. I felt her pain at what she had once done. Her hate for her own self-assurance and her own cowardice. Her reluctance to fight with me – and her readiness to fight to the end.

It all came down to me not wanting to let her have the prophecy without having thought the matter through properly.

'Now you understand me!' I retorted, flinging a Triple Key back at her.

It was the most absurd combat of my life. We stood there facing each other, brimming over with Power, with death-dealing spells trembling on the tips of our fingers – but without feeling the slightest hate for each other, understanding each other to the very depths of our souls . . .

And then the air around us was filled with a loud crackling and Others started pouring out of the portals that had opened up.

Fan had summoned the Inquisition.

Arina called up the situation instantly. A gust of fiery wind swept out in all directions, more as a distraction than a real attempt to delay the Inquisitors. Then I saw Arina smiling, standing in the middle of the ring of fire in a man's trousers and jacket that were too large for her. With painful slowness, it seemed to me, although it could hardly have taken more than a second, Arina pulled a wallet – my wallet! – out of the jacket's inside pocket and opened it. The flash stick jumped out onto her palm . . . and Arina disappeared. The wallet hung in the air for a moment, like in a cartoon film, and then fell.

Arina had probably been clutching the Minoan Sphere in her left hand the whole time.

I lowered my eyes to examine myself.

Yes, the long skirt and turquoise blouse had looked better on Arina than on me. And what was worse, her clothes were obviously too small for me and were already coming apart at the seams.

'Halt!' barked one of the Inquisitors when I leaned down to get my wallet.

'Mr Anton Gorodetsky offered resistance to the criminal and is not guilty in any way,' Fan said quickly. 'There should be no charges against him!'

Perhaps Fan possessed incontrovertible authority, or perhaps the Inquisitors were simply obsessed by dreams of catching Arina – but in any case all five or six of them disappeared into the portals that had opened up again.

'It's useless,' I said, clutching the wallet in my hand. 'A Minoan Sphere can't be traced. There'll be an entire tree of false trails branching out to eternity.'

'They are obliged to try,' Fan said politely. 'It is their job. Can I help with your clothes?'

'I'll manage,' I said, frowning. 'I'll apply a false appearance, and I have spare clothes at the hotel.'

'A very elegant spell,' Fan said. 'I simply can't imagine for what purpose it was created.'

'Arina's a great joker,' I said, sitting down and pouring myself some tea. 'The old crone – she tricked me after all . . .'

'But she left you your documents and money.'

'What's true is true,' I agreed. 'She always did have style. But that flash stick . . .'

Fan spread his hands helplessly. The shield that he had pumped full of Power, which made the Taiwanese look slightly hazy, was slowly dissolving into the Twilight.

'What are you going to do now?' he asked.

'I don't know,' I replied. 'I'll probably finish my tea, go back to the hotel and get changed. And then I'm going home.'

Part Three

DUBIOUS DOINGS

PROLOGUE

ANTON GORODETSKY WAS watching TV.

He wasn't one of those people who don't have a television on principle, or who proudly declare that they haven't switched it on for years. To tell the truth, he did watch it sometimes – the news almost every day, and even some film or other a couple of times a year, if he came across it on the airwaves by chance.

But right now he was watching TV thoughtfully, with serious intent. And the fact that he was switching from channel to channel every five seconds by no means indicated that he wasn't concentrating.

Click.

'Accused, why did you go to visit the victim?'

'Well . . . I . . . wanted to have a drink with him . . . And he . . .'

Click.

'. . . the verdict of the court is thirteen years' imprisonment to be served in a strict-regime penal colony. The defence have already stated that they will appeal, and the guilt of the accused is in no way . . .'

Click.

'. . . went off course and failed to enter orbit. But the specialists emphasise that the satellite was insured . . .'

Click.

'. . . the size of the average pension will increase by eleven per cent to five thousand, nine hundred and seventy-four roubles . . .'

Click.

'. . . and those terrible years, the decades of repression and tyranny, did not break the artist's spirit, he carried on working and exhibiting his works, in defiance of the Communist regime . . .'

Click.

'. . . advanced technologies. The scientists tell us that using them to produce nanotechnological cement will make possible a significant improvement in the quality . . .'

Click.

'. . . it is proposed to remove the children from the family, since the parents' level of income is inadequate to provide appropriate care . . .'

Click.

'What I say is this, commander: if we try to withdraw, their blocking units will gun us down, but if we surrender, then at least there's some kind of chance . . .'

Click.

'. . . the largest in Europe! And this is indisputable proof that the policy being pursued is correct . . .'

Click.

'The oysters in this restaurant are the best in Moscow, but the wine really is quite pricey – I couldn't find anything decent for less than five or six thousand . . .'

Gorodetsky turned the television off, even though he still had ten channels left. He rubbed the bridge of his nose.

Anyone who said TV wasn't worth watching was a fool. It was

just that you ought to do it once every three or four months. That way it was more than just a blurred flickering in your eyes.

But, of course, if you only watched it every three or four years, that was even more instructive.

He walked over to the window and looked at the low grey sky hanging over the city. Then he slowly rubbed his hand over the cold glass.

The clouds parted and a chink opened up in the sky – a tiny little eye of dark blue. Somewhere behind the shroud of clouds the sun was setting.

Anton shoved his hands into his pockets, took out the little round earphones and set them in his ears. He clicked the button on the player. The band Picnic came up.

> The city's fierce lights
> And harsh neon brightness
> Shove from behind and jostle me on,
> But I stroll along,
> Breathe it all in,
> And what is mine it cannot take from me.
>
> One minute more lingering in this breeze,
> In this Crooked Kingdom I feel at my ease.
>
> Here money won't wait
> Until it gets burned,
> Its power brings happiness, takes it away.
> But that's not for me,
> I'm wandering free
> And the dark streets are calling my name.
> He's playing his game,
> It's always the same,

> And one out of two people pauses to see.
> But I'm not that one,
> I'm drunk, having fun,
> And I'm only just beginning to breathe . . .

The gap in the clouds closed up. Anton raised his hand – and then lowered it again.

It would close over anyway.

He walked through into the kitchen, opened a small cupboard and took out a bottle of cognac that had already been started. He glanced round stealthily, poured a little into a paunchy glass and downed it barbarously, in a single gulp.

The bottle gave a despairing sigh. Anton screwed up his eyes and looked at it, trying to determine who had cast that spell.

Svetlana.

Anton poured a second dose, put the sighing bottle away in the cupboard and walked through into the sitting room. He stood in front of a cupboard with glass doors, studying the wooden chalice standing on one of the shelves.

Of course, artefacts of that kind really ought to be kept in the Watch office. But after studying it for a week, none of the analysts had been able to discover how to read the prophecy concealed in the chalice (or even if it was really there) and the apartment of two Higher Others (actually three, if you counted Nadya) was effectively defended against any kind of intrusion.

And so, on Gesar's suggestion, Erasmus's chalice had been returned to Gorodetsky. It was returned without enthusiasm – the Inquisition was very displeased that Anton had not tried to summon them to detain Arina. But Gesar had come up with a convincing argument: Erasmus might have tuned the chalice in some way so that the prophecy could only be revealed to Gorodetsky.

Gesar could always come up with a convincing argument if he really wanted to.

Anton looked at the chalice for a while, then opened the cupboard and picked it up. He held it to one ear, then the other. Then he walked into the kitchen, splashed some cognac into the chalice and drank it.

Naturally, the prophecy was not revealed.

'Daddy?'

Anton was standing by the window with the chalice, lost in thought, and he hadn't noticed that Nadya had come back from school.

'What, my love?'

'Did you . . .' Nadya sniffed demonstratively, but she asked diplomatically: 'Did you part the clouds?'

'I admit it. Just a little bit.'

'I noticed.'

Nadya shifted from one foot to the other at the door. She either wanted to ask him about something or she had something to tell him. Anton looked at his daughter and suddenly – completely out of the blue – he realised that his daughter was not completely a child any longer, that she was already treading the mysterious path that leads from childhood to youth, the path on which talking dolls, teddy bears and beloved parents are left behind, abandoned and forgotten . . .

Nadya had only just stepped onto this path, but there would be no return from it, there could not be . . .

'Did you want to ask me something?' said Anton.

'Daddy, that chalice thing . . . I touched it too.'

Anton nodded, realising it wasn't physical touch that was meant.

'I think there's something there. But it's really well hidden: you can't get it out, no matter how cunning or strong you are.'

'If cunning or strength was enough, the Inquisition would already have understood everything,' Anton said with a nod.

'I think there's some very clever release mechanism,' Nadya went on, brightening up. 'You have to do something that you would never ever think of. That you wouldn't ever do. And then the prophecy will be revealed.'

Anton looked at the chalice in his hand.

Then he nodded again.

'In that case, we'll probably never find out.'

'Are you upset?'

'No,' said Anton. 'Not really. That is, not at all.'

CHAPTER 1

He was a fine young man, one of those who had come into the Watch the year before, and was dreaming of becoming a field operative. An honest Fourth-Level, with every chance of advancing further. His name was Alexander – or Sasha – and only recently he had been studying at the Moscow Aviation Institute and dreaming of becoming a space-flight engineer. People like that only became Light Ones, because in 2012 in Russia only a complete child or a holy fool could dream of becoming a cosmonaut.

'Anton Sergeevich,' – he was trying hard to speak calmly and collectedly, but there was still a slight tremble in his voice – 'are you certain they'll come here?' I shrugged, took out a pack of cigarettes, lit up and offered one to Sasha, taking no notice of his grimace of disapproval. He started fidgeting, then reached uncertainly for a cigarette.

I pulled the pack away.

'Don't. First, never smoke. Second, never do anything that authority figures suggest if you don't like it. If I jump off the bridge, will you do the same?'

'If necessary, I will!' Sasha declared resolutely.

I looked down into the grey water of the river Moscow with

the lighted street lamps reflected in it (in Moscow the stars in the sky aren't often visible). I nodded.

'That's always the most important thing, understanding whether it's necessary or not . . . Sasha, they'll come here, because this is where the Call's directed. When I was a little bit older than you, but probably not any stronger, it was very hard for me even to sense the vampire Call and to follow it. But now I can do a little bit more . . . and I know that the vampire is walking along the Bersenevskaya Embankment, and the girl is walking along the Prechistenka Embankment. Just recently it has become highly fashionable among vampires to take their victim on a bridge, then throw the body into the water. By the time it's fished out, no one can tell what the person died of.'

'Why can't they tell?' Sasha asked indignantly. 'What about the loss of blood? And the marks from the fangs?'

'Just think about it,' I said, blowing out a cloud of smoke. 'You're a forensic pathologist. They bring you a body fished out of the water, considerably damaged, battered against the riverbank or the supports of a bridge . . .'

Sasha started turning pale. He was still young. A good lad, but young . . .

'Even if you notice that there are small wounds of some kind on the body and there is almost no blood in it, what are you going to think? That there are vampires walking the streets of Moscow? Or that some young fool in love leapt into the water and spiked herself on a piece of metal as she fell?'

'I would consider all the possibilities,' Sasha decided.

'That's why you're in the Watch,' I said.

Sasha paused while he glanced vigilantly to the left and the right. Then he asked timidly: 'Won't the church stop them?'

I glanced at the massive, attractively illuminated building and shook my head.

'Not this one, it won't stop them. In general vampires aren't afraid of religion – if they believed in God, they wouldn't have become vampires. But you're right in the sense that a genuine church, a shrine, can protect the victim. If it's close by and the victim believes. Do you understand? It doesn't frighten the vampire, it protects the victim.'

'I think I understand,' said Sasha, nodding thoughtfully. 'But why won't this one help?'

'There are many factors,' I replied evasively.

Sasha stood there, fiddling with a little lock dangling on the railings of the bridge. A funny habit that modern lovers have – come to the bridge, kiss, hang up a lock – and it's as if they have locked up their love.

But love shouldn't be locked up. That's not what it's given to us for.

'I can sense him,' Sasha exclaimed excitedly. 'He's coming! From the left!'

'I know,' I said.

'He won't . . .'

'He won't sense that we're Others and he won't even see what we really look like,' I reassured him – without telling him that instead of me the vampire would see a skinny young guy with an earring in one ear, and instead of Sasha he would see a dejected girl. A standard sight for this spot – lovers who have fallen out.

'I can sense the girl too,' Sasha said with relief. 'There she is, walking along . . . why, she's almost a child!'

I turned my head slightly. The girl walked past us, gazing blindly straight ahead, and I agreed: 'Yes, only fourteen or fifteen. That's bad. If she was ten . . .'

'What's bad about it?' Sasha asked in amazement.

Hadn't he done his lessons? Did he really not remember that licences were issued . . .

'They've disappeared!' Sasha exclaimed excitedly.

I myself saw the vampire, who looked as young as my partner, take a step towards the girl and smile – his fangs had not extended yet, there was just a faint hint . . . and they both disappeared.

'Let's go,' I said, pitching my cigarette end over the parapet into the water with a snap of my fingers. I sensed my shadow rather than saw it – and stepped into it.

Cold. The usual piercing cold of the Twilight. The world around was veiled in grey and slowed down, sounds became viscous, lingering and distant. Underfoot there was an uninterrupted covering of blue moss. Our feet sank into it like an expensive carpet.

The vampire was standing a few steps away from us, very young and handsome, aristocratically pale. He was genuinely young, too, not just disguising himself as youthful: he was the real thing – otherwise his Twilight image as an Other would have been quite different.

The vampire was standing there, holding the girl and kissing her on the lips. Kissing, not biting. Out of the corner of his eye he looked at me and at Sasha, who entered the Twilight clumsily behind me.

'Night Watch – everyone leave the Twilight,' I said in a humdrum voice.

I was really hoping that the vampire would expose his fangs and throw himself at me. Or make a run for it. Or start shouting that he hadn't done anything wrong, he'd only kissed a pretty girl . . .

The vampire stopped kissing the girl and carefully set her aside – she froze like a doll. Then, with a note of resentment in his voice, he asked: 'What is the problem here?'

'Anton Gorodetsky, Night Watch of the City of Moscow,' I said, already understanding everything. 'Show me your registration.'

'Well, good evening,' the vampire said politely, unbuttoning his shirt, through which I could see the blue lines of a registration mark. 'Pleased to meet you, Anton. I've heard a lot about you.'

'Denis Liubimov, vampire, Sixth-Level,' I said, reading from the mark. 'You are under arrest for unlicensed contact with a human being.'

'Why do you assume it's unlicensed?' Denis asked. 'Here!'

A thin sheet of 'parchment paper' unfurled in his hand. I could have spent a long time drearily checking all the numbers, signatures, seals and magical signs . . . Only I could see perfectly well that the licence was genuine.

'She's not fifteen yet,' I said for some reason.

'And I'm twenty,' Denis said. 'Licences are issued beginning from the age of twelve, if there are no Others among the immediate relatives. It's all legal.'

Sasha started breathing heavily behind me.

'It's your right,' I said in an absolutely flat voice. I looked down at my feet – and the blue moss stirred as if someone had splashed petrol on it and set it on fire. 'But you are really very young, Denis. I don't dispute your rights, but I would like to remind you that many vampires live for hundreds of years without using their licences to hunt. Instead you can be granted various kinds of privileges under the terms of agreement number sixty-four, article seventeen, of the third of July—'

'I have read and signed all the required documents, I know my rights and obligations,' the vampire said politely. 'I can confirm once again that everything will be done as humanely as possible, painlessly and quickly. And now, gentlemen of the Watch, I ask you . . . please leave the Twilight!'

'Why?' Sasha suddenly exclaimed. 'Tell me why, you ugly vampire scum!'

I swung round and grabbed Sasha firmly by the shoulder. The

last thing we needed was a complaint from a vampire to the Day Watch about unprovoked insults and discrimination on the grounds of nutritional preferences.

But this was a modern vampire – young, polite and restrained.

'Because such are the laws of nature,' he explained amiably. 'Because people constantly take great pleasure in devouring each other. Most often in a figurative sense, but far more cruelly and painfully than vampires or werewolves. I did not choose my destiny, I did not choose my way of life – or death, if you prefer. But I will not pretend to be a sheep when I am a wolf. So now leave us . . . The Call is weakening, the girl could come round and become frightened, and you will be to blame!'

'Remember one thing,' I said without turning away. 'You may be a wolf, but we are wolfhounds.'

I was already on my way out of the Twilight, dragging Sasha along, when I heard a shout from behind me: 'My father kept an Irish wolfhound, a fine dog. Only they don't live long.'

I had to grab hold of Sasha and thrust him bodily against the parapet, otherwise he would have gone dashing back into the Twilight.

'Why he, he . . .' the young watchman fumed.

'He mocked us and provoked us, especially you,' I said. 'Calm down. He's within his rights.'

'But now he'll kill the young girl!'

'Yes, most likely,' I said. I took out a cigarette and lit up. 'Do you know how many people are killed in Moscow in a single night? And, by the way, most of them are killed by other humans, not by Others.'

'But—'

'We're not knights in search of a damsel in distress,' I said.

'We're police! We guard and protect!'

'No, we're not even police. We're bureaucrats who ensure the observance of laws that we don't even like. We're dogs who guard the herd against the wolves, but we don't bite the shepherds who cook kebabs in the evenings. Calm down.'

Alexander took a step back, staring at me in horror. Then he shook his head and said with genuine revulsion:

'I don't believe it. Honestly, I just don't believe it! You, Anton Gorodetsky . . . you're a hero, you've done so much . . . they told us about you in our classes, I watched the training films about how you—'

'The training films have actors in them,' I said. 'And in the classes they tell you legends.'

There was a rustling sound behind my back. The girl's limp body appeared in mid-air, hung there for a second, then flew over the parapet and hurtled down towards the water.

A second later the vampire appeared, looking pink-cheeked, cheerful and handsome. With a slight inclination of the head, as if he was saying goodbye, he swung round and dashed away from us across the bridge at an incredible speed.

Below us, in the cold, dirty water of the river Moscow, there was a barely audible splash.

Sasha stared at me, glassy-eyed.

'Remember, I told you the important thing is to understand whether it's necessary to jump or not?' I asked.

Sasha didn't answer.

'Well, that's the entire problem here,' I explained. I spat the cigarette over the parapet – and jumped after it.

The river struck my legs like repulsive, heavy meat jelly that instantly liquefied, turning into icy autumnal water. I went right under, opened my eyes and looked at the lights shining through the water. If I didn't look too hard, I could have taken them for stars . . .

The girl's body was slowly sinking quite near me. I had already made two broad strokes when the sound of a sharp blow struck my ears – another body had hit the water.

'Are you stupid?' I asked, once I was sure that Sasha had stopped coughing up water. 'Why did you jump, if you can't swim?'

'But you, you said . . .' he groaned, sitting up.

'What did I say?'

'That you . . . have to . . .'

'That you always have to understand what you're doing,' I reminded him pitilessly. 'You're a Magician. An Other. A Light One. So you should be especially ashamed of being a fool!'

I had dragged Sasha and the girl through the water against the current and out onto the bank at a spot where there weren't many people – thankfully, the abilities of an Other allowed me to perform tricks like that. We were sitting on the dirty embankment, beside the car park in front of the monstrously ugly statue of Columbus, to which Peter the Great's head had been attached. Peter-Christopher gazed contemptuously over our heads into his own bronze-yellow distance.

'The girl . . .' Sasha groaned.

'Lying over there,' I said, nodding in her direction. 'I dragged you both out. Thanks, you were a great help . . .'

'Is she alive?' Sasha asked hopefully.

'She's not dead,' I said, after glancing at her aura.

'What?' exclaimed Sasha, finally sitting up properly and looking round. 'That bastard—'

'Could have finished her off completely. But I managed to nettle him, with your help. So she isn't dead – she'll be a vampire.'

A sombre-faced pair walked by – a solid-looking man in a suit and tie and an even more sturdily built man with a bull-neck, wearing a suit slightly too large for him. I automatically extended the Sphere of Inattention to cover the poor girl, but even so the owner of the powerful neck turned his head and slipped his hand in under the flap of his jacket. Good bodyguards are like that – they can sense us Others . . .

'What shall we do?' asked Sasha.

'First, get dry,' I said. 'Do you remember the spells? Well done! Second, get up, it's dirty and cold here, we're still young men, we don't want prostate problems. Third, I'll go home, get washed and sleep.'

'What about me?' Sasha asked in a quiet voice.

'You'll stay here and wait for the girl to come round. Call the Day Watch . . . say "Situation six, no complications." If you don't remember the number or you're too squeamish to talk with Dark Ones – ask our operations officer. Is your mobile okay?'

'It's protected . . .'

'Smart boy. Before the Dark Ones arrive – and they won't hurry – have a talk with the girl. Explain that she has been bitten by a vampire, that now she will also become – essentially she already has become – a vampire. Well, all the rights and obligations . . . You hand her over to the Dark Ones, and they'll find a teacher for her. That Denis, for instance. That's all, after that your work's over.'

I got up and shook myself down. My clothing gave off clouds of steam that smelled of rotting wood and oil. It was a good job I was wearing my windcheater: you couldn't clean a good suit after the river Moscow's water, not even with magic . . .

The Mercedes with the boss and his bodyguard in it was already trundling out of the car park. I raised my hand, transmitting a light command. Remoralisation or the Breath of Teresa wouldn't do the trick here.

The Mercedes braked gently to a halt. I opened the back door: the owner of the car was sitting beside the driver in that manner that nouveau-riche second-raters have.

'Drive along the embankment for the time being,' I ordered the bodyguard. And before I slammed the door, I shouted to Sasha: 'Oh, by the way, you passed the practical exam. You can take tomorrow to recover – in situations like this I usually get drunk, but you can think up something of your own. And the day after tomorrow, report to the operations section. You're hired.'

On that day Gesar had been in an elated mood since the morning. At the briefing meeting he smiled, told an irrelevant joke that was funny but rather crude, unexpectedly increased the science department's budget for the next quarter, gave Olga Ignat's playful little hug when she was simply walking by and approved Ignat's business trip to Lvov 'for an exchange of experience', although everybody knew perfectly well that Ignat was from Lvov and he simply wanted to visit his relatives and friends.

My account of Alexander's practical exam was also received favourably. The only question was one that I was expecting.

'And are you sure it wouldn't have been better for the girl to die than become undead?' the boss asked, toying with his ballpoint pen.

'No, I'm not,' I replied honestly. 'But I didn't have a chance to ask her, and I didn't want to decide for her. At the end of the day, she has enough time with a relatively healthy psyche before she is totally transformed. If she should choose differently . . . And then, it was extremely useful for Alexander to realise that our actions don't always produce the desired result. I'm sure he got the point.'

'Convincing,' Gesar said, nodding, and signed the order for Alexander's enrolment as a full-time member of staff with a flourish.

Basically, it was a day when you could get Gesar to okay anything, or almost anything. And I tried to take advantage of that when I stayed behind after the gathering started to disperse.

'Questions, Anton?'

'Yes, I have one. About Erasmus.'

'Have you guessed how to reveal his prophecy?' Gesar asked.

'Not yet, although I've had one inkling of an idea. But everything here's so interconnected . . . Boris Ignatievich, tell me, that bonsai you sent him – can you tell me what magic is concealed in it?'

'No,' Gesar snapped.

Well, it was worth a try . . .

'I wouldn't bother my head about the old prophecy,' Gesar continued, without looking at me. 'It either went off and was never realised, or it all happened ages ago. But finding out what the boy wanted to tell us, now that really would be interesting.'

'Arina twisted me round her little finger,' I said, repenting for my sins, and not for the first time. 'But even I'm not certain that there was anything on that flash stick . . .'

'Remember the unwritten law that anything that can go wrong, will go wrong – there was something there, all right . . .' Gesar sighed and closed his laptop. 'Sit down, Anton. Let's talk. I understand what's bothering you.'

'Arina's prophecy,' I admitted. 'Or rather, her friend's . . . What if she's right and the prophecy does come true?'

Gesar shrugged.

'Maybe she's right, and the prophecy will come true. Maybe it already did, despite all her cunning tricks – the Germans occupied Little Russia, the Japanese invaded Siberia, they hanged Bolsheviks . . .'

'The war will last nine years?'

'The First World War began in 1914, the Civil War in Russia ended in 1923. Can you do the sum?'

'It ended in 1922,' I protested stubbornly.

'Oh, these historians! In Yakutia, in Kamchatka and Chukotka, it was 1923!' Gesar growled. 'Who are you arguing with? Were you there? I fought against Bologov's Cossacks and their shaman in 1923! And the basmachi carried on their bloody struggle after that . . .'

'That's not what I'm arguing about,' I said in a conciliatory tone. 'If the count includes 1914 and 1922, that makes exactly nine years.'

Gesar raised his hands thoughtfully and started bending down the fingers. Then he looked at me and turned crimson.

'So what *are* you arguing about? It's all happened!'

'Not all of it,' I said morosely. '"A third of the people die of starvation . . ."'

'Famine in the Volga region, Kazakhstan, Little Russia . . . Not a third, of course, but let's grant the Prophets the right to pile on the tragedy.'

'"The world absorbs the rest of the nation . . ."'

'What country hasn't been absorbed into the world nowadays?' asked Gesar, raising one eyebrow in surprise. 'Globalisation, Anton! Everybody has dissolved in everybody! I went into a toilet in Paris, and there were graffiti scratched on the wall in fourteen languages!'

'"Moscow consumed by flames . . ."'

'Prophecies are always allegorical,' Gesar snapped. 'The old Moscow has perished, there's nothing left of it but the Kremlin – but the Kremlin isn't Moscow.'

'"With the loss of his heir, the tsar is deranged . . ."'

Gesar pondered for a moment. Then he said: 'Well, that is the result of Arina's interference. She treated the heir to the throne's illness, if she's not lying, so he didn't die – as he should have done . . . But one way or another, all the rest has happened. The silly old fool has simply gone gaga. She wants to suffer a bit, don't you know. She has destroyed Russia! What a laugh! The whole world and its uncle have been trying to destroy Russia for a thousand years, but it's still there, and it will stay there!'

'Thank you,' I said sincerely, getting up. 'I was feeling pretty lousy about it.'

'Anton, I've lived in many different places,' Gesar said in a gentle voice. 'Tibet . . . China . . . India . . . Flanders . . .'

'Not Holland?' I asked.

'Zeelandic Flanders,' Gesar replied. 'Now it's part of Holland, that's right. The point, Anton, is that you can get stuck on any country. I love Tibet, and India, and Flanders. And Russia, of course! But with the passing years you come to realise that the most important things are your family, your friends, your work. And as for countries . . . we're all citizens of humankind, we have emerged from it, but we live and work for its sake. We're all Others! That's what is most important. Don't be afraid of that old Witch's nonsense. Sleeping for all that time had a bad effect on her. Don't seek for meaning in Erasmus's old lump of wood: if even Arina didn't covet it – and she could have stolen it from you a hundred times – it means there isn't any meaning in it. But when it comes to Innokentii's prophecy, of course, that's where you really blundered! That would be really worth knowing!'

I hung my head repentantly.

'You definitely erased everything from the toy phone?' Gesar asked casually.

'Yes. I gave it to the lab guys.'

'They couldn't fish anything out of it,' Gesar sighed. 'A tiny microchip, completely written over, the old information completely erased . . . And you didn't keep another flash stick?'

'I don't have another one. They've checked already.'

'That's bad,' said Gesar, sighing heavily again. 'The most valuable piece of information you obtained in Formosa is that the Tiger is not exactly what we thought: he tries to spur the Prophets on to make their prophesies, not eliminate them! But he behaved quite differently here! He himself stated that the prophecy must not be uttered! And that makes the prophecy interesting – but now it's out of our reach!'

'It's my fault . . .'

'Drop it,' said Gesar, with a wave of his hand. Yes, he was clearly in an excellent mood. 'What's done is done. No point raking over old coals. I don't have any assignments for you today, you can take care of your own business. Ah yes . . . you are granted the right to one seventh-level benign intervention!'

'If only I'd had it yesterday evening!'

'You would have saved the girl, and the vampire would have been given a new licence. You know that!'

I shrugged and walked out of the office.

CHAPTER 2

THE MAIN ADVANTAGE that someone at the top has, at least in an organisation like the Night Watch, is the freedom to plan his own day.

I actually always had more than enough work. Officially I had been made responsible for supervising trainees, monitoring teaching in the school and inspecting patrols. In the tedious bureaucratic language that is self-generated in any organisation, whether it's the accounts office of a pipe-rolling mill or an alliance of anarchistic romantic artists, my job was titled 'Deputy Director for the Training and Professional Development of Personnel'.

Doesn't actually sound too exhausting, right? But I had practically no free time left. Unless I took an arbitrary decision to rake all the papers to one corner of the desk, switch off my work mobile and do something that was strictly optional. Then it miraculously turned out that the Watch was capable of existing without one of its deputy directors for as long as you could wish. But the moment I turned back to work, I was swamped by a tsunami of applications, requests, complaints, instructions and schedules.

As a child I didn't like school, as a young man I didn't like college – and I went through all that to end up supervising the training programme in a magical police force! I wonder whether, if I had remained a programmer, or taken up architecture – that was what my parents wanted, we had some well-known architect or other in our family – educational work would have caught up with me anyway?

Probably it would. Anybody, even an Other, can only change the form of his life, not its content. In one old computer game a wicked witch had the habit of asking people she met: 'What can change human nature?' – and afterwards she took great pleasure in killing them. Because no one could find the right answer . . .

But although Nature cannot be changed, she can always be deceived. For a while.

And so I sat at the desk in my office for a few minutes, looking through the papers and smoking a cigarette. About a year earlier Igor, in a burst of fanatical enthusiasm for the healthy lifestyle, had launched a campaign to prohibit smoking in the Watch's office premises. In general terms everybody, including the smokers, agreed with his arguments. But when it came down to the specifics, opinions differed widely. Naturally, in areas where non-smokers worked, no one smoked anyway. In communal areas it was permitted, but only if no one objected. Everyone took their dose of poison either in the smoking rooms or in their own offices – and when all was said and done, it didn't take that much magic to rid rooms of the smell of tobacco. But Igor insisted on having everything his way, railing about the stench of tobacco, holding up the example of civilised Europe, pressing home the point that it was embarrassing when colleagues visited us from there. (Although I hadn't noticed the European Others suffering much when they drank vodka at receptions, smoked in their rooms or, for instance, bought hundreds of suspiciously cheap 'licenced' movie DVDs and music CDs in the shops.)

The campaign came to a sudden end when Gesar, after listening benevolently to Igor speaking on his proposal, remarked: 'That's right, everyone should smoke pipes or hookahs, not stinking cigarettes . . .' Igor should have stopped short there and then, but in the heat of the moment he blurted out that hookahs, pipes and cigars were even worse than cigarettes: 'The stench is really horrible!' Gesar's face darkened and he asked whether from now on, when he wanted to focus on thinking through important problems, he would have to run out into the street with his hookah. And then he asked if there was no difference between the climate in Europe, where you could go outside in your shirtsleeves in December, and the climate in Russia, where even in Moscow minus twenty Celsius was a common occurrence.

After that the subject somehow just folded of its own accord. For a while Igor walked around looking offended and ostentatiously withdrew from any areas where anyone was smoking. But then his enthusiastic endorsement of the healthy lifestyle was replaced by the struggle against the discrimination suffered by Others with low levels of magical Power.

Since I wasn't expecting a visit from Igor, I smoked unashamedly as I looked through the accumulation of papers.

A schedule of classes for novice Others. That could wait.

A plan for the advanced training of Fourth- and Fifth-Level Others in order to identify the more powerful magicians among them. That was a bit more interesting. Peering attentively at the sheet of paper, I read this remarkable phrase: 'The goal of holding this advanced training programme is advanced training for the purposes of determining . . .' After that I suddenly started feeling bored, signed the papers and dropped them into the 'Approved' file. The sheets faded and disappeared, teleported off to their authors.

So, what next?

A schedule of classes for patrol members on the subject of 'Certain aspects of interaction with members of the Day Watch in situations where "wild" Others have been discovered and apprehended.' I glanced through the lesson summaries with great interest. Olga was intending to teach the classes, which was already interesting in itself. And the subject was a burning issue of perennial interest – by no means all Others were found and initiated by members of the Watches, quite often people discovered their own magical powers independently . . . and then things could get really messy, regardless of whether they were Dark Ones or Light Ones.

So I actually marked the first class in my diary, in order to attend it myself. Not as an inspector, simply as one of the students. It was always useful to learn something new.

And what was this?

Olga again?

Amusing. She must have been bitten by the teaching bug. A lecture for Watch members on the subject of 'The Watches' response in cases of technological and social catastrophe. Specific aspects of interaction with the human agencies of law enforcement.' And two remarks. The first was 'attendance desirable' – so it was only nominally an open lecture with optional attendance: in fact, everyone was recommended to attend. The second was 'invited guest – a non-Other'.

That was really interesting!

And the lecture had begun half an hour ago . . . I wondered why neither Olga nor Gesar had said a word to me about it.

I decided that my desk work was over for the day and stood up. I could consider this as attendance at a recommended lecture and an inspection at the same time. That note – 'attendance desirable' – had freed my hands. Simply turning up at Olga's lecture would have been awkward, it would have looked like an official visit. But this way it was all fine and dandy – I'd just come to learn something.

* * *

The lecture hall was absolutely crammed and I felt like a total idiot. Everybody must have been there, apart from Gesar (he had nothing to learn, even from Olga) and the guys in the duty office.

As I walked in, the crowd burst into laughter. I even hesitated in the doorway. But fortunately they weren't laughing at me. It was quite dark by the door and no one had even noticed me.

Olga was standing on a small dais beside a lectern, looking out into the hall with a smile on her face. When the laughter died away, she said: 'And then I said: "Franz, why have you got both gloves on the right hand?" He looked at Willem, blushed and shouted: "Well, damn me, so that was your hand!"'

The audience laughed until it groaned. It guffawed, chuckled, grunted and squealed. It had obviously been a very funny story – but I'd only caught the very end.

There's nothing more pathetic than a man who has heard the end of a joke and starts asking plaintively: 'What was that about, what was it? What happened at the beginning?'

'And what did Willem say?' someone shouted out from the hall.

Olga was apparently expecting this question and she had the answer ready.

'Willem lowered his eyes sheepishly and replied: "Yes, Herr Franz, but it wasn't my hand."'

The audience collapsed in paroxysms of laughter, even louder than before. I sighed, slumped against the wall and waited.

It took a couple of minutes for order to be restored. After that Olga, evidently considering that she had the audience eating out of the palm of her hand, announced: 'And now meet our guest, Senior Police Sergeant Dmitry Pastukhov!'

This was getting more and more interesting! Mentally congratulating myself on taking up the strategically correct position by the door, I squatted down on my haunches. And when Olga stepped down off the dais, clapping her hands, my old, if rather superficial, acquaintance Dmitry Pastukhov mounted it with an embarrassed expression on his face.

'Hello,' Dmitry said, with a smile that was awkward but basically friendly and sincere. 'I am very pleased, I really am, to have been invited here.'

The audience suddenly burst into applause.

'Of course, I'm not Franz, and I'm not Willem,' Pastukhov continued, encouraged by this approval. 'But a job's a job, in any country at any time. Right? So ask what you like, and I'll answer – only don't forget, I'm a senior sergeant, not some high-up . . .'

'Why have you been stuck as a sergeant for so long?' a young girl from the research department piped up from the audience.

'If I'd known you were going to invite me to speak, I'd have become a general!' said Pastukhov, laughing the question off. He didn't seem very keen to discuss the leisurely progress of his career.

But the audience was in a friendly mood. Alisher was the first to get up and ask a question.

'Dima – may I call you Dima?'

'Of course!'

'Let's discuss the following situation. There's some kind of disturbance taking place in a city. The police are trying to restore order. They haven't got enough men. The crowd is setting fire to cars, looting shops, beating up peaceful passers-by. And then two men approach you, an ordinary sergeant on patrol duty. One says he can pacify the crowd, the people will feel ashamed and all go home. The other says he can frighten the crowd, make the people feel pain and they will go running home. Whose help would you accept?'

'The first to approach me!' Pastukhov replied without a moment's thought.

'But if they both approach you at once?' Alisher persisted. 'And you can only accept help from one of them?'

Pastukhov pondered for literally a second. Then he said confidently: 'The one who will frighten them and cause them pain. Would you like to know why?'

Well, would you believe it! There was a pretty decent speaker hiding away inside my police acquaintance! Or had Olga somehow, before his appearance, stimulated his ability to communicate with the audience?

'Why?' Alisher asked sympathetically.

'Because feeling ashamed is for kids who've scrawled four-letter words on a fence!' Pastukhov declared confidently. 'And even then . . . these days, not even a kid feels ashamed of that. People who feel ashamed and go on their way . . . they'll just get up to no good all over again! But if they feel pain and fear – that gets through to their brains, and their livers, that gets stored in their subconscious minds. Especially since . . . well, you know who we're talking about here?'

'Who?' asked Alisher, fascinated.

'Individuals involved in committing group criminal offences!' said Pastukhov, energetically waving one hand through the air. 'Mass disturbances, breaches of the rules of conduct of gatherings and demonstrations, an unsanctioned public assembly, the destruction of private property, delinquency, thuggery, robbery, hooliganism, bodily harm . . . Basically, the whole works! And can you find them all afterwards, arrest them and put them on trial for what they've done? No way! Probably ten fall guys will be picked and given a good beating as an example, and the rest will get away with a bit of a fright. So it would be good to punish them in the process of suppressing the illegal activity. So, one – let it be painful! And, two – let it be frightening!'

He glanced triumphantly round the hall.

The audience was silent. Thinking. But this was far from being the censorious silence of Light Others appalled by human cruelty.

Everyone was simply silent as they thought over his words. And it seemed as if they were willing to agree with them.

And by and large I agreed with Pastukhov too.

I didn't like it! But I agreed with him.

'Dmitry, may I ask you another question, then?' said Olga, rejoining the conversation. 'On a slightly different subject, but nonetheless . . . There's a ship sailing over the sea. A large one, with many passengers on board, very many. The hold springs a leak. There aren't enough lifeboats. They can't wait for help – it simply won't get there in time. The captain realises they won't be able to save everyone, but the passengers aren't yet aware of the situation. What would you do?'

Pastukhov knitted his brows. Then he asked hopefully: 'This is a kind of test, right? We had a visit from a psychologist, he asked questions like that . . .'

'No, no!' Olga said, shaking her head. 'It's not a test, not that. Simply a question. What do you think should be done in a situation like that?'

'Well, probably they should put the children in the lifeboats,' said Pastukhov, after thinking for a moment. 'And the women, if they'll fit.'

He was speaking sincerely, I could see that. And I immediately started to like the senior sergeant a lot more than when he was talking about the corrective power of pain and fear.

'Not even all the children will fit in!' said Olga. 'And it's by no means certain that they'll survive in the lifeboats without any grown-ups, anyway.'

Pastukhov knitted his brows.

'They could save those who are most deserving . . .' he said thoughtfully. 'You know, distinguished people with special honours and such . . .' He rubbed the bridge of his nose and objected to his own idea. 'No, that's no good. Who's going to decide, eh?

Who's worthy, who isn't . . . you'd end up with a real set-to. I'd probably do nothing.'

'Nothing?' asked Olga. Curiously, not judgementally.

'Nothing!' Pastukhov replied, speaking firmly this time. 'Well, you know, of course I'd order the crew to pump the water out, block off the hole with some kind of plug . . .'

'They use patches for that!' someone well informed on maritime matters told him from the hall.

'With a patch, then,' Pastukhov agreed. 'But otherwise – let the musicians play and the waiters serve the food . . .'

He must have watched *Titanic* just recently, I thought.

'But who's going to be saved?' Olga carried on questioning him.

'Whoever manages to get away,' Pastukhov said, with a shrug. 'Whoever realises that the ship is sinking, that there aren't enough lifeboats. That would be the fairest way of all. Afterwards, when everybody realises, you could try to impose some kind of order.'

'Thank you, that's a very valuable opinion,' said Olga. 'Any more questions?'

'Dmitry, this is a different situation . . .' said someone in the audience. 'You're an ordinary person, a cop, I mean, a *polizei* . . . uh, sorry. An ordinary policeman who knows nothing about Others. At night you come across a creature who behaves exactly as if he's a vampire – or a werewolf, say. What would you do?'

'Take out my pistol and attempt to detain him,' Pastukhov replied.

The audience seemed to be surprised. There was total silence. Pastukhov shuffled his feet.

'Don't go thinking that I'm some crazy, gung-ho kind of hero,' he said guiltily. 'But what would I think? That it was some sort of psycho who'd dressed himself up as a vampire or a werewolf. That means he can be arrested. What can he do against a pistol?

But if I know – the way I know a little bit about you – well then, of course, no. I'd run for it! But you wanted to know how an ordinary cop – a policemen, that is, would react . . .'

I quietly opened the door a bit and walked out of the hall.

Somehow I didn't like what was going on. Since when had they started preparing the Night Watch for interacting with the human agencies of law enforcement? The humans were on their own and we were on our own. That was the way it had always been. Or maybe not always?

No, I definitely didn't like this.

I looked round. Over at one side, beside a little projecting wall, Las was standing, smoking stealthily and hiding the cigarette in his fist like a schoolboy.

'What are you up to?' I asked, taken by surprise.

'What can a cop tell me that I don't already know?' Las asked rhetorically. 'Though I remember I met one cop who played a Vivaldi concerto on the flute. Now that *did* surprise me!'

'Well, why shouldn't a man have a hobby like that?' I asked, shrugging. 'No matter if he's a policeman to the depths of his soul – if he enjoys playing, let him!'

'Right, but not standing under the falling snow in winter, on duty!' Las protested. He thought for a second and added. 'His playing was lousy anyway, I tell you honestly. Definitely a C-minus.'

I shook my head. I had never encountered any militiamen or policemen who played the flute. In general I hadn't come across even a tenth as many amusing little scenes as Las saw all around him. I'd come across plenty that were beastly and abominable, but not the amusing kind.

'In the first place,' I began, 'I wasn't invited to the lecture.'

Las nodded understandingly and whispered: 'Yes, I would have been offended too!'

'In the second place, I find the whole subject rather strange,' I went on, ignoring the jibe. 'Are we preparing for a series of cataclysms or something?'

'There's no stability,' said Las. 'The terrorists have seized another plane.'

'What plane?' I asked, pricking up my ears.

Las looked at me suspiciously. Then he shut his cigarette end in a pocket ashtray and waved his hand about to disperse the smoke.

'Forget it. It's just a figure of speech. Anton, take a look around you! At the human world. You're all Great Ones, mighty magicians, you're not interested in watching ordinary life. But the world's in a fever, financial crisis after financial crisis, currencies skipping up and down, governments falling in countries all over the place, revolution after revolution in the underdeveloped countries. And meanwhile our enemy is cunning and powerful, he's on the offensive.'

'We're supposed to have a truce with the Dark Ones,' I remarked. 'And Zabulon's not being any more malign than usual . . .'

'Zabulon! Ha!' said Las and laughed sarcastically. 'He's small fry. Our enemy is the Prince of Darkness.'

'The devil?' I said. 'Well, there are no specific grounds for believing that he exists . . . Did you get baptised, then?'

'Do you need to ask?' Las proudly pushed his fingers in behind his collar and showed me a brand new shiny little cross. 'I got baptised, I confessed, took the sacrament – the works!'

'A good job you didn't receive extreme unction,' I quipped. 'That's it, then. The forces of evil are doomed now.'

'Don't mock,' Las said in an offended voice.

I suddenly felt awkward. In the final analysis, faith is every individual's personal matter. Whether he's an Other or a human being . . . Take Arina, the witchiest of witches, but she still believed!

'Sorry, I was wrong,' I said. 'Since it's impossible in principle to prove that God does or doesn't exist . . .'

Las patted me on the shoulder patronisingly.

'That's okay. I understand. But you won't deny that the world is seeing an increase in conflicts between countries that can't be resolved by peaceful methods, financial instability is on the increase and all the traditional economic, political and social models are imploding?'

'I won't,' I admitted.

'Well then, in these conditions the Watch is absolutely obliged to prepare to take measures for the protection of the human herd.'

I thought I must have misheard.

'The human what?'

'Herd. Well, population,' Las said, frowning.

'You're not very polite about human beings,' I said.

'Well, have they deserved any better?' Las asked in surprise. 'Two thousand years since people were given the Good News! And what's changed in all that time? We have the same old wars and violence, infamy and abomination!'

'Overall there has been some progress,' I said, disagreeing. 'In wartime they used to annihilate people or turn them into slaves, the peasants starved to death . . .'

'And now in wartime they torture them and poison them with gas in concentration camps, bomb them with high-precision smart bombs or, in the very best of cases, they occupy countries economically and turn them into powerless satellites. And where there is no war – they dumb down their own people and treat them like cattle.' Las spread his hands emphatically. 'All those Genghis Khans, Xerxeses and Caligulas were more honest, I reckon. So far, there is nothing to respect human beings for.'

I started getting a bit wound up at this point.

'Las, we're the Night Watch. We protect people, we don't despise them.'

Las pulled a wry face.

'Listen, Anton. You're, you know . . . a Higher Magician and all that. One of the high-ups. But can we talk off the record, just as friends?'

'Sure, go on.'

'Then don't give me that razzmatazz about how we protect people,' Las said calmly. 'We control them – just a little bit. And we prevent the Day Watch from controlling people the way they think is right. What kind of protection is it, when we issue licences to vampires to hunt people? What kind of protection is it, if for every good deed that we do the Dark Ones are granted the right to work evil? We protect ourselves! Our way of thinking, our comfortable existence, our long lives and lack of human problems. Sure, we're good, and the Dark Ones are bad! That's why we don't entirely regard human beings as cattle. But we don't consider them equal to ourselves!'

'We do,' I said stubbornly.

'Oh, yes?' Las laughed. 'When did you last live life as a human, Anton? So that you had to count the money left in your pocket until payday, grovel to some petty human bureaucrat to get some absurd little piece of paper with a stamp on it, wander round grimy, filthy health centres trying to get exhausted doctors to treat you, spend two hours stuck in a traffic jam because half of Moscow has been blocked off for some big shot, or dodge a car with a flashing light and "special" number plates hurtling along the wrong side of the road?'

'There are plenty of people in Moscow who don't count every kopeck and don't grovel to bureaucrats . . .' I began.

'Of course, and they regard the people around them as cattle,' Las said. 'All those other people who don't have a flashing light or a couple of credit cards from major foreign banks in their wallet. And if you behave like those who reckon they're above the common folk – and, I'm sorry, that's exactly how you do behave when you calculate the lines of probability, remoralise roughnecks just for a minute or two when you run into them, pay in a shop with your bank card from work, which has no limit—'

'Why do you think our Watch bank cards don't have any limit?' I asked in amazement.

'I checked it,' Las chuckled. 'Seems like you try to live within the pay that's supposed to be transferred to your account. Count it all up some time, out of curiosity – you'll soon see that you've been spending two or three times as much as you earn for a long time! The only limit is your internal sense of measure . . . and that has a way of getting stretched. So, Anton, if you behave like those people who are used to thinking of themselves as above everyone else you're absolutely no different from them.'

'I don't drive through red lights with a flashing beacon!' I growled.

'Of course not. You drive through the crossroads in the Twilight, or you apply a Sphere of Inattention to your car, so that everyone brakes without even knowing why. What's the difference between your magic and a flashing light? There isn't any! You think of yourself as a member of a higher race too – only, of course, with greater reason. You *are* a member of a higher race! You're an Other. A Light Other. So you wish people well. But it's a long, long time since you lived the life of ordinary people and you couldn't live that way. You wouldn't last even a single day.'

'I would,' I said stubbornly.

'That's what you think,' said Las, frowning. 'Anyway . . . I like humans, I wish them well. But I don't idealise them. And since they behave like cattle, that's the way I have to relate to them. No way am I going to pretend that there's no difference between me and Vasya the yard-keeper.'

'There isn't any difference, except that we have magical abilities,' I said. 'Absolutely none. We have the same morality, the same dreams . . . the whole kit and caboodle!' I raised my hands, touched the Twilight and felt for my own aura. 'Block for twenty-four hours.'

'I was absolutely certain you would do that,' Las said. 'Well, go on, try it. Only twenty-four hours is too ambitious to start with. A couple of hours would have been enough for you.'

'I queued for passport control in the airport for an hour,' I said. 'It was okay, not a peep out of me.'

'A pity it wasn't two,' Las sighed. 'Then you would have been more careful now . . . Right, then, we'll talk tomorrow.'

'Right, then,' I said and nodded.

'Shall I give you a lift home?' Las asked.

I just snorted disdainfully and headed for the exit.

CHAPTER 3

There's a simple way to understand what a blind man feels in this life: close your eyes and try to do something. Something ordinary, not difficult. Something you normally do anyway 'without looking' – take a spoon out of a drawer in a table, light a cigarette, put a CD in a music centre. It only takes five minutes at the most to understand everything and know that you'll never forget it.

Or you can try a more humane experiment. Tie a load of about ten kilogrammes, wrapped in a big, soft pillow, to your stomach. Only the load has to be something fragile, and so precious that you would be absolutely distraught if you lost it. Then walk around like that for twenty-four hours. And sleep with this load . . .

Even like that you can't get the full comparison, but somehow men who have been through that kind of training start jumping to their feet as if they've been scalded when they catch sight of a pregnant woman standing in public transport.

Magic, of course, is not given to us from birth (if we don't count my daughter, that is) and it's not as priceless as a child. Magic is merely an additional convenience in life. Just like that damned flashing light on an expensive car . . . or a Duma deputy's ID that makes him 'uncheckable', brings traffic cops out in red blotches and makes them salute the offender with black hate in their hearts. So surely I would be able to manage without magic for just twenty-four hours?

Although, of course, it would have been good to leave myself the Sphere of Inattention. As the magical version of the flashing light . . . no, to hell with it!

Mind you, I was very well aware of just why my thoughts kept coming back to that crappy piece of transparent blue plastic that squawked and flashed on the roofs of Mercs and BMWs. I was driving home in the daytime, but I had been rash enough to try it at rush hour (incidentally, after the new mayor of Moscow dedicated a massively broad lane on every major thoroughfare to public transport, rush hour in Moscow had stretched out to fill the whole day and a large part of the night) and the bureaucrats' cars overtaking me in the oncoming lane had begun to provoke despairing envy and burning hatred simultaneously. I tried to recall if I'd ever seen vehicles with special signals like these in any other country at all – apart, that is, from police cars and ambulances. I could only remember a few odd cases – one in London, one in either Spain or Italy.

But on my right there was an empty lane, separated off by a solid line. For some reason the cars with the flashing lights didn't enter it, although you'd have thought they had no reason to feel shy. During the half-hour that I spent in a slow-crawling queue, two buses and a couple of cars with black-tinted windows and no number plates drove along the dedicated lane. In one of the cars – a hulking great Lexus SUV – the window on the driver's side was lowered. The driver was a swarthy young man with a mobile phone in his hand. He was hardly even looking at the road. People like him used to be called 'individuals of Caucasian nationality' in the police bulletins, but recently they'd started using the more politically correct expression 'natives of the Northern

Caucasus region', which in the popular daily vernacular had rapidly been reduced simply to 'natives'.

It would have been okay if buses and taxis had been driving along the dedicated lane in an unbroken stream, the way they do everywhere else in the world! Then it wouldn't have been so offensive. It would have been clear that I was paying with my time for the comfort of riding in a car, while people using public transport were granted the right to ride past the traffic jams.

Only there weren't any buses to be seen. But even so, apart from a few especially self-confident 'natives', the drivers didn't venture into the special lane.

I lit a cigarette. Then I crushed the cigarette into the ashtray and started turning to the right. They weren't exactly delighted to let me through, but they did it calmly – the jam had given drivers a sense of unity but had not yet driven them berserk. Once I was through the four lines of cars that were driving in three lanes, I turned grimly out onto the dedicated lane and put my foot down.

So what if they have put up speed cameras all over the place now! Let them send me a fine in the post, I don't give a damn, I'll just pay it . . . I moved on at a brisk pace, glancing at the speedometer every now and then to avoid exceeding sixty kilometres an hour. The Lexus loomed up ahead in the distance. Along the side of the road 'natives of Central Asia' were picking in relaxed style at the asphalt and the hard autumn ground. For every man with a pick there were three or four standing about aimlessly or observing the slow-flowing river of glittering cars with curiosity. The *gastarbeiters* were finishing stripping the asphalt off the pavement in order to replace it with paving slabs, after the new fashion. Occasional pedestrians manoeuvred between them, skipping from little islands of surviving asphalt to the more even patches of earth. A young mother shoved her baby-buggy forward with dour intensity, as if she didn't notice the nightmare all around her. I suddenly imagined a young woman just like her, somewhere near here seventy years earlier, pushing a barrow filled with earth from the anti-tank trenches that were being dug around Moscow with the fascists already at the approaches. But while her grinding labour had been a significant feat of heroism, nowadays this heroic feat had become a meaningless torment.

The line of *gastarbeiters* came to an end, giving way to dug-up pavement with stacks of sombre grey concrete slabs standing along it like columns. I wondered what had prevented them from laying the slabs along this section of pavement first, and then starting to break up the next one.

There was no answer to that question. But at the end of the mutilated pavement, where it was a bit less muddy, there was a traffic-police patrol car parked, and two young guys in mouse-grey greatcoats waved their striped batons at me gleefully.

I squeezed in close to the kerb, braked to a halt and lowered the window.

'Senior Sergeant Roman Tarasov!' the young, ruddy-faced policeman who walked over announced briskly.

'Common driver Gorodetsky!' I replied, for some reason just as briskly and even playfully, holding out the documents for the car and my licence.

'We're infringing the rules!' the sergeant said, grinning.

'Yes, indeed,' I agreed, not attempting to deny it. 'I couldn't bear sitting in that traffic jam any longer.'

'This lane is the lane for public transport!' the policeman explained to me, as if he was talking to a child. 'Can't you see that, then?'

'I can,' I admitted. 'But I can also see a Lexus that just drove past you. And I haven't seen a single bus for the last quarter of an hour.'

The sergeant lost a bit of his *joie de vivre*, but he carried on smiling.

'A Lexus – that's a big car, almost like a bus . . .' Apparently that was an attempt at a joke. 'But even if there are no buses, that's no excuse for infringing the rules!'

'Agreed, that's no excuse,' I said, nodding. 'But, just the same, why didn't you stop the Lexus?'

The sergeant looked at me as if I was an idiot.

'You mean you didn't see his number plates?'

'I didn't,' I said. 'But then, there weren't any to see! By the way, that's another infringement . . . and the windows were tinted darker than the standards allow. A whole bunch of infringements.'

'A whole bunch . . .' said the sergeant, wincing as if he had toothache. 'The lads stopped one of those "bunches" once – and they got thrown out on their ear, lucky not to get taken to court! And do you know how I got this job?'

'How?' I asked, beginning to feel rather surprised.

The policeman's face assumed the expression of mixed caution and squeamishness with which normal people regard someone who's got a few screws loose.

'Driving onto the lane for public transport traffic,' he said drily. 'Fine: three thousand roubles.'

'I accept that,' I agreed again. 'Write out a receipt.'

This time he looked at me really warily.

'I think you were in a hurry, driver Gorodetsky . . .'

'I was.'

'And your car . . . isn't a Lexus,' he remarked in a flash of brilliant insight.

'A correct observation!' I exclaimed. 'It's a Ford!'

'We could try to resolve the situation – for half,' the policeman said in a very low voice. 'And writing out a receipt takes so long . . .'

I could feel the laughter welling up inside me. He was so very hungry. Of course, for the last seventeen years I hadn't lived the way other people did. But, even so, I did remember a thing or two.

They hadn't changed at all since my first meeting with Pastukhov at the Exhibition of Economic Achievements metro station. 'I tell you what, Roman, write me out the fine,' I said. 'I'd really like to save a bit of money and not waste time. Only it makes me feel sick. Do you understand?'

His face seemed to shudder.

'Do you think it doesn't make *me* feel sick?' Roman asked in a quiet voice. 'Don't dare stop some of them . . . And then there's others that wave their fancy IDs at you . . . and they've closed down all the factories in my parents' town, and you can't buy anything on a pension . . . and I . . .' He faltered, waved his hand through the air and looked at me. He held out my documents. 'Drive on.'

'What about the fine?' I asked.

'Forget it!' He swung round and walked back to his partner.

I watched him go. Sometimes remoralisation doesn't require magic. It was just a pity that this kind of wizardry didn't work for long – and it didn't always work . . . not on everybody.

As I drove slowly back into the lane on the right, I heard the sergeant's partner exclaim: 'You what?'

'Well, you know – he's a popular actor, in theatre and films . . .' Tarasov lied clumsily. 'Let him go.'

I raised the window, squeezed in between a dusty Nissan and a battered old Volga, blinked my emergency lights to thank them for letting me in. And looked at my watch.

Not bad: I'd be home in an hour and a half.

From here it was about twenty minutes on foot by the direct route, through the side streets and courtyards . . .

* * *

In actual fact I drove up to the building a quarter of an hour later – some switch or other had tripped in the mysterious mechanism of Moscow traffic jams and the pace of the cars became almost lively. I stopped in front of the building, in my usual spot, and recalled that a long time ago I'd cast a spell on this convenient patch of asphalt to prevent other people from parking there. Should I stick consistently to my principles and move the car? That would be stupid – no one else would park on this spot anyway.

So I decided not to count magic employed previously as a breach of terms, climbed out of the car and locked it. Now I would go home, and I wouldn't need my abilities as an Other there either . . .

My mobile jingled. I looked at the screen.

'Dearest, buy some black and white bread, vegetable oil, ten eggs, sausages. And the toilet paper's running out.'

Sveta always writes texts with capital letters and punctuation marks. It amuses some people and makes other angry, for some reason. I like it.

I shrugged and set off towards the nearest supermarket, the Crossroads. As everyone knows, since ancient times crossroads have been regarded as the meeting places of evil forces, vampires and dark sorcerers – no wonder that was where they preferred to bury them, after first hammering an aspen stake through their chests with texts from Holy Writ attached to it, just to make sure. That was probably how the first road signs had appeared . . .

The modern-day supermarkets that had incautiously taken this name were not particularly well respected in Moscow, owing to a certain lack of chic and the low-income range of their clientele. But I always felt more comfortable there than in upmarket places with sparser crowds like Alphabet of Taste, Gourmet Globe or Seventh Continent.

I didn't have far to walk – it only took five minutes. But even so I had time to think with bitter sarcasm that today, having abjured the use of magic, I was bound to get into some kind of scrape. The young checkout girl would short-change me and give me lip. An old pensioner at the checkout would count the change in her hand and sob bitterly as she took the chicken thighs and millet off the conveyor belt and put them back in the basket. A beardless youth would try to buy cheap vodka or fortified wine, and the checkout girl (the same one who was going to short-change me) would pretend that she didn't notice his age.

Basically, something unpleasant was bound to happen, something on which, in normal circumstances, I could use the weak remoralisation spells available to me because of my rank – Reproach, Crying Shame, or even Disgrace – in order to restore justice and punish vice.

But even now I had no intention of giving in. I was going to show everyone, and in the first place myself, that I was capable of living like an ordinary human being while preserving my dignity and making the life around me better. I would shame the checkout girl (dammit, how had I got landed with this girl I'd never even seen?), pay for the old woman, who would bless me as I walked away, and lecture the youth sternly on the harmfulness of consuming alcohol in adolescence. Basically, I was going to do everything that I always did, only without magic.

It had worked with the traffic police!

So when I grasped a basket and set out on my journey round the shop (right, oil – there it is . . . the eggs are close by) I was ready for anything. Sausages . . . bread . . . the toilet paper's near the entrance, I'll pick it up there . . .

Standing in the queue for the checkout, I automatically picked up a round lollipop and a chocolate egg with a surprise in it off the counter. I thought about how for the last few months these traditional treats had no longer roused the same childish delight in Nadya that they once had.

What could be done about it? Children grow up faster than we can grasp what's happening.

There was an old woman in the queue. And a youth with some kind of bottle. And the checkout girl was young and lippy-looking, with a piercing in her nose.

I braced myself inwardly.

The old woman set out on the conveyor belt a chicken, a bag of grain (what was this, did my clairvoyant abilities still work, even when my magic was blocked?) and, rather unexpectedly, a bottle of Crimean Cahors wine. And then a plastic card appeared from her little old purse.

'My terminal's not working, only cash,' the checkout girl began.

'Am I supposed to know the terminal's not working?' asked the old woman, instantly joining battle.

'I put up a sign,' said the checkout girl. Then she deftly raked together the old woman's purchases, got up and carried them to the next conveyor belt. 'Leila, let the granny through ahead of the queue.'

The old woman moved to the next checkout, muttering something indignantly, although she did growl 'Thank you' to the girl with the pierced nose. The queues waited patiently. The youth fidgeted nervously, looking at his watch, but he stayed where he was. I studied the sign: *Sorry, we are temporarily unable to accept bank cards.*

A man who looked like a building labourer bought two packs of two-minute noodles and a can of strong beer, and then set off towards the chemist's stand with a confident stride. I had no doubt that he was going to buy either 'antiseptic liquid, 96 per cent ethyl alcohol' or 'tincture of hawthorn', which possessed the additional advantage of having a pleasant smell. And then the youth who came after him didn't buy any alcohol at all, but some kind of vitaminised lemonade 'made with natural ingredients'. Maybe he was intending to mix this lemonade with tincture of hawthorn too, of course. But I decided not to think badly of people. Otherwise I would start thinking of them as inferior too.

The girl quickly rang up my purchases and even treated me to a weary workaday smile before she turned to the next customer. I walked thoughtfully towards the doors.

On the one hand, Las was wrong: I could live without magic, no problem. But on the other, it turned out that I really had lost the habit, if a simple trek to the shop had become a reason for me to anticipate heroics . . .

And incidentally, what was that Las had said about our bank cards from the Watch?

I walked towards the ATMs. Took out my card and twirled it in my hands. It had been issued by some bank I'd never heard of called the Commonwealth Bank of Australia, which seemed basically rather strange. Didn't Russia have enough of its own banks or branches of well-known foreign ones? I stuck the card in the slot and entered the pin code. Right, let's try it . . . *Balance request.* No information. Naturally, the ATM belonged to Raiffeisen, and I'd never seen any ATMs belonging to the Commonwealth Bank of Australia in Russia. I probably ought to look for them in Australia. And I thought I'd seen their logo in Taiwan, too . . . But I'd never even thought of checking my balance.

I wondered what the point was of the Night Watch providing its staff members with cards from a bank that didn't conduct any business or have any offices in Russia.

Well . . . for instance, so that they couldn't check their balance.

But then, what was the point of that?

I selected *Withdraw cash* on the menu. Then *Another amount.* I smiled at the pun. Another amount for an Other . . . The usual limit for a single withdrawal of cash was thirty thousand roubles.

I punched in 30 500 and pressed *Enter.*

The ATM thought for a second and started rustling banknotes.

I entered the pin code again. Went to withdraw cash. Selected the dollar menu. Paused before I entered the sum.

No, this was raving lunacy.

25 000. *Enter.*

No way could an ATM issue me two hundred and fifty hundred-dollar notes!

Something inside the machine started chirring. A stack of hundred-dollar notes slid halfway out. I pulled it out and stuck it in my pocket, as if I was dreaming. The ATM didn't ask for the pin code again – it started counting out more notes. I stood there, trying to hide the slot with the money in it from curious eyes – the European tact in such matters hadn't yet caught on in Russia.

Another stack of money.

The rustling of notes as another portion was counted out . . .

What was I going to do with twenty-five thousand greenbacks? I could buy a new car with that, but what did I need it for?

And the answer was basically this:

Light Others aren't ascetics or saints who have renounced money. We like to dress in beautiful clothes and eat good food. We won't say no to a new TV. Or to a new car.

But, unlike the Dark Ones, we feel . . . awkward about it, I suppose. It's as if we try to live according to the utopian Communist slogan: 'From each according to his abilities, to each according to his needs.' Only we assess our abilities ourselves – and sometimes rather critically. And as a result we reduce the level of our needs.

What can be done to allow convinced altruists to indulge themselves whenever they feel like it? The answer's simple – cure them of the habit of counting. Here are your bank cards, lads. Your pay (and believe me, the boss knows how much you've earned) is transferred to your account . . . Enjoy.

We were probably the only organisation in the world, whether human or Other, in which the boss tried to deceive his rank-and-file colleagues by increasing their pay.

Or rather, by not setting any limit to it.

That was funny.

'Not the smartest thing for an Other who has blocked his abilities to do,' a quiet voice said behind me. 'I mean walking round Moscow in the evening with your pockets stuffed with bucks.'

'I think walking round London or New York with that kind of money wouldn't be too wise, either,' I replied without turning round. 'I knew you were following me, Arina.'

The witch laughed quietly. I finished stuffing the money into my pockets and turned to face her.

She was looking superb. As always.

'Did you deliberately block your magic?' she asked. 'To lure me out?'

'No,' I admitted honestly. 'I had a bet . . . with a colleague.'

'About whether you could live without magic? Well, how is it?' There was a note of unfeigned interest in Arina's voice.

'A mass of unpleasant little details, but I can get by.'

'But I can't,' Arina sighed. 'I'd turn into a decrepit old ruin . . . And by the way, you're not being entirely honest. You blocked your magic, but you still have the health of an Other, your magical aura's visible – and no vampire or werewolf would dare to attack you.'

'I blocked what I could,' I said morosely. 'Why don't you tell me what you're going to do?'

'Me?' Arina asked in genuine surprise. 'I'll see you home, to make sure no one hurts you. We'll have a talk on the way – I swear not to work any evil! You won't attack me, will you?'

Naturally, I could have removed the magical block that I had set up myself. But that would have taken a few minutes and Arina would have sensed it.

'Until I get home – no, I won't.'

'Great,' the witch said delightedly. 'Let's get a move on. It's getting dark already and the forces of evil are coming out to hunt!'

It occurred to me that the sight of Arina would be enough to make any force of evil who had the slightest inkling about magic fill his pants, but I didn't verbalise this banal thought. Smiling at each other, we walked out of the supermarket and headed for my apartment block.

I wasn't at all surprised that Arina knew exactly where I lived.

'What do you make of the prophecy?' Arina asked casually as soon as we were a few steps away from the shop.

'Nothing. You stole the flash stick.'

'Oh, I'm sorry, I forgot to apologise for that bit of petty larceny,' Arina replied, not embarrassed in the least. 'But I can't believe that a computer specialist didn't keep a copy.'

'Gesar didn't believe that, either,' I sighed. 'They turned the whole place upside down, checked my PC and my laptop . . . took away the toy . . .'

'Oh, don't play the hypocrite,' Arina snorted, 'As if you didn't keep a copy, and somewhere where they wouldn't find it! You could have sent it to an e-mail address, for instance.'

'I did think about that,' I said. 'But that's dead easy to trace too.'

'All the same, you have that file,' Arina said confidently. 'By the way . . . would you like me just to give you back the flash stick? I don't need it any more.'

'I'll destroy it, Arina. You can take it to Gesar, he was interested.'

'Oh, woe is me, I don't want to go to Gesar,' said Arina, fluttering her hands. 'It's you I'm interested in. What are we going to do?'

'I already told you – I haven't heard the prophecy!' I replied irritably. 'I haven't heard it! And I don't want to hear it!'

Arina walked along for a while in silence, thinking about something. Then she said: 'You'll have to listen to it. It's important, Anton. Believe me.'

'And then the Tiger will come for me? And I'll have to choose between revealing the prophecy to humans or dying? Thank you kindly! I'll leave that choice to you!'

'Anton, it's all much more complicated than you think.'

'Life is always more complicated than we imagine. Stop this! I'm sick of it, do you understand? I'm sick of deciding for other people! I'm sick of defending the Night Watch! I'm sick of fighting for good! I'm sick of everything!'

I didn't realise at first that I was standing there shouting and the infrequent passers-by were keeping well away from us. Arina stopped too and looked at me sombrely. Then she said: 'Anton, I understand you. And I'm not exactly overjoyed at what's happening, either. But you must hear this prophecy. And you *will* hear it.'

'And how will you make that happen?' I asked. 'Will you force me? Will you break your oaths again?'

'Again?' Arina asked in surprise. 'I didn't break anything. I didn't swear that I wouldn't purloin your trousers and the flash stick.' She giggled, then turned serious. 'No, Anton, and I don't intend to exploit your temporary helplessness to force you to listen to the prophecy. You'll do that yourself.'

I laughed and lengthened my stride. Arina hurried after me.

'Anton, do you remember the joke about how to make a cat lick itself under its tail?'

'No.'

'You should: it may be a child's joke, but it demonstrates various approaches to solving a problem. As usual, representatives of three different nationalities were involved. The American hypnotised the cat. The Frenchman spent ages training it painstakingly—'

'I think it was the Chinese who trained it,' I said without stopping.

'That's not important. And the Russian rubbed mustard on the cat, after which it started licking itself voluntarily with passion and gusto. You'll listen to the prophecy yourself, Anton – with passion and gusto!'

'And what's going to be the mustard?' I asked.

'Your daughter. The boy's prophecy concerns Nadya.'

'What?' I exclaimed, looking round.

Arina spread her hands expressively.

'You heard what. And don't look at me like that, it's not my fault. See you, Anton! When you want to talk to me about the prophecy, summon me. Just summon me through the Twilight – I'll hear you.'

She waved her hand to give me a glimpse of the Minoan Sphere and disappeared.

Lousy old witch, crazy senile schemer . . .

Yes, of course.

But she'd given me a good slathering of mustard. No mistaking that professional touch.

I only remembered that I'd forgotten to buy the toilet paper after I got out of the lift.

CHAPTER 4

APPARENTLY SVETLANA HAD understood everything the moment I walked in the door. But she only asked the question late in the evening, when we were already in bed.

'Have you blocked your magic?'

'Uh-huh.' I didn't attempt to deny it, but I tried not to get involved in explanations. 'The block will run out tomorrow.'

'I see. For a dare?'

'For a dare.'

Svetlana put down the book that she was reading in bed for the second evening in a row and glanced into my eyes. I tensed up, expecting some ironic comment or at least the question: 'What the hell for?'

'Was it hard, Anton?' Svetlana asked.

'Yes,' I admitted. 'I never realised before that I'm always doing something with magic – little bits and pieces, but I do them . . .'

'I understand.'

'It's hard to understand,' I said, smiling to soften the unintended harshness of my words. 'Until you try, it looks dead easy.'

'Anton, I haven't used magic outside the home for four years now.'

'What!' I sat up on the bed. 'But that's stupid!'

'Yes, I know,' said Svetlana, nodding.

'But why?'

'I felt like I was becoming less and less human,' Svetlana replied. 'Almost imperceptibly. At first it seemed miraculous – solving every problem with a single movement, only worrying about the balance between good and evil . . . Then I realised that I never solved any problems but my own. I started trying to reassure myself that there was nothing wrong with that. That the Night Watch couldn't exterminate evil . . . that that wasn't its job in any case: all we can do is not allow good to be defeated, humans have to strive for all the rest themselves. Well, you know . . . And the things they teach young Others in school – the ones with the most passionate hearts join the Watch afterwards, and the ones with cool heads simply live as Others among humans. And then it started making me feel . . .' She paused, trying to find the right word.

'Sick?' I asked with avid curiosity.

'Uncomfortable.' Svetlana shook her head: 'Not sick. We really do try to do good, after all. But . . . uncomfortable. You know, it's . . . Rumata Estorsky probably felt that way just before he took out his swords and stood facing the door that the storm troopers were breaking down.'

'I understand,' I said with a nod.

'I love you precisely because you do understand and I don't have to explain to you who Rumata was,' Svetlana said seriously and smiled. 'And then . . . I realised that I would end up like he did.'

'I went through something like that,' I said.

'You coped. You're a man, you react differently. If push comes to shove, you can always get drunk and abuse Gesar. But I realised that I would just fly off the handle and run wild, create a real mess . . . And I stopped using magic. Well – apart from at home. I hate ironing the laundry!'

'Why didn't you say anything to me?' I asked.

'You were busy. You were saving the world.'

'I'm sorry,' I said. I felt unbearably ashamed. 'I'm sorry.'

'What for?'

'For being a blind, self-satisfied ass. For not seeing . . .'

'You couldn't have seen anything, I didn't put up a block. I just stopped using magic.'

I looked into Svetlana's eyes. Then I glanced at the bedroom door.

'She's asleep,' said Svetlana.

After that we didn't need any magic.

In the dead of night I lay in bed, listening to my wife's breathing and thinking about prophecies.

There were two of them – and something about them didn't add up . . .

No, there weren't just two of them. That was my mistake.

There was a third one, too. The prophecy that Svetlana would have a daughter, who would become an Absolute Enchantress. An Other of boundless Power. Someone who could alter the balance of Light and Darkness, change the entire existing order of things.

Somehow I'd almost forgotten about that. But after all, it was a prophecy that had come true. Olga had rewritten Svetlana's destiny for its sake, and for its sake Gesar had brought us together, intrigued, taken risks, got involved in confrontations with Zabulon and the Inquisition. The stakes were monstrously high – and now suddenly it was all over? Zabulon had resigned himself to defeat?

But that could never happen . . .

So that game wasn't over yet. It was still going on. The prophecy had been realised: Nadya was an Absolute Enchantress, but the prophecy hadn't specified what that would lead to.

All right. Let's hold that fact in our memory, it's obviously important. Nadya is one of the pieces on the chessboard. Maybe the most important figure – the White Queen.

What was next?

The boy Kesha's prophecy. Arina already knew it – so the Tiger was after her . . . Or was he? According to the classical theory, the Tiger tried to eliminate the Prophet in order to prevent a prophecy from being pronounced and realised. And that fitted perfectly with what I had seen with my own eyes and heard with my own ears. When he stormed the Night Watch office, the Tiger had said: 'The prophecy must not be heard.'

Right? Right.

But in the old Chinese magician's opinion, that wasn't the goal that the Tiger pursued at all. His goal was to 'shake up' the prophets, urge them on to declare their prophecies to humans, so that the prophecies would come true – and change human life in one way or another, make sure that the human anthill didn't stop developing. A coherent theory that was confirmed by Fan Wen-yan's own story . . . The Tiger 'hassled' the prophets until they performed their duty – or firmly decided never to proclaim the prophecy. Clearly, the prophecy that Wen-yan had heard foretold something very bad for China – and the magician had been prepared to die in order to save his country. The Tiger had realised that and had left – he didn't need any pointless sacrifices.

But then why, in Kesha's case, had the Tiger said that 'the prophecy must not be heard'? So was it special in some way? Something that went beyond those that brought the world Sputniks, miniskirts or rock music? And at the same time, if Arina could be trusted, it concerned my daughter.

A riddle.

So, let's start from the other end. Who is the Tiger? Once again, in Wen-yan's opinion – and apparently he had studied this question more thoroughly than all our European sages – the Tiger was not simply an Other, changed and guided by the Twilight. He was more complicated than that. He was . . . well, to a certain extent, you could say that he was alive. Alive and intelligent.

Like the Twilight itself.

Basically, he *was* the Twilight, in a form accessible to our eyes . . .

I felt a frosty chill creep across my skin. Someone was walking over my grave, as the Americans say.

Someone . . . A Tiger in a coat!

The Twilight . . .

There it was all around me. Accessible to Others, but barely even capable of being sensed by humans. The source of Power – and simultaneously its consumer.

And, if Wen-yan could be believed, alive and intelligent.

How was that possible? How could a nothingness be intelligent? A matryoshka doll with seven dimensions, one of which is our world, with the others ranging from a cold desert to a pale copy of the real world. Intelligence had to have some material vehicle.

Or did it really have to have anything?

After all, we didn't even know what the magical Power that we used was. Our scientists were all, to a man, poor magicians, but with wise heads, and they had investigated this matter throughout the twentieth century and carried on in the twenty-first. Our scientists – meaning not only Light Ones and not only Russians. Others throughout the world had sought to understand their own nature, when necessary even involving human scientists and feeding precisely calculated crumbs of information to the Pentagon, the CIA and secret Soviet research institutes. Specially trained Others had collaborated with human scientists, demonstrating certain facets of their abilities – too little for them to be taken with unconditional seriousness, but enough to inflame curiosity and get entire laboratories with multimillion budgets set to work.

Nothing.

There is a Power that we can sense. It is emitted by all living things, but to the greatest extent by humans. (They are followed by whales, dolphins, pigs, dogs and rats – as it happens, monkeys don't even make the top ten.) Others can sense Power, see it as an aura, they can assess it and record it. And also consume it, naturally – amass it within themselves. So that later, by entering the Twilight, or simply summoning up its mental image, they can perform magical actions.

How? The Chinese magician was quite right – how did the Twilight, which was non-material, transform Power, which was not registered by any instruments, into a perfectly material fireball or a Triple Blade that sliced through metal and stone? Our thoughts and desires were only the switches. Or, to use computer terminology, the commands. But all the invisible work that allowed us to work miracles took place beyond our awareness and beyond our control. It was carried out by the Twilight. So, the Twilight was either an inconceivable non-material computer, tuned to carry out the desires of Others – but then that raised the question of who created it and programmed it – or an inconceivable non-material rational being. A superbeing . . .

In principle, there wasn't really any great difference here. A machine consisting of energy fields, say, or an equally exotic supermind. Was it all-powerful?

Probably not. By definition, only God was omnipotent and omnipresent. I wasn't prepared to believe that if the Supreme Being existed, He was concerned with realising the desires of a bunch of Others. That contradicted both theology and common sense. And the facts that we had at our disposal, too. The Tiger or a Mirror, for instance, were not like a manifestation of divine will, almighty and omnipotent. But they *were* like the behaviour of a very powerful and intelligent being. The behaviour of God? No, not by a long way.

And what was it that every living creature feared?

That was an easy one.

Death.

So . . . that meant that one way or another, the boy Kesha's prophecy was dangerous for the Twilight. And that was why the Tiger didn't want it to be heard.

Logical?

Yes.

Then we could take that as a starting point.

Now for the other prophecy. The one that was shouted into a hollow tree by a quite different boy who lived in Britain a long, long time ago. A prophecy that had been slumbering, stored away in a wooden chalice for almost three hundred years.

Did it have anything to do with me?

Or did it announce the independence of the United States of North America, the discovery of penicillin or the sinking of the *Titanic*?

No. In matters such as prophecy, there was no such thing as coincidence. If it had come into my hands, if I had guessed – of course, if I really had guessed . . . how I could hear it . . .

These were two links in a single chain.

But between them was a third link, the prophecy about the Absolute Enchantress Nadezhda . . .

And I didn't have any options. I was a cat who had been smeared with mustard under his tail – and I was going to lick it off, with passion and with gusto.

Because my daughter's fate was at stake.

And because I really didn't like the dream that I had had, about Nadya screaming at me with hate in her voice: 'Daddy, what have you done to us?' And it wasn't just a dream generated by nervous stress, a drop of strong drink and a song about a magician who was a poor student of his art that had surfaced from my subconscious. It was a case of precognition, what ordinary people call a 'prophetic dream'.

I got out of bed quietly, so as not to wake Svetlana. The bed creaked treacherously and I froze, but my wife didn't wake up. I went to the sitting room, closed the door to the bedroom and switched on a dim standard lamp.

In a modern home, if you don't happen to be a fanatical opponent of progress, and especially if you're keen on gadgets, there are many electronic devices capable of carrying information. All of them at my home had been checked. The desk PC and the laptop. And Nadya's netbook. And Svetlana's tablet. And the mobile phones. And the alarm clock, on which you could record your own music to wake you up. And all the flash sticks. And the answering machine on the landline phone. Even the teddy bear that had a chip in it with the phrase 'I love you, Nadenka' recorded on it by Svetlana had been checked – with apologies. They hadn't forgotten my MP3 player, either.

Many Others, especially those who have been alive for more than a hundred years, have a pretty poor grasp of electronics and modern technology in general. In this respect, Gesar is a sophisticated Other, a smart guy who tries to get some idea of what's what.

And that was why, for this supremely polite search, he had sent really young Others who weren't powerful magicians but who understood very well where a microchip with the recording of the prophecy could be hidden.

These young guys had checked everything but had not found anything, although they had special instruments that I'd only seen in the movies, capable of identifying any memory card at a distance even if it wasn't plugged into anything. I had thanked them – they'd found a couple of flash sticks that I'd lost around the flat a long time ago . . .

But they didn't find the prophecy.

Naturally. I hadn't made a copy on an electronic medium. I'm not an idiot.

I opened the drawer of the sideboard, crammed with all sorts of old electronic junk, and took out an old Sony minidisc player. A dead-end branch in the development of electronics, the kind of thing that no one uses now except people who are especially fond of shocking the public (or who are exceptionally thrifty). The battery in it had died a long time ago.

But there was a separate container that could be attached, and I stuck a battery in that, then screwed the container to the player (all fair and square, a sound, reliable screw, not some kind of flimsy clip-on fastening) and pressed the play button. Vysotsky's hoarse voice started sounding in my earphones:

In remote Murom's dark, secret, forested parts,
Evil spirits sow fear in all travellers' hearts.
Like wandering corpses, they wail and they howl,
And the birds there don't sing, they mutter and growl.

Oh, it's dark and creepy lost in the murk!
In enchanted swamps female hobgoblins lurk,
They'll grab you and drag you down out of sight.
Fierce wood demons wander the woods day and night.
On foot or on horseback, they'll give you a fright
Oh, it's dark and creepy lost in the murk!

Once lost in that deep forest gloom,
Peasant, merchant or soldier brave,
Drunk or sober, they are all doomed
And there's no way they can be saved.
Whatever reason brings them there
They all simply vanish into empty air . . .

I didn't really have to listen, but I did. Right to the end of the song. To the final couplet.

> The spirits fought a battle that ended it all,
> They all fought to the death, as old greybeards recall,
> And that was what made the dread disappear.
> Now people go to the forest with nothing to fear
> And now it's not dark and creepy at all!

Then I pressed the stop button and glanced round furtively. The doors of the bedroom and the nursery were closed. Naturally, I couldn't check the Twilight right now but our home was surrounded by such powerful defensive spells that even Gesar and Zabulon working together would have taken hours to break through them. The spells were an entitlement of my rank – and since Nadya lived here . . .

Did I want to hear the prophecy?

I knew now for certain that it existed. Arina had said as much. There was no point in hoping that Kesha hadn't pressed the button on the toy phone. Or that the prophecy was about the price of oil or the presidential elections . . .

I sighed, closed my eyes and pressed the button.

Silence. With crackling, like from an old-fashioned record.

'You are Anton Gorodetsky, Higher Light Magician . . .' a childish voice said quietly. My hands started trembling as they clutched the minidisc player – someone wasn't just walking over my grave, they were dancing jigs and reels on it. 'Because of you . . . all of us will be released . . .'

Released? What did that mean?

'The Tiger's coming, the Tiger's coming, the Tiger's coming,' said Kesha, suddenly speaking rapidly, almost incoherently . . . 'A long time. A long, long time . . . Nadya Gorodetskaya! Nadya can do it, Nadya can . . .'

I actually jerked up off my chair when the hasty muttering was interrupted by my daughter's name.

'You can't divide anything by zero, you can't divide anything by zero . . .' the voice reminded me like the feverish ravings of some star pupil. 'Anything multiplied by zero is zero, anything multiplied . . . Kill the Tiger! Kill the Tiger and you kill the Twilight! Kill the Tig—'

The recording came to an end. The toy phone only had a small memory chip.

A few seconds of silence – and Vysotsky started singing again in mid-line . . .

In a strange country everything's queer,
You could get lost, you could just disappear.
It can raise goose bumps thinking too long
About all the strange things that could go wrong.
The ground cracks apart, raising a doubt:
Will you leap boldly, or just chicken out?
And that's the basic complication
Of such a tricky situation.

I took off the headphones, turned the player off and tossed it back into the drawer.

Basically, I'd understood quite a lot.

'The Tiger's coming, the Tiger's coming for you . . .' No comment required.

'The Twilight is falling asleep . . . not enough Power, not enough, not enough . . . the prophecies have been waiting . . . A long time. A long, long time.' The Twilight was short of Power? That was kind of strange. Was there really not enough grief and joy in the world? Well – let's just accept it. 'The prophecies have been waiting . . .' Which prophecies did that mean? The one that

Wen-yan had not made known? The one that Arina had 'retarded'? Possibly.

I imagined the flood of emotions that would be precipitated by the destruction of Russia – or China . . . It wouldn't be a momentary thing, it would last for years, decades. It would be insanity. The world was imperfect enough already, it was full of conflicts, torn apart by small wars and global crises. And even if peace and prosperity were established throughout the world, human beings were such brutes, they'd always find some reason to suffer!

Well, okay, let's accept that the Twilight is short of incoming Power. Assume that's a fact.

'Nadya can . . . You can't divide by zero, you can't divide by zero . . . Anything multiplied by zero is zero, anything multiplied by zero . . .' I thought I understood what this meant, too. Nadya was a Zero-Level Enchantress. An Absolute Enchantress. In theory there were no limits to her power. Of course, she didn't really understand how to control it . . . but that was only a matter of practice.

What did 'you can't divide by zero' mean? Not in mathematics, but in this particular case? And what did 'anything multiplied by zero is zero' mean?

I looked at the closed doors of the nursery and the bedroom again. I crept out into the hallway, feeling like a criminal, and took the cigarettes and the lighter off the shelf. I don't smoke at home, not even on the balcony – but I had just realised that I really needed a smoke now. I pulled on my anorak, went out onto the balcony and closed the door firmly behind me. I lit up and launched a thin stream of smoke into the night sky.

Who were the Others?

Rational beings, capable of using Power.

The Twilight, with the Tiger as its embodiment, was also a rational entity, capable of using Power.

Different in kind, but also a rational being . . .

Who was the most powerful Other?

Nadya was the most powerful. A Zero-Level Enchantress.

And the Twilight was also zero-level.

The terms 'stronger' and 'weaker' were inapplicable here. Even among the Great Ones, whose Power could not meaningfully be measured, there were some differences in the level of Power, and that was why those who invented the most cunning spells, used them more quickly and struck at unexpected points were victorious. But the Power of the Twilight and Nadya's Power were identical. The Twilight possessed all the Power that flowed into it. And Nadya, in some miraculous way, was also capable of controlling all the Power in the world.

Could the Twilight destroy Nadya?

Could Nadya destroy the Twilight?

That was the question.

And to judge from the words of the prophecy, she could.

'Kill the Tiger and you kill the Twilight!'

You can't divide by zero – the Twilight couldn't destroy Nadya. It seemed that that was physically impossible. And I was very glad about that.

If you multiply anything by zero, the result is zero.

What did that mean? That Nadya was capable of destroying the Twilight? And what would happen to her if she did? Would she be killed too? Or lose her magical abilities?

I didn't want that for my daughter.

That was the whole picture. I wasn't going to reveal the prophecy. And I was going to destroy the recording.

What about the Tiger?

He wouldn't come for me. It wasn't in his interest, he didn't want the prophecy to be made known to humans. That was what he had said himself. But I wouldn't tell anyone, and he ought to understand that. I couldn't vouch for Arina, but the Tiger could take care of her . . .

I finished my cigarette and flung the butt off the balcony in a slovenly gesture. I followed its flight down from the seventh floor – the small dot of fire sliced through the darkness until it was lost to view in the circle of light round a street lamp.

Right at the feet of the man standing there . . .

I grabbed hold of the railing as I looked down. At the young man in a light-coloured raincoat. At the Tiger looking up at me.

The Tiger raised his hand and waved to me, either in greeting or farewell. Then he turned and walked away into the darkness.

I took out another cigarette, then put it back in the pack. I went back into the flat, hung up my anorak, rinsed out my mouth in the bathroom so as not to stink of tobacco, and sneaked quietly into the bedroom. Svetlana was sleeping. I lay down and fell asleep too – easily and perfectly calmly.

CHAPTER 5

FROM EARLY MORNING those mystical forces responsible for the roads of Moscow (forces that seem more mysterious to me than any Tiger) were well-disposed. I slipped out easily onto the Third Ring Road, and the traffic on it was moving at a lively pace. In the direction I needed, of course – all the cars going in the other direction were barely crawling along – but that was the usual way of things.

I moved into the left lane and switched on the radio. First my heart was gladdened by a strident song with the chorus: 'Young teen fluff-head. She's a lame-brain child.' Another station was broadcasting an interview with an opposition politician who was abusing the authorities in almost obscene language and claiming there was no free speech in the country. As a matter of fact, in any country with a culture of free speech, at the end of that broadcast the politician would have been served with a summons for slander, defamation of character and insinuation. So I carried on wandering through the Moscow airwaves until I came to rest at a station that was broadcasting foreign popular music.

'Turn it down a bit, Anton,' a voice said behind me.

I squinted at the rear-view mirror. Yes, real skill didn't depend on age. Skill like teleporting into a moving car that was protected, and doing it completely unnoticed . . .

'Arina, I didn't invite you.'

'But you listened to the prophecy,' said the witch, stating a fact.

'Of course. You're very persuasive.'

'And?'

'And nothing.'

Arina paused. Then she said ingratiatingly: 'Do you understand what this prophecy is about? Your daughter can destroy the Tiger.'

'And the Twilight,' I said. 'A wonderful prospect.'

Arina tossed her head angrily.

'Anton! Come to your senses! You know about the prophecy that I tried to prevent from happening . . .'

'I know that if through some incredible disaster the Twilight is destroyed,' I said, keeping my eyes on the road, 'then all our Power will be reduced to nothing. It will drain off into the void – or remain in this world . . . that's not important. But we will no longer be able to heal people, to protect them . . .'

'As if we really healed them and protected them very much anyway,' Arina said. Not scathingly, more sadly.

'We do what we can,' I said, shrugging. 'Perhaps it's not for a former Dark One and Witches' leader to reproach the Night Watch on that score?'

'Ah yes, I'm a well-known Baba Yaga,' Arina snickered. 'I used to eat little Ivans for supper and send the swan-geese off to plunder and loot.'

'I'm not claiming that,' I said soberly. 'I'm even prepared to concede that you personally scrubbed down fine young heroes in the bathhouse and inspired them for the battle against evil.'

Arina laughed unexpectedly. 'You know, you're right! That did happen a couple of times . . .'

'But like any witch, you worked both good and evil,' I continued.

'And without distinction. But *I* try to stick to good. So don't go reproaching me.'

'I'm not reproaching you,' Arina said with surprising meekness. 'But you've heard the prophecy, haven't you? The Twilight is short of Power. Power is produced by human emotions. Life has clearly become too calm . . .'

'Oh, it's really calm!' I exclaimed. 'Not a day goes by without a new war. And there's no problem with sex in the world, either. The consumer society consumes, the Third World fights battles, ships sink, typhoons rage and roar, power stations explode – the world's awash with emotions. And there's Hollywood trying its best, too: people certainly aren't short of spectacles.'

'So it means that isn't enough,' Arina said stubbornly. 'It means that the way everything's going doesn't suit the Twilight. It wants major upheavals. The downfall of kingdoms, mass human migrations, holocausts and apocalypses . . .'

'And what has that got to do with us?'

'If I understand correctly, Fan Wen-yan refused to promulgate a prophecy that would have destroyed China as a unified power,' said Arina. 'I did something similar with a prophecy about Russia. Unfortunately' – a note of genuine sorrow appeared in her voice – 'I didn't have the wits to die and halt the prophecy completely. I only delayed it. But the Twilight needs Power. And it will get it – when our country perishes.'

'That's your opinion,' I said. 'I don't think that sort of thing happens because of causes that are . . . let's call them mystical. It's not the invention of the miniskirt, you know! Gesar believes that you really did change the prophecy, and that's why everything foretold in it has already happened – but in a mild form. The revolutions, and the occupations . . .'

'I wish I could agree with the old intriguer,' said Arina. 'But where's the guarantee?'

'Where's the guarantee that Nadya can destroy the Tiger?' I asked. 'The incoherent exclamations of a third-year schoolboy? Highly convincing! And what will happen if the Twilight is killed? Will magic simply disappear? Or will it be the end of life on Earth? Or the end of reason? Do you understand how it's all arranged? I don't! And the old programmer's law says: "If it works, don't touch it!"'

Arina didn't answer.

'And just why have you decided that the Twilight is an enemy?' I went on. 'And that it's in some way involved in realising the prophecies? Don't get your apples and oranges mixed up. Say my daughter does go and destroy the Tiger. And the Twilight with it. Magic disappears. But the prophecies remain the same as they were. They come true. Do you understand? What then? We won't even be able to do the little bit that we can do now! Because we'll have become ordinary human beings!'

'I'd like to believe Gesar,' said Arina. 'And you, too. But what if I'm right? What lies behind your words, Anton? Genuine anxiety for people? For peace, for our country, for your nearest and dearest? Or simply the fear of a magician living his own special, interesting, comfortable life? The fear of losing his abilities and becoming like everyone else!'

'Permit me to remind you,' I said, unable to stop myself, 'that if you lose your abilities, you'll be transformed into a decrepit old woman. Or disintegrate completely, into dust.'

'Yes,' Arina said in a quiet voice. 'You're right. But that has nothing to do with the case. I'm prepared to pay that price.'

'Well, I'm not! And in particular I'm not prepared to decide for others. For Sveta. For Nadya. For Kesha. For all the Others who exist and will exist.'

'But you'll have to, won't you, Anton?' Arina said with just a hint of a threat.

'You think so?' I asked. 'What will you do? Reveal the prophecy to humans? It doesn't state that the Tiger will be killed. It only tells us that Nadya can kill the Tiger. Do you want to make her do it? That will be pretty hard. And not only because you'll have to get past me and Svetlana . . . I don't know how I'll manage, but Sveta will twist you into a fancy pretzel. She's a mother. Do you understand that? But you'd still have to persuade Nadya. Battles like that aren't won through fear. And Nadya won't destroy the Tiger. She's very fond of furry little animals in general.'

'Furry little animals . . .' Arina laughed bitterly. 'Is that right? I'll think of something.'

'You can tell the prophecy to humans,' I said magnanimously. 'If that's what you want. There's nothing inevitable in it. All you'll achieve is to set the Tiger on your own trail.'

'I'll think of something,' Arina repeated stubbornly. 'For instance . . . wait, where are you going?'

'What do you mean, where?' I asked. 'To work. I turn through the gates right here.'

There was a pop behind me – and Arina disappeared. The Night Watch office is shielded by so many magical barriers that Arina could have been left stuck outside the gates for ever – despite all her great wisdom and the power of the Minoan Sphere.

I parked in my own space, with a gloating laugh, only to discover three of our guys getting into our SUV field vehicle – Semyon, Las and Alisher! A strange kind of team! I clambered out of the car and waved to them.

'Where are you off to?'

'Another Schuchart's turned up. Want to go with us?'

'What level?' I asked.

'Fourth. But the guy's pumped himself full of Power.'

The picture of Arina tormented by demons flew right out of

my head, along with all the prophecies in the world. When someone throws a Schuchart, it's bad. Very bad. I know: it nearly happened to me once. And as yesterday evening had made clear, it could even have happened to Svetlana . . .

And if this young guy had already pumped himself up to the gills . . .

'Let's go,' I said as I climbed into the car. Las was in the driving seat. He turned and looked at me intently.

'Yes, thanks for reminding me,' I said, then closed my eyes and started removing the block on my magical abilities. 'Note that this is a matter of urgent necessity. I think I've already proved that I was right!'

Las didn't argue. He just stepped on the gas.

The area around Luzhniki Stadium was quiet. I got out of the car first and looked round. Yes – this was bad. Judging from the amount of litter on the approaches to the stadium, quite a lot of people had passed this way. And the number of *polizei* at the entrances suggested the same. What a lot of fine puns we sacrificed when we took up that German term and dropped the good old Russian 'filth'.

But it was quiet.

'What's going on here?' I asked Alisher. 'It's a bit early for any kind of sports events.'

'A concert,' Las said curtly.

'Thank God it's not football,' I murmured. 'But what band is it? And why are they playing in the morning – is it a special children's performance?'

'Almost. The All-Russian Youth Competition for New Performers, the final. All sorts of rock bands from Perm and Yekaterinburg, original genre artistes from Kaluga and Syktyvkar, folk-rhyme declaimers from the Urals . . .'

'Well, then, there can't be many spectators here,' I said dismissively. 'Although maybe I shouldn't be so sceptical – Yekaterinburg has produced heaps of tremendous groups . . .'

'Someone had the bright idea of providing the performers with an audience. They've bussed in school kids, twenty thousand of them. And soldiers too, as part of their cultural programme – at least ten thousand.'

'Dammit!' I said, lengthening my stride. 'Alisher, I'll make contact. You brief me and handle liaison with the Day Watch. Las, you take up position among the school kids. If necessary, put them all out with Morpheus. Semyon, you back me up, okay?'

'There isn't really much to brief you on . . .' Alisher said, frowning. 'Valentin Loktev, twenty-five years old, Fourth-Level, not specialised, studied in our school five years ago, didn't join the Watch . . .'

The image that Alisher had sent took shape in my memory: a young guy with a nose twisted slightly to one side, sharp but rather coarse facial features, without any breeding or inner strength.

'A sportsman, is he?' I asked. 'I seem to remember him. I saw him at the school a couple of times, when I was giving lectures.'

'A sportsman,' Alisher chuckled. 'A chess-player! And his nose is flattened like that from fighting when he was a little kid and a teenager. He's from the outskirts, a district well known for the direct approach to settling disagreements.'

'I get it,' I said.

As we reached the entrance I picked out a member of the Day Watch in the crowd – a young vampire, dressed in a deliberately bright, challenging style. To look at he was the same age as our Schuchart, about twenty-five. The vampire was standing there, slouching against the metal barriers near the entrance.

'Hi there, Gorodetsky!' he exclaimed, identifying me instantly.

I have a certain reputation among the vampires. And you couldn't even really say that it's a bad one. It's kind of complicated.

But at least they all know me.

'Anton Gorodetsky, Night Watch,' I said, preferring to introduce myself formally in any case, and not slip into an informal tone. 'What's happening?'

The vampire didn't take up my cool tone.

'Ah, the usual business with you Light Ones. Some young guy wants universal good and justice. And right now, straight away, as usual. He's sitting in the stand, sector B, up at the top, pumping Power out of everyone on all sides.'

'We get some interesting cases with you Dark Ones as well,' I said. 'When you get the urge for a drop of hot blood . . . and off you go into the dark streets at night.'

The vampire licked his lips. But he carried on smiling.

'Tell me about it, Anton. The young folk these days have got so wild. We struggle and strain, trying to educate them . . . frighten them – with your name, by the way. Tell them Gorodetsky will come and dematerialise them . . .'

I realised I was taking a hopeless beating in this duel of words. So I pretended it had never even happened.

'Right then, we're onto it,' I said. 'Your assistance is no longer required, you can go.'

'I'll stand here for a while and watch,' the vampire chuckled. What was his name . . . I'd seen his picture at briefings in the Night Watch office, but his name had completely slipped my mind. Something very ordinary, either Sasha or Andrei . . . 'It's not every day you see Light Ones clobbering their own.'

That finally got my back up.

'Fine,' I said, spreading my hands. 'You can observe. But bear in mind that if I can't disarm the guy immediately – and I can't guarantee anything – then the first thing he'll probably start doing is clobbering bloodsuckers. That's a bad character trait we Light Ones have – we dislike the Lower Others most of all.'

His face twitched briefly, but then he smiled again.

'I can't argue with that. You do have a bent for discrimination. Thanks for the warning – I'll be careful.'

I walked past the Day Watch representative, imagining to myself (with great pleasure) how I could flatten that insolent vampire with a Press and then rip off his registration mark, and he would crumble into grey ash.

What was it with the vampires these days? Insolent, smug . . . First that one who was hunting near Bolotnaya Square, and now this one . . .

The policemen at the entrance moved towards me uncertainly. They could sense that something was wrong – their instincts told them that the people in the stadium were behaving oddly . . .

What kind of nonsense is this? What instincts? These are people, not animals!

'Show me your invitation, citizen,' said a rosy-cheeked young man in uniform, blocking my way.

'You're not concerned about my invitation,' I said morosely, waving my hand in the style of the Jedi knights. The vampire behind me giggled audibly.

'I'm not concerned about your invitation,' the policeman agreed, stepping back. His comrade, who had also been affected by the mild spell, backed away to allow me through.

And then I saw a familiar face ahead of me. This policeman hadn't been affected by the spell, and now he was waving his arms, desperately trying to attract my attention.

Yes indeed. Anyone who has experienced magical compulsion tries not to repeat the experience.

'Hi, Dima,' I said, walking over to Pastukhov. 'What are you doing here? It's not your district, is it?'

'I've been shipped in with the reinforcements,' said the senior sergeant. Despite the cold weather, he was streaming with sweat. 'Tell me, Anton – what's happening?'

'A minor emergency,' I said dismissively. 'Don't bother your head about it, it's our job.'

'And tell me, over there . . . behind you . . . is that . . . ?' He hesitated.

'A vampire,' I replied honestly. 'Don't worry, he's on duty too. He's bad, but not dangerous right now. He won't do anything to anyone.'

'Can I stick with you?' Pastukhov implored me desperately. 'I'm like one of the gang, right? I help you, we work together . . . I gave a lecture to your colleagues yesterday . . .'

Probably he simply didn't want to stay near a vampire, even a 'safe' one. But on the other hand . . . why not? There was something intriguing about the idea of working in tandem with a member of the human forces of law and order.

'Let's go,' I said. 'Only stay behind me and don't interfere, all right?'

Pastukhov nodded and then crossed himself clumsily.

Valentin Loktev was a young man of rather unprepossessing appearance. The only noteworthy feature he possessed were his immense eyebrows, which reminded me of the former leader of the USSR, Leonid Brezhnev. But the General Secretary of the Central Committee of the Communist Party of the Soviet Union also had a massive and impressive figure that somehow harmonised with his giant eyebrows – as well as a post that allowed him to determine people's fate and the destiny of the entire world with a single flourish of them. But the beetle-browed Loktev was a skinny young guy with an otherwise absolutely ordinary appearance.

Maybe, of course, if he were to occupy a post like Brezhnev's, that would lend him charisma, the way it so often happens.

Loktev was sitting well apart from the other spectators. As Pastukhov and I climbed up to him, I examined the audience curiously. They looked kind of dejected. Some rock band was performing on the stage, laying down frenzied heavy metal, and the spectators periodically seemed to come to life and start moving about . . . and then slump back into indifference again.

The Light Magician Valya Loktev was pumping their energy out of them. Pumping out the Power that was swirling about, mingled with positive emotions. And that is basically what every Schuchart does.

'Light vampires' like this got their name from readers and admirers of the Strugatsky Brothers. In their novel *Roadside Picnic*, there's a wonderful character by the name of Schuchart, and at the end of the book he approaches the Golden Orb that grants wishes, shouting out (or muttering to himself – ah, I can't remember . . .) the only good wish that he can think of: 'Happiness for all, and let no one leave feeling short-changed!'

Naturally, malicious tongues rehashed this agonised *cri de coeur* from a member of the intelligentsia into the phrase: 'Happiness for all and let no one who feels short-changed leave!' Which, of course, changes the whole idea substantially. But at the same time it introduces a certain honest realism into a fantastic story.

'Schucharts' is the term we in the Watch use for Light Ones who one day simply snap in the face of the imperfection of the universe, decide to work good all over the place and run amok. The problem with this is that the good they work immediately gives the Dark Ones the right to work evil of equal strength . . . Of course, Dark Ones are not all born villains, thirsting to torment everyone around them simply to satisfy their own malice. In daily life many Dark Ones are perfectly pleasant. But they mostly derive their Power from the negative feelings of the humans around them. And in general they have no real regard for them, so when they're given the right to Dark intervention they quickly make up for all the good caused by a 'Schuchart'. And, as a rule, with interest.

In general, Schucharts are not very powerful – Fourth- or Fifth-Level, only rarely Third. (Those who are more powerful than that are usually more intelligent and mature.) That's why, once they've chosen the path of militant good, 'Schucharts' set out for places where they can load up with Power from positive emotions – a good concert, the premiere of a long-awaited film, a sports event at which the fans of the winning team are in the majority, or even a children's New Year party. And there they pump themselves full of energy – so much energy that it makes dealing with them a problem, even for Higher Magicians.

And then off they go, working good on all sides. Until they're stopped.

By any possible means.

One day I almost became a 'Schuchart' myself. But I had either the wits or the luck to realise exactly what I ought to do . . . what I was gathering the energy of human happiness for.

I wasn't sure about the young man Valentin.

As I approached, I could see quite clearly just how full he had pumped himself. Right up to the eyeballs, as they say – he couldn't accumulate any more Power and was flinging everything he pumped out into a Sphere of Negation. I could tell at a glance that no spell of mine would pierce that defence. Maybe Gesar could have done something. Thanks to his technique. But there was no certainty that even he could have done anything straight away.

So, a Sphere of Negation. A spell that weak Others are really fond of – it allows them to oppose far more powerful magicians.

Right, now we know you, Valentin.

'May I sit down?' I asked as I approached the young man. Pastukhov had stopped a little distance away and started watching the stage in a very unnatural manner.

'Have a seat, Anton,' Valentin said. And he added, trying to speak as impressively as possible: 'Only don't try anything stupid, all right?'

'There's nothing stupid left for me to try here,' I sighed as I sat down.

Valentin snorted.

'It was always interesting to listen to you, Anton. You added a special kind of twist to the way you put things.'

'That comes with age,' I said, surveying the stand. 'If you happen to live that long . . . So what are you doing, kiddo?'

'You can see that,' he replied with an adamant edge to his voice.

'Sure, I can see. You're pumping in Power. But what have you taken it into your head to do? Remoralise everyone here? Annihilate the Dark Ones? Scatter the clouds and improve the weather?'

'There, now you're talking plain nonsense,' Valentin said scornfully. 'Do you take me for a total fool?'

'No, for a noble idealist with a passionate heart,' I replied seriously.

'I realise perfectly well that remoralising everyone haphazardly won't do any good,' said Valentin. 'For your information, I've studied the history of those who've already tried to do that.'

'And did that history teach you anything?' I asked.

'Of course.'

Valentin paused for a moment, peering into the stand. He was clearly waiting to seize the moment to suck in the next spurt of energy. I had to suppress a puerile desire to beat him to it and imbibe the spectators' Power. It would be amusing . . . but no, better not nettle the young guy.

'Valya, what is it that's got you so wound up, anyway?'

'The world's full of injustice,' Valentin replied immediately.

'I won't argue with that. But there was something specific, wasn't there?'

Valentin thought for moment.

'Yes, probably. The old woman.'

'What old woman?'

'My neighbour. She's almost eighty already. Lives alone. Her children are either dead, or they don't visit her. Yesterday I was walking along and I saw her in front of a shop – standing there, crying . . . counting the kopecks in her hand. How can that happen, Anton? How can we let people suffer like that?'

I sighed.

'So it's not the Dark Ones you're protesting about, then? Not about the vampires who hunt people? Not about the Dark Magicians and Sorceresses?'

'Them too,' Valentin replied quickly. 'But they come second. I just can't bear to see the way people suffer!'

'By the way, did you help the old woman?' I asked casually.

'What do you mean?'

'Did you ask her why she was crying? Was it because she didn't have enough money for bread and kefir? Or had she lost her purse? Or was she simply senile, squirrelling away all her money for her funeral? That happens to old women sometimes, you know.'

'I can't help all the old women in Russia,' Valentin said resentfully.

'Why only in Russia?' I asked in surprise. 'Do you know how badly the old women and children in Africa suffer? You're not a racist, are you?'

'No!' Valentin exclaimed indignantly. 'But there are other people there, and Others too. I think that's their duty.'

'I can agree with that,' I said. 'But even so! You're an Other. Sure, you're a Light One, but the abilities of an Other allow you to live a pretty decent life, within the limits of the law and morality. You've probably got a thousand or two in your pocket. Did you help the old woman?'

'Drop the cheap rhetoric, Gorodetsky!'Valentin suddenly shouted out loud. 'I ran away! I was ashamed! You can't plug a hole in a dam with your finger!'

'Yes, you can,' I replied confidently. 'If it's a small hole, and a strong finger. You're an Other. But, first and foremost, you're a man. You didn't help the one and only old woman you came across – so what do you want to use the Power for?'

'I'm going to the Kremlin,' Valentin said in an icy voice.

'And what?' I asked. 'I hope you won't start killing everyone on your way, like a certain Don Rumata?'

Valentin gave me a puzzled look.

'That's from a different book, not the one about Schuchart,' I explained. 'Don't bother your head about it. So what is it that you want?'

'I'll remoralise them,' said Valentin. 'All of them. From the president to the . . . to the Kremlin office manager.'

'Let's say you do,' I stated. 'You'll break through the defences set up by both the Watches, especially to deal with those who want to intervene like this, and you'll alter the nature of all the people who have anything to do with power. The president, the ministers, the Duma deputies . . . So?'

Valentin actually started puffing and panting with indignation.

'What do you mean, "so"? Corruption would come to an end, the laws would be observed. It would straighten out people's lives!'

'But you won't remoralise all the people in the country,' I said gently. 'The Dark Ones will be granted the right to payback. And so?'

'So if the authorities have high moral standards . . .'

'Then in a few days they'll be gobbled up by those who aren't affected by your spell. Who won't have any pangs of conscience, doubts, hesitations. An honest politician is an oxymoron. The new arrivals will immediately remind your highly moral elite of all their sins – and they'll start beating their breasts and repenting without that in any case.'

'Then they can step down!'

'But the new ones won't be any better.'

'So am I supposed just to do nothing?' Valentin asked, outraged. 'Are people simply doomed to suffering? What do you suggest: "Don't touch it until it starts to stink"?'

'Better: "Don't touch if it still works",' I told him. 'Valentin, the whole problem is that the regime is a reflection of society. Crooked and grotesque, but still a reflection. And as long as most of the citizens of a country – if they happened to gain power – would steal and regard themselves as better than other people, no remoralisation of the ruling circles will change anything. Those politicians who acquire a conscience will leave. And new ones without consciences will take their places. It's people who have to change, society—'

'You already said that,' Valentin growled.

'Uh-huh. And I can say it again.'

'No, Anton,' Valentin said firmly. 'I don't believe it. That's your fatigue talking – your pessimism. As well – pardon me for mentioning it – as your own self-interest.'

'How's that?' I asked in amazement.

'The status quo suits the Night Watch,' Valentin said dismally. 'You feed your own sense of self-importance, have a fine life, and you're afraid of serious changes in society. Maybe you're simply afraid of being left with nothing to do. If there's less evil in life, not only will the Day Watch shrink, you won't be needed either!'

I just shook my head. It had suddenly become quite clear to me that I was wasting my time arguing. Valentin wanted to do good. Swiftly and effectively, with all the bells and whistles. And here was I muttering something to him about human nature, about how it was impossible to wave a magic wand and bring happiness to everyone.

'And you won't stop me,' said Valentin, working himself up even more. 'I'll go to the Kremlin – the president's addressing the Duma there today. And I'll bring them all to their senses! I've worked out the whole thing. I'll have enough Power to repel any of your spells, with plenty left over for a mass remoralisation.'

'The Sphere of Negation?' I asked.

'Uh-huh,' said Valentin, nodding proudly.

'A good spell,' I admitted. 'You really will be able to block any of my magic, and you can draw Power from it, too.'

Valentin smiled. He looked like a schoolboy who has earned words of praise from a strict teacher.

There was no point in dragging things out any longer. I stuck my hand in the pocket of my anorak and took out a short telescopic truncheon. I shook it and it snapped out to its full length.

'Ah . . .' said Valentin, starting to get to his feet. He had realised belatedly what was happening.

I shoved him gently in the chest with my free left hand – as I was expecting, Valentin flung his hands up to protect himself against the harmless blow. And that was when I whacked him with the truncheon, swinging hard so that the dense rubber with the heavy metal core thudded dully against the top of the hapless Other's head.

Valentin's eyes rolled up and he went limp. I held him up by his anorak as I sat him back down on his chair. Pastukhov was there beside me immediately, holding his own far heavier truncheon at the ready.

'Easy now, everything's fine,' I told him. 'Right . . . just a moment . . .'

Oh, the young guy had really pumped himself full! I absorbed as much Power as I could and then started simply releasing it into space. With no one controlling it any more, the Sphere of Negation no longer impeded me. The people in the stands livened up, started applauding and yelling. The music started playing louder.

What is the point of teaching them? All that effort, but instead of the Magician's Shield, which protects against everything, they still use the Sphere of Negation. He could at least have set a weak Crystal Shield under the Sphere . . .

Ah, these young people.

When I'd finished, I cast the Clamps spell on him, blocking his magical abilities completely. The Clamps can only be used on an Other who is unconscious, and they only hold for a few hours. But that would be enough.

'He's alive,' Pastukhov declared in relief after examining Valentin. 'Listen – he's one of yours, a Light One, isn't he?'

'If he's a Light One, that doesn't necessarily mean he's one of ours,' I sighed. Semyon was already walking towards us.

'And what's going to happen to him now?' Pastukhov asked. He seemed almost to sympathise with the young guy.

'A trial,' I said, shrugging. 'He didn't have time to actually do anything – he'll get five to ten years' deprivation of rights. That means living without magic.'

'Well, that's not so terrible,' said Pastukhov, relaxing.

'You think so?' I sighed. 'Ah, but it is – if you're already used to it – And he is.'

CHAPTER 6

GESAR LOOKED AT me with an expression of affronted amazement. No, he wasn't just affronted, he was seriously disappointed. That was probably the kind of look a great artist would give his pupil if he found out the pupil had been stealing his brushes and paint and had drawn moustaches on several pictures of lovely ladies just for the fun of it.

'Why?' Gesar asked bitterly, flinging my old minidisc player down on the desk in anger. 'Why the hell didn't you give me the prophecy straight away?'

'Because it's too dangerous,' I explained. 'I didn't want to get the entire leadership of the Watch involved in this business. The Tiger would have come—'

'And eaten us all up,' Gesar snorted. 'I can't see anything terrible in the prophecy.'

'Really?' I asked, astonished.

'It doesn't actually forecast anything at all,' Gesar said calmly. 'All it does is articulate the possibility that an Absolute Enchantress is capable of destroying the Twilight. You don't think that's news to me, do you?'

Now it was my turn to gape at the boss in absolute disbelief.

'It's simply axiomatic,' Gesar continued. 'An absolute force is capable of destroying everything. Doesn't it frighten you that your daughter is capable of blowing up the planet?'

'What?' I bleated lamely.

'Blow it up. Incinerate it. Flood it. And all exclusively by magical means – she draws Power from an effectively infinite source, she has enough to do all that. And she can destroy the Twilight the same way.'

'How?' I asked.

'Maybe collapse all the levels together,' Gesar explained casually. 'Then the whole world would be overgrown with blue moss and a second moon would appear in the sky – although most of the time it would be hidden from sight by the fluorescent clouds. Basically, there would be an incredible transposition of spatial dimensions. One hell of a cataclysm. Maybe magic would be preserved if that happened, or maybe not . . . But there is a second possibility, also quite likely. The world won't change, but we won't be able to enter the Twilight. The level of magic will start to decline . . . and then, even in this case, there are various alternatives.'

He got so carried away that I realised he'd been wanting to talk all this over with someone for a long time.

'I, for instance, believe that magic would be completely lost to people,' he explained. 'But Zabulon believes the opposite – that those people with the highest magical temperatures, who nowadays don't possess even the weakest of clairvoyant abilities, would become Great Magicians!'

'Zabulon?' I asked stupidly. 'You've discussed this with him?'

'Yes, Zabulon,' Gesar replied firmly. 'You should understand, Anton, that there are some things so important for all Others that all enmity is forgotten in the effort to understand them.'

'But if there's no Twilight, how will these human-Others use magic?'

'They won't need to enter the Twilight. They'll operate with just their own internal energy – although perhaps in time they'll discover a way to pump energy directly out of other people . . . and we'll become practically immune to magic,' Gesar laughed. 'You can't give an electric shock to someone who doesn't conduct electricity.'

He paused and then sighed.

'But we'd have a really tough time, of course. We could forget all about having such a long life.'

'So Kesha's prophecy isn't dangerous, and it doesn't contain anything new,' I said thoughtfully. 'And perhaps it's not the first of that kind?'

Gesar didn't say anything, but he smiled.

'Then why was the Tiger so afraid that the prophecy would be heard?'

'Because there really is a chance that someone will try to destroy the Twilight,' Gesar said calmly. 'For instance, as we see, your girl-friend Ar—'

I frowned.

'A certain Witch of your acquaintance,' said Gesar, correcting his mistake. 'As you've already seen, she has a definite bee in her bonnet – she's afraid that her careless interference with a prophecy has brought disaster down on the country. And she's not the only one, either. There are radical Dark Ones, for instance.'

'But what do they want? Are they prepared to lose their Power?'

'They believe that magic will simply change. And they hope that their own personal Power will be increased in the process. There are radical Light Ones, too. Today, for instance, you were working with a lad who wanted to make people happy by making the human authorities super-moral. That's a standard situation, isn't it? But there are other Light Ones who are tormented by the awareness of their own Power. And they'd like it if there was no magic, if people lived without any wizardry at all!'

'But do many of them know that the Twilight can be destroyed – and who is capable of doing it?'

'Fortunately for you and Nadya, not many,' Gesar said drily. 'Or they would try to influence her.'

'So what should I do?' I asked. Suddenly I felt like what I really was – despite the rank of Higher One that had come my way by chance: a novice Magician, a rank-and-file Other, the pupil of a wise Magician.

'Why, nothing, Anton,' said Gesar, with a careless gesture. 'Only try not to hide anything else from me, all right? And don't let anyone know anything. I don't think the Tiger's going to come for us. He realises that we won't reveal the prophecy to anyone. And even if Arina does reveal it, it's still only possible, not inevitable.'

'Are you going to hunt for her?'

'Not with any serious commitment,' Gesar said, shrugging. 'If you get a chance, give her my advice. Either to go back to sleep again, for ten or twelve years or thereabouts. Or turn herself in. She could turn herself in to me, by the way. I'd try to protect her against the Inquisition and obtain the mildest possible sentence.'

I nodded.

'Thank you, Boris Ignatievich.'

'I can't put a thank-you in my pocket,' he growled and glanced at the screen of his computer. 'All right, off you go . . . conspirator. I've got work to do.'

'By the way, about pockets . . .' I said, suddenly remembering. 'Tell me, how much money can I withdraw with my bank card?'

'That depends on your rank,' said Gesar, without looking at me. 'Anton, this is all nonsense, you should understand that.'

'It can't be total nonsense,' I said stubbornly. 'Yesterday I went up to an ATM . . .'

'Anton, tell me: what value do you think human money has in an organisation with even one Fourth- or Fifth-Level Clairvoyant?' Gesar asked.

'None,' I answered after a moment's thought.

'That's the whole point. Simply from fluctuations in exchange rates and share values, even in the most stable of years, the Watches can earn any amount of money they like. And since a normal Other isn't interested in the human attributes of wealth and prosperity, I can't see any point in limiting my staff members' access. Not even Dark Others suffer from that kind of vanity.'

'But it seems kind of—' I began.

'Do you want a Bentley?' Gesar asked, looking up at me with a stony stare.

'What the hell for?' I asked in amazement. 'To attract the curses of the envious people all around me? I wouldn't mind buying some kind of Japanese four-by-four, though. We drove to the dacha in the summer: the road was thick with mud and we got stuck.'

'Then buy one,' Gesar said blithely. 'The natural circulation of money stimulates economic activity, and is ultimately beneficial to people. And especially since Japan has been hit by an earthquake – you'll be helping them.'

'Boss, tell me honestly, will you – can you justify absolutely *anything* you like from the perspective of goodness and justice?' I asked.

Gesar thought for a moment. He scratched the tip of his nose.

'Basically, probably yes. But don't you fret about that. It comes to everybody with age.'

At one o'clock I went to the canteen. I didn't really feel like eating – the events of the morning must have killed my appetite. I just picked at my chicken Kiev and left most of it. Our chef Aunty Klava gave me a reproachful glance as she surveyed the dining hall from the serving hatch, so I had to go through a whole pantomime to demonstrate that my trouser belt would barely close, I was really getting out of shape and that was the only reason I hadn't eaten up my full portion. Aunty Klava was appeased. I poured myself a glass of her remarkable cranberry mors, downed it in one, took another and sat back down at my table. The canteen was almost empty: after all, it was the middle of the day and the operations staff were either catching up on their sleep or spending time with their families – those who had them, that is. In another hour or two people would start congregating for lunch.

'Is the mors good, Anton?' Klava called to me across the canteen.

'Great!' I declared quite sincerely, and the chef smiled in delight.

You know, there's something to all those quack theories about the influence a name has on a person's character, after all. All those Andreis, Alexanders and Sergeis or Lenas, Mashas and Natashas can be absolutely anybody at all. But once a name deviates just a little bit from the perennially popular list, it starts to have an influence.

With the name Klava, for instance, it's good to be a chef. Not necessarily fat, but sturdy. And from the age of twenty-five you'll be known as 'Aunty Klava'. Because 'Aunty' and 'Klava' are inseparable somehow.

But how does the name 'Anton' influence someone, for instance?

I pondered for a moment, recalling the Antons I had known. One Anton, for example, was a robust, amiable individual, a good family man and conscientious professional. And at the same time an inveterate practical joker and composer of scabrous verse. But then another Anton had been a bookworm, entirely unsuited for real life.

So probably the name Anton wasn't rare enough to influence people at all.

I picked up my plate and empty glasses, so as to take them over to the sink for washing, but Aunty Klava came across without making a sound and took them out of my hands.

'Go on, off you go and work. The idea of it, Great Ones carrying dirty dishes around . . .'

'I'm not a Great One,' I muttered.

'A Higher One, are you?' Klava asked, and then continued: 'You are, and that means you'll be a Great One. Off you go.'

I set off to my office, feeling awkward. And about ten metres before I reached the door I heard the mobile phone that I had forgotten on the desk ringing.

And I suddenly had an ominous kind of feeling.

I lengthened my stride, bounded up to the door and hastily unlocked it. Damn, what kind of stupid habit was that? Why would I want to lock my door in the Night Watch, when there weren't any outsiders here? But all the same I did it . . .

The phone was lying on the desk, still ringing. Stubbornly and insistently. Somehow it was clear that it wouldn't carry on ringing for long – and this call was very important for whoever was making it.

But, at the same time, I didn't want to answer it.

'Hello,' I said, raising the phone to my ear.

'Antoine!' Erasmus Darwin exclaimed with genuine feeling that I could sense through all the digital relay stations, fibre-optic cables and satellites suspended in the sky that bridged the two and a half thousand kilometres between us. 'I am exceedingly glad to hear your voice! I hope you are presently in good health and a positive frame of mind?'

'Thank you, Erasmus,' I replied, sitting on the edge of the desk. 'Yes, I am in good health and a positive frame of mind.'

'I am most gratified to hear that,' said Erasmus. 'Are you presently in Muscovy, or has duty carried you further afield to regions unknown?'

'Yes, I'm in Moscow,' I confessed.

I didn't like the way Erasmus was talking. He was far too agitated. Speaking just a little bit more hastily than usual. And I could hear some kind of noise in the background. Not loud, but unpleasant.

'What a pity that we can only speak for two and a half minutes!' said Erasmus.

'Why?' I asked in surprise. 'Er . . . is your mobile phone running down? Or is there no money in the account?'

Erasmus laughed quietly.

'No, no! There's enough money in it to last to the end of my life. Antoine . . . please. I can't carry on guessing about the Great Gesar's present. Tell me, Antoine! What is the secret of the bonsai that he sent me?'

The noise in the phone grew louder.

I hesitated for a moment.

'Erasmus, I don't know for sure. I haven't asked Gesar. But I think I've realised what the truth is.'

'Well, well?' Erasmus asked eagerly.

'It's just a little tree in a pot. Just a bonsai. Without any magic. Gesar's idea of a joke.'

Erasmus said nothing for a second, while the noise in the earpiece grew louder. Then he burst into laughter.

'Gesar! Oh, the cunning old Tibetan fox! I'd been told that he likes wacky jokes! Thank you, Antoine! I had to find out. I had to hear the answer. Otherwise it was just too upsetting!'

'Erasmus, what's going on?' I asked. 'Pardon me for asking, but are you drunk?'

'Yes, a little bit,' he admitted. I heard a distinct gulp. 'But this is such a rare whisky . . . so very old. I was keeping it for a special occasion . . .'

'Erasmus, what's happening there?' I shouted.

'It's the Tiger,' the prophet replied very calmly. 'I deceived you ever so slightly, Antoine. Don't hold it against me. I carved two chalices out of the tree into which I shouted my prophecy.'

'You've found out what your own prophecy was?' I cried, jumping up off my chair. I ran to the window. Right now: who was there on the premises right now? No one . . . but if I really hurried, there were people walking by in the street . . . 'Erasmus, hold on for a minute! I'll hand the phone to someone, you tell them.'

'Don't bother, Antoine,' Erasmus told me. 'It's all predetermined. Don't bother! And don't try to discover my prophecy, please. It won't bring you joy and a long life. Don't be angry that I gave you the chalice. Forget about it, bury it.'

'I can't promise you that I'll do that,' I said honestly.

Erasmus sighed into the phone.

'Then forgive me. I only have twenty seconds left. The Tiger's about to break through my defences. I'm putting my will into a briefcase – a crocodile-skin briefcase . . . there. It will be lying on the table in the kitchen.'

'Erasmus, I'm very sorry!' I exclaimed. 'Maybe there's something I can do?'

'Contact the London Day Watch. Ask them . . . to tidy up my home.' He paused for a moment, and then said quite calmly and clearly, in good Russian: 'Farewell, Moscow Magician Anton Gorodetsky.'

First the noise in the earpiece fell silent.

And then the connection was broken.

I looked at the screen. Length of conversation: two minutes, twenty-eight seconds. I had heard Erasmus Darwin's final prophecy even as he spoke it.

Erasmus was a good Prophet.

Or rather, he had been.

And in general, not a bad Other. For a Dark One, quite remarkable.

I walked over to the window, opened it and lit a cigarette. It was cold and overcast, threatening rain.

That was how Olga found me – smoking at the window. She walked up without saying a word and took out her slim 'feminine' cigarettes. When she had emerged from her confinement in the body of an owl thirteen years earlier, she had smoked Belomor *papyroses* at first – the height of chic back in her time. Only she had soon found her bearings in a changed world.

'What's wrong, Anton?' she asked. 'You look really terrible.'

'Erasmus phoned me.'

'Darwin? What did he want?'

'To say goodbye. He had another chalice with the prophecy sealed inside it – and he couldn't resist the temptation. He found out his own prophecy . . . and then the Tiger came.'

Olga swore. Coarsely, like a man. She asked: 'Is there nothing we can do?'

'No. He only had two and a half minutes – he wanted to say goodbye. And he asked me not to try to find out the prophecy, no matter what.'

'Destroy the chalice,' Olga said firmly. 'Anton, don't play games with prophecies. It's a good thing that Kesha's prophecy turned out to be so vague – incredibly vague, if you ask me. But any prophecy is potentially dangerous.'

I wasn't surprised that Gesar had already shared his information with her. Or that Olga had immediately come to me and was concerned for my safety: that was in her nature. But there was something bothering me. Something wasn't right. But Olga gave me a demanding look and I nodded reluctantly.

'All right.'

'Today.'

'All right.'

'I feel like I ought to keep tabs on you, Anton.'

'Olga, I swear. I'll go back home today and destroy the chalice.'

She looked into my eyes and nodded, reassured.

'Thank you. Maybe everything will be all right. Probably it was wrong—' she said and stopped.

'What was wrong?' I asked. 'You mean it was wrong of Gesar and you to think up that trick with the Chalk of Destiny? Wrong to turn my daughter into a Zero-Level Enchantress?'

'Who could tell then that she would be yours . . .' Olga replied sombrely.

'Why did you need to do it at all? A massive shift like that in the balance between the Watches . . . I can just imagine the kind of concessions it cost.'

'Let's just say we did it on credit,' Olga said casually.

'Meaning?'

'We'll be settling up with the Dark Ones for fifty years.'

I didn't say anything to that.

'I suppose it would be pointless to ask what the Dark Ones were granted the right to in exchange for Nadya's appearance?'

'Absolutely pointless,' Olga replied sharply. 'Let's just drop the subject.'

'But why? What did you need to do it for? A Zero-Level Enchantress is a violation of the equilibrium, a disruption of the balance, it . . . it's like an atomic weapon that's made in order not to be used . . .'

I understood the whole thing myself before I'd even finished speaking.

'It's not against the Dark Ones, is it?' I asked Olga. 'That's why Zabulon agreed . . . that's why the Inquisition turned a blind eye . . .'

For a long moment Olga didn't answer. The dead cigarette end trembled in her fingers.

'Nadya's a weapon against the Twilight, right?' I said. 'She's the only Other capable of destroying the Twilight – of destroying the entire world of magic. You . . . you had suspected for a long time . . . for a long time that the Twilight was not simply an environment, not just energy – but a person. And you were afraid. That was why Gesar consulted with Zabulon. And you involved the Inquisition too, right? And it was decided that the Others needed a deterrent, just in case . . . in case the Twilight should suddenly stop carrying out our petty whims and become far too active. How did you decide what colour she would be? Did you toss a coin? Zabulon took heads and Gesar took tails? Doesn't it bother you that you're raising a child as a living weapon?'

'I had no part in it!' Olga replied abruptly. 'If you remember, I was still a stuffed bird.'

'But you held the Chalk!'

'I was desperate not to spend another fifty years in the cupboard, Anton! And I didn't realise what it was all about at first. Do you think Gesar let me in on all the details straight away? Oh, sure – it sometimes seems to me that he hides his own plans from himself!'

'I'll tell Nadya everything,' I said. 'She has a right to know. So that no one can try to use her without her knowledge.'

Olga sighed.

'No one intends to use her. It's just a precaution. Don't burden the child with it, let her grow up.'

'I'll think about it,' I said and closed the window. 'But all of you really are . . .'

Olga narrowed her eyes as she looked at me.

'Really are what? If the leaders of the Watches have arrived at the valid suspicion that the Twilight is an active force, that it possesses will and desires – what would you have us do? The Twilight doesn't enter into contact with us: its most real manifestation is the Tiger – and he's not very talkative. So what would you have us do? Rely on its goodwill? But who can say that we understand the good in the same way? Better to have an Other in reserve who can stand up against the Twilight in a crisis. And bear in mind, by the way, that your daughter is effectively under the care and protection of both Watches! She's a communal weapon!'

'She's not a weapon,' I said wearily. 'She's a person.'

'She's not an ordinary person, she's an Other!'

'All that's nothing but words, Olga,' I said, starting to stride round the office. I looked at her and asked: 'You don't think that the Twilight really is harmful? That it would be better to destroy it? Maybe I should ask my daughter . . .'

'But are you certain that she would survive the Twilight?' asked Olga. 'She's an Absolute Enchantress. All the Power in the world flows through her. Are you sure that Nadya can live at all without it?'

'Bastards,' I said. 'You're all such bastards . . .'

Olga simply shrugged, as if to say: Think what you like.

'Contact the London Day Watch, will you?' I asked her. 'They need to visit Erasmus's house. His will is lying on the kitchen table, in a crocodile-skin briefcase.'

'Where are you going?' Olga shouted after me.

'Home. Consider me on leave.' As I closed the door, I couldn't resist adding: 'Indefinitely'.

CHAPTER 7

One bad thing about an ordinary city flat is that it's hard to burn a large object in it. Especially if the object's magical, which means that in order to avoid unpleasant consequences it's best to burn it with ordinary fire.

Now, if only I'd had a flat with a fireplace in it! Then I'd have tossed the wooden chalice into the blazing heap of wood, closed down the damper of the hearth a bit and watched as the prophecy for which Erasmus had died disappeared for ever.

But just what was this prophecy? And why had Arina and I both got away scot-free with listening to Kesha's prophecy, which the Tiger had wanted so badly to prevent that he had even spoken in human language? And in any case, it was strange, preposterous: not a prophecy, but an information bulletin – it could have been included in Wikipedia . . .

I glanced round the balcony. Maybe I could light a little fire here? I could handle the fire brigade if I had to . . .

But we had a good balcony, glassed-in, with an insulated wood-laminate floor. Svetlana would bite my head off if a burnt spot appeared on that wood. If only there had been some ceramic tiles left over after the renovation work . . . but we'd used up every last one.

After I'd wasted enough time trying to come up with something, I went back into the flat, through into the kitchen, opened the oven and took out the steel baking tray. That would do the job.

But then, why go back out onto the balcony? Erasmus's wooden chalice wasn't very big, it fitted into the oven perfectly.

I held it in my hands again for a moment. It was made very precisely, lovingly. Perhaps not with any special skill, but with genuine care and application.

So there had been two of them. It was a pity to do this, of course. Quite apart from the cunningly concealed magical filling, the chalice was interesting in its own right. An ancient relic . . .

But the prophecy concealed in the chalices had already killed its owner.

Oh no. Enough sacrifices. Down with prophecies. I put the chalice on the baking tray and went to get a bottle of lighter fluid. (I'd been using those cheap gas lighters for ages, but the bottle had been standing in the cupboard, waiting for its time to come.)

'May you rest easy in the Twilight, Erasmus,' I said, dousing the chalice generously with petrol.

The front door slammed.

'Daddy! I'm home!' Nadya shouted. 'Anna Tikhonovna fell ill and let us off the last lesson!'

Sveta had been going to collect Nadya from school that day.

'Okay,' I shouted back, squatting down in front of the oven with a box of matches in my hand.

'I've brought visitors.'

'Yes?' I asked, looking round.

Nadya appeared in the doorway. Then Kesha appeared awkwardly behind her.

'Hi, Innokentii,' I said. For some reason I wasn't surprised by his visit. 'How are things?'

'Fine . . .' he said and hesitated, not looking up. 'The lessons are interesting.'

'That's great,' I said in the vigorous tone that grown-ups use for talking to children.

'Kesha's mum is working late,' Nadya explained. 'I invited him over to our place. Mummy promised to take him home afterwards.'

'But where is mummy?'

'She drove us to the entrance and then went to get some toilet paper,' Nadya said, with a giggle. There's an age at which the very words 'toilet paper' sound remarkably funny, especially if you say them in front of someone the same age as you.

'Yes, I forgot to buy any yesterday,' I said in a repentant voice.

Nadya looked round and shouted into the hallway: 'No, those are mummy's slippers, the green ones are for visitors!'

'Have we got lots of visitors, then?' I asked, getting up.

'Not really lots,' said Nadya, slightly embarrassed. 'Just Aunty Arina as well. We met her in the entrance. She was coming to see us.'

I took a couple of swift strides and positioned myself between the children and the hallway. My left hand was still holding the box of matches. But the fingers of my right hand were already folded into the Shield sign.

'Anton,' Arina shouted from the hallway. 'Peace, friendship, chewing gum!'

She glanced in cautiously from the corridor.

'I come in peace!' she said, smiling broadly. 'No evil here. You can see that the children are fine!'

Nadya seemed to have realised that she had acted rashly. She didn't make a sound, but she grabbed hold of Kesha's hand and dragged him in further behind me.

And I felt a bottomless well of Power seething and brimming over just a metre away from me.

'Nadya,' I said in a quiet voice. 'You know perfectly well that you shouldn't bring strange . . . people back home.'

'But she's not an ordinary person,' said Nadya, trying to make excuses. 'She's an Other . . . a Light One.'

'She used to be a Dark One,' I said. 'But that's not the point: there are some Light Ones who don't have a single white spot left on them.'

'Anton, you're being insulting!' Arina exclaimed indignantly.

She looked entirely peaceable. A long dress, long hair arranged in a bun, looking like an elderly village school teacher. The large fluffy slippers on her feet completed the picture.

'What have you come for?' I asked.

I wasn't really afraid. Svetlana would arrive in a moment. I was in my own flat – and at home the very walls lend you strength, every Other knows that. And in addition, I had my daughter beside me. Not very skilful, but infinitely powerful. And if she struck out – with anything at all – Arina would go flying out through the wall.

'As I understand it, you've decided to do away with the chalice,' Arina said. 'I'd like to watch that. May I?'

'I'm going to burn it,' I said. 'And don't try to change my mind.'

Something elusive glinted for a moment in her eyes. Could it really have been relief?

'I swear that I won't! But can I just watch? And then I'll leave! I swear—'

'I've had enough of your oaths!' I growled. 'You should be thankful that the children are here. Nadya, Kesha! Stand over there, in the corner! I'm just going to burn this lump of wood, then Arina will say bye-bye and leave. Okay?'

'Can I say "See you later, alligator"?' Arina asked, smiling sweetly.

'How come you have such a good knowledge of 1950s slang?' I asked. 'You were asleep then!'

'I've been watching a lot of movies just recently,' she said. 'I don't like the modern ones very much, they're spiteful. But fifty years ago people knew how to make good-hearted films.'

'A good-hearted Baba-Yaga,' I snorted and prepared to strike the match. Arina watched me attentively, not looking as if she wanted to interfere. But one of her hands was tightly clenched on something. 'The Minoan Sphere!' I said, realising what it was. 'Put it on the floor and take a couple of steps back!'

She didn't argue. That should probably have put me on my guard. She opened her hand, showed me the small sphere of white marble . . . so that's what you look like, you famous Minoan Sphere, the Inquisition's headache number one. Then she squatted down, carefully placed the sphere on the floor and set it rolling in my direction. Either the floor of the flat wasn't very even, or Arina's hand trembled, but the sphere rolled under the shoe locker.

'Anton, I'm playing fair and square.'

Oh, but I don't believe in honest Witches at all – and not very much in honest Others . . .

'No sudden movements,' I said, just in case. I lit the match and threw it into the oven, trying to keep my eyes on Arina.

There was a flash of flame. Quiet a powerful one – the concentration of petrol fumes must have built up. Nadya even cried out – but, like the fine young fellow he was, Kesha stepped forward towards the stove, to face up to the danger.

'That's it,' I said to Arina. 'Happy now?'

Arina was gazing intently into the oven.

'So, you made up your mind after all, daddy?' Nadya asked in a deliberately loud voice, evidently ashamed of being frightened.

'Yes. No one should hear this prophecy,' I said. 'It has already . . . done enough damage today.'

Arina suddenly laughed.

'Ah, Anton,' she said. 'Straight, honest, simple and naive. So you still haven't realised?'

'Daddy, I think the prophecy is revealed when the chalice is destroyed . . .' whispered Nadya.

I managed to turn round in time. I even managed to take a step towards the open oven, towards the wooden chalice blazing with a bluish flame . . .

But the next second the threshold of destruction that Erasmus had implanted in his handiwork was reached.

And I was on the edge of a dark forest at night.

About five metres away from me I could just barely make out a village track running through the darkness. Beyond it were fields, and beyond the fields were dim lights that I guessed at rather than saw with my eyes. Yes, the electricity supply wasn't so good back then – or rather, there wasn't any.

There were two shadows darting about in silence on the track. One was almost incorporeal and moved with incredible speed. The other was moving fast, too, but was far more material – and it was carrying a glowing blue whip in its hand. The blows of the whip occasionally connected with its adversary, but didn't seem to cause him any serious injury at all.

I suddenly realised that I was starting to respect Zabulon. He hadn't abandoned his underage pupil to be torn to pieces by the Tiger. The Great Dark Magician had accepted the challenge of a combat that should have been his last.

I heard strange sounds beside me, as if someone was being sick. I dragged my eyes away from the magical duel, and saw a thick old oak tree. There was a hole in the oak at about the level of my chest, and protruding from the hole were Erasmus Darwin's legs. He ought to have been fourteen years old but he seemed to be only the same height as Kesha, and he had only half as much bulk as the modern young Prophet. So the idea of historically increasing rates of development was clearly no myth after all.

'He's coming for us,' I heard suddenly in a barely audible whisper from the hollow tree. I took a step closer and leaned down towards Erasmus's back. The illusion of the world around me was complete – I even caught a faint smell of sweat and fear coming from the boy. 'The Executioner's coming to make you talk, the Executioner's coming to make you keep quiet . . .'

Yes, that was right. They used to call him the Executioner then.

'The Executioner needs blood, the Executioner needs flesh . . .' Erasmus muttered. 'The Executioner will drink the blood, the Executioner will eat the flesh, the Executioner will take the soul . . . Not enough, not enough, not enough blood, flesh, souls . . . Never enough, never enough, never enough . . . the Executioner is falling asleep . . .'

That night, separated from me by an abyss of time, was warm. But I was shivering violently.

He was saying almost the same thing as Kesha!

Only in different words . . . the words of his own time . . .

'The Executioner will come, the Executioner will never stop, the Executioner doesn't sleep, the Executioner is ready for work . . . Only a maiden, born through deception, the daughter of a Great Enchantress who has rejected her Power, the daughter of a Great Magician who has taken Power that is not his own, only a girl, a girl will be able to kill the Executioner . . . the girl Elpis, the daughter of deception, the girl Elpis, the Executioner's sister . . .'

Feeling as if I was about to black out, I noted that Erasmus had received a good classical education. In Greek, Elpis means the same as Nadezhda means in Russian: Hope.

I had to leave. Turn away. Plug my ears. Not listen.

But I couldn't do it.

And what good would it do anyway, when my daughter Nadya, the boy-prophet Kesha and the old witch Arina were there, like disembodied shadows beside me, listening to Erasmus's mutterings?

But not a single human being . . .

'The Executioner is all the Power of the world,' Erasmus continued, making his confession to the tree. 'The Executioner is all the magic of the world. The girl can kill the Executioner. The girl can kill magic. Kill the Executioner and you kill magic! Kill the Executioner and you kill magic . . .'

But no, after all there was nothing really terrible happening. It was the same prophecy. The same one that Kesha had spoken. It hadn't frightened the Tiger, so what was the meaning of this situation?

It was a preamble.

An introduction.

A harbinger of the real prophecy.

I flung my hands up and covered my ears. But the world around me was only an illusion, living according to its own laws, and I carried on hearing everything.

First – Zabulon's despairing cry. And then his strangled howl: 'Mercy! I will leave, Executioner! Spare me!'

If he ever learned that I had witnessed his shame I was done for. No treaties or obligations would ever stop Zabulon from thirsting for my death a hundred times more keenly than before . . .

And then I heard Erasmus's voice. Slower and more powerful. No longer a frightened boy's voice, but the voice of a maturing man.

'You, magician from a harsh northern country, who heard not what you should have heard at the proper time, but have come here as a disembodied shadow and learned what you did not wish to know . . . The Executioner will die and magic will quit our world. Your choice. Her Power. His fate. The Executioner will come and you will have to decide. But whatever you may decide, you will never know peace again.'

'I've never known it anyway!' I shouted. I wanted to grab hold of Erasmus, drag him out of the hollow tree and lash him hard across the cheeks – to make him shut up. But I knew that my hands would pass straight through the Prophet's body.

'I pity you – and forgive me,' Erasmus said and fell silent. The legs protruding from the hole in the tree twitched and went limp. He had clearly lost consciousness.

As I stood there, I didn't realise immediately that I was sobbing and tears were running down my cheeks. Zabulon was groaning somewhere close by. The Tiger walked up to the tree unhurriedly. He stood there, looking at the part of Erasmus that was visible. He was the same as in our time – young, with a genial, serene face. Only the clothes he was wearing were old-fashioned and terribly uncomfortable, to my way of thinking. The Tiger looked at Erasmus for a few seconds. Then he turned his head and looked at me. As if he could see me.

And he smiled – sadly and understandingly.

We were all still in the poses in which the prophecy had caught us. Me with my hand stretched out to the blazing chalice. Nadya huddled up against the fridge, Kesha valiantly protecting her with his body. Arina off at one side, giggling quietly and tramping her feet on the spot. Had the old witch really gone out of her mind?

'Was that a prophecy?' asked Kesha.

I didn't answer. I touched my face – it was wet with tears. I looked down at my feet – they were covered in dust.

Very slick. So had this not been simply an illusion, but something like a journey in time?

'I think I said something like that too, only I've forgotten it . . .' Kesha added quietly. 'But that was about the Tiger . . .'

'The chip in the toy was too small,' I replied. 'Not everything was recorded.'

'I never did trust technology,' said Arina. And she cackled with laughter.

'Daddy, am I going to have to fight someone?' Nadya asked. 'And kill him?'

I looked at Arina. The witch was as happy as if she had stuffed herself with her own witch's toadstools in toad sauce.

'What are you so delighted about?' I asked. 'Do you realise what's happened? We've heard the prophecy for which the Tiger killed Erasmus Darwin today.'

'Killed him?' Arina asked, knitting her brows. But the smile remained on her face. 'I'm sorry for the old alcoholic, I really am. But I'm glad that everything has been settled. Now we can get this over and done with, Anton! You and me – or rather, your daughter. But we'll help. The Tiger will come and Nadya will destroy him.'

'I think you didn't hear the prophecy clearly,' I said. 'It's for me to decide. Do you understand?'

I stepped towards my daughter and put my arms round her.

'It's for me to decide whether Nadya kills the Tiger.'

'I don't want to kill anyone,' Nadya said quickly. 'Daddy, I don't want to!'

'I'm afraid you don't have any choice any more,' Arina said calmly. 'The Executioner will die and magic will quit our world. It has been said! If we tell the prophecy to humans – it will come true.'

'And what if we don't tell them?' I asked.

'Then the Tiger will come and kill all the Others who know the prophecy,' Arina said, smiling. 'I'm ready. I'll die anyway when the Twilight disappears, as you already know: ordinary people don't live as long as I have.'

'You're the one to blame,' I said. 'You're involved in this somehow. You knew how to activate the prophecy, didn't you? Had you known for a long time?'

'I suspected,' Arina said calmly. 'It's basically an old witch's method, to make a spell dependent on the destruction of some valuable item. Then you can hope it will only be used in a case of extreme need. But you were absolutely right, Anton, I couldn't have influenced your daughter. I couldn't have enchanted an Absolute Enchantress. I had to make sure that she had no choice and you didn't either.'

'There's always a choice,' said Nadya, slipping out from under my arm and giving Arina an angry look. 'I won't kill anyone! Not even if I get killed!'

'But your daddy will be killed too,' Arina said. 'And Kesha also, as it happens. Will you be able just to watch the Tiger kill them?'

Nadya's face fell.

'So you couldn't have influenced Nadya,' I said. 'But what about Erasmus?'

Arina lowered her eyes for a moment.

'It was only curiosity . . . As you know, it killed the cat. And that old Irish drunkard, too.'

'Why?'

'To give you a nudge. Erasmus had foretold that you would hear his final prophecy. So he had to get in touch with you. And you had to panic. And make up your mind to destroy the chalice.'

'All you needed to do after that was make sure Nadya got home in time,' I said, nodding. 'And not alone – so that I would feel responsibility for someone else's child as well. I won't even ask if Anna Tikhonovna's illness was a coincidence.'

'At our age, Anton, your health gets so frail!' Arina exclaimed. 'Well, I'm sorry! Forgive an old witch! You understand it's not for myself! It's for a higher goal!'

'What goal?'

'To put an end to all this! No more feeding the Twilight! No more paying for our Power with human suffering!'

'Arina, you don't even know if that prophecy is active – and what it really said! Maybe all those disasters have already overtaken our country and they're over now!'

Arina shrugged and said in a firm voice: 'Even so. What we do is repugnant in the sight of God. And if we can put an end to it, then we must.'

I suddenly felt a pricking in the tips of my fingers. A sharp sensation, just for a second.

The sentry spells around our building had been triggered, the spells that had been cast a long, long time ago by Gesar and – as I now realised – by Zabulon. The spells guarding the Absolute Enchantress. The Enchantress that the Great Ones were holding in reserve as a Doomsday weapon.

I looked out of the window. And saw the Tiger walking towards our building from a side street.

It was very easy to see him – he wasn't trying to hide, he wasn't trying to walk round the defences or remove them. He was simply breaking through them – probably in exactly the same way as he had broken through the defences of our office when he came for Kesha. The Tiger looked like a man cast out of white-hot metal. As he walked along, a firestorm raged around him. Branches of trees burst into flames. Parked cars overturned with their alarms screeching. A stray tomcat driven crazy by what was happening started dashing about in front of the advancing Tiger, as if it couldn't decide which way to run.

Cats see on all levels of the Twilight. Maybe right then it was seeing something inconceivable even for a cat that could follow the stealthy movements of werewolves in the night and observe the flights of witches in the twilight sky.

The Tiger stopped, facing the cat. Leaned down and stroked it. Then walked on.

The cat instantly forgot about its panic, sat down in the middle of the courtyard and started licking itself.

And the Tiger moved on towards our entrance.

'Daddy, I'm afraid,' Nadya told me. She and Kesha were standing at the window, watching the Tiger.

'You have to hit him,' Arina said hastily. 'Just hit him. With pure energy. A Press. But with all your strength! Do you understand?'

A bolt of lightning from the sky struck the Tiger. It was good that there were clouds in the sky: people would at least find some kind of explanation for themselves . . .

The Tiger froze at the centre of a crater of smoking, shattered asphalt. He shook his head. Clambered out. And walked on.

'Daddy, your phone . . . it's ringing . . .' said Nadya.

I slapped at my pockets and took out my mobile. Without taking my eyes off the Tiger, I said: 'Yes, Gesar.'

'What are you up to now!' the boss howled.

'I'm sorry, I was duped. I . . . I've found out Erasmus's prophecy.'

Gesar swore.

'Open a portal, boss,' I told him. 'I just need a little bit of time to decide what to do . . .'

'I can't open a portal,' Gesar said in a quiet voice. 'I'm sorry, Anton. But . . . it's as if the Twilight has gone absolutely crazy. I can't do anything.'

'But what should we do?' I asked. 'Erasmus's prophecy . . .'

'No, don't tell me,' Gesar interrupted. 'Don't do that! Although . . . no. If everything's the way I was afraid it would be . . .'

'It probably is,' I said, pressing up against the glass to see the Tiger opening the door of our stairwell. Something glinted down there too and the floor shuddered under my feet. But I was under no illusions about the Tiger being vulnerable to Gesar's and Zabulon's traps.

'You have to decide for yourself, Anton,' Gesar said eventually. And I sensed how his voice had changed. How old it had become. Ancient. I would have called it an Old Testament voice if Gesar had had even the slightest connection with Christianity. 'You have more right to do that than I do.'

'Why? Because I'm more of a human being?' I asked.

The seconds still left to me were ticking away, but I couldn't make a decision. And it was very important for me to hear Gesar's answer.

'Because I have wronged you very badly and I'm tired of feeling guilty.'

'What is it about today? Everybody keeps apologising to me,' I said and broke off the connection.

I looked at Arina. The witch kept glancing warily at the hallway and then looking back greedily at me.

'What have you decided, Anton? There's no more time.'

'There's always time,' I said and held out my hand.

The Minoan Sphere shot out from under the shoe locker like a bullet and landed softly in my hand. Oho, it was really heavy!

And then the doorbell rang!

He was being very proper today, our Executioner-Tiger!

'Nadya, Kesha, hold on tight to me!' I ordered. The children clung to me and I put my arms round them, just to be sure.

'You bastard!' Arina squealed and leapt at me.

How could I activate the Sphere? Probably just wish: the energy was pumped into it beforehand, and the route too, probably . . .

I squeezed the cold little marble sphere in my palm and wished, wished desperately, to be as far away from there as possible.

And at that very second Arina grabbed my shoulder so tightly that it hurt.

CHAPTER 8

WITH A PORTAL, you simply step through it. And you get the illusion of being in total control of what's happening, even of being personally involved in it all. Lift a foot . . . take a step . . . stick your head out in a different place. Drag everything else through . . . half in Moscow, half in the Seychelles, and no problems . . . except that it's all a bit creepy.

The Dark Ones' paths through the lower levels of the Twilight are hard and dangerous. I don't really know why – after all, no one lives there – but a couple of times I've seen Dark Ones emerge from journeys like that battered and bleeding. I don't know, maybe they do battle with their own internal phantoms down there.

But the Minoan Sphere dragged us through space unceremoniously, in one single mighty jerk of power. It wasn't painful, or disgusting, no one was sick or even felt queasy. But it did leave an unpleasant kind of sensation behind, as if just for a moment I had been Gulliver in Brobdingnag, a living toy in the hands of giants.

By and large and on the whole, I liked aeroplanes better.

We couldn't keep our feet at the end of the journey. I tumbled over onto Arina and Nadya landed on Kesha. I got up and offered the witch my hand without saying a word.

'Ah, you saucy thing!' Arina exclaimed skittishly as she got up. 'Whatever happens, a man only ever has one thing on his mind!'

I really did like her, after all. Despite her witchy nature . . .

Beside me Nadya had already jumped off Kesha, her entire manner demonstrating that she would rather have fallen into a heap of rubbish than land on some boy or other.

But overall, no one was actually hurt.

'Daddy, where are we?' asked Nadya.

I looked round.

A little wooden-walled house with one room. Walls covered with wallpaper that had faded with age. Furnished with a table and a couple of chairs, a sideboard, an iron bedstead with little nickel balls on the headboard – the kind that used to be all the fashion in the 1930s – a ponderous ancient television, bookshelves . . . but almost no books.

That was right, the Inquisition had taken them all away when it cleaned out Arina's home.

It was strange that they hadn't burnt the house down.

I said so out loud.

'Strange that the Inquisition didn't burn the house. I thought that was standard procedure for a fugitive witch's home.'

'They set fire to it. Only it's not that easy to burn my house,' Arina replied, straightening her dress. 'This is my land. The village I come from used to stand here. I was born here and apparently I'll die here. Burn the house, do whatever you like to it – it will just spring back up out of the ground.'

I believed her.

The house had a well-lived-in feel to it. Apparently Arina must have made her base here, wisely deciding that no one would bother to check the site of her burnt-out home. There was an open packet of cheap sweets on the table, and in the sideboard a carton of milk and half a loaf of white bread, carefully wrapped in a clean rag.

'But they carried off all the books,' Arina sighed. 'I've begun restoring my library little by little, but I don't know myself what for. After all, I won't have time to finish the job.'

I stepped towards the bookshelves and touched the spine of one of the books.

Aliada Ansata.

The Witch's Herbal.

None of the others had anything to do with magic. Ten volumes of Pushkin, including two or three volumes printed in his lifetime. The fourth volume of Harry Potter, a collection of Ralph Stout's detective stories and a little volume of Bunin's verse, *Leaf Fall* – also an old pre-revolutionary edition. Apparently witches sometimes simply wanted something to read.

'I'm sorry, Arina,' I said sincerely. 'For your house – and for you.'

'No need to feel sorry for me,' she replied calmly. 'My day is done. Either the Tiger will polish me off or old age will get me, as soon as the magic dries up. It's easier for you Magicians. You'll just start to age like everyone else. You're still young.'

'Arina, I don't want to destroy the Twilight,' I said.

The witch said nothing for a moment. Then she asked: 'Why not?'

'For numerous reasons. In short, I don't believe that the Twilight works evil . . . or only evil,' I corrected myself.

'Did the Tiger seem benign to you?' Arina asked me.

'None of us are benign when someone's trying to destroy us.'

'That's not what's bothering you,' Arina said calmly. 'It's something else. What you'll tell your daughter when she grows up and realises that she could have been a supremely powerful Enchantress, but has become an ordinary human being. The fact that your wife will get old and wrinkles will cover her face and behind every glance there'll be the question: "Why this?" And you'll be old and sick too, doddery and gasping for breath, with a stabbing pain in your side, struggling to make ends meet on a meagre pension and groaning over the injustice of the world . . . no longer able to defend yourself, let alone help anyone else. You've tried what it's like living without magic for one evening. And it frightened you.'

I didn't answer.

'But you don't have any choice,' Arina went on. 'I know that you like me – not as a woman, but as a person. And I like you. But Wen-yan killed the friend he loved more than himself. Only that could prove to the Twilight that he would keep the secret of the prophecy. And that prophecy probably only promised disaster for a billion Chinese, but ours will kill the Twilight itself. Our prophecy must either die with us or be fulfilled. Any move leads to defeat.'

'In chess that's called a zugzwang,' Kesha put in out of the blue.

I looked at him and asked: 'But do you know what I should do?'

Kesha looked at me as if I was an idiot and exclaimed: 'I'm ten years old – how should I know?'

'In the movies, when things get critical, a little child always suggests a brilliant move to the hero,' said Arina. 'Don't be surprised, Kesha. When grown men don't know what to do, not only will they ask a child, they'll even ask a woman . . . Anton, make your mind up. The Tiger won't take long to find us.'

'Can you recharge the Sphere?' I asked, holding out the little ball of marble.

'It's completely drained,' Arina replied after inspecting the artefact. 'It wasn't intended for dragging four Others through space. If it isn't completely dead, it will take at least five years to recover. A pity – it's unique, it opens a portal from anywhere at all at any time, in any circumstances. No, Anton. You can't run away any longer.'

'Can I have a sweet?' Kesha asked.

'Of course,' Arina agreed hospitably. 'I can give you some bread and milk, too. Nadya, would you like some bread and milk?'

The lad was in a well-balanced state of mind. I wondered what that meant. After all, he was a Prophet, and if we were about to be killed, he ought to foresee it.

So had I made up my mind?

'I'll just have a smoke, Arina,' I said. 'All right?'

'The door's open,' the witch said calmly as she took an odd assortment of cups out of the sideboard.

'Aren't you afraid that the Tiger might be out there already and he'll just splat me?' I asked as I opened the door.

'Well, that would solve all our problems!' Arina exclaimed. 'Surely a daughter would avenge her father?'

Nadya looked at me in fright.

'Daddy, don't go!'

'Nadya, don't be afraid,' I said. 'Arina's right, it doesn't make sense for the Tiger to kill me. 'Tell me, can you open a portal?'

Nadya paused for a second, then shook her head.

'I'm sorry, daddy. It's like the Twilight's boiling. It's all ripples and bubbles . . .'

I couldn't imagine what she was seeing and where. As far as I could see, the Twilight was still the Twilight. Perfectly normal.

On the first level, at least.

I sighed, opened the door and walked out into the evening forest gloom. Arina's little house stood right in the middle of the forest, without any fences, vegetable plots or other extravagances. There was only one path that led to it.

The one and only item of convenience here was a fallen tree fairly close by. It had fallen in just the right spot and a few of its branches had been trimmed off, transforming it into a kind of natural bench.

I stood there, looking at the bench and the individual sitting on it.

Then I walked up, sat down beside the Tiger, took out my cigarettes and asked him: 'Like one?'

The young man in a formal business suit and light-coloured raincoat looked at me for a while without answering. Then he said: 'Smoking's bad for your health.'

'It's okay for Others,' I said glibly.

'If I disappear, your Power disappears too,' the Tiger reminded me. But he took a cigarette. It lit up on its own in his hand. The Tiger took a drag, removed the cigarette from his mouth, looked at it quizzically and shrugged.

'Who are you?' I asked.

'That's the wrong question,' said the Tiger, shaking his head. 'What's the point of asking that? You can't check what I say, can you? I could say that I'm God, when I'm really the devil.'

'But even so, if you did answer me, what would you say?'

The Tiger looked at me curiously.

'I'd say that I'm the Twilight. That I'm a person. That I'm a reflection of the consolidated mind of all the people who have become Others, lived their lives and departed – departed into me. That I want to live, although you can't even imagine what my life is like. That I have my own interests, which you can't understand. But all of this is just words spoken for you.'

'Good,' I said. 'Good. Then tell me, what do you want?'

'The wrong question again!' said the Tiger, frowning. 'The wrong one! But if you want an answer, then my reply is that I want to live. Simply live.'

'Why do you kill the Prophets?'

The Tiger took his time answering this one. And I suddenly noticed that the cigarette he was smoking wasn't getting any shorter. The doctors' and tobacco magnates' nightmare – an everlasting cigarette . . .

'Do all prophecies have to be heard?'

'But killing . . .'

'Is that a member of the Night Watch, who has personally killed Dark Others, speaking?' asked the Tiger.

'You mean to say that you are Good?'

'I am not Good. I am not Evil. I am the Twilight. I want to live, and my life is people. Everything that is good for humankind is good for me. Everything that is harmful to it is harmful to me too.'

I looked at the hut and saw three faces in the window. Arina, Nadya and Kesha. Nadya and Arina looked tense. Kesha was drinking milk.

'But prophecies often bring good. And you allow them to be heard and carry them out.'

'I do?' the Tiger asked, with a clear note of amazement in his voice. 'A prophecy is a ruptured abscess. Cassandra was not to blame for the fall of Troy. And neither was I. It is the will of humankind, its aspirations and anticipations that erupt into the world through the prophets. And once they have broken through, they come to pass. I can hurry them along and I can delay them . . . sometimes. No more than that.'

'And the prophecy that Arina is frightened about?' I asked. 'The one she tried to annul and merely . . . postponed. Or has it already happened?'

The Tiger shrugged.

'Once again, what does my answer mean to you? I could say something that will reassure you. But how will you know that it's the truth?'

'Tell me anyway,' I insisted.

'I don't demolish kingdoms and unleash wars,' the Tiger said quietly. 'I have seen the fall of Sumerian Kish and the long death of Uruk, the ruination of Assyria and the destruction of Babylon. I have seen great empires crumble and small states fade away. I have seen armies marching in an endless stream for three days and nights, seen cities plundered and prisoners killed. I have seen evil out of which grows good and good that is pitiless and brings death. But all of this is not I. And it is not even you, the Others, who imagine yourselves to be the shepherds of humankind. All of this is human beings. All of this is their love and hate, courage and cowardice. Are you, like Arina, concerned for the fate of your nation and your country? I have no answer for you. Just as I had no answer for Wen-yan. And no answer for Erasmus. In the end only people decide if they are going to live or die. I am an executioner. But I am not a judge. Great joy is as useful to me as great sorrow. But the joy and sorrow are chosen by people.'

'So what should I do?'

This time around the Tiger paused longer. Then he said: 'I want to live. If you tell people the prophecy . . . then it will be fulfilled. That means that people don't need magic any longer. They don't want anyone who is different from the rest. Anyone who craves what is strange. Who pushes and pulls humanity along. Then I shall die. And I can also die if I fight your daughter.'

He paused before adding: 'But there is a chance. She's only a child and she might not be able to manage it.'

'But is there another way out?' I asked. 'So that you will not die and all of us will not die . . .'

The Tiger shrugged and replied: 'See how well you have already understood everything for yourself. The answer was in your question.'

I nodded.

'That's a shame.'

We sat there in silence for a while. I smoked a second cigarette, then a third one. It was completely dark already. Darkness falls quickly in the forest, in the forest there is no twilight. A fluttering candle flame started twinkling in the window.

'I'm sorry,' the Tiger said unexpectedly.

'I'm sick of you all apologising to me!' I howled, jumping up. 'I've had enough of it!'

'You have to make up your mind what to do, Anton,' the Tiger said.

'Give me five minutes,' I said.

'Ten,' the Tiger said, carrying on smoking. The spot of light flared up and faded away repeatedly as I walked towards the hut.

The children were sitting, quiet and alert, at the table, on which two candles were burning. Arina was still standing at the window, gazing at the Tiger.

'Have you decided?' she asked without turning towards me.

'Nadya . . .' I began, looking at my daughter. I could barely make out her face in the candlelight. 'Will you do what I ask you to do?'

'What?' she asked tensely.

'We have only two choices,' I said, gazing at her. It was a good thing I had been able to see her grown up – even if it had been in a dream.

In a dream that must not come true.

'There are always three,' Nadya said stubbornly. 'In all the fairy tales, there are always three paths.'

'It can't be helped, this isn't a proper fairy tale,' I said and tried to laugh. 'Only two. Kill the Tiger – and destroy all the magic in the world. All the Others will become ordinary people. And there could be all sorts of cataclysms . . . I don't know.'

'Magic has become an evil,' Arina said intensely. 'People must—'

'People must be people,' I responded. 'If there's no magic, they'll find some other way of destroying themselves.'

'So have you decided to let the Tiger kill us?' Arina exclaimed.

'And there's a second way,' I said, glancing at my daughter. 'To prove to the Tiger . . . to prove to the Twilight that we will never reveal the prophecy. We won't tell any people about it. Then it won't come true. And the Tiger won't have to kill us.'

'To make the Tiger believe that, you need a sacrifice,' Arina snorted. 'A terrible, irrevocable sacrifice . . .' She paused for a moment and then screeched in outraged indignation: 'Anton, you want to kill—'

'Daddy, do you want me to kill you?' Nadya asked.

Arina was a former Dark One. And Dark Ones take everything the wrong way. Unlike Light Ones.

I shook my head.

'No, my love, I don't want to leave you with that burden. And anyway, there's still Arina, isn't there? Promise me. Simply promise that you'll never tell anyone Erasmus's prophecy. And you swear too, Kesha.'

'He'll kill the boy,' Arina said quickly. 'The Tiger will kill him. Tear him to pieces in front of your daughter – won't that be a fine psychological trauma for her?'

Kesha exclaimed passionately: 'I won't tell anyone! Not anyone!'

'Swear,' I repeated. 'So that what I'm about to do won't be in vain. Swear.'

Kesha started nodding desperately.

Nadya got halfway up off her stool.

'Don't,' I told her and turned to Arina.

'You'll never do it,' Arina said quickly. 'We're both Higher Ones, but I've got more experience, Anton.'

I didn't say anything . . .

About what Edgar had once told me. At the Cosmodrome in Baikonur, when I was standing facing Kostya Savushkin, my friend and a Higher Vampire, who was planning to turn all the people of the world into Others . . .

The Power ran through me, and the chill of it scorched my fingers. Arina put up a shield – she didn't understand what I was doing.

Some things are hard to understand for someone who has been a Dark One for too long.

The Twilight shuddered as the white stone walls rose up through it. Space seemed to expand: the table at which the children were sitting was carried off into the distance, the ceiling dissolved and its place was taken by a gleaming white dome, the floor was covered over with marble slabs.

I didn't have quite enough Power after all. But I had an unlimited source right beside me: I reached out to my daughter and scooped some up – and the space around me assumed its final form.

A round hall about ten metres in diameter, with a domed ceiling.

No windows and no doors.

Nothing.

Gleaming white stone, in which Arina and I were imprisoned.

For ever.

The Sarcophagus of Time – the Inquisition's most terrible spell of all. A spell that worked on the victim and the executioner.

'You've lost your mind,' Arina whispered and sat down on the floor.

'Probably,' I said, sitting down beside her.

There was air in there and it would probably always stay fresh.

There was even Twilight – but there was no way out of the Sarcophagus onto any of its levels.

If Edgar had been right, prisoners in the Sarcophagus didn't feel either hunger or thirst.

They were allowed to carry on going out of their minds for all eternity, without any physical suffering.

'It's impossible to break open,' said Arina. 'Do you understand? There's no way. Not even your daughter can do it.'

I shrugged.

A patch of white stone ten metres across. A capsule adrift in eternity.

I wondered if the expansion of the Universe would be followed by contraction and a new Big Bang. If it was, then we had some kind of chance.

I started laughing, imagining billions of years of incarceration. Arina reached out and gave me a resounding slap on the cheek.

I stopped laughing.

'Do you really believe him?' Arina asked. 'The Twilight?'

'I don't know. The only thing I do believe is that people make their own destiny. People, and not the Twilight. And not you and me.'

Arina said nothing for a moment, then spread her arms helplessly.

'Well . . . we'll never know the answer now, anyway. Never.'

I reached into my pocket, took out the pack of cigarettes and glanced into it. Two left.

There was no point in economising in the face of eternity.

'Want one?' I asked.

Arina nodded feebly. She wasn't even frightened – after all, she had been heading for death anyway. She was thoughtful. As if what I'd done had astounded her.

I stuck both cigarettes in my mouth, lit them and handed one to Arina. She looked at me in surprise.

'I saw that in some old American movie,' I explained. 'I've always wanted to do it.'

'Our great moderniser Peter brought this lousy herb to Russia. I asked him not to,' Arina muttered.

'Don't lie – you were born after Peter was already dead,' I protested.

'Better get used to it, we've got nothing to do now except tell tall tales,' Arina retorted and took a drag. 'Although, of course, there will be other amusements. After all, it's eternity, you understand,'

I took the cigarette out of my mouth and stubbed it out on the floor, looking over Arina's head – at the gap opening up in the wall of the impenetrable Sarcophagus.

The Tiger stood there in the gap, with a seething grey haze behind him. I even thought I could see the 'bubbles' that Nadya had talked about.

'Impressive,' said the Tiger, walking into the Sarcophagus. 'Did you know that in the entire history of the Inquisition this spell has only been used three times?'

I shook my head. Arina was already on her feet – she seemed to be preparing to fight.

'In principle, it's perfectly convincing,' the Tiger continued, walking unhurriedly towards me. He ignored Arina. 'But didn't it strike you that your daughter might draw an unexpected conclusion?'

'What kind of conclusion?' I asked.

The Tiger grabbed me by the collar and hauled me up into the air without the slightest effort.

'For instance, that if the Twilight dies, her beloved daddy will come back from the Sarcophagus.'

'Is that true?' I wheezed, clutching at my throat and trying to loosen my collar.

'No! But is she really going to believe me?'

The next moment the Tiger lunged forward – and we passed through the wall.

Arina's scream broke off behind me, as if it had been chopped off with a knife.

Once again we were standing in the little house lost in the depths of the forest outside Moscow.

'Daddy!' shouted Nadya, dashing towards me. The Tiger let go of my collar and moved a few steps away. I hugged my daughter and looked at him. The Tiger looked morosely at Kesha, standing beside him. The boy seemed to have turned to stone.

'Don't even think about it!' I said.

'But what guarantees do I have?' he asked in a low voice.

'None. We get by without guarantees all our lives – you'll just have to get used to doing the same.'

The Tiger fixed Kesha with a piercing stare. Then he said: 'Boy-Prophet – for my own safety, I ought to kill you . . .'

'I don't want you to!' Kesha exclaimed, terrified, and started backing away awkwardly in my direction.

'All right. That's what we'll write: Innokentii Tolkov refused,' said the Tiger. And he disappeared.

The three of us were left alone together.

'Has he really gone?' asked Nadya. 'What do you think, daddy?'

'I think . . .' I said, rubbing my throat and coughing to clear it – the Tiger had almost strangled me as he dragged me out of the Sarcophagus, he didn't know his own strength – 'I think any being that has a sense of humour can't be all bad.'

Nadya sobbed and hugged me even tighter. Kesha hesitated for a second, then walked up and nuzzled against me awkwardly from the other side.

'Everything's fine, just fine,' I said. 'It's all over now.'

'But where's Arina?' Nadya asked in a low voice.

'In the Sarcophagus of Time,' I replied.

'Does that mean for ever?'

'That means that never before has anyone ended up in a Sarcophagus that is impossible to get out of, with a Minoan Sphere that can open portals from absolutely anywhere . . . I don't know, Nadya. Probably not even the Tiger knows that.'

I myself didn't know whether what I'd said was really the truth or an attempt to console my daughter.

And I was even less sure if I wanted the ancient witch to make her inconceivable escape from that dungeon. It was basically fine by me if she stayed there until the end of time.

'Shall I try to open a portal?' asked Nadya. 'The Twilight is settling down . . .'

'In ten minutes and thirty seconds the Great Gesar and Great Zabulon will open a portal to us,' Kesha suddenly announced. His voice had changed. As often happens with young prophets, the fright had started him prophesying. 'Next week you will explain your actions at the Inquisition Tribunal in Prague . . .'

'That much I can figure out for myself,' I whispered, gazing at the tousled hair on the top of Kesha's head.

'You are Anton Gorodetsky,' the boy continued. 'You are a Light Other. You are Nadya's father. Because of you . . . all of us . . . all of us . . .'

I held my breath.

But there was silence

'Did I say something?' Kesha asked timidly.

Isn't that always the way!

Just when you really want to know if you did the right thing or not.

But no one will ever answer that question for you.

Not even the Twilight.